D0251297

WITHDRAWN

FELICITY CARROL
AND THE
MURDEROUS
MENACE

ALSO BY PATRICIA MARCANTONIO

Felicity Carrol and the Perilous Pursuit

FELICITY CARROL
AND THE
MURDEROUS MENACE

A FELICITY CARROL MYSTERY

———◆———

Patricia Marcantonio

NEW YORK

Published in the United States by Crooked Lane Books, an imprint of The Quick Brown Fox & Company LLC.

Crooked Lane Books and its logo are trademarks of The Quick Brown Fox & Company LLC.

Library of Congress Catalog-in-Publication data available upon request.

ISBN (hardcover): 978-1-64385-289-8
ISBN (ebook): 978-1-64385-310-9

Cover design by Shira Atakpu
Book design by Jennifer Canzone

Printed in the United States.

www.crookedlanebooks.com

Crooked Lane Books
34 West 27th St., 10th Floor
New York, NY 10001

First Edition: February 2020

10 9 8 7 6 5 4 3 2 1

To Marguerite and Gabrielle, both strong and beautiful

All things bright and beautiful,
All creatures great and small,
All things wise and wonderful;
The Lord God made them all.

—Mrs. C.F. Alexander, 1848

Chapter 1

London, England

"Apples, apples," Felicity Carrol sang out in a whiny voice. She held out the fruit to the woman who passed. "Juicy and sweet, dearie. Only a penny." Her cockney accent was as perfect as the apple she offered.

Standing almost a head taller, the woman ignored Felicity with a wave of her right hand and then crossed Warwick Road. The woman had no little finger. Felicity took in the woman's scent of lavender, vanilla, and murder.

Bessie Denner was suspected of killing three husbands with arsenic. The Deadly Widow had finally appeared.

Taking a bite out of the apple, which was as good as she had advertised, Felicity watched the woman walk into Simons Apothecary. The suspect wore an expensive though gaudy blue satin dress and a hat with the largest ostrich feather imaginable, which made her even taller.

In contrast, Felicity wore a plain dress, apron, and shawl, all topped with an oversized bonnet. She was proud of her disguise, having based it on those of other vendors she had seen on the streets. Her wares lay in a wooden tray hung around her waist with a leather belt. Three days before she had started her apple selling right in front of Simons Apothecary. On that first day, however, owner Alfred Simons had yelled at her to move on, in less than polite terms, and added a little shove for good measure. Slight and short, Simons had eyes that resembled a mole's, especially when he threw curses at Felicity in her apple vendor disguise. So she had moved directly across the street. The vantage point had proved sufficient. Through the apothecary's window, Felicity had spotted the woman with the big feathered hat pitch her arms around Alfred Simons and plant an ardent kiss on him.

"*Complice*," Felicity whispered. The French word for accomplice sounded so much better in this case.

Felicity had smelled Bessie Denner's lavender and vanilla fragrance before. Like a mist over a cemetery, the scent had lingered on the clothes of Denner's latest kill. Felicity had examined the newly deceased Michael Spencer in the London coroner's mortuary. The victim had been dressed as he had appeared in life, a barrister's clerk natty from his toenails to his tie. Despite the conservative clothing, the face had revealed a kindness even in rigor mortis.

The coroner reported arsenic poisoning as the cause of death.

"They did one of those tests to find the stuff," said Mr. Hobson, a clerk at the coroner's office.

"The Marsh test," Felicity said.

"That's the one."

Felicity found irony in the fact that arsenic came from nature, existing in minerals and crystal form. But ever since ancient days, arsenic had become the perfect murder weapon because the lethal substance could be slipped undetected into food or drink. Arsenic had been unofficially labeled the poison of the kings on account of its regular use when one noble wanted another dead, presumably to move up the ranks. British chemist James Marsh had devised the first really successful test for the presence of arsenic in bodies in

1836. Using sulfuric acid and zinc, his method effectively detected minute traces of the poison. As a result, the test now bore his name. She had to determine how the poison had been administered.

With a ruler, Felicity opened the mouth of the deceased Michael Spencer. Arsenic carried the smell of almonds, though not fresh ones—rather something reminiscent of stale decay. There was no almond smell in the dead man's mouth.

"He didn't ingest the poison?" she asked Hobson.

"The coroner found arsenic in his system, but not in his throat or stomach."

She proceeded to sniff the rest of the body. This was where she smelled the lavender and vanilla on the deceased's shirt and coat.

Hobson stood and watched. Though her first visit to the coroner's office had been met with resistance and unfriendliness, today the clerk had opened the door with a smile. She and Hobson had become acquainted during her first-ever investigation, which she now referred to as the King Arthur Affair. She'd had to initially bribe him to allow her to inspect one of the victims of the killer, who had been preoccupied with the Arthurian legend. When she'd returned to the mortuary for other investigations, she'd had to pay only a small remuneration to the clerk. Felicity had now come to like Hobson, who knew everything in the world about cats, since he owned two.

"Hobson, come here, please," Felicity said. "Take a whiff of the deceased's hands and tell me what you smell."

Hobson took a long sniff. "Beeswax, paraffin, and peppermint?"

"Excellent, Mr. Hobson. Just what I thought. I suspect the smell came from an ointment because the victim suffered from arthritis. Notice how the knuckles on his fingers are oversized."

"Mean anything?" the clerk said.

"Not at this time, but the investigation is young."

Michael Spencer had become the third suspected victim of the Deadly Widow, the title bestowed by the *Illustrated Police News*.

Not necessarily a creative title, but one most accurate. Although sensational and often lurid, the penny newspaper made its living reporting stories about crime, many of them without a resolution. Regularly, Felicity combed its pages, as well as those of the *Times*, seeking out such cases.

The unsolved. The baffling. These cases had become her vocation.

Felicity Margaret Carrol of Surrey was one the wealthiest heiresses in England. She had inherited the magnificent Carrol Manor and thousands of acres of land, not to mention a cotton mill, shipping line, and thousands of pounds from investments. But instead of using the riches to attract a husband, as most young ladies in their early twenties would have done, she had found other ways to spend her money. She had increased wages for those who worked at her family's businesses and started a foundation to help children in the poverty-laden East End.

But solving the unsolvable and pursuing justice were her main occupation.

Felicity had an utter distaste for the usual role young ladies played in their Victorian society and was determined to forge a path in the opposite direction. Tapping her vast financial resources to aid in her investigations, she utilized all her intelligence, scientific talents, and exceptional memory to recall anything she had read to help bring justice to those who might otherwise get none. She had so much in life, and she wanted to give to those who'd had everything taken from them by murder. She gave back by tracking down their killers. This had been her passion for the past year. She received tremendous satisfaction in making sure the people who thought they could get away with homicide ended up with their hands bound by the metal handcuffs of the Metropolitan Police.

To her dismay, there were many cases where the killer remained free, including Bessie Denner. Felicity had read about Denner in the *Illustrated Police News*. The story had even earned a spot on the cover. In an obvious ploy to sell more issues, the penny magazine's drawing depicted an overly beautiful young woman sitting in her chair darning a sock in front of a fire in a quaint parlor. Smiling, she looked over at a nondescript older man sipping tea—tea allegedly containing arsenic. The magazine drawing did show the woman was missing a little finger on her right hand. That detail had been based on testimony from friends of the victims who had seen the woman accompanying her soon-to-be-dead spouses.

The police reported that the wife had become the chief suspect because she'd departed with the victims' money and valuables. By the time Felicity read about the case, the Deadly Widow had already dispatched two husbands in such a poisonous fashion. According to the autopsy reports, the men had died from arsenic, but there was no presence of it in the throat or stomach in either case. That left the police wondering how the widow had passed on the toxin.

The Metropolitan Police hadn't investigated for several months because their leads had been exhausted. The Deadly Widow had disappeared—until she struck again.

Then Felicity read about the death of Michael Spencer in the *Times* and had the opportunity to examine what could be a fresh kill of the Deadly Widow.

Friends and neighbors called Spencer a man of good character. Childless and not physically attractive, he made wooden toys for children at a nearby orphanage and helped unfortunates at his church. Though only a clerk, he had recently inherited money from his father's clothing store. Being a frugal man, he had placed the seven-hundred-pound legacy away until he could realize his vision of becoming a clergyman in the country. Above all, he longed for the love of a good woman and his own children.

He got neither.

Instead, Michael Spencer met Bessie Denner. The *Illustrated Police News* drawing had greatly embellished her looks. In reality, Bessie Denner was one of those broad-of-shoulder women with the glowing cheeks of a milkmaid who could wrestle a cow to the ground.

Ten years younger than Spencer, the woman did possess provocative curves, deep round eyes, cherub cheeks, and full lips. Not so much a beauty, though she projected herself as one.

After examining Michael Spencer's body, Felicity had then set off to talk with his neighbors. One of them was an old woman with wiry white hair.

"You some kind of detective?" the neighbor asked in a creaky voice when she answered the door.

"Just a citizen interested in justice for Mr. Spencer," Felicity replied earnestly. Whereas she had often turned to subterfuge in previous investigations, Felicity didn't lie this time.

The neighbor thought about that, grinned with brown teeth, and asked Felicity to follow her into an insignificant parlor. The woman sat back in a worn chair and proceeded to tell Felicity all she could about Bessie Denner.

"I knew she was up to no good. Courting Michael that way, like a lioness after prey. Putting on airs like a lady. She used his loneliness against him."

"She does sound despicable," Felicity said.

"I had a better term come to mind," the old woman replied, and huffed a bit of snuff from a worn tin.

"Did you notice that she had only nine fingers?"

"She always wore gloves when I saw her."

Felicity smiled. "That's a good detail. Did she smell of lavender and vanilla?"

"Stank of the stuff, really." The neighbor pinched more snuff and sneezed mightily into a threadbare handkerchief.

"Did Mr. Spencer ever talk to you about Bessie?"

The neighbor spit into a tin she kept next to her chair. "Only that he loved her and wanted to take care of her and about how sweet she treated him. He bought her anything she wanted. But I heard her yelling at him like a banshee."

"About what?"

"Money. When was he going to go to the bank for his inheritance? When was he going to buy her more pretty things? When were they going traveling in style? I swear that Bessie woman looked at Michael like he was the Bank of England."

Not exactly information Felicity could use to track down the killer. But the woman's other observations about Bessie Denner's character were useful. She was not only greedy but mean.

"Sorry I couldn't be of more help," the older woman said, as if reading Felicity's thoughts.

"Oh, but you have been most helpful."

The woman gave a tired smile and began rubbing her hands, which were gnarled as dying tree roots. The smile became a grimace.

"In much pain?" Felicity, who had a medical degree from the University of London, recognized an acute case of arthritis.

"Agony. Poor Michael suffered from the same ailment in his hands. All that holding a pen at the barrister's office."

Spencer's hands had showed signs of arthritis when Felicity examined the body. They had also smelled of beeswax, paraffin, and peppermint.

A rush of excitement came to Felicity at a possible connection.

"Did Mr. Spencer say whether Bessie gave him anything to help him with his pain?"

The neighbor gathered her shawl tighter. "Matter of fact, she did. An ointment he rubbed on his hands all the time. I wanted to use some, but Michael said it didn't help him much and not to bother. Bessie insisted he keep using the stuff, so he did just to please her. He'd do anything for that woman."

"Ever see the ointment pot?" Felicity said.

"Kept it in his pocket, he did."

"Anything written on it?"

The old woman's eyes lightened at the memory. "Why, it said 'Simons Ointment.'"

Felicity smiled at the discovery and bid the neighbor goodbye.

"Get that murderous slut." The old woman raised her eyebrows and took in more snuff.

Back at her London house, Felicity had reread the police and postmortem reports on the first two murdered husbands. Although she easily recalled anything she read, she still reviewed the information for absolute certainty. She also turned to the dependable solicitor firm of Morton & Morton, which had proved of value again and again—for a fee, of course—in her past investigations. She requested from them a narrative on each of the dead spouses.

Denner's victims had all been lonely older men without children but with money. Each had had medical problems. One man complained of a bad left knee obtained while serving in the army. The other dealt with gout in both legs. And Michael Spencer suffered from arthritis in his hands. After learning this, Felicity sat back and visualized how Bessie Denner had committed the crimes. The woman must have given her husbands the tainted ointment to use on their aching legs, knee, and hands. Over time, the poison killed them. Denner took all their money and promptly vanished. She preyed on men who only wanted love, which infuriated Felicity. Her determination to track down Bessie Denner intensified.

Next Felicity talked with hospital nurses and doctors, although none had ever heard about a Simons Ointment. One nurse did mention a Simons Apothecary on Warwick Road. And that was what had finally led Felicity to start her reconnaissance. In her disguise as an apple vendor, she had waited for the Deadly Widow to appear. And appear she did.

From Felicity's observations over the next few days, Denner and Alfred Simons lived upstairs from the shop. From time to time, he locked the door and put up a GONE TO TEA sign, and they both retired upstairs for what Felicity surmised was a romantic interlude. Either that or plotting another murder. Bessie Denner's association with the apothecary made the most perfect sense—criminally speaking. No doubt *he* had worked up the ointment Denner had used to deliver the fatal arsenic. At the crime scenes, police probably thought nothing of seeing an ointment pot in the home of an older man, nor would they have considered testing the ingredients for poison.

One day, Denner left by herself, wearing a girlish white outfit bedecked with ribbons. Felicity set aside her apple vendor tray in a nearby alley and followed. Denner moved her hips and sashayed as if she were the only person in the world who mattered. At a café, she fluffed her hair and entered. Felicity hurried to the other side of the street and located a good place from which to see without being seen. She used a telescope to aid her surveillance.

At a table, Denner sat with a man who resembled her other victims. Older, well dressed, and a little too starved for attention from females. The last was readily apparent in how the man threw his head back to laugh and how his cheeks reddened when Denner reached over and touched his hand. Here, potentially, was dead husband number four.

Felicity had to hurry.

Abandoning her apple vendor disguise, Felicity rented a second-story room in a boarding house across the street from the apothecary. The site provided a good view. She realized she needed to make Scotland Yard aware of the murderous widow's whereabouts. First, she wanted to confirm that Bessie Denner and her associate had whipped up the lethal ointment in the apothecary. That meant she had to see the mixture for herself. But rarely did the couple leave together during the day. Either one or the other left on errands and returned with food or supplies. Denner also went out by herself in various new dresses, no doubt to woo the older man Felicity had seen in the café.

Sharing the watch in the rented room was Helen Wilkins. Felicity's friend and maid had insisted on helping catch the probable killer of three men.

"She's a shame to all women," Helen had said. "Besides, I can't have you staying in a room by yourself."

"Then we shall do this together, Hellie," Felicity replied.

Helen had previously told Felicity she had gotten used to her young mistress's sometimes peculiar activities during her investigations, although Helen still tried her best to make sure Felicity wasn't harmed. For her part, Felicity didn't like to get Helen involved as she pursued killers. Helen had raised Felicity ever since her mother died when she was six months old. Her father, Samuel Reuter Carrol, had abandoned Felicity to Helen, servants, nannies, and governesses at Carrol Manor. So Felicity considered Helen family, and therefore was protective of her. At the same time, Felicity greatly appreciated Helen's love and respected her strength, which had made Felicity feel less lonely growing up.

On this occasion, Felicity didn't reject her offer to help. In the room, Helen took shifts watching the apothecary while Felicity slept or vice versa. One Sunday afternoon while Felicity napped in the rented room, Helen woke her. "Miss, Miss. They're *both* leaving," she whispered.

Felicity rushed to the window. Dressed in another flamboyant outfit, Denner, accompanied by Simons, was leaving down Warwick Road, laughing as she went. He had on a nice suit.

"Looks like they're going out on the town," Helen said.

"Then I'm going over there to find more evidence for Scotland Yard. Please watch for them. When they're returning to the shop, hang a white cloth in the window and I'll hurry out."

Helen wished her good luck.

In her past exploration of the apothecary, Felicity had spotted a back door, which faced an alley. She went to work on the locked door. When she had begun her investigations into crime, she'd learned from a grizzled locksmith how to get past a lock. Obviously, there would be needed clues behind secured doors. Initially Felicity had been bothered about illegally entering private premises, but if suspected wrongdoing could be stopped by doing so, she didn't believe Scotland Yard would mind. Then again, she didn't always mention that the evidence she discovered had required a skeleton key to obtain.

Once through the door, she stepped into a back room filled with supplies and Denner's signature scent of lavender and vanilla. Not knowing how long Denner and Simons would be gone, Felicity quickened her search for the ceramic Simons Ointment pots. Without trying to disturb anything, she glanced in boxes and drawers in the back room. Nothing.

She couldn't search the shop itself in case someone saw her through the windows. She looked up at the ceiling while she considered where to look next.

Their flat upstairs. Of course. She hurried up the stairs.

The door was unlocked. She had anticipated an ostentatious room of inequity, but instead saw a well-ordered parlor and kitchen with pricey furniture probably bought at the expense of three dead men.

Felicity stood in the middle of the room. Denner and Simons had no motive for murder other than money. She swore she felt their greed crawling up her arms and legs like stinging insects. The couple, and Denner in particular, had thrown away human life to live more comfortably. An impulse to smash every item in the room out of rage for the victims flashed through Felicity's mind. She let it pass and breathed in calmly.

Think.

Judging from their overt actions, these people clearly had no remorse. They had been so obvious in their scheming, so Felicity looked in an obvious place. She rushed to the bedroom, located toward the back of the building. There, on top of a small dresser, sat ten small white ceramic ointment pots, all looking like a set of vertebrae. The words SIMONS OINTMENT were printed on each. She opened one and smelled. Beeswax, paraffin, and peppermint. With her skeleton tool, she scooped out a bit and placed it in one of the envelopes she always carried to store evidence. She smoothed over the mixture in the pot with her gloved hand to erase any sign of disturbance. Then she returned to the parlor. Glancing out the window, she spotted Helen waving a white cloth frantically. Daring to spy outside, Felicity saw the couple a few shops down from the apothecary.

Time to leave. Felicity rushed down the stairs and out the back door at almost the exact moment she heard the couple enter through the front.

At her London home on Grosvenor Square where she and Helen had been staying during the investigation, Felicity had avoided any experiments that might start a fire. At Carrol Manor in Surrey, an experiment with a voltaic battery had gone more than wrong, resulting in a fire that had burned down the east wing of the mansion along with some of her father's valuable art pieces. She had rebuilt her new laboratory a safe distance from the house this time.

With utmost care and a bucket of water nearby, Felicity conducted the test for arsenic in the ointment sample. The result revealed the presence of the poison.

Her next visit: Scotland Yard.

★　★　★

Inspector Stuart Marshal was all muscle in crumpled tweed. He sat at his desk at Four Whitehall Place, headquarters of the Metropolitan Police, better known as Scotland Yard. The better-known moniker came from the building's situation. It backed up to a court and street named Great Scotland Yard, supposedly called that because the land had once been owned by a man named Scott sometime during the Middle Ages.

Inspector Marshal didn't appear to care about history. Judging by his dress, he didn't care about fashion, either. He cared only about solving crimes. His dense fingers intertwined as Felicity went through the details leading to the discovery of Bessie Denner's whereabouts. Felicity had originally asked to see her friend Inspector Jackson Davies but had been told he was ill that day. The answer troubled her, because she hadn't seen Davies for a while, but she didn't have time to explore his absence. Still, she had talked with Inspector Marshal previously and liked his slow-burning strength.

Since the King Arthur Affair, Scotland Yard inspectors had listened to Felicity and taken her theories seriously. Most of the time, at any rate. The police were also discreet, which she appreciated. Felicity had asked to stay in the background, and the police accommodated her request. She referred to herself as a private citizen who just happened to help unravel mysteries and find murderers. She assumed another reason Scotland Yard inspectors kept her name out of the newspapers was to save themselves embarrassment. The police probably didn't want to give too much credit to a young woman for solving what they couldn't. No matter, the recognition and cooperation were gratifying, albeit covertly so.

"In conclusion, Inspector Marshal, I believe Bessie Denner is working with Alfred Simons, who runs Simons Apothecary." Felicity wrapped up her account.

"You really saw Bessie's nine fingers, eh?" Marshal said in a voice that sounded filled with pebbles.

"I counted them myself." She liked teasing the police. It was a vice, she had to admit.

The inspector placed his huge hands on the desk.

"The neighbor of her latest victim will tell you about the Simons Ointment," Felicity said. "You will also find arsenic mixed in with similar ointments in their flat above the shop." She didn't mention how she had learned that particular fact. "And we must hurry, Inspector Marshal. I believe Bessie Denner is planning to wed husband number four very soon."

"Know the man's name?"

"Not at this time, but give me twenty-four hours and I'll find out." She said this a bit too eagerly.

"Not necessary. We'll get officers together and go down there today."

Felicity smiled. "I expected no less, Inspector."

"Miss Carrol, your tips have proven very helpful in the past in apprehending criminals, and I'm sure this one will be the same."

When men complimented her beauty, she usually disregarded the praise. But this praise Felicity accepted heartily.

"Can I ask why you're doing all this, Miss Carrol?" His head slanted as if he was taking a closer look at her.

"Because it must be done, Inspector," she said with such seriousness, his eyes fluttered trying to think of a response.

"Can't fault you there." He threaded his fingers again. "But you're a very strange young woman. Anyone ever tell you that?"

"Frequently."

Inspector Stuart Marshal kept to his word. At three that afternoon, the Metropolitan Police appeared at Simons Apothecary. With swift action, two officers brought out a cursing and screaming Bessie Denner and placed her in back of the police carriage. Her accessory, Alfred Simons, on the other hand, cried like an infant and had to be dragged along.

From the window across the street, Felicity and Helen watched. "Miss Felicity, you probably saved lives today—again." Helen placed a hand on her shoulder.

Felicity tried not to be so delighted with the outcome. As she had told Inspector Marshal, the work was necessary. Still, she felt light with accomplishment.

"Hellie, let's go to tea."

CHAPTER 2

Felicity rode through the color blue. Bluebells spread over the ground, giving her the feeling of galloping through an upside-down sky. Her horse kicked up dirt and flowers as she traveled through spring in the woodlands of Carrol Manor.

She breathed in the season, the days of buds and renewal. Her favorite time of the year, when the earth got a second chance at life. She believed in second chances. She had received one and, just like the earth, welcomed it. As she rode, her braid slapped her back and the breeze skimmed her cheeks. The air carried the fragrance of grass and nectar. Ah, springtime.

She promptly sneezed so hard she had to grasp the reins. She laughed. Ah, springtime pollen.

With its huge house and thousands of acres, the estate had been her place of respite and rejuvenation ever since her father died more than one year ago. A dreadful thought, but true. When her father lived, Carrol Manor had been his house more than hers. The same had been true of their London home. He had rarely visited the manor during her childhood, and when he had, he'd hardly spoken to her. Usually he had walked past as if she were another piece of expensive furniture, albeit one with dents. Then she would rush to her room and cry. Somewhere along the way, she had stopped crying and stopped trying to please him, substituting education for a father's love. Yet she had always hoped her father would start acting like the kind of parent she had always dreamed of. Warmhearted and open. Accepting of her. She'd never stopped dreaming right until the day he passed away.

After an argument at their London house, her father had died due to a heart condition he'd refused to talk about. They had fought over her first murder investigation, which he found unladylike. She'd confronted him about his neglect. He had won the quarrel by dying.

Logic had told her she wasn't to blame, but she continued to claim fault for what had happened. She suffered from guilt over how their relationship had ended. The mood tailed her like a spy, ducking in darkness and not daring to come into the light. Some days she eluded it. Other days the shame came so close she swore she could feel its heady breath on her neck.

After he died, Helen tried to comfort Felicity. Helen swore her father did love her but wasn't the type to bare his emotions. Felicity just kissed her former nanny's cheek and thanked her for the well-meaning falsehood.

In truth, Felicity had gained a satisfying sense of freedom after his death, which in turn generated more guilt. She was freer because she no longer had to work hard to win his love or approval. With such thoughts came to mind the writings of Publius Cornelius Tacitus, a senator and historian of the Roman Empire. "To show resentment at a reproach is to acknowledge that one may have deserved it," Tacitus wrote. He should have known what he was talking about. If anyone should feel guilty about what they did, it was the Romans.

Guiding her horse over a hedge, Felicity hoped the guilt she carried would fall off along the way. But it clung to her. She rode back toward Carrol Manor. After years of feeling like a visitor there, she had grown to love the place because of the people who lived there. The people who raised her, like Helen and the other servants. They were her home and family now.

★ ★ ★

John Ryan met Felicity as she rode up to the stables. "The contraption's been acting wild again."

"How many dishes this time?"

"Just a few. Well, maybe more."

Felicity got down off her horse and led him into the stable. Then she and Ryan, the head groundskeeper, headed to the workshop located in a separate building behind the manor. Ryan and other workers were assembling a dish-washing machine.

Felicity had read about the device in the *Times*. Josephine Cochrane had designed the machine in a shed behind her house in a town called Shelbyville, Illinois, in the United States. With help from a mechanic, Cochrane had come up with the idea of using water pressure to clean plates, cups, and saucers. She placed the dishes in wire compartments, which went inside a copper boiler. Hot water shot out from the bottom and cleaned the contents. Cochrane, who obtained a patent in late 1886, claimed she had invented the machine to help women who faced washing dishes after making a meal for their family. She also had to deal with debt after her husband died. Felicity respected how the American had recognized a need and met it.

Felicity had written to Josephine Cochran and paid well for a copy of her plans for the device. She wanted to save the servants of Carrol Manor time and work with the machine.

From the look on John Ryan's face, the kindly and extremely competent Irishman had taken great pleasure in building the dish machine, although he and the others had had a mishap or two, not to mention several dozen broken dishes.

The machine was smoking when Felicity and Ryan entered the workshop.

"Bloody hell," Ryan hissed in his Irish brogue, then apologized to Felicity.

"The same words crossed my mind."

After allowing the smoke to clear, Felicity studied the machine. Still in her riding clothes, she got down on her hands and knees on the dirty wooden floor of the workshop. Even if she had been wearing an expensive gown, she would have done the same thing to decipher the problem. "Mr. Ryan, I believe one of the wires in the dish compartments has come loose and stopped up the motor." She pointed to the trouble spot.

Ryan gazed at it and shook his head in agreement. "Good eye, Miss Felicity. We'll fix it and have another go."

"Excellent. After we get this running, I'd like to discuss constructing a windmill to generate power."

"Sounds interesting, Miss."

They both coughed from the still-present smoke.

The dish-wash machine was just one of the modernizations Felicity planned to bring to Carrol Manor.

The installation of electric lights throughout the manor, including in the servant rooms, had been completed the previous fall. Although some of the workers had confessed a scare at light blazing on with a switch, within a month there were no complaints. Many even confessed they enjoyed no longer having to go about the house lighting and then extinguishing candles and lamps, as well as not having to stumble about in a dark room. In the evening, the manor's windows glowed white with the electricity in place of the yellow from the candles. Felicity thought it looked like progress from afar.

But her proudest achievement was bringing education to the manor. She had hired a young teacher to instruct the servants' children, and any adult servant, for that matter, on how to read and write. A schoolroom had been set up in one corner of the manor's ballroom. Many of the employees attended, which pleased her immensely. Once they did learn to read, the servants were invited to borrow any of the books in the manor's extensive library. Felicity considered adding another teacher to include lessons in history, mathematics, and art and planned to put similar schools in place at the family mills and shipping line.

She loved to learn and had spent four years studying an array of subjects from chemistry to literature at the University of London and gaining degrees in medicine and history. Her father, however, had disapproved of her education and wanted her married off. When she was old enough, he requested that she attend balls and other social events to meet a suitable young man—the only times he did talk with her. Felicity hated the balls, teas, and galas. The other young women in attendance were vacant as empty palaces, the men solely interested in her fortune. Felicity soon grew bored with their simple conversations about fashion, home, and other social activities. In turn, the women eyed her with suspicion. She wasn't one of them, but something else entirely. Turning the manor's ballroom into a school was an infinitely better use for the space than swirling gowns, dress coats, and hollow conversations.

Yet Felicity's main preoccupation was crime. Located away from the manor, her new crime laboratory held the latest scientific equipment. There she also kept files on the murder cases she had solved and the ones still requiring attention, as well as books on the oldest and newest methods of criminal investigation.

She imagined her grandfather Anthony Carrol, who had built the grand place, whirling in his grave at all the changes. Good thing she didn't believe in that sort of thing.

After leaving the workshop, Felicity traveled through the kitchen, greeted the staff, and picked up an apple from a bowl on a counter. She headed upstairs to her room to read books on crime detection, which was one of her favorite pastimes when she wasn't busy with her own investigations. Felicity prepared to continue reading the works of French chemistry professor Mathieu Orfila, who had started publishing in 1814. Among his many achievements, he had studied the way a body decomposed and the effects of asphyxiation and was credited as the first person to utilize a microscope to evaluate blood and semen stains. He appeared regularly as a medical expert in criminal cases.

As she started to read, a knock sounded on the door. "Come in."

"Sorry to bother you, but this note was delivered and marked urgent." Helen held the paper out for Felicity.

"Thank you, Hellie."

"Ring if you need me." Helen left quietly. Felicity had already started to read the note.

Written on plain white paper, the handwriting was neat but almost childlike.

To Miss Felicity Carrol, Carrol Manor, Surrey,

I have heard Jackson speak of you fondly and often. My son is a proud man and would not ask for your help, but I am not too proud to ask. I love my son very much and he does need your assistance.

Please come visit him.

It is a matter of life or death.

With all the best,
Mrs. Joanna Davies

Life or death.

Felicity set down the book, bolted out of her chair, and began to change her clothes. The note seemed to burn in her hand from its desperation.

With as much haste as she could manage, she would be in London by early evening.

★ ★ ★

The horses pulling her carriage couldn't go fast enough for Felicity. She had asked her driver, Matthew, to hurry, and he did, but her concern about Jackson Davies seemed to lengthen the minutes into intolerable hours.

She had not talked with her friend for several months. Her frequent notes to him to join her for dinner at Carrol Manor or tea when she visited London had gone unanswered. She had even stopped by his office at Scotland Yard on occasion. Every time, she had been told he was out on a case, and so she had left him another note. She was curious about what crimes had kept him busy and why he hadn't told her about them. She was also vexed because he seemed to be shutting her out of his life.

They had met during the King Arthur Affair. During their earlier encounters, they sparred each time they talked. He attempted to keep her out of the investigation, and she wanted him to listen to her theories. He wanted evidence. She had deductions and science. They were pugilists with words.

When she solved the case, Davies apologized and promised to trust and listen to her from then on. Afterward, they met regularly. When she worked on her own investigations to locate murderers and needed his help, he supplied support and information. Sometimes he came to her and presented facts of a case and sought her insights and whatever data she could obtain thanks to her financial resources. She learned much about police procedures from him and taught him new investigative methods, though he remained skeptical of them. Yet they came to trust each other. Despite their vastly different stations in life, they found a comfortable state in between. They had both lost their fathers and were strident about obtaining justice for victims of murder and other crimes.

When not working on their own inquiries into lawbreaking, they met for lunch or dinner, where they discussed events of the world and England or merely laughed at each other's bad jokes. When he visited Carrol Manor, they walked out to the private lake on the estate and sat and listened to the night.

Felicity believed Inspector Jackson Davies resembled one of those handsome actors in Shakespearean plays she had seen: the squarest of jaws, features that could have been chiseled by Michelangelo or even one of the lesser Renaissance sculptors, dark-amber eyes hinting of a hidden forest. When she had finally confessed this to him, he had taken offense. To prove her point, which she was prone to do, she had taken him to a production of *Hamlet* at St James's Theatre on King Street. He had never attended a play before, and she had the greatest pleasure in knowing what a teacher must feel giving a student a basic lesson in life. Davies's mouth opened in awe at the Louis XIV–style interior of the theater, and throughout he smiled at the play's action.

"Well?" she asked him afterward.

"That Hamlet fella should have just had his uncle arrested for the murder of his father," Davies said in an accent suggesting his East End roots. "Let the law deal with the killer, I say."

"Ah, but testimony from the ghost of Hamlet's father isn't admissible in court," she said.

He blew out a laugh. "You're right. I did like the sword fighting, although half the time I couldn't understand what in blazes they were talking about."

It was her turn to laugh.

"And I still think I look more like a Scotland Yard inspector than an actor in those ruffles and tights," he added.

"That, Jackson Davies, is your opinion. Come on now. I'll buy you dinner."

"Good. You have more money than I do."

Felicity's mind didn't change, however. She believed her friend much better looking than the thespian who played the mad Dane on the stage.

Then, last August, Davies had told her he had been assigned to the case of a prostitute who had been brutally mutilated in Whitechapel, a district of the East End known for its poverty, crime, and congestion.

"We'll have this nasty fellow caught in a week," Davies said to her at lunch at the Crown's Place, which had become one of their spots to meet. Located near the London coroner's office, the tavern sold good food and ale at a reasonable price. She was more at home there than at any of the expensive restaurants where she and her father had dined.

A month later, she and Davies were meeting for tea at the Café Royal on Regent Street. Davies had arrived wearing a rumpled shirt, and his face held on to a shadow of a beard. This was quite out of character for the inspector, who usually took great care with his appearance. His eyes were liquid with anger and lack of sleep as he talked about the hunt for the Whitechapel killer.

"This man, Felicity, this man is insane," he said.

"From what I read in the *Times*, you don't have to convince me," Felicity replied.

"The way he damages the women." He closed his eyes and grimaced, as if seeing the bodies.

She placed her hand on his. "You look like you haven't slept in weeks, Jackson."

"Too much to do," he said, almost to himself, then downed his tea. "I can't stay, Felicity."

"You've barely gotten here."

He squeezed her hand. "I'm sorry. I'll be in touch." And he hurried out of the restaurant.

They hadn't talked since that day. Over the following months, more prostitutes had become the victims of the grisly homicides thought to be the work of this maniacal killer.

The murderer was never apprehended.

Instead of reading about a new method for criminal investigation, Felicity sometimes sat in the library at Carrol Manor or in her bedroom at the London house and thought about Jackson Davies. After months without contact, she had begun reviewing their many conversations and wondered if she had said or done anything to cause him to break off contact with her. Felicity missed her friend. She had so few that his loss was akin to facing the tempestuous English Channel with a canoe and a spoon to paddle across. Her other good friends in the world were Helen and John Ryan. But she couldn't talk about crime with them. Jackson Davies made her think, and she cherished him for it. She admired most his desire for justice, which was as potent as her own.

On the carriage ride to see him, Felicity bit her upper lip. She should have told him how much his friendship meant to her. Yes, he was intelligent and attractive, humorous and generous. He treated her with regard and as an equal. Although they still verbally jousted, they could talk about anything, and just as important, he accepted her aptitude for solving crimes. She had never seen him through the haze of one of those misty-colored romantic lights. That's because she didn't dream of a Prince Charming as much as she did catching a heinous criminal. She also doubted Jackson thought of her as a princess to be rescued. Theirs was a relationship of mutual esteem. Perhaps that was a type of love. She hadn't decided. She just knew she was worried about him.

"Please, Matthew, hurry on," she shouted up to her driver.

She hoped she wasn't too late.

CHAPTER 3

Inspector Jackson Davies's flat lay on the border between the East End and the rest of London. The East End's poverty faded close to his doorstep but could still be seen from a distance. Children in rags, working men, dismal streets. Shocking despair.

He resided on the second floor of a standard brick building appearing much like the ones on either side. Felicity rushed up the stairs as soon as Matthew stopped the carriage.

Joanna Davies answered Felicity's knock. Davies's mother appeared as her son had described her: a tall, handsome woman. Her friend must have inherited some of his looks from her—same thick black hair, same green-brown eyes. As soon as Felicity stepped into the parlor, Joanna hugged her, which made Felicity taste rising tears.

"My dear Miss Carrol. I'm so grateful you came." Joanna's voice was as warm as fresh bread from the oven.

"Jackson is my friend. I'll always come to his aid." Felicity hugged her back.

Joanna wiped at tears with her ironed apron.

"And please call me Felicity."

"Joanna."

Felicity nodded.

"Jackson will be so happy to see you." Joanna motioned for her to sit.

Davies's flat was tidy and masculine, with a dark rug, dark curtains, and dark furniture. A short shelf held books, a majority of them about police procedures. He had once told Felicity his place could fit into her library at Carrol Manor, and he had been absolutely correct. Four boxes stacked in one corner of the room drew her attention.

The room smelled of him—the sweet tobacco she had bought him for his birthday, with a little bay rum thrown in for good measure. Felicity sat down on a small dark-blue couch, while Joanna took a seat across from her.

"What's wrong with Jackson?" she asked his mother.

The woman's eyes shifted to a closed door to the left. "My son is very ill. The doctor says he has fluid in his lungs."

"But when did this happen? How did this happen?" She was also upset that he hadn't informed her of his illness

Joanna's hands balled up her apron. "His physical condition has been worsening over the last months, Felicity. He's almost worked himself to death investigating that ghastly case."

"The Whitechapel murders." The words dried Felicity's tongue.

"Aye. He didn't eat or sleep well while he tried to find the man who butchered those women."

"Those killings halted in early November."

"But Jackson didn't."

"That's not surprising. Your son is a driven young man."

"He thought of nothing else but catching that killer. He'd work his regular shift on other cases and then go prowling throughout Whitechapel searching for evidence." Joanna pointed to the boxes. "His papers are there. I picked them up when he fell sick. They were scattered all over the house, along with shocking photographs of the victims. They are dreadful, my dear. Dreadful. To think my son lived with that horror for months."

"No wonder he became ill."

"Jackson seemed to be getting better until one week ago. Then he collapsed and took to his bed." As she talked, Joanna's voice fractured with sadness. "I'm afraid for my boy."

Felicity clenched her hands to maintain her emotion. A display of worry would do no one any good, and she *was* worried. "May I see him now, Joanna?"

With a brave smile, Joanna got up, knocked on the door, and looked in. She nodded to Felicity and lightly touched her back when she entered the room.

Felicity had a lot of experience with a splintering heart: the death of her mother and then her older brother, the neglect of her father ever since she could remember, his death after their row over her independence.

But nothing had prepared her for the ache that rose in her when she saw what had befallen Scotland Yard inspector Jackson Davies.

He was lying flat on his bed, his head turned toward the windows. His whole being seemed to withdraw into the bedcovers. Felicity walked over to his bed and sat on a chair next to it. She took his hand, which was cool and insubstantial to her touch. She recalled when he had taken her hand at her father's funeral. There had been such strength within his grasp.

He turned his face toward hers. His deep-set cheeks and the shading around his eyes attested to a loss of more than twenty pounds. His color reminded her of old paper. His thick black hair lay limp against the pillow, and his white bed shirt was rumpled and sweaty. Most painful to see were his eyes. Once animated with intelligence and drive, they were now dull with defeat. She wanted to weep. *Be resilient for him*, she told herself.

Felicity smiled. "Inspector, are you trying to annoy me?"

Throughout their meetings, he had told her she annoyed him with her all her questions and theories. This time she hoped to make him smile. At this moment she wanted that more than anything in the world.

He did smile, through lips looking as if they had not tasted water in years. "Bless me, Felicity Carrol."

She leaned over to kiss his cheek. The intimate gesture was natural and at the same time astounded her with a new realization. This man *was* important to her.

He sat up a little, though he struggled in the attempt. She aided him and placed a pillow at his back.

"I suppose my mother contacted you. I wish she hadn't." He looked at his hands.

"I'm very angry *you* didn't let me know about your condition. Then again, you're always very proud and stubborn."

"Guilty." He coughed up what sounded like phlegm into a handkerchief. With watery eyes, he looked up at her and smiled once more.

She was happy he could do so. "Your mother says you've labored way too hard on this horrendous Whitechapel homicide case. So much so that you've driven yourself to exhaustion, and now what sounds like a bout of pneumonia."

"Just a cold." What color remained in his cheeks paled even more, and he shook with a chill.

Pulling up the blanket, she tucked it around him. "Remember I have a degree in medicine, so no more of that. You've never lied to me before, so don't start now, Inspector Jackson Davies." She gripped his hand tighter. "I know you. Once you undertake an investigation, you don't stop until it's settled."

"This one certainly wasn't."

"And because of that, you're wallowing in loss and consider yourself a failure because you haven't found the killer who preyed on Whitechapel. Your record of arrest has been superlative until now, and you can't accept the disappointment."

"That your diagnosis, Dr. Carrol?" he said with bitterness.

"It is. You possess a commanding sense of justice and there has been none in this case, which has literally sickened you. But, Jackson, spending so much time on this particular crime smacks of mania. A fixation that has poisoned your mind and harmed your body." She half hoped her truthfulness would snap him back to health, if for no other reason than to argue with her.

But he laid his head back on the pillow and sighed so deeply, Felicity feared he might not have any breath left.

He stared at her. "As usual, you're right." He spoke quietly.

A tear ran down his cheek. Felicity had never seen a man cry before, and her spirit wept with him. She took out her handkerchief and dotted at his face.

"To hear out loud what I've been thinking all along is very disturbing," he said.

"And aren't you glad I was the one who said it?" She smiled.

"Your ability to aggravate me beyond any reason hasn't faded." He sat up a little more.

"Now that's the Jackson Davies I know. Sarcastic, proud, and self-righteous."

"I'm not self-righteous."

"Jackson, there have been other cases you haven't solved. Why is this one so different?"

"Because the killer is a madman and he's still out there. During the course of my career, I've encountered many bad things in London and in the East End in particular. But the horror of these crimes . . . they chill my very core." He placed his hand on hers and squeezed. "They make me question how good can survive in a world that produced such a fiend. It is as if heaven has moved even farther away from us."

"There will always be good in the world with men like you."

"Felicity, you don't realize how much work the Yard put into tracking down this maniac."

She made a clicking noise with her tongue. "I do read and I do remember. Teams of policemen went house to house in Whitechapel. More than two thousand people were questioned, three hundred people seriously investigated, and some eighty men held under suspicion."

He sat up even more.

"Surgeons, physicians, and even butchers were considered suspects because of the types of mutilations made with a knife and the removal of organs from some of the victims. Police surgeon Thomas Bond even consulted on the killer's character. After reviewing the postmortem reports and other facts, Mr. Bond called the Whitechapel killer a lonely man with episodes of homicidal and erotic mania. All in all, these crimes have called forth all the vast resources of the Metropolitan Police. Despite that, the murderer remained at large." She placed her hand on his. "See, Jackson. I have kept up on the case."

"I should've known."

"Yes, you should have."

He laughed and began to cough again. Rough and wet sounds emanated from his lungs. His face reddened.

"Joanna, come quickly." Felicity stood up and called.

The woman rushed into the room, holding a small glass container.

"Jackson, breathe slowly." Felicity took his hand again. "That's brilliant. Now hold that air. Command it to fill your lungs."

"Take this, my love." His mother placed a dropper full of liquid from the glass into his mouth. She turned toward Felicity. "The doctor said this will help his lungs."

His breathing steadied.

"There now," Joanna said and kissed the top of his head. "I'm making broth for the both of you. Go on with your chat now, and I'll let you know when it's ready." She left.

"I like your mother very much, Jackson," Felicity said.

"She's my heart."

"Then you're fortunate." Felicity dotted away perspiration from his head and chest.

He ran his fingers through his hair. "To have made myself sick this way . . . I'm ashamed, Felicity."

"You shouldn't be. No other man I know would care so much, Jackson. You gave almost everything—even your health—to solve terrible crimes. I greatly admire that."

His smile filled with gratitude.

"Your mother said you took a turn a week ago. What caused this?"

From underneath his pillow he took out a folded newspaper story and handed it to her, his hands shaking.

BIZARRE KILLER STRIKES
IN MINING TOWN

The prosperous and wild mining town of Placer, Montana, is home to thousands of souls who labor at the several mines and smelters on its outskirts, all for the prize of silver, gold, and copper.

In the early-morning hours of March 29, 1889, Mr. Joe Maxwell was heading home from his long day at the Big Strike Mine when he literally stumbled across a grisly scene. The body of Lily "Big Lil" Rawlins lay in an alley off Melton Street, which is located in the center of the town's notorious red-light district, home to its many brothels.

Rawlins had been a prostitute and was the victim of a fiendish and revolting murder. Two wounds from ear to ear sliced her throat deep enough that her head was nearly severed from her body. Her torso also suffered foul and horrendous mutilations.

The town law ruled out robbery as the motive, as twenty dollars remained in the victim's nearby purse.

Thirty-three years of age, Lily Rawlins had been a frequent imbiber of liquor. The poor victim had earned her name "Big Lil" because she weighed two hundred and eighty pounds. The murder took place within four blocks of her residence on Viceroy Street. She left behind no family that authorities could locate.

Town sheriff Thomas Pike reported that no one had been arrested in the atrocious murder.

The crime echoes the horrifying slaughter of five prostitutes between August and November 1888 in the Whitechapel district of the East End of London. The suspect in those murders has never been apprehended despite a massive hunt by Scotland Yard.

In those terrifying cases, the killer slashed the throat of each victim and viciously mutilated their bodies.

"Where'd you get this article? It didn't come from the *Times* or any London paper, or I would have recalled the information," Felicity said.

"The story was published in the *New York Times*. A colleague at Scotland Yard gave it to me. He has a relative in the States who sent it to him because of our work on the Whitechapel murders."

"I understand why you relapsed. You believe the killer has relocated to America."

"He's gone to continue his repulsive work, and unless we hurry, there will be more victims. I've got to go there. To Montana." His voice sounded rough, as if he had eaten gravel.

Felicity gave him a sip of water from a glass on a table near his bed. His chest rose and fell with effort.

"You aren't going anywhere, Inspector Jackson Davies. If you do, then this killer will have claimed one more victim, and that I can't allow." She looked down at the newspaper in her hand. "I'm going."

"What?" He attempted to sit up, but she held him down.

"There's nothing wrong with your ears."

"This man is more dangerous than any you've encountered. Even I'm afraid of him."

"That reinforces the point that he must be stopped. I shall simply go there and see what I can learn about the murder. If your hunch is accurate and it is the Whitechapel killer, then when you have recovered, you can join me. You can arrest him and make sure he faces the law, and the hangman."

"I know you, Felicity Margaret Carrol. You don't do anything simply."

"Hush, now." Felicity rose and called for Joanna Davies to join them. Felicity took the woman's hand. "Joanna, I'm going on a journey on Jackson's behalf. Before I leave, I'm going to hire the best physician available to care for him, along with a nurse to help you. You shall have anything you need to see he gets well."

The look on Joanna's face was all the thanks Felicity needed. She turned to Jackson, who closed his eyes.

"If anything should happen to you . . ." he said.

"Nothing will happen. We both want to find this killer and make sure he gets what he deserves. Justice is my goal in life also, Jackson."

"I'm your friend. I can't let you go."

Felicity took his hand in both of hers. "*Because* I'm your friend, I must go."

She would track down Jack the Ripper.

CHAPTER 4

Felicity sat in the library at Carrol Manor and read more of the files Jackson Davies had given her. She attempted to assimilate the information with the detached eye of a scientist or detective. But her toes chilled as if she were wriggling them in dirt over a fresh grave.

Five prostitutes killed in or near Whitechapel over the course of four months. All mutilated in a nightmarish manner. The more she read, the more she comprehended why the Scotland Yard inspector and her friend had become fixated on arresting this murderer.

Helen Wilkins rapped on the open library door, and she was startled.

"Anything wrong, Hellie?" Felicity bade her enter the room.

"No, Miss Felicity. I'm thinking you might want a chaperone for your trip to Montana. And since you didn't mention you had one, I'd like to offer my services."

Earlier in the day, Felicity had announced to the servants her pending trip to the United States. She hadn't even thought about a companion.

"Montana is a long way, Hellie."

"I raised you, and I mean to protect you." Helen stood up like a soldier ready for combat.

"We're going to what could be an uncivilized place, perhaps even a hazardous one."

"I grew up in the streets of Spitalfields. After that, any place is a ride in the country."

Helen often mentioned her roots in the tough part of London and how that upbringing had made her tough as well. Yes, she was, but Helen was also loving and capable of great gentleness.

"You sure, Hellie?"

"Even Indians won't scare me." She paused. "Will we run into Indians?"

"I don't believe so where we're going."

"Then why are you going, Miss Felicity?"

Helen was one of the few people who knew about Felicity's work solving murders and other crimes. "To track down a killer. And one of the most enigmatic ones we may ever confront."

"Well, every young woman should have a hobby." Helen winked.

Felicity warmed with gratitude. "Then we're off to Montana, my girl."

★   ★   ★

Her hands on her hips, Felicity talked more to herself than to the two maids in her bedroom. "What shall I do about the chemicals? I'll just have to take the essentials and hope American apothecaries have the ones I may require."

She pointed to one of the four open steamer trunks in the room. "Gertie, please pack the books I've set in the corner."

Felicity could have used one more trunk but was making do because her personal items had not yet been packed. She had kept the clothing selections simple because she doubted she'd be attending any balls or teas where they were heading. She hoped so, anyway.

A young housemaid stood in the doorway. "Your solicitor is here, Miss."

"Please show him to the small sitting room downstairs and send on the tea. Thank you, Maggie."

After her father's death, Felicity had given much thought to terminating the employ of this particular solicitor. Martin Jameson had been her father's friend, and the solicitor's arrogance more than equaled her father's. He wore superiority over others like a pearl stickpin. And not unlike her own parent, the solicitor didn't hide his disapproval of her. Both men had condemned her pursuit of education and freedom instead of matrimony and becoming an acceptable young woman of English society. When she inherited the estate and holdings, she had asked Jameson for all the financial reports of her family's assets, investments, and companies. With such a request, she had hoped he might not want to be employed by a woman, but Jameson had told her he had promised her father to look after her and sent on the reports.

The solicitor had been with their family for years and she couldn't dismiss him so easily, although she scolded herself for sentimentality. She also had to admit to herself that she kept him on partly out of the guilt she still felt about her father's death.

The rotund Jameson stood and bowed slightly as she entered the sitting room. She asked him to take a seat and the servants to leave. "Thank you for coming on the shortest of notices, Mr. Jameson."

"I am always at your service, Miss Carrol, as I promised your late father."

Whenever she spoke with him, he always reminded her of that. She cleared her throat. "In the next few days, I will travel to America for what may be an extended period of time. I'm going to a place called Placer, Montana."

"Montana?"

One side of her mouth bowed up in a smile. "Sounds barbaric, doesn't it?"

"I am sure the place will live up to the name." His nostrils were alert, as if smelling mess. He was a man of expensive tastes and grim manner, leaving Felicity to wonder if he had ever laughed out loud in his life.

The servant entered with the tea.

"Maggie, I'll pour for Mr. Jameson and myself." The servant curtsied and left. Felicity turned her attention back to the solicitor. "I require your services for additional items related to my trip."

Jameson sniffed. "Proceed."

"I need a good-sized house in Placer, Montana. Certainly nowhere as large as Carrol Manor. Three or four bedrooms will suffice. In addition, I'd like someone to run errands for me, someone very familiar with the town. This person must also be discreet and trustworthy. Lastly, I require a line of credit to pay for my expenses. Even an American town like Placer must have a bank." She handed him a list. "My necessities for this journey."

He sniffed again.

Felicity handed him another document. "If anything should happen to me while I'm away, here's my last will and testament. I mean for the servants to be taken care of, especially those who have served my family for years and raised me."

"Miss Carrol, what could possibly happen to you?"

"Please, let me continue. Since I'm unmarried, it's my intention that Carrol Manor be turned into a school for girls. This school will be open to any who want to attend, regardless of their station, rich or poor. The assets from the family's mill and shipping revenue will fund this endeavor. The instructions are included in the papers." She'd had the firm of Morton & Morton draw up her will.

"A school?" Jameson's cheeks flamed with indignation. "This house has been in your family for three generations."

"And I can think of no better future for the manor than helping young girls obtain an education. Please take the document, Mr. Jameson."

He touched the will as if it were soiled and exhaled more disapproval. "But how can you, a young woman, travel alone halfway around the world? This isn't prudent, wise, or decent. People will be shocked."

"Miss Helen Wilkins will accompany me. She's an impeccable chaperone. And I believe Placer, Montana, is less than one-quarter of the way around the world." She couldn't resist a poke at Jameson's crusty exterior.

"Miss Carrol, may I ask the reason for your expedition to America?"

Felicity had prepared for this inquiry. She had created a good diversion story to avoid any more questions—or at least she hoped she had. She had also rehearsed the fabrication like an actress learning a role.

She stood up to aid in the performance. "I intend to become a writer of crime and mystery stories. They're frightfully entertaining and quite popular." She made the announcement with deliberation and pride. Then she waited, expecting a sneer, argument, and lecture in propriety from Martin Jameson. In their place, disquiet passed over his face as if all he had ever known had been called into question.

"Whatever in God's name inspired you to take up such an enterprise?"

"Edgar Allan Poe."

"Poe?"

"'The Murders in the Rue Morgue,' 'The Pit and the Pendulum,' and all his other tales of horror and crime." She put a measure of admiration in her voice, which was not feigned. She did love his writing. "Mr. Poe is my ideal. He was American, you know. So what better way to start this new authorial undertaking than in the United States?"

"Crime writing?"

"Jane Austen and the Brontës penned stories of romance, but this genre is much more exciting."

Mention of the famous English writers softened his condemning expression—only faintly. *Remarkable*, Felicity thought. So a woman writer was more acceptable than a female investigating murder. She couldn't understand why. But if nothing else, Jameson already thought her eccentric, so he might accept this writer invention. Even if he didn't, she was going forward with her plans.

"Why this Montana place, Miss Carrol?"

"A very interesting crime has been committed there, one that has inspired my first book. Of course, London is no stranger to murder." Felicity hadn't intended to bring up the topic, but it provided a reference the solicitor might understand.

"Whitechapel," Jameson whispered, as if the word was an obscenity.

Any Londoner who read the *Times* knew about the Whitechapel killer, but she hadn't thought this highly proper solicitor would mention a clearly scandalous case. This surprised her.

"Precisely, Mr. Jameson. I've studied the murders and read all the newspaper articles." That was true.

The teacup clattered in his hand until he set it on the table.

"I know I should take up painting or the piano, but crime writing intrigues me so. On the positive side, I won't torch the house with pen and ink as I did with my science experiments." She knew her late father had told Jameson about that particular incident. "And who knows? I might become as famous as Mr. Poe, under a pseudonym, naturally." She extended her hand. "In any event, thank you for helping me in these preparations and for all you've done for my family, Mr. Jameson."

Sniffing again, he stood to leave but remained stationary and didn't shake her hand. His full eyebrows jerked together.

"Do we have more business to discuss, sir?"

"Miss Carrol, as your solicitor and as a friend to your late father, I recommend you seriously consider the possible consequences of digging into what should be left buried."

"Whatever do you mean?"

"The past should remain untouched. Dredging it up will only bring pain and destruction. I can say no more at the moment."

"You haven't said much."

"Good day." Nodding his balding head, the solicitor departed.

Felicity scratched her chin over the solicitor's comment, which sounded more like a polite threat than legal counsel. But she couldn't waste any energy on his secrets.

Returning to her bedroom to finish packing, Felicity threw one of her petticoats to the floor. With Martin Jameson, she had surrendered to what society expected of her. Taking a chaperone, indeed. She wanted to go alone. But if she did disregard that convention, she would probably offend the men who managed the family businesses. And she needed them to keep the hundreds of people employed at her companies, as well as to generate the revenue to fund her investigations into crimes. She detested the rules of English social order as much as she hated ignorance, but she knew enough to choose which battles to undertake. Traveling with a chaperone was one she wouldn't fight. She also had to admit she was looking forward to Helen's company on this trip.

Now with the journey two days away, Felicity picked up her petticoat from the floor and placed it over one of the trunks. On her dressing table, she unfolded the newspaper article Jackson Davies had given her. Felicity placed the clipping on top of a thick packet of papers, secured it with string, and packed it. She had one more stop to make.

CHAPTER 5

The London cabby's eyes and cheeks were degrees of red. Felicity surmised that whiskey was the source, based on the smell of his clothing. Still, he had a trustworthy face—the look of a hardworking man with a back bowed from hauling around people all day in the black hansom cab. His brown horse was a sturdy strutter, brushed and spritely, which told Felicity the driver cared for the animal that helped him make a living.

Felicity hired him outside the Regency Hotel on Kensington High Street, where she and Helen had rooms. In the morning, their boat was scheduled to cross the great pond for America. While Helen rested at the hotel, Felicity took a carriage to the East End of London.

"You really want to go there?" the driver asked Felicity when she told him her destination.

"I do."

He brushed a gloved hand under his nose. "You must be very brave, Miss."

"I can only hope so."

He helped her into his cab, which mercifully did not smell of whiskey.

"Come now, Daisy," the cabby called from his tall seat in back of the carriage. With a click or two of his tongue, he drove Felicity to the East End. Once there, they crossed an invisible border from affluence to misery. The world of invention and progress had halted at the border of the East End, one of the most poverty-stricken sections of the city.

Little had changed since the last time Felicity had visited this part of London. The cab passed the King Cock public house, which looked even worse in the day. There she had met a thief of antiquities during her very first murder investigation—the one that had directed her path to catching criminals. That case had ended well.

With hands closed tightly on her lap, Felicity hoped for a similar outcome in her next undertaking. Success was imperative to save her friend Jackson Davies. He needed her. And in all her years, she had never been needed before by another human being. The sensation was humbling, wonderful, and petrifying.

Because of the poverty of the area, the sky seemed murkier in the East End than anyplace else in London, although the hour had just struck noon and the sky was clear enough. Putting her hand to her mouth, Felicity choked on the smell of rot and stale beer. While horse manure from constant carriage traffic stank up many of London's streets, the stench was worse in this section of London because the roadways were not cleaned as often. She did not fault the people who resided there. With low-paying jobs, they could afford only crowded housing with inadequate sanitation. From these conditions grew slums and crime and more squalor. The attitude of English society—the people who had way more money, that is—was that the poor were poor because they were sinners. She thought those who spouted such ignorance should keep their mouths shut and learn what it was like to live with little money, prospects, or education.

"Don't tarry too long in this place, Miss," the cabby said as Felicity got out at George Street. "It's not the safest place for a lady."

"I will be fine. Please wait here as I asked."

"You paid me well to wait, and that I will." He crossed his arms and nodded to seal the agreement.

She asked directions of a police officer with a young man's whiskers and eyes darting at every sound. Even he did not want to be there. Through Morton & Morton, she had asked John McCarthy, the building owner, to meet her. A huge man who wheezed as much as he breathed, he stood in front of the door to Thirteen Miller's Court. McCarthy leered at her approach.

"In between renters for the moment. No one likes to stay here very long 'cause of what happened." The man threw a terrific sneeze into a gray handkerchief and opened the lock. "I'll be in the room next door if you need anything. Stay as long as you like, love."

Anemic sunlight through the window only emphasized the room's dinge. Against one wall, a small bed was bent as an old man's arm. Splintered wood made up the table, two chairs, and floor in the twelve-foot-square room. The building smelled of cabbage soup. Removing her gloves, Felicity's fingers traced the furniture and the mantel of the small fireplace.

This was where Mary Jane Kelly had died.

Felicity recalled the details of Kelly's final night from reading Metropolitan Police, postmortem, and inquest reports, as well as many newspaper narratives about what had passed the morning of November 9, 1888.

Before midnight, Mary Jane Kelly had left a pub by herself and set off to the tiny flat at Thirteen Miller's Court. The threadbare red shawl she wore probably provided little protection from the nip of the November night. Inside the room, she warmed up a bit of greasy fish and potatoes she had saved from her previous night's dinner but pushed the plate away after two bites. How far her life had toppled— from working as a domestic servant, to being a clerk in a shop on Commercial Street, to servicing clients in a high-class brothel in the

West End, and finally to rambling the thoroughfares of the lower depths of Whitechapel. Closing her eyes, she began to sing "A Violet From Mother's Grave," an American tune. Those who knew her said Mary Jane had a lovely voice that didn't belong in the East End.

"*They all have left me in sorrow here to roam. While life does remain, in memoriam I'll retain this small violet I plucked from Mother's grave,*" Kelly sang.

However, not all appreciated her voice. An upstairs neighbor woman pounded on the floor and screamed, "Shut it. Don't you know it's one in the bloody morning!"

Mary Jane kept on singing. "*No one's left to cheer me now within that good old home.*"

Although it was nearing two o'clock, Kelly ventured out into the dark streets one more time. Somewhere she met a stranger, whom she invited back to her flat. A knife replied to her invitation.

At eleven later that morning, a man knocked on her door to collect the rent she owed. The place was mute as a church on Monday. He tried the door, but it was locked. One of the panes was missing in the window by the door. He shouted for Kelly to wake up and pay up. Still, she didn't respond. He pulled aside the shabby curtain.

Blood was everywhere.

All the way to the Commercial Street Police Station, the man yelled, "Murder! Murder!"

Building owner John McCarthy heard the shouting and met the police in front of Mary Jane Kelly's room. Since this was his building, McCarthy insisted on wielding the ax against the locked door. When the door gave way and he entered, his eyes went to the woman's clothing over the chair and her worn boots by the fireplace. They were the sole normalcy in the room. In the middle of the bed lay Mary Jane Kelly's body, or what was left of it. Her lovely hair was wavy as seaweed, undulating in a current of red.

The savage killing of the prostitutes had started on August 31, 1888, in Whitechapel, the center of the End East. Police appeared helpless as the killer kept up his spree, often leaving bodies out on the nighttime streets. Mary Jane Kelly was the last of the five women murdered. By the time he was finished, this so-called Jack the Ripper had spread alarm around the area and the whole of the East End because no one knew where he might strike next.

After Mary Jane Kelly, the murders stopped as abruptly as they had begun. The killer was never captured. He seemed to have vanished like a nightmare in the morning, but leaving the sleeper fretful and afraid of repeating the dream.

Felicity breathed out and closed the door behind her. She thanked McCarthy, though she had paid him well to let her into the tiny flat.

This time he didn't ogle her. "You're not the only person who wanted to see this place in the day."

"I'm sure."

"Reporters. Writers. The curious. Damn 'em all. What's your reason, Miss?"

She gave a last look at Thirteen Miller's Court. "To finish what a friend couldn't."

His eyes constricted with bafflement.

"What was she like, Mary Jane Kelly?" Felicity said.

McCarthy shut the door and locked it. "She's dead now. What's it matter?"

"You were there, Mr. McCarthy. You saw what happened to her in that room."

"I did." His eyes were wet with anxiety.

"And that's why it does matter." Felicity left the man and began walking back to the waiting carriage on George Street.

Her steps sounded hollow under her feet. She felt as if a solar eclipse had shaded the sun and the light might never return to warm the earth. She had been shocked by the cruel details she had read in the reports about Mary Jane Kelly and the other Whitechapel victims, but they were only words. To actually stand in the room where the woman had been slain made the murders real and the killer more dangerous.

With each new investigation Felicity had undertaken, she had questioned herself. Whether her knowledge of science, history, physics, medicine, and all those other subjects she had studied would help her solve a crime. Whether she would be up to the task, whether she could work up an inner strength to look past the horror for clues that would lead her to the murderer.

This case was no exception.

Hurrying on, she had no time for such doubt. Later, she would weep for the lost, when the culprit was behind bars waiting for execution. Now she had to ready herself for a long voyage.

Within another house near the East End, Inspector Jackson Davies lay in a bed. He had been wrecked like a ship pounding against unforgiving rocks. The energetic young man she had verbally scrapped with, annoyed, and befriended was now a phantom in his own life.

Inspector Davies had become obsessed with arresting the fiend who had killed Mary Jane Kelly and the other women in Whitechapel. He had spent hours, days, weeks, and months working the scarce clues he and other inspectors could unearth in a truly puzzling case. He had revisited each crime scene over and over. Followed suspects who had turned out to be innocent. He had neglected his family, his health, and his friends, including Felicity, all in the name of justice. But despite his labors, the killer had evaporated into obscurity once he had satisfied his yearning for death.

Thanks to her astounding talent for retaining all she read, Felicity recalled every word in the newspaper article Davies had given her. Her friend was right. The lead in a remote mining town on another continent was one that had to be examined. Jackson Davies could not make the trip, but giving Felicity the newspaper clipping amounted to handing over a challenge, albeit with reluctance.

Now it was up to her to find Jack the Ripper, even if it meant a trip to the wilds of Montana.

CHAPTER 6

Placer, Montana

Felicity and Helen stepped out of the stagecoach, and the ground shook. Horses clomped dirt. Buildings tremored.

"My heavens," exclaimed Helen, who turned around and tried to get back in the coach.

"What an introduction," said Felicity, who gently tugged on the back of Helen's dress to stop her. "We've come all this way, Hellie. We can't go back now."

"Oh yes, we can."

Felicity straightened her velvet hat while their trunks were removed from the coach. At a café across from the station, a man leaned against the porch. A star glinted on his leather vest. A lawman of the West—how exciting just to see one! She noticed how he examined the face of every man in the vicinity. He was searching for someone, and from his severe gaze, she was glad it was not her.

Then the man's focus landed on Felicity and Helen, and he ambled toward them as if he had more than time on his side.

"This is our lucky day, Helen. I wanted to meet the sheriff, and I believe here he comes."

"I wouldn't call that lucky," Helen replied, and pulled at her wrinkled dress. "He's probably come to throw us out of town."

"Don't be so negative, Hellie." Even if he threw them out, she'd come back, because she had a goal to achieve.

The sheriff walked straight, though perhaps a little too much so, as if he followed only a trail he trusted. With his longish dark-brown hair, he could have been a good-looking young Allan Quatermain pursuing adventure in Africa rather than a lawman upholding order in an unruly Montana town. As if he had heard her thoughts, the man licked his fingers to tame a few errant strands of hair behind his ears.

Pay attention, Felicity chided herself. *You're acting like a silly schoolgirl, not that you ever were one.*

"Welcome to Placer," the sheriff told Felicity. His voice sounded like an American sunset, rich and rough.

"This place is certainly a long way from New York."

"Or anywhere." Helen adjusted her hat. Her thumb pointed back at the stagecoach. "My insides have never been so shaken around as in that contraption." She turned to Felicity. "And Miss, you said nothing about earthquakes in Montana."

Before Felicity could answer, the man held up his hand. He noted his short shadow, took a watch out of a vest pocket, and smiled. "Wait one more minute, ma'am."

Helen mouthed *ma'am* to Felicity, and they both tried not to laugh.

A whistle blew in the distance, and the whole town rattled once again. In the street, horses reared and whinnied. Dogs barked. Windows shook.

"Another earthquake!" Helen started to climb back into the stagecoach, and Felicity again pulled at the back of her dress.

"No earthquake, Helen. A dynamite explosion. If I'm not mistaken, the sound originated from the west."

"You're right, ma'am. It's the noontime blasting at the mines."
The sheriff scratched his head.

From his face, Felicity could tell he was wondering how a
woman knew about dynamite.

"I suppose the blasting takes place during the day so as not to
wake everyone," she said.

"That's the general idea. You two sound British."

"Your powers of observation are keen. Are you the welcoming committee?" The corners of Felicity's mouth quirked up with
mischievousness. The sheriff replied with a smile he probably used
to impress women.

"Sheriff Tom Pike, at your service." He tipped up his hat.

"This is fortuitous. Exactly the person I wanted to meet,"
Felicity said.

"How lucky can a fella get?"

Brilliant. Another sarcastic man. Her mouth straightened with
determination. "I've come to Placer to learn about the murder of
Lily Rawlins."

Pike lost his amiable exterior and instead became a wooden pillar.

She pointed at the star on his chest. "You *are* the sheriff, aren't
you?"

"Last I looked, ma'am."

"Enough *ma'am*. My name is Felicity Carrol, and this is Miss
Helen Wilkins."

Pike shook their hands. "A pleasure. But what's all this about
Lily Rawlins? You a Pinkerton detective or something?"

Helen laughed.

"Heavens, no. But what a delightful compliment." Felicity's
eyes widened.

"When you came out of the stagecoach, I told myself spring
had arrived. Lovely and refreshing like the flowers on the moun-
tainside," Pike said.

"How poetic of you, Sheriff."

"Then you opened your mouth." Pike's brow creased with irritation.

Even in America, I have this effect on men, Felicity thought. But she couldn't worry about annoying this interesting fellow.

"Hundreds of people from all over the United States and other countries land in Placer to work in the mines and smelters or to seek their own golden vein in the ground. It's my duty to find out who's arrived in my town."

"Not only poetic but efficient," Felicity said.

"You two are among the most extraordinary I've ever seen."

"How kind of you. Wait, was that a compliment?" Felicity said.

"I'm not sure."

"Now, about Lily Rawlins."

"This is some sort of record, ma'am. You got into town a few minutes ago and have already put me in a God-awful mood."

"I suspect you woke up that way, Sheriff," Felicity replied.

"Why you asking about Big Lil? Her death isn't exactly the nicest subject for a lady to discuss." His tone turned harsh, as if he hoped to scare her away.

Felicity brushed dust from her skirt. "My dear sheriff, if you're not a lady, then how can you determine what is proper?"

He took off his hat and ran a hand through his hair. "Listen here, Miss Carrol . . ."

"Excuse my forwardness. This is the middle of the street and not the most conducive time or place for a conversation. Can we meet tomorrow for tea?" From her purse, she took out a handkerchief and dotted her forehead. "I have purchased a home at Fifty-Six Bullion Boulevard. Funny name."

"Not to men digging for gold. And tea is fine, Miss Carrol."

A wagon with two men stopped in front of the station. Felicity had telegraphed for one to haul her, Helen, and their trunks into town. "Say two o'clock, Sheriff?"

His nod was sharp. "I can see you're smart as well as beautiful. Me, I only had a few years of school, but I'm good at two things. The law and reading people. I can interpret a person's character as easily as reading horse tracks in the dirt." He leaned over her, which was easy, because he was a good head taller. "Already I can tell you're hiding something under your bustle. I'd also wager my best gun there are more riddles to you than the number of mining tunnels under Placer."

"But I'm not wearing a bustle." Felicity smiled. "Now, I must see to our transportation."

She and Helen left to supervise the loading of the trunks. When the men finished, one sat in the back of the wagon while the driver helped them up to the seat. As the wagon pulled out, Felicity watched Sheriff Tom Pike walk into a general store.

"Cowboys," she muttered. So far, she found that their attitudes toward women echoed those of the conservative Englishmen she had left back home. Yet the men of the American West were different, and not only because of the guns on their hips. She saw in them a muted wildness from having to survive the evident harshness of the land. The sheriff had that air, along with inquisitive eyes. Too inquisitive.

She faced front in the wagon, which traveled farther into Placer. Working with a New York attorney, her family solicitor Martin Jameson had succeeded in finding a house for her and Helen. Via telegrams received at stops on her journey across America, Jameson had informed her the property was located in a part of town where the respected and well-bred people resided. Through his American counterpart, he had also hired the services of a trustworthy older man who had worked for the former homeowner. Felicity didn't doubt Jameson's efforts. He probably couldn't stand the notion of a young Englishwoman alone with a servant in a Godforsaken place like Montana.

On their trip via steamship, railroad, and stagecoach, Felicity had read about mining to understand the source of Placer's wealth and reason for its existence. The bustling town served as a hub for the extraction of gold, silver, and copper from the Rocky Mountains located to the west and south. After refinement at smelters, the precious metals were transported by horse and wagon to a rail station twenty miles away for shipment to cities.

During the train leg of their trip, Felicity had also acquired a valuable detail not noted in any book. It had come from a smartly dressed farm-implement salesman who eyed her as if he could see straight to her bloomers. "Placer has the largest red-light district west of Independence, Missouri."

"How disgusting." Felicity had feigned ladylike offense. "I suppose that's well known in the West."

"To the right people." Even his wink was lecherous.

Especially a killer who sought out prostitutes, Felicity thought.

"Let me tell you more," he said.

Before he could, Helen tapped the man's shoulder and pointed him in the other direction. "On your way."

Placer, Montana, was larger than Felicity had expected. People in fashionable clothes strolled on clean wooden sidewalks along the wide and busy Main Avenue. Men on horses, in wagons, and on carriages rode over the grated dirt streets. Electric poles dotted both sides of Main, and men were erecting more poles on side streets. Newer brick and wood structures housed shops, hotels, banks, restaurants, express offices, and even a drugstore advertising medicines and soda water. Another group of men worked on a clock tower atop the sizable white stone building of the new courthouse, or so their driver told them.

They drove off of Main Avenue, and the mood changed.

A horse lay dead and bloated in the middle of a side street. In an alley, a man in a leather apron thrust an ax down on the thick neck of a cow. Under the animal curled ribbons of blood. From another cow hung on a hook, a man jerked out purplish entrails. A flow of pack mules, horses, and oxen towing wagons stirred a layer of dust over the streets, which were covered with brown lumps of manure.

"Whew, what a stink," Helen declared.

The stench of the animals did nothing to conceal another, fouler odor. Burning wood, sulfur, and greasy coal all mixed with sewage and tallow. Felicity commented as much to the wagon driver.

"Most of the stink comes from the big smelters, Miss." The driver's yellow bush of hair matched his yellow teeth. He pointed a craggy finger toward huge dark structures on the western edge of town. "But here we're heaven on earth compared to Butte. In that town, I seen people's noses bleed from the smoke."

"Miss Carrol, Miss Carrol." Helen tapped Felicity's shoulder. "Indians!"

Three men with black braids and decorated blankets over their shoulders led two packhorses down the street. Although the men held fierce long-barreled rifles, their faces were solemn and conquered. A woman wearing a shoddy dress and the same expression as the men dragged her feet as she carried a baby on her back. These Indians were quite different from how the dime store novels depicted them—bedecked with feathers, arrows, and menace. Still, the men appeared more than capable of declaring war on the government of the United States.

"Just wait till I tell the people back home." Helen bounced in her seat like a child. "They'll never believe I saw real Indians."

"A new world." Felicity said, not referring to just the Indians. In England, she perceived history in the cobblestones and castles. Ever since she had disembarked in America, she had been struck by an untamed rawness of this new land. In the West, there were no historical buildings anywhere because history was being made. How exhilarating.

The buckboard reached the north section of Placer. Large, well-built houses of stone and wood ruled the streets. An abundance of flowers, shrubs, and trees surrounded them.

"Greenery. For a moment, I thought this Montana town was devoid of any," Felicity said.

"This must be where the ladies and gents live," Helen said.

They stopped at a white two-story house built on a low hill. A granite block fence with a black iron gate encompassed a yard bursting with flowers. Granite steps led to a veranda wrapping around the front and sides of the house. The exterior boasted fairy-tale ornamentation of gables, stained glass, and carved wood over the windows. Two sturdy marble columns in front of the main door provided an aura of strength.

"Quite lovely," Felicity remarked to Helen.

"Not Carrol Manor, but it'll do."

An older man rushed out of the house to help Felicity and Helen. Short and muscular, the man had a thick white handlebar mustache that contrasted with his thinning white hair. "Miss Felicity?"

She straightened her hat, which had slipped to the side from the bumpy ride. "I am."

"The name is Robert Lowery." His hand jutted out to take hers.

Felicity liked this American custom. People gripping the hands of those they had barely met. England was a country of distant nods, curtsies, and bows. Handshakes in her homeland were weak gestures, a mere brushing of the fingers. Embracing this cultural difference wholeheartedly, she grabbed Lowery's hand. "Delighted to meet you." She shook so hard, the old man's head bounced. "May I present Miss Helen Wilkins."

"I'm very lucky to be in the company of two such lovely ladies."

Helen blushed. "You're a smooth-talking man, Mr. Lowery."

His expansive smile revealed a missing front tooth.

Upon entering the house, Felicity reminded herself to write a generous thank-you note to Martin Jameson. "Perfect."

"The house used to belong to Judge Mitchell Sauter." Lowery spoke in fatherly tones. "He got struck down by a runaway ore wagon and died. Didn't have no living relatives, so your people got a good deal on the place, furniture and all."

"I'm sorry to have benefited from another's misfortune, but this is very satisfactory." Felicity took off her hat.

A bedroom, good-sized front parlor, dining room, library, and kitchen lay on the ground floor. Two more bedrooms were upstairs. Felicity beamed when she opened the double doors to the library. Shelves of books lined three of the four walls. A well-used reading chair sat in the corner by a window. Most important, the former owner had installed electric lights. "The judge must have been a truly enlightened fellow," she said to Lowery.

"He did like to keep up with the times."

The judge had also liked his comforts. Carved marble fireplaces with intricate tile work seemed to be as much for decoration as heat. Intricate crystal chandeliers hung over the dining-room table. Thick Oriental rugs covered parquet floors. Paintings of landscapes and still-lifes dotted walls about the house.

Glancing in each room, Felicity was happy with her decision not to take up residence in one of the deluxe hotels on Main Avenue. She wanted to get the feel of the town, to be one of its residents and live among them. Besides, she didn't want to burn down a hotel and its guests if one of her experiments went wrong as it had at Carrol Manor. She had confidence in her chemistry skills but didn't want to take a chance.

"I live in a small room at the back of the kitchen, but I can move out to the carriage house if you'd like," Lowery said.

"Nonsense. This is your home also."

Another gap-toothed smile appeared.

Felicity directed Helen to the bedroom near the staircase. "Will you be comfortable here? I'd like to sleep in the room next to my laboratory upstairs."

Helen peeked in. "A fine chamber. And my lumbago won't put up an argument. Now excuse me. I want to see what an American kitchen looks like." She rubbed her hands together in anticipation.

Felicity instructed the drivers on where to place the trunks. She addressed the older man. "Mr. Lowery, is my laboratory all prepared?"

"Yes, Miss Felicity. We got a telegraph from your people and did what you asked. I hope you'll find it to your liking."

"I'm sure it will be admirable."

He nodded at the compliment. "Those packages were sent to you all the way from Denver, Colorado, and Boston, Massachusetts."

Several parcels and boxes sat on the dining table, as well as a good-sized crate on the floor. The packages contained a microscope, vials of chemicals, and laboratory equipment. Another package held a new typewriter.

Lowery's mouth slackened as Felicity inspected the contents. "Excuse me, Miss, you a doctor?"

"Merely an interested bystander."

His bushy eyebrows knotted at her answer.

The crate held a new English Compact Reversible camera shipped from the Blair Company in Boston. Also packed were boxes of dry plates, sensitized photographic paper, print frames, and processing chemicals. Although the Eastman Company had revolutionized photography with its new roll film, Felicity had chosen the large dry plates because of the superior quality they produced in the prints. The Metropolitan Police had started taking photographs with the Whitechapel murders, and she had seen the effectiveness of preserving the scenes where the killings had taken place. The photographs suspended time for a closer search for clues.

She asked the wagon driver and Lowery to place the crate and parcels in her laboratory.

As soon as they left, Felicity inspected a metal and wooden cross-bow and a dozen bolts in a flat wooden box. The bolts were metal, thin, and sharp. She disliked the thought of weapons, but this murderer was dangerous, and she wanted protection for Helen and herself. She replaced the weapon in the box, which went under her bed.

When the older man finished his tasks, Felicity asked him into the library and shut the doors. "I have another subject to discuss with you, Mr. Lowery, one I hope shall remain between the two of us."

He winked. "I can keep my mouth shut, Miss."

"That's what I'm counting on. I understand you're a man who knows almost everything that happens in this town, particularly events of a criminal nature."

"Before I worked for the judge, I used to be a jailer under ol' Sheriff Pike. I still got lots of friends in the sheriff's office and around town."

"Excellent. Then please inform me immediately of any major crime in town about which you may hear. Be it any time, night or day, I want to know. You'll be handsomely compensated for such information, over and above your salary as a retainer."

"I'm at your service, Miss."

"I knew I could count on you and your discretion. Incidentally, old Sheriff Pike must be related to the young Sheriff Pike."

"That's his boy, and a good man he is."

Back in the dining room, Helen wiped her hands on the apron she had donned. Her traveling hat was still on her head. "A finely equipped kitchen, Miss Felicity. Maybe this Montana isn't such a barbarous place."

"Excellent. Now, as they say in the vernacular of the West, can you please rustle us up some tea and sandwiches?"

CHAPTER 7

Because of her unfamiliarity with the town and to save time, Felicity asked Robert Lowery to drive her to the *Placer Gazette* office later in the afternoon. She wanted to begin her inquiries as soon as possible. For the visit, she had changed into a sober black serge dress with a small white lace collar. A perfect costume for the part of a writer. She had also purchased a notebook, not unlike the one her friend Jackson Davies carried. Of course, she didn't need it, because she could recall details with her remarkable memory. Still, the notebook gave the costume a bit more credence.

While the horses clopped along, Felicity marveled at the distance she had traveled. Across the ocean and much of the United States, yes, but also an existence and a half away from her life in England. With such a new start, she could begin the chase in earnest. No constrictive rules of Victorian society here.

Just a killer.

The bell over the door tinkled as Felicity entered the newspaper office on Broadway Street, a road off of Main. The office was one long room with a counter at the front, a few desks behind, and a printing press in the back. Felicity could see through to the back door from where she stood near the front. The building was permeated by the smell of ink and coffee, both equally strong and black.

As if she were an inspecting general, the men cracked to attention. They adjusted jackets. Squared shoulders. Sucked in bellies. A tall boy carrying an armful of papers stopped, his Adam's apple bobbing with a gulp. The exception was an older man scribbling away at one of the desks. He gave her little notice and went back to his writing.

A man in his twenties raced to the counter. "May I help you, Miss?"

"I suspect you don't get many female visitors."

"No, Miss. I mean, yes, Miss."

Felicity wanted to make him feel at ease, but did not. She had to be taken seriously. "I want to read all the stories you have published about the murder of Lily Rawlins. I will pay one dollar for each newspaper, if that is sufficient."

The older man at the desk put up his ink pen. His face drew into a powerful scowl. Men in the back of the long room halted their typesetting. The boy leaned on his broom.

"Big Lil?" the young man said.

"Correct."

He consulted with the older man in a whisper. As the young man bent to hear instructions, the older man lifted unkempt eyebrows and gave a strident nod, as if he had never agreed to anything in his life. In a while, the young man returned with three newspapers.

One item had been printed on the front page of the March 29 afternoon edition under the headline PROSTITUTE'S MUTILATED BODY FOUND IN RED DISTRICT. Much of the article about the murder of Lily Rawlins contained the same information Felicity had read in the *New York Times* story Davies had given her, thankfully with a few more facts.

Hands at its side, the body lay on its back with a horrendous slice to the throat and abdomen. The front of the woman's garments was drawn up to her chin and soaked in blood.

"I won't be able to have a good night's sleep ever again after witnessing such a sight," said Mr. Joe Maxwell, who had stumbled upon the corpse in the alley.

Big Lil, as the pitiful victim was called, lived in and worked out of one of the so-called "cribs" on Viceroy Street, where many of the town's soiled doves reside and take in clients.

Sheriff Tom Pike reported to the Gazette *that he had not found a knife in the alley or close about. The sheriff also estimated that the murder must have taken place between eleven thirty at night and two in the morning. He surmised the time because the deceased had last been spotted at the Lost Horse Bar about fifteen after eleven. Barman Barrett Young said Lily Rawlins had drunk at least six beers, all bought for her by men in the establishment. After joking that she was "closed for business," Rawlins had made her way home.*

The dead woman's purse lay near the body and contained twenty dollars.

Sheriff Pike has made no arrest in the shocking killing.

As a side note, Mrs. Josephine Miller, a waitress at the Red Hawk Café, fainted after she accidentally glimpsed the carnage on her way to work.

Another article printed two days later reported that the killer had still not been arrested. The story ended with:

The Rev. T. Phoenix from the Church of the Morning on Walton Avenue is taking up a collection to bury murder victim Lily Rawlins. Rev. Phoenix ministers to many ladies of the evening.

The next day's newspaper reported that Lily Rawlins was scheduled to be buried at Pauper Grounds. The murderer had not been caught.

Felicity asked to talk with the person who had written the stories. The old man who had ignored her took his time getting to the counter. His cuffs were threadbare and dotted with ink. His head seemed perpetually bent forward, probably from squinting too closely at words and distasteful events.

"I am Clark Andrews." He did not offer a hand to shake.

Felicity introduced herself. "I have questions about Lily Rawlins's murder."

"Everything is in the stories I wrote." He wore gruffness like his worn gray suit. "There isn't any more, Miss. And just why are you interested, anyway?"

"I'm a writer of crime novels in England." She attempted to sound artsy.

"What's the matter? Don't the English commit any crimes?"

"Very clever, Mr. Andrews. I can see why you are a writer. Please, can you help me?" She pulled out the notebook and a fountain pen from her purse. The paper was stained with ink, as were the fingers of her white gloves. "My fountain pen leaked," she said, embarrassed by the spill and feeling a touch foolish.

A rough laugh broke from the newspaperman. "I'm busy. Lots of news happens in Placer. Besides, how you can write a book when you can't even manage a pen?"

"But Mr. Andrews."

"But nothing, young lady. Females should stay close to hearth and stove. They should be tending the children and not unearthing wicked crimes no decent woman should even think about."

Felicity had heard those words all her life and had grown an armor to them, although the backward thinking still irritated her now and again. Using her handkerchief to clean the ink as best she could, Felicity wondered how she could obtain anything from this man. She had discounted much of what her father had told her over the years but did remember his familiar adage: money will lead you through any door.

"How thoughtless of me, Mr. Andrews. I realize you're busy. Allow me to pay you for your time. I hope twenty dollars will do." From her purse, she drew out an ink-stained twenty-dollar gold piece and placed it on the counter. She did not wipe off the ink.

Andrews gazed at the money, at Felicity, and back to the money. His hand slid out over the twenty dollars. "Well then, ask your questions."

"Besides the gruesome mutilations to Lily Rawlins, were there any other unusual details you didn't include in your articles?'

He hocked up a cough and the information. "Not all the coins were in her purse."

She inclined forward so close to him she smelled the whiskey he must have had for lunch. "No?"

"Five one-dollar pieces were laid on the ground at her feet."

"Can you draw a diagram of where the coins were located?"

On her notebook, he sketched a stick figure and five coins in a semicircle under the feet.

"What a fascinating piece of information." Not only telling but familiar, or so she had read in the files given to her by Jackson Davies. "Were there any suspicious footprints in the alley?"

The reporter smirked. "It had rained that morning, so the alley was muddy as a drained riverbed by the time the body was discovered. When I arrived, you couldn't pick out the killer's footprints from anyone else's, including mine."

"One of your articles stated that Lily Rawlins was buried in Pauper Grounds. What is that, precisely?"

"Twenty dollars is too little compensation for all these questions." His severity resurfaced.

Twenty dollars *was* a good sum. But Felicity understood she was also paying to graze over this man's obviously cantankerous nature. "Then we shall make it another twenty." She brought out another gold piece.

He took the money. "Pauper Grounds is where all the destitutes, criminals, and harridans are buried. You'll find it near the Placer Cemetery about five miles northwest of town."

"Has a murder similar to this one ever occurred before in Placer? I mean, one of this, ah, viciousness."

The man's smirk waned, and he breathed out more liquor-imbued breath. "I've reported on many a murder and other acts of violence for the *Gazette*, and I've never seen anything like this."

"One more query, Mr. Andrews."

He rolled his eyes.

"What were your impressions of the crime?"

"Don't get your meaning, young lady."

"What thoughts entered your mind when you saw the body?"

The newspaperman sucked air between crooked teeth. "I thought a monster had come to town."

She thanked the reporter, and he grumbled a reply.

Outside the newspaper office, Felicity's legs turned as heavy as the gigantic gates outside Carrol Manor. Her mind slowed. She wanted to do more, but the journey to Placer and unpacking had left her exhausted.

Robert Lowery dozed in the wagon. She called to him softly, not wanting to startle the older man. His eyes fluttered awake.

"Sorry for making you wait so long, Mr. Lowery."

He climbed off the buckboard to help her up. "Don't think nothing of it, Miss. It's my job. Your face is a bit drawn, if you don't mind me saying so."

"I do need rest. But that can wait until after we visit Pauper Grounds."

★　★　★

The west end of Placer appeared to have been built on nothing but hills and grit. Houses and other buildings clung to the inclines as if to prevent themselves from falling off the side. The effect was that of a town folding in on itself like the pages in a book about to be closed. Sad wooden shacks and brick boarding houses were chaotically bunched together along dirt roads.

One section of a hill had been scarred laterally, as if a giant's fingers had scrapped over it, burrowing for treasure. Tremendous piles of gray rocks, mounds of timber to brace mine shafts, and rail tracks on wooden skeletons covered the barren landscape. Working men and horses resembled industrious insects outside a gray hive.

Brutal A-shaped steel frames stood over the mine shafts. They supported ponderous cables, which lowered metal cages full of workers and supplies and brought out ore cars. According to Felicity's reading, the frames were called gallows. Such an apt name, since they created the appearance of a modern Golgotha. Farther on were the smelters, huge, arklike structures. At more than one hundred feet high, the smelter stacks bellowed demons' breath. Out of the buildings flowed lines of slag, the waste from the copper smelting. The hot melted excess of silica and iron coursed down the hills to large pools of red below.

Felicity had long admired the mechanical inventions of the decade, from electric light to the phonograph to the steam turbine. Marvelous ingenuity to help mankind. Soon after her father died, she had begun researching machinery that would be safer for the workers at her family mills in Lancashire as well as increase productivity. The mill manager had objected and groused until she explained how profits would be amplified. Still, she had also become increasingly dismayed at how some recent inventions had been perverted. Blue skies became black over such industries; science turned into greed, and benefit into death. She had hopes of science benefiting humanity but was realistic enough to know it could also be used to destroy.

The starkness of the mines and smelters and the land around them also stirred memories of the ruins of Pompeii. At the University of London, Felicity had studied ancient Rome and wanted to see where history actually took place. So she and Helen had taken a trip there during a Christmas break. The eruption of Mount Vesuvius in AD 79 had petrified the residents and structures with ash and cataclysm. Nature had been responsible for the sullen and gray wasteland of Pompeii. In Placer, the bleak landscape was all for the sake of commerce.

When the road bent north and away from the area, Felicity was relieved. Up the hill lay Placer Cemetery, with stately marble stones, metal crosses, and wrought-iron fences marking family graves. The grounds here were cleared of rubble and weed. Set a few yards away, Pauper Grounds had seen no such care. Many of the wooden markers had fallen with time and weather. Sprawls of long grass grew between and on the graves. When Felicity got down from the wagon, she tried to take care where she stepped, but she had no idea where people had been buried. She could not remember a more depressing spot.

LILY RAWLINS, 1856–1889 had been carved into a simple wooden sign erected in one corner of Pauper Grounds. In time, the marker would collapse into nothing, just like those on the surrounding graves. Felicity stood at the foot of the mound. She suspected the victim had lived a poor life that held no surprises. Lily Rawlins's first and last surprise had probably come when she died in that dirty alley.

Felicity had wanted to place roses at the grave site, but Placer had no flower shop. In their place, she renewed her vow to find the man who had left Lily Rawlins in a place where even the dead had been forgotten.

CHAPTER 8

From the library window, Felicity observed Sheriff Tom Pike approaching the house on Bullion Boulevard. She shook her head. His right hand rested on the gun in his holster.

"I should assure him there'll be no shootouts during tea," Felicity said out loud.

Inspector Jackson Davies and Sheriff Tom Pike shared many characteristics. Both were good-looking men, sure in their jobs. She had won Davies over with her modern crime-investigating techniques and deductions. Well, some of them. Others he had dismissed with maddening swiftness. Now she would have to do the same with this Montana sheriff.

Pike cut the classic figure of a western lawman, just as in the dime novels she had read. But there was a troubled set to his mouth as if he was tired from keeping something unsaid. He had a secret as well.

She answered the door. "So good of you to come, Sheriff. And so prompt." She led him to the parlor.

"Thanks for asking me. Now, Miss Carrol."

Before Pike could say more, Helen brought the tea service and curtsied to him. "Nice to see you again, sir."

"Call me Tom."

"Tom, sir."

He smiled, and Felicity noticed one dimple in his left cheek. "Thank you, Hellie."

"You're welcome, Miss." Before she left, Helen winked at Felicity as if saying, *He is quite handsome, you know.*

"Sheriff, do you take sugar?"

"No, thanks."

"Lemon or milk?"

"No."

Felicity offered him the cup. "You do like tea? Maybe, we should brew coffee."

"Tea is fine."

"Biscuit?"

"Nothing."

"Helen's scones are absolutely delicious."

"Miss Carrol, please."

He breathed with exasperation. The sheriff was probably used to dealing with harsh criminals. Obviously, tea and biscuits left him quite disconcerted, which Felicity thought a bit endearing.

"Try the cucumber sandwiches. They're Helen's specialty."

He held his large hand up against the plate of sandwiches she offered. "I don't want coffee, biscuits, or those cucumber things. I want to know why you've come to Placer."

"Ah," she said with deliberation.

"What?"

"You're one of those get-straight-to-the point men. Do you treat all visitors in this manner?" She sipped from her cup.

"Just the ones who ask about murder." He crossed his arms.

Felicity recognized an obstacle. She had seen them all her life. But his cooperation was essential if she was going to conduct her investigation in his jurisdiction. "Very well. I shall tell you."

"I'm all ears."

"I don't understand."

"It means I'm ready to listen to whatever you have to tell me."

"An American expression." Felicity cleared her throat. "I write crime and mystery stories, which are unpublished at this point, but I soon hope to remedy that. I'm here because I read about Lily Rawlins in the *New York Times*, and it inspired an idea for my new book."

"What kind of book?"

"A novel about a man who kills prostitutes. Naturally, I'll change the name of the town and the deceased if you think it best."

As she spoke, the skin on her arms itched. The deception was difficult to maintain with the sheriff. His dark-brown eyes examined her as if she were an organism under her own microscope. When they met, he had said he was good at reading people. Maybe he was. As a result, her mouth parched with the untrue words, and she had the most upsetting sense that the more truth she hid, the more she might divulge. The only thing to do was lie very well.

She smiled. "My dear readers will welcome any particulars you're willing to share about the crime. Your observations will be extremely valuable."

"I wouldn't want to let down your readers—when you get them."

Like Inspector Jackson Davies, this sheriff employed sarcasm. *Must be a male law enforcement officer affectation*, she concluded. "I'll ignore that ridicule, Sheriff."

"Didn't know it was." He had a nice smile, which she ignored also.

"I've read the newspaper accounts about Lily Rawlins's death but want your view of the incident. I'm also planning to visit the alley where Lily Rawlins's body was discovered. After we finish our tea, of course."

"What?" He stood up, flipping the spoon in his teacup. He caught the spoon in midair. "The murder took place in the Red District, which is no place for a lady such as yourself. It's the roughest part of town, which is saying a lot."

"Such a violent place. I had no idea. I must remember to make note of that."

"The Red District is populated with gambling houses, brothels, saloons, and opium dens, not to mention the men out for a good time no matter the cost. And let's not forget, the varmints who'll steal you blind or kill for a good pair of boots. Hell, some of my deputies even hate going there at night, and they're packing guns." He pointed the spoon at her when making each point.

"Such vivid descriptions. Sheriff, I'm surprised *you're* not a writer."

Pike set the spoon in the cup and exhaled. "Last year, more than two hundred people died in Placer. Some fifty of them were killed in the mines or smelters. Thirty passed on from old age or disease. Five people were hung. The rest were either shot or knifed to death, and the majority of those killings took place in the Red District." His voice lowered with warning. "You're not going to like what you see there." He said each word carefully.

She dabbed her mouth with a napkin. "I appreciate your concern, Sheriff. If it makes you feel any better, you can go with me." She handed him a plate. "Try a scone."

★   ★   ★

Sheriff Tom Pike clasped the reins so hard his knuckles blanched. He drove Felicity's buckboard with his horse tied at the back. His head appeared ready to blow like the dynamite at noon. She infuriated men with her questions, which she wasn't going to ever stop doing. Still, she had to say something. He had agreed to escort her, after all. "I'm grateful you decided to accompany me. I'm sure you have many other things to do."

"If I let you go alone and something bad happened, it'd lay heavy on my conscience, Miss."

"What could possibly happen on a nice day like this?" she said, with such exaggerated sincerity that he returned a flash of a smile. She exhaled with pleasure at having dulled his temper for the moment, at any rate.

He directed the wagon to Ore Avenue, which measured twice as wide as many of the other streets she had seen in Placer. Poles with five rows of electrical wires stood on each side. Huge wagons loaded with timber and pipe rambled up the road. Groups of bearded men with lunch tins ambled toward the mines and smelters, while another group with dirty faces and clothing moved the other direction. The traffic from the men and wagons created a rumbling noise.

"Why is this route so busy?" she asked loudly.

"Ore Avenue is the main road to haul equipment to the mining and smelter operations yonder. The mining companies use the same road to move out the gold, silver, and copper."

"What happens when the minerals are depleted, Sheriff?"

"We'll dry up and blow away." He guided the wagon left.

The surroundings began to change as they drove on. No electric lights here. The roads were bumpier. Saloons, gambling houses, and shanties replaced the markets, banks, and more commercial businesses of Ore Avenue. Felicity smelled frying bacon and beer.

"Welcome to the Red District," the sheriff pronounced.

"How did it get that name?"

"From the red lights or curtains in the windows of the girls' cribs. Kind of an advertisement for their business."

She had read about the cribs. They were the houses where the prostitutes lived. "Were you acquainted with Lily Rawlins?"

Pike nodded, regret in his eyes.

"Tell me about her."

"Big Lil Rawlins had the tiniest feet of any whore in Placer, Montana. Dainty as angel cake, small as a child's." His cheeks reddened. "I didn't mean to say *whore*, ma'am."

"I'm not offended, Sheriff. Please go on."

"Well, anyone who knew Lil, client or otherwise, wondered how such little things could hold up a woman of such girth and immorality. Lil often bragged she washed her feet in milk twice a week and paid an old Chinese woman to dig dirt from under her toenails since she could not reach. Besides food and beer, Lil's whoring profits bought the best shoes from San Francisco, which she considered the only ones good enough for her pearly gems."

"She sounds like a unique individual."

"Big Lil liked to drink, but a lot of the soiled doves do. She had a poke of indecent jokes and had men laughing till they choked. Big Lil could be your best friend, unless she filled herself with beer; then she could get ornery as a skunk with fleas. Like most women in her trade, she wanted to get rich. But they don't."

"Why not?"

"Generally they drink themselves to the grave or become addicted to opium or laudanum. Some also kill themselves to escape the life."

"Big Lil was drunk that night, wasn't she?"

He gave a nod. "She might not have realized her predicament and died without pain. I hope so, anyway."

"The man who stumbled upon her body."

"Joe Maxwell."

"I'd very much like an interview with him."

The sheriff stared straight ahead. "Good luck finding him. A week after he stumbled onto Big Lil's body, Joe left town. He told me he didn't like the kind of people who lived here, 'least not the kind who'd do that to a woman."

At a battered sign with the writing VICEROY STREET, Pike turned the wagon again. They drove past sorry wooden buildings with long front porches and five doors set in each. Next to those were small shacks built end to end. The names of different women were hand-painted over the doors in fancy lettering. MARIA. MOLLY. RUTH. ANNIE. On they went.

"Are these the cribs, Sheriff?"

Pike mumbled a yes. "They belong to the girls of the line."

"Girls of the line?"

"What people call the prostitutes who live there."

The scene troubled Felicity. Not only because sadness coated the place like dust, but because these women were now targeted by a madman and Big Lil Rawlins was the first to fall. That is, if Jackson Davies's suspicions were correct.

They continued on until they reached Melton Street four roads over. Stopping at an alley between a dingy café and an abandoned building, Pike helped Felicity from the wagon. Mice scrambled out from under one of the porches. Befouled water streamed along the middle of the alley.

At the sound of a splash, they whipped around to see a grossly fat woman tossing slop from a bucket into the alley across the street. The fat woman blew her nose at them and retreated into one of the buildings. Red humiliation brushed over Pike's cheeks.

"Where did Mr. Maxwell find the victim?" Felicity asked.

"You can't miss the spot."

She entered the alley, which she estimated was ten feet wide and thirty feet in length. Midway, black spatters covered the west wall. Gruesome patterns in old blood, but still providing a narrative.

Felicity's stomach constricted. The murderer had stood perhaps in the very place where her own shoes were now planted on the compacted dirt. His knife dripping blood. His mind a savage thing. Stomping dust from her boots, she couldn't afford the emotional diversion. "What do you think took place that night, Sheriff Pike?"

Pike walked to the entrance of the alley. "I speculate the man waited here. He propositioned Big Lil as she passed, and she didn't say no." The sheriff stepped backward into the alley. "I reckon he got behind her and put one arm over her mouth to keep her from screaming. With his other hand, he finished her with the knife."

"From the arrangement of the blood spots, I believe that's exactly what happened."

"What are you talking about?"

Her hand swept over the main spray. "The killer sliced her throat here. Notice the largest amount of blood from the neck wound. Lily Rawlins then fell to the ground, where he continued to disfigure her body. He must have been methodical and knew what he was doing, because there is less blood closer to the ground."

Pike looked over the blood spots and Felicity as if he had never seen either of them before.

"Sheriff, in what direction were Lily Rawlins' feet pointed?"

"Toward Melton Street."

"Ah."

"What *ah*?"

"The man must be left-handed. I'll demonstrate."

"That I'd like to see."

Using the fingers of her left hand, Felicity drew an imaginary knife across her throat and thrust her arm toward the west wall. "See, the blood flew onto this side of the alley. If he had been right-handed, there'd have been more blood on the other wall. One more point: the culprit must have been taller than Lily Rawlins." She made her explanation defined, specific. Not too preachy or academic to avoid aggravating the sheriff any more than she had to.

"You're telling me you know all this just by the blood?"

"How tall was Lily Rawlins?"

"About five feet."

"Note how the spatters of blood point down slightly, indicating her assailant was taller. If he had been the same size as her, the blood spots would have been more level along the wall." She again brandished the pretend weapon to prove her theory.

"I'll be a son of a bitch. Sorry, Miss."

"Merely the science of force and energy."

"Do all book writers ask this many questions?"

"If we don't ask, how are we to learn?" Felicity knew she had won the point when the sheriff tugged at his vest.

"You're nosier than ten women in a sewing circle. And you're wearing at my nerves."

"Then one more question."

"Shoot."

"What?"

"Never mind, Miss Carrol, just ask."

She promised herself to become more acquainted with American lingo. "Why do you believe Lily Rawlins was killed?"

Pike took off his hat. He ran his hand through his longish hair as if letting something go. Felicity noted a cast of sympathy shadowing his face, as if he had lost a family member in the alley. Those vulnerabilities, albeit small ones, made him more attractive.

He turned to her. "Whenever there's a murder, for better or worse, there's a reason. Over money. A woman, an insult, a mining claim. Too much liquor. But with this one, I can't see a clear reason other than to spill blood and cause pain." He replaced his hat.

So close to the truth, Sheriff, Felicity thought.

"I've coped with shootouts, swindles, bar fights, and murders where the killers didn't cut up their victims like that." Pike hit the side of the alley with his fist. "Whatever the reason, it smells to heaven."

"*Hamlet!*"

"I'm not a buffoon, however much you may think so."

"On the contrary, Sheriff. I'm very impressed." She marveled that this lawman knew Shakespeare, but Pike only stiffened with skepticism. He apparently didn't know how to handle her compliment either. She had to return to business. "For my book, I want to absorb the atmosphere. Don't let me keep you from your duties. I can find my way back."

"Check the time." An order.

She glanced at her watch. A little past five. Shadows began to edge along the alley.

"If you think I'm going to leave you here alone, you're crazier than a roomful of drunks on a Saturday night."

"A colorful metaphor." Felicity sighed, because she clearly wasn't going to get rid of him. "Very well. I must take photographs."

"Why?"

"As a reference. They'll help me describe the place when I start writing."

"Damn if that doesn't sound reasonable."

From the back of the wagon, Felicity drew out the camera, dry plates, and a wooden tripod. To take the most effective photographs, she had studied the work of Mathew Brady, who had brilliantly captured the American Civil War. Like him, she hoped her photographs would convey a story and not just reflect reality. She had also taught herself how to develop plates and had become an avid reader of the *British Journal of Photography*.

Felicity took two photographs of the alley and two more of the blood on the walls. While she worked, Pike stood in the alley smoking a short cigar and watched her every action. His acute interest made his eyes grow darker.

When she finished, he helped her load the camera equipment into the buckboard. "Now that you're done with your little picture taking, I have questions of my own."

"It's frightfully late."

"You're not getting away so easy, Miss Carrol."

"Felicity, please."

"Miss Carrol," he emphasized. "You might be a writer as you say, but why come all the way to Placer?"

Good questions, and ones she didn't wish to answer at the moment. But she had to convince him of her story, so she mixed in a bit of truth. "I wanted to study the crime with my own eyes to give my writing authenticity. I intend to thoroughly investigate the circumstances of Lily Rawlins's death. I saw her grave, and with time, it will soon pass into oblivion. If I write about her, I shall preserve a bit of her life in print. That's something, isn't it?"

She turned away, but Pike took hold of her left arm.

Felicity swiveled her body to face him. She understood his frustration, so she didn't get angry. "No need to manhandle me." Her voice was steady.

"We do our best to keep crime at bay, but this place is treacherous. If you're not careful, you're going to get hurt nosing around the Red District. I don't care if you're the next Harriet Beecher Stowe, it might be best for all around if you and your woman friend leave Placer tomorrow."

Felicity shook his hand off. "Sheriff, I'm not disregarding your warnings. I shall use all caution. If it eases your mind, I can take care of myself, and I'm not afraid."

"That's even worse." He expelled a gust of breath. "Sorry I grabbed your arm."

Like so many men, he was unaccustomed to apologizing. "I believe you rather enjoyed it." Her mouth turned up.

"I believe you're right. I've never met anyone quite like you."

"Just your typical Englishwoman."

"I seriously doubt that, Miss Carrol. Do you want to have dinner with me tomorrow night?" His eyebrows rose, his own impetuousness seeming to surprise him.

She was astonished as well. Never had she received a dinner invitation after being told to leave town.

"I will dine with you, provided you don't arrest me for asking too many questions," she said as he helped her up into the wagon.

"Pick you up at six. Until then, stay out of damn trouble."

CHAPTER 9

Hands shook Felicity awake. A candle flickered above her head.

"Hellie?" Felicity could not yet focus.

"Apologize for waking you, Miss, but Mr. Lowery says to tell you another woman has been murdered."

★　★　★

Felicity declined Robert Lowery's offer to drive her to the blacksmith shop on Mulligan Road, but she did seek his directions. In the back of the wagon, she placed her camera and satchel full of investigation tools and took up the reins. Back home, driving a carriage by herself and without a host of servants and chaperones was tantamount to a Lady Godiva ride in front of Westminster Palace.

But this was not home.

The early-morning sun covered the town in a copper hue, which she believed most appropriate in a town obsessed with the metal. Drawing her shawl tight about her shoulders, she shuddered at the prospect of what lay behind the blacksmith shop. Yet she clicked her tongue to speed up the horses.

The forest-green wooden building had a large square opening in the middle and two windows on each side. Over the door, the sign read KENRICK BLACKSMITH. Iron rings of varying sizes leaned against the front wall, as did a worn iron bench. Two horses snorted in a small corral on the left side of the building. Inside, the muscular smithy pounded metal on anvil, emitting sparks with each stroke. Keeping his head to his work, he acted as if death hadn't dropped by his business. After tying her horses across the street, Felicity picked up her equipment and walked behind the building.

Tom Pike shouted at the dozen or so people who stood over the body. "Everybody back away, dammit. Give the doc room to work. This isn't no traveling show for you to gawk at." The curious obeyed but muttered at their forced retreat. Pike motioned to his deputies. "Don't let anybody within a hundred feet of here."

Two working men stood beside Felicity. One asked the other, "Who's dead?"

"Another whore," his friend replied.

"There's plenty of 'em left. I say we go get breakfast."

Evidently having had their fill of murder, the men and others departed. That gave Felicity a better vantage point. A slender man in a dark suit bent over the body. A black physician's bag sat on the ground beside him. Dense red hair topped his head and filled in his full mustache and beard. Standing close to the scene of the murder was Clark Andrews, still wearing the same gray suit and grimace he had worn the day Felicity met him at the *Gazette* office. The newspaper reporter shook his head as he jotted notes. The reporter's presence gave her an idea.

Felicity walked around a beefy young deputy.

"Ho, there," he said, and stepped in front of her.

"I'm a writer, too. If Mr. Andrews from the *Gazette* newspaper is allowed near the body, then so am I."

His hefty arms held her back. "I don't know what you're talking about, lady. So stay put."

"I must get closer," she added with indignation.

"You ain't getting no closer. I got orders."

"Sheriff! Oh, Sheriff!" Felicity waved at Pike, who was watching the doctor examine the body.

Pike strode over to her, took his hat off, and slapped it against his leg. "What in the blazes are you doing here?"

"I must examine the remains."

Pike stepped in front of Felicity, which did little to block her view. "Why do you want to see such a thing?"

"Because it's important for the book I'm writing."

"I thought you were writing about Big Lil's murder."

"Now there are two. That makes for a better story."

"A female shouldn't witness this."

"Never mind my gender. Think of me as a writer."

"It's hard not to think of you as a woman. Besides, this is official town business."

"You allowed Mr. Andrews to view the body. Why not me? We are both writers. Besides, I might be able to sell this story to the *Times* of London."

Pike flushed as if he had no good argument. "You can have your turn after Dr. Lennox completes his job. But if you have nightmares for the rest of your life, don't blame me, sister. Let her through, Wilbur."

With ease, Felicity ducked under the big deputy's arms and positioned herself off to the side for a good view. The body lay parallel to the back wall of the blacksmith building and about one yard away from it. The right arm lay across the chest with the other arm at the side. The left leg was drawn up.

Felicity covered her mouth at the sight of all the blood. Saturating the woman's dress. Forming a muddy pool on the ground. Staining the wall.

Two acute gashes crossed the victim's neck and severed the jugular vein, which explained the copious amount of blood. A slit long as the woman's forearm had been made in the center of her abdomen. The bright-red tissue underneath the wounds contrasted with the pale skin in such a way that the killer seemed to have allowed something feral to escape.

The doctor drew the victim's dress down over her legs and brushed his hand over the open eyes to close them. After wiping his bloody hands on a white cloth, he wrote in a small notebook. He took off his wire-framed glasses to clean them. Throughout, his face lacked any reaction, but his movements were precise and abrupt, as though he was inconvenienced by having to be there. Replacing his stovepipe hat, the doctor joined the sheriff standing a few feet from the body.

Wearing a singed leather apron, the blacksmith pushed open the back door of his shop. His face looked like burned steel. "Why'd they have to pick my business for their dirty work?" he said to no one in particular.

"Russ, you'll have to take that up with the murderer," Pike replied.

Clark Andrews waved over the blacksmith and started asking him questions.

"Still want to see this?" Pike asked Felicity.

"I'm not running away, Sheriff."

"I hoped you might."

"I never retreat."

He motioned for her to proceed.

Felicity crouched down. There was no torn clothing or lacerations on the victim's hands from fighting off the assailant. So there hadn't been much of a struggle. This told her the victim had known the murderer or was killed quickly.

A mess of footprints in numerous sizes and shapes marred the ground all around the victim. "Sloppy, sloppy," Felicity said.

A glint in the dirt. A plain silver ring had been partially buried at the foot of the body. Felicity glanced around. Pike was talking with the doctor and no one else looked her way, so she picked the ring up with a handkerchief and placed it in her pocket. The middle finger on the woman's right hand was bruised. The killer had ripped off the ring. Why?

Felicity stood and frowned. The setting was chaotic. Children and dogs ran by. Deputies shouted at everyone to get back. Horses and carriages trod along the street nearby. The blacksmith had returned inside and pounded away at the anvil. To gather more details about the murder, she needed time with the body, and this was not the place.

"I thought you were going to fall over." Pike was behind her.

"This ground is uneven."

"I understand." His voice softened.

"Who is she, Sheriff?" Felicity said.

"Mattie Morgan. Another prostitute. She lived in one of the cribs a few streets over on Viceroy. The blacksmith spotted her body at five this morning, but the doctor says she had probably been dead for two to three hours."

She stooped down again to feel the stiffness in the body's jaw and neck muscles, where rigor mortis usually began. The doctor was correct. She stood up. "I'm going to shoot photographs now."

Pike dropped his shoulders. "Suit yourself. She's beyond caring. But make it quick. I've called for a wagon to carry off the body."

"To where?"

"The undertaker, Quigley and Son. And I'm afraid our dinner is off tonight."

"Understandable."

Felicity peered into the camera's viewer at the image of Mattie Morgan's body. Through her inquiries into various crimes, Felicity had attempted to remain the observer, but the task was difficult at the pitiful sight of lives stolen away by murder. Yet she had found a balance. A way to stay dispassionate enough to seek out clues but let in some anger to drive her on to find the killer.

Click. She took a photograph of the body but also experienced a jolt of terror. The same type of wounds. The position of the bodies. The awful mutilations. The man's cunning and sick ceremony. And as heartbreaking as the brutality was, the loneliness of the figure alone on the dirt. Tremors attacked Felicity's hands, and she wrung them to stop the shaking.

Felicity took four photographs of the body from different angles. She backed up for a wider view of the location, which included Tom Pike conversing with one of his deputies and the doctor walking away from the blacksmith shop.

While Felicity began packing her photography equipment, the sheriff summoned two men leaning against the wall and sharing a cigarette. The men covered the body with a wool blanket, each lifting one end. On the way to the wagon, the woman's bloody hand slipped out and seemed to wave a farewell.

"Sheriff, when you arrived at the scene of the murder, did you notice any distinguishing footprints near the body? With all this trampling around, I suppose a clear footprint is going to be impossible to distinguish." Felicity could almost hear Pike's teeth grind together at her question.

"For your information, I did locate one clear footprint between the body and the wall. A good shoe made it, not a work boot. Then again, the print may not belong to the man who killed Mattie Morgan. That satisfy your interest?"

"More like ignite it."

"What good news."

"More sarcasm, Sheriff. And I've made your neck veins protrude like ropes." She admitted to herself she felt a bite of pleasure at challenging this too-serious lawman.

His hand went to his neck, which he rubbed. "You're calling me a bad lawman. You're saying I'm not doing a good job here."

"I said no such thing."

"Well, you say it even when you say something else."

"I'm confident you'll do your very best with what's available to you."

"There you go again. I'm not sure how to take that. You insinuating we're nothing but backward hicks?"

"Not necessarily."

Pike's teeth grinded again. "Thanks for your confidence, ma'am." He started walking. "You've seen the body, so you might as well see this, too. Come on."

He led her to an empty corral on the other side of the blacksmith shop with a trough in one corner. Red spotted the wood and ground around it. "The killer washed the blood off. He must have been covered with it after what he did to Mattie Morgan."

Felicity peered into the water. Her reflection made an unsettling vision in scarlet. A young woman's face, steadfast but masking revulsion and traces of doubt. She turned away.

"Sheriff, may I read the postmortem report on Lily Rawlins?"

"Why?"

"To determine whether the wounds on Mattie Morgan are similar to those inflicted on Lily Rawlins. From preliminary reports, they appear to be alike."

"So?"

"Then they were killed by the same man."

"That possibility's been ruminating around in my head."

"Maybe it is time to stop ruminating."

Pike bit his lower lip and stomped off.

"Hold on, Sheriff. Does that mean I can't read the report?"

He skidded to a halt. "It's not pleasant."

"I've encountered unpleasant matters in my life. I think I shall be fine."

Pike put on his hat and didn't turn around. "Come to my office and I'll give you a copy."

★　★　★

Marcus Quigley had red-rimmed eyes, as if he perpetually cried over his patrons.

A forty-dollar contribution to the undertaker gave Felicity admittance for a private inspection of Mattie Morgan's body. Pike and the doctor were scheduled to arrive later for the autopsy at the funeral parlor on north Main Avenue. The less they knew about her visit, the better. Another ten dollars bought Quigley's silence.

Saying he didn't feel right leaving a stranger with the deceased, the undertaker sat on a stool in the corner of the workroom where the body lay on a metal-topped table. "My pa passed on seven years ago, and I got the business by default." Quigley spoke in tranquil tones, a habit no doubt picked up from talking with the bereaved. "It's a good business, but I do sometimes miss conversations with the living."

"Mr. Quigley, I've talked with people who were no more alive than the clients on your table." Felicity lifted tools out of her satchel.

He slapped a knee and chuckled. "That's a good one."

Felicity wore a light wool outfit she usually reserved for riding horses. It allowed better movement, and she didn't have to deal with a bustle. She put on white gloves and one of Helen's aprons. Her inspection started with the victim's clothing, which had begun to stiffen with drying blood. Two red smudges marked the lower part of the victim's skirt, where the killer must have cleaned the knife on the fabric. Fortunately, Quigley had installed electric lights that provided more illumination than the usual kerosene lamps.

Over each part of the body, Felicity made unhurried passes with a magnifying glass. A purple bruise had formed on both sides of the body's jaw, obviously from where the killer subdued her with his arm. Several strands of wavy hair about three to five inches in length were stuck in the blood under the woman's right ear and on the hem of the dress. Mattie Morgan's hair was longer, blonde, and straight. The hairs Felicity discovered appeared red-hued, although the blood might have tinted them. The microscope at her laboratory would reveal their true color. The hair samples went into an envelope.

Placing a white piece of paper beneath the body's hands, Felicity took scrapings from under the fingernails.

"Why you doing that?" Quigley picked his teeth with his own nail.

Felicity remained concentrated on her work. She blew back a piece of her hair that had fallen over her eyes. "The woman might have scratched her assailant. If so, he'll have scratch marks on his face or body. Such evidence will help convict him in a court of law when he is apprehended."

"I get it," Quigley said, then gave a big yawn.

Felicity calmed her breathing and inspected the wounds. They were alike in placement to those found on Lily Rawlins's body, according to the postmortem report she had obtained from Sheriff Pike. The cut to Mattie Morgan's abdomen was exact and straight. No surgeon could have been more detailed.

With a gulp and grit, she inspected inside the body cavity. The heart and liver had been removed and placed in the wrong location.

"Where'd you learn to look at a body that way?" the undertaker asked.

"At medical school." She had forgotten he was even there.

"You a doctor?"

"I could be but have other interests. Excuse me, I must focus, Mr. Quigley."

"Sure, sure."

Using tongs and her magnifying glass, she saw the detached organs had clean cuts. No tearing of the flesh or unnecessary nicks. They had been separated by an expert hand, signifying a disciplined side of the murderer. The discipline, however, disappeared when it came to the female parts of the victim. There were several knife wounds of different depths. The randomness of them suggested rage.

After sketching the body in a notebook, Felicity noted the placement of the wounds. On each injury, Felicity pushed the skin together, and the wound tapered at both ends. Such a shape indicated a double-edged knife, according to her study of forensic medicine. Many of the wounds measured one inch wide. Felicity slid a thin ruler into the wound, which stopped at six and a half inches. She gained a clear picture of the knife.

Thin, long, double-edged.

Sodden with blood, the woman's dingy drawers showed no traces of seminal fluid, which signified the victim had not been sexually violated. Felicity imagined young women back home swooning at the idea she had even made such an examination. But she had studied bodily fluids, including blood, during her medical studies. This was part of a crime and had to be studied as such. With logic and objectivity.

As she examined the body, her mind whizzed over case files from the London Metropolitan Police for comparisons to what she was seeing. She didn't want to miss any vital clues in her sleuthing.

"Poor soul. Tore to bits." Undertaker Quigley got up from his stool in the corner. "The same as old Big Lil. Somebody sure don't like girls of the line." The undertaker smoothed the victim's hair. "A pretty girl. Too bad."

Felicity fully regarded the young woman's face, which she had neglected to do at the blacksmith shop. She had been paying too much attention to the physical evidence. Even with a chin and cheeks spotted with blood, Mattie Morgan appeared peaceful, a fair sleeping beauty with no hope of ever awaking. "Yes, very pretty."

But there was no time to digress. The killer didn't dally, and neither could she. Using ink and a brush, Felicity painted the thumb and forefinger of the body's right hand. She pressed the fingers on a piece of paper for a clear impression.

"What you doing now, ma'am?"

"Gathering fingerprints."

"Why?"

"So I can identify the victim."

"We know she's Mattie Morgan."

Felicity sighed with patience. "We must distinguish her fingerprints from those of her killer." She cleaned the ink off the body's fingers with alcohol. She didn't want Pike and the doctor to know about her visit.

"That sounds confusing," said the undertaker. "Give me a body and I'll do the rest. By the way, ma'am, you got ink on your nose."

CHAPTER 10

Even with ample light from the early-afternoon sun and the electric bulb overhead, Felicity rubbed her eyes and moved the kerosene lamp closer to the microscope. For the last three hours, she had analyzed the evidence collected from the body of Mattie Morgan. Thanks to the carpentry skills of Robert Lowery, the large upstairs bedroom had been transformed into a laboratory based on her own design to aid in her investigation.

A wooden counter running the length of one wall held the microscope and a typewriter, where she wrote up the notes on what she had discovered. At the back were beakers, tongs, tubes, and medicine droppers, as well as Erlenmeyer flasks for any chemistry experiments she might have to conduct. A shelf to hold bottles of chemicals had been built above the counter. Set against another wall was a shelf with science and medical books, many from her studies at the university, along with pamphlets about investigation procedures used by the Metropolitan Police Service. Although she had memorized the information, having the books there gave her comfort. She liked the feeling of being surrounded by knowledge.

Working at the counter, Felicity viewed the hairs plucked from Mattie Morgan's dress and those found near the neck wound.

Under the microscope, they were wavy and a somber red. The hair might very well have come from one of the men who had visited the victim professionally. They might also belong to the murderer. She placed the strands in an envelope after carefully marking its contents and placing it in a wooden box she had assigned to collect evidence in this case.

The ring Felicity had picked up at the slain prostitute's feet was plain silver, probably a wedding ring judging by the placement on her left hand. Usually prostitutes weren't married, so Mattie Morgan must have been widowed. Holding the ring with tweezers, Felicity applied finely ground charcoal to both sides and brushed away the excess. Back home, she had spent many hours teaching herself how to collect fingerprints from a variety of materials and record them. Although not recognized by courts as evidence, fingerprints were helpful tools in her investigations.

Under the magnifying glass appeared ridges of a thumbprint on the outside of the ring and part of the index finger on the inside. She compared the prints to the ones she had obtained from Mattie Mason. They matched.

The killer had left no prints. He had probably worn gloves, and that revealed something about the man. He was careful.

Through the microscope lens, she studied the scrapings from under the victim's fingernails. Nothing but dirt. Still, they might be important later, so she placed them in another envelope.

Upon completion of her work, she set the magnifying glass and microscope at the back of the counter. In a voice like a metronome, her science tutor Terrance Smyth had repeated, *Keep your station organized. Place your equipment away in an orderly fashion so you can easily find an item when needed the next time.* She could almost hear Master Smyth say, "Well done, and bravo" about her tidiness and technique, although she doubted his approval of what she was analyzing these days.

Felicity straightened. From stooping over the counter, her lower back had tightened. She checked her watch. "They're ready."

Hours before, she had placed a wooden rack on the grass in the back of the house. The rack held five small wooden frames with negative plates over a piece of photographic paper. The sun had provided the light to expose the images onto the paper. Now she removed the frames from the rack and headed to the cellar, where she had set up a photographic laboratory, again thanks to Robert Lowery's expert carpentry talents.

The cellar was accessible from an outside door at the back of the house near the kitchen. A packed dirt floor gave off the pleasant odor of a newly watered field. Shelves with boxes of potatoes, carrots, and apples as well as canned goods lined one wall. Against the other wall of the cellar, Lowery had built a short counter, upon which Felicity had placed porcelain basins for the photograph-processing chemicals.

Although the former owner of the house had installed electric lights upstairs, he had neglected the cellar. Felicity had remedied that. She had hired a man from Montana Electric, the company bringing the service to Placer, to run a wire to the cellar and install two lights. One lightbulb hung over the photography darkroom. Another bulb lit the shelves of food as a convenience to Helen for whenever she needed to fetch supplies.

Felicity lit a candle in a lantern of yellow glass to give her enough light to see, but not enough to expose the photographic paper. Heavy black curtains had been hung on three sides of the counter to block any daylight. Felicity drew the curtains and pushed up the sleeves of her blouse. Removing the photographic paper and plate negative from the wooden frames, she slipped the paper into the developer bath. An image began to appear in the faint light— a close-up of Mattie Morgan's pretty face. With tongs, Felicity placed the print into another basin filled with a soda compound to halt the developing. Last, the print went into a basin of water to rinse off the chemicals. With a clothespin, she hung the photograph on a piece of line she had strung up and then repeated the process with the other prints.

While they dried, Felicity went upstairs to eat. The kitchen door was ajar, but she didn't enter. Inside, Helen and Robert Lowery drank coffee at the table and chatted in soothing, intimate tones, as if they had known each other more than one week. Their perceptible warmth for one another created a cozy haze about them like a cocoon of friendship. Helen appeared to be a woman ten years younger.

Felicity grinned at her own dullness. *What a grand mistress of observation you are,* she told herself. How could she have missed such obvious clues? Hadn't she noticed how Lowery rushed to help Helen with the smallest chore? How Helen had begun baking apple pies after Lowery claimed they were his favorites? How they eagerly headed to the market together and took longer and longer to return? Attention to the gruesome murders had blinded her to everything else. To the good things, the surprising things least expected, particularly for Helen.

"Good for you, Hellie," Felicity whispered.

So as not to disturb them, Felicity skipped lunch, going around the front of the house and into the library to read until the prints were dry.

Felicity returned to her laboratory upstairs for closer inspection of the photographs she had taken of Mattie Morgan's body and the scene of the crime. Using the magnifying glass, she searched for anything she might have overlooked while at the blacksmith shop.

In the black-and-white photographs, the blood appeared the color of oil on the dirt and walls of the building and the body looked smaller and lonely. Other than what Felicity had witnessed there, no details emerged.

Pictured in the wide-angle photograph, Pike and one of his deputies stood near the body, their heads bowed in conversation. A blur in a black coat, Dr. Lennox was departing the site. But another figure stood out among the commotion of the day, and Felicity hadn't noticed her when she took the photograph. A woman stood to the right of the blacksmith building. Felicity aimed the magnifying glass over the image. The attractive woman wore a stylish dress and a large hat with feathery plumes. Part of her face was revealed.

The woman was smiling, albeit sedately.

"She's probably the type who also attends executions," Felicity said out loud.

With a knock, Helen entered, carrying a tray. "Excuse the intrusion, Miss, but I brought you tea and a bit of roast beef. You picked at your breakfast like a bird this morning and had no lunch."

"Thank you, Hellie. I'll eat in the dining room."

"Good. I don't how anybody could have an appetite in this room."

Helen referred to the wall across from the counter, which was covered with photographs of the murdered victims.

More to make Helen happy than to satisfy hunger, Felicity ate. "Sit and talk with me, please."

"It ain't proper, Miss."

"Hellie, it's not proper to reject my invitation." Felicity fetched another cup from the cabinet and poured tea for Helen. "Besides, your brother, Mr. Horace Wilkins, is nowhere around to remind us what is correct."

"Thank goodness."

Like Helen, Horace Wilkins had worked for the Carrol family for many years. While he had treated her late father with the highest respect and admiration, he hadn't shown Felicity the same. Though Wilkins didn't say it outright, he also blamed her for her father's death. His accusations came in the form of even frostier indifference. Happily for Felicity and Helen, Wilkins had gone to work for Martin Jameson after her father died. Theirs was a match made in hellish propriety.

Helen didn't sip her tea, and her brow was weighed down with worry.

"What's wrong?" Felicity said.

"I hope I'm not being impertinent, Miss. Even though this is America, I worry about what people will say about you going around town without an escort, or me, your chaperone."

Felicity had told Helen about their reason for coming to Placer and trusted Helen not to say anything. However, the truth about their mission or any of the other criminal investigations Felicity undertook didn't stop Helen from trying to protect her.

"This is a new country, Hellie. I'm enjoying independence here and must say I find it invigorating. America also means a new freedom for you, too."

"Me?"

"Without a doubt. We're no longer Miss Felicity Carrol and her servant Helen. We're just Felicity and Helen, friends and companions."

"You still pay me, and rather well."

"A mere detail. You give more than you'll ever receive in pounds and shillings."

Helen puffed out her chest and grinned. "Blimey. My prune of a brother would bust his collar button if he heard such a sentiment."

"I suspect you're right. So what do you think about Placer? Still worried about an Indian attack?" Felicity cut a piece of roast beef.

"I'm beginning to change my mind about this town."

"Wonderful. And I'm extremely pleased with our Mr. Lowery. A hard worker, kind, and generous. I've also noticed he's shaved every day this week. He wants to impress you." Felicity used her best innocent voice.

Helen choked on her tea. Felicity patted her back. "Oh Hellie, forgive me."

"Don't know what you're talking about, Miss," she answered with embellished indignation, but she couldn't hold on to the stern face. They both began to laugh. Helen stood. "Time I got back to my work."

"Me as well." Felicity stood and brushed crumbs off her skirt.

"Where you off to, then?"

"To see a doctor."

"Feeling all right, Miss?"

Felicity smiled. "That depends on what I find out."

★   ★   ★

Felicity knocked one more time at the office on Front Street and waited. As she raised her fist for another try, Dr. William Lennox opened the door to a slit.

"What do you want, then?"

"I saw you with Sheriff Tom Pike at the scene of Mattie Morgan's death."

"Is the sheriff here?" The doctor's eyes darted about the porch and then fixed on Felicity as if she peddled bottled plague.

"Afraid not. He's quite busy today. I don't want to bother him."

The physician opened the door wider. Impatience, suspicion, and perhaps a touch of nervousness advanced over his face. "You're the writer. Sheriff Pike mentioned you might be calling. He's an honorable man." The doctor had a Scottish accent thick as haggis.

"Oh, yes. A man who can be trusted."

Money had helped her obtain information from newspaperman Clark Andrews. She hoped Tom Pike's name might act as currency for the physician, as if the very mention was an entry into a gentlemen's club. The sheriff had advised her that the doctor kept to himself outside his medical practice, didn't like women, and was friendly as a case of scurvy.

He snuffled and waved her inside.

Antiseptic.

The word best describing the doctor's large sitting room. White walls. Expensive but scarce pieces of furniture. The essentials and no more. No vases, crystal, knickknacks, lace-covered tables, or Tiffany lamps that decorated other fashionable homes. No portraits of loved ones. The rooms were a space the doctor merely occupied. An artist's easel stood in a corner.

Behind open double doors lay his surgery, with an examination table, cupboards, and a wooden-and-glass case stocked with medical tools and supplies.

A young man wearing a white jacket brought in the tea service.

"Where are your gloves?" the doctor asked the servant as he placed the tray on the table.

"In my pocket, Doctor."

"You know I dislike dirty hands, and your fingernails are filthy."

Lennox's rudeness infuriated Felicity, who believed no one had the right to speak to their employees in such a manner. She gave an encouraging nod to the young man.

"Sorry, Doctor. Won't happen no more." The servant put on the white gloves.

"Anymore."

"What?"

"It won't happen anymore," Lennox corrected him.

"Well, it won't."

"You may leave." Lennox shooed him away.

After the servant left, Felicity and Lennox sat without talking. He didn't move, but his eyes went to the tea service. She relented and poured for them both.

"At last, a decent cup in America." She sipped and then rubbed her hands together in delight. He didn't acknowledge the praise. The doctor appeared to be in his late thirties or early forties. His clothing was flawless and precise as his office. The hands on his lap were large but well tended as a woman's, with long, tapering, pristine fingernails. His dense red hair was parted to one side.

She held up her teacup, which had Chinese markings.

"Ever visited China, Dr. Lennox?"

"No." His reply was stern.

"Afternoon tea is what I do miss about home. I served a cup to the sheriff, but I don't believe he liked it much." Mentioning Pike's name again couldn't hurt, since talking with Lennox was akin to crowding herself into a corset three sizes too small. She sipped her cup and looked around the room. The wall decor consisted of two paintings. One depicted a castle in a green field. Another was of a woman's hands in repose.

"Fine paintings. Did you do them, Doctor?"

"How did you know I paint?"

"The easel."

"Of course." He glanced at his pocket watch and then replaced it in his vest pocket.

"Whose hands are they?"

"My mother's."

"Is she here? How lovely to meet her."

"She died seven years ago from typhus," Lennox answered with vexation.

"I'm very sorry. I suppose you trained in Edinburgh?"

"Miss Carrol, I've had enough of this line of questions. They're unbelievably personal and entirely irrelevant to the issue at hand. I don't wish to discuss my history with you any further."

She set down her cup. "So enough pleasantries." Though he had been anything but pleasant. "I examined Mattie Morgan's wounds but require more information about Lily Rawlins's injuries."

"Everything was in the postmortem report." He took out his pocket watch again. After a glance at it, his eyes fixated on what seemed to be an object a great distance from the sitting room.

"The sheriff was kind enough to share a copy, but reports can't necessarily give you the entire picture. Please indulge me, Doctor. My writing will greatly benefit from your expertise."

A distinct grumble emitted from the man. "You prone to fainting spells? Many women are. I daresay it appears to be a prerequisite of the gender."

"I've never fainted in my life, Doctor."

"Always a first time." He tugged at his beard and tapped his feet as if counting out the seconds he had to tolerate her.

"Your report did brilliantly describe the site of the several stab wounds on Lily Rawlins's body, but you didn't note the length or depth of them."

"They were not important, since she died from the severe cuts to her throat."

"Did they measure about an inch wide?" She held out two fingers to demonstrate the length.

"Perhaps. Yes."

"Did the wounds taper at each end?"

He put his head down for the answer. "Now that you mention it."

"And the depth of the wounds?"

"Six inches or thereabouts."

"I'm particularly interested in the mutilations."

"Quite horrific." He stood. "This is all in my report."

His glasses reflected sunlight right into Felicity's eyes. She adjusted her position so she could see his eyes. "In other words, were they comparable to those of Mattie Morgan?"

He nodded sharply. "Except the most recent murder was even more brutal." He pulled a handkerchief from his pocket and dotted his forehead. "The most appalling sight I've ever beheld."

Felicity lifted an eyebrow. The physician could have been lecturing on the growth of mold. She folded her hands on her lap. "Did the killer also stab Lily Rawlins—well, to put it delicately, in her womanly parts?" His neck muscles bulged at the question. "Doctor?"

"Yes."

"How many times?"

"Six." More irritation from him. "Very few people are aware of those unnatural wounds, which is why I didn't record them. That, and they were indecent. Why do you ask?"

"In crimes against women, the question seems logical. Anything else?"

"An act completely vulgar and beastly." He coughed into his handkerchief. "Are you quite finished with this inquisition?"

"With your patience, Doctor, a few more questions. Is it your opinion that the same man killed the two women?"

"I don't have enough information to make that assumption."

The data was all there, Doctor. You failed to make the connection, Felicity thought.

"Given the meticulous removal of the organs, do you believe the killer had knowledge of anatomy?" she asked in a nonchalant manner. A book by a former Scotland Yard inspector counseled that the best way to catch a person off his guard was to surprise him with an unexpected line of inquiry in an unexpected manner. The result: his mouth would say what his mind wouldn't.

The physician remained stoic. "Perhaps a butcher, someone who deals with animals."

"Even a doctor?" She wanted to elicit any emotional response from this statue of a man. Finally, his eyes were on her. Shakespeare had written about the eyes being the windows to the soul, but even the Bard might have been confounded by those of Dr. William Lennox. His green eyes were the portals to an abyss.

"Absolutely, a physician. I must point out, my dear Miss Carrol, there are only two within one hundred miles, including me. Consequently, your supposition is as empty as it is asinine."

She could have sworn his hair bristled.

"You appear to be well acquainted with anatomy yourself, Miss Carrol. Maybe you're the murderer."

"I did study medicine at the University of London. Alas, I have a good alibi."

"Droll, I'm sure." Lennox poured another cup of tea for himself.

"Forgive me for all the questions, Doctor. The curiosity of a writer. May I have another cup of this delicious tea?"

"As far as this visit is concerned, teatime is over." Dr. Lennox placed his watch back in his pocket.

Felicity left the physician's office and glanced back. She didn't give much credence to intuition because it wasn't scientific or rational, but she felt as if a cool hand brushed over her back. She turned around. Dr. Lennox looked at her through the window. He closed the curtains. She had met many unfriendly men in her short life, but Dr. Lennox ranked high among them. He cared for the health of people, but the doctor apparently didn't like them very much.

Back in her laboratory, Felicity reviewed what she had collected and admitted the evidence amounted to very little.

The only clear fact, though an important one, emerged out of the unknowns. The wounds on Mattie Morgan and Lily Rawlins were similar, made by the same knife, probably wielded by the same man.

She pivoted in her chair at the counter to face the opposite wall. Faces of dead women in several photographs were pinned up in a nightmarish exhibit. The facts of their deaths created a puzzle to be solved.

Spending the afternoon reading, she fell asleep in a chair in her laboratory. She dreamed she was a young girl playing near the lake on the estate at Carrol Manor. A storm rose, rivaling a biblical tempest. The winds threw her into the swirling water, where she thrashed about with panic in the wet gloom. A hand plunged into the water and dragged her to the shore. Mattie Morgan had rescued her. The wounds on Mattie's neck flapped like the gills of a suffocating fish.

CHAPTER 11

Sue the Madam leaned against a pine bar in a large ornate parlor. Amber-colored curls piled atop her head like a decadent dessert. Her lips stood out as the reddest red on a plump powdered face. In a lacy, revealing nightgown over a white corset and underthings, the madam's body was a series of puffed pillows. She reminded Felicity of a grand dowager of the carnal.

"Harry, a glass of beer for me and one for my guest. You like beer, don't you, honey?" Sue asked.

"Simply love it," Felicity lied.

Never before had Felicity met a madam or visited a brothel, which was not unusual for a young woman of means in England. She wasn't shocked to be there. Nor did she judge the women who chose to make a living selling themselves. If they had the education and resources, she was sure they might have selected jobs requiring them to make more use of their minds and talents than their bodies.

The brothel decor was gaudy, with bright-red wallpaper, strands of beads in doorways, gold tassels, statues of naked women, and more trappings to entice and excite the male visitors. She wondered if the British counterparts looked the same. Over the bar hung two large paintings of naked and rather heavy women lying in suggestive positions. Felicity had seen nudes before in museums, but the sensuality of these two left her a bit embarrassed. She sipped the beer, which was heady. It was her first taste and somewhat sour.

"Those paintings arrived from San Francisco," Sue said with pride. "The men love them."

"No doubt."

Felicity had examined the body. Now she wanted to learn about the personality and habits of the latest victim. The killer might have spotted the girl in this very establishment. "I'm here about Mattie Morgan."

Sue took a noisy sip of beer before answering. "Damn shame. Makes me want to cry every time I think of her."

Before going into business for herself as a girl of the line, Mattie Morgan had worked at Sue's Place, according to an article printed in the *Gazette*. However, the story didn't say how long Mattie Morgan had worked there or when she had left. Located in the middle of the Red District, Sue's Place had earned a reputation for employing the prettiest and most thieving prostitutes in town. That was according to Robert Lowery, who had blushed when Felicity asked him what he'd heard about the brothel.

"Men visit the place with lush yearnings and depart with empty pants pockets. Sheriff Pike's arrested a few of the girls caught stealing, but Sue paid their fine and made them return the money," Lowery had said. "'Course that's what I heard." He blushed one more time.

Sue the Madam took a seat on a red-and-white-striped silk sofa. "This came all the way from New York City. No one can sit on it but me, and woe to anyone who tries." She ran her fingers along the fabric.

"It's very beautiful." Felicity took a seat across from the madam, who said she was happy to talk with a woman writer. Sue said she had read all of Jane Austen's books and loved the romance. Such a pleasing revelation that an owner of a brothel in Montana read Austen.

"When was the last time Mattie worked here?" Felicity asked.

"Been months and months."

A disappointment. "What kind of person was she?"

The madam moved her bottom to sink deeper into the couch. "Mattie was a real sweet girl and a good seamstress who used to make beautiful dresses for the girls here. Mattie said she was saving up to go back to San Francisco. That's where she was from."

"Was she popular with the men who visit here?" Felicity hoped that was a polite way to ask the question.

"She used to be darn pretty when she worked for me. Men paid up to five, six dollars for her any time of the day. All that changed when she started smoking too much opium. The drug wears away at prettiness like water on a rock. Finally, I had to let her go." Sue had an airy and syrupy voice.

"Did she favor any particular opium den?"

"Heard from the girls that Mattie was a regular at Lo Han's off of Viceroy." The madam's eyes went to the door, and her red mouth hitched into a corpulent smile. "Why, Tom Pike."

Felicity took another sip of beer.

Pike walked over to the women. Sue rose to her feet and greeted him with a formidable embrace about his chest.

"You're breaking my ribs, Sue." He panted theatrically and gently extricated himself from her mutton arms and vast bosom.

"Tom, I haven't seen you here since Max Freed shot that Frenchman over my best dove."

"How could I forget?"

Sue pinched one of his cheeks. "You get better looking every day. Have a beer, Tom." She signaled for the barman to bring one. "I'm just talking to Miss . . . Miss . . . Honey, I forgot your name."

"I know Miss Carrol. This young woman is like a stone in my boot," Pike said.

"Sheriff." Felicity gave a nod and wished he would go away.

"Leave her be, Tom. She's just asking about Mattie, poor thing," Sue said.

The barman brought him a beer. Pike sat in a chair next to Felicity. "If Miss Carrol doesn't mind, I also have questions for you, Sue."

"I'd love to hear yours, Sheriff," Felicity said.

His eyes stared up to heaven for a moment, then to the madam. "Sue, any of your girls complained about customers who got rough or pulled a knife?"

"What a good query, Sheriff," Felicity interjected.

"Thanks. Well, Sue?"

"My girls shout like pigs if any of them so much as gets a scratch. Earl back there deals with any brigands." She addressed a beast of a man cleaning glasses behind the bar. "Earl, you run into anybody like that? Somebody mean? Somebody with a knife?"

"No, Miss Sue. Can't say I have." Despite his bulk, Earl had a voice high and melodious as a woman's.

"When was the last time you saw Mattie?" Pike asked the madam.

"I already asked that. She said months ago," Felicity volunteered. "Miss Sue, in your establishment, have you noted a man dressed in a long black coat, gold chain in his waistcoat, gray gloves, white spats? A man wearing a black bowler hat and new shiny shoes?" Felicity tried to discount Pike's stare at the specifics, but the question was essential. No one had ever seen the face of the Whitechapel murderer, but one witness had described the clothing worn by a man talking with Mary Jane Kelly the night of her death.

Sue shook her head in the negative. "He sure sounds like a dandy."

"Do you have any more questions, Sheriff?" Felicity asked.

"No," he replied with a severe look. He turned to the madam and smiled. "Thanks, Sue."

"Sorry I couldn't be more helpful."

With effort, the madam rose from the sofa, hooked her arm in Pike's, and walked him to the door. Felicity followed. "How come you never want to spend time with any of my girls, Tom? I got the best house in Placer, the best doves, the best prices. Like the sign out front says, 'All the comforts of home.'" She blinked eyelashes to tempt him.

Felicity smiled at his discomfort.

Pike put on this hat. "Us lawmen just don't make that kind of money, Sue."

The madam pinched his cheek again. "Well, quit getting so dang handsome."

Outside, Felicity enjoyed the clean air. The stench of cheap toilet water, stale beer, and tobacco had made it hard to breathe inside.

"I should throw you in jail for meddling in this case," he told Felicity.

She had heard the threat before.

"And what was all that with the clothing?" Pike said.

Her lie had to be quick, maybe not good, but fast. "In my book, the killer will dress as a gentleman, and I wanted her reaction. Her dandy remark was very clever. I'll add that description."

His rigid face told her he didn't believe her. He walked off, leaving his horse hitched in front of Sue's Place. Felicity hurried to catch up.

"Where you going now, Sheriff?"

"To Mattie Morgan's crib."

"I'd love to go along."

"No."

"Then I suppose I'll just go on my own. But I'd rather have your company." His cooperation was better than not. And like Jackson Davies, he challenged her and she loved it. For example, his good question about whether a man had threatened any of the women at the brothel with a knife.

Pike grunted a "Fine, then."

"Madam Sue mentioned Mattie Morgan had an opium habit and was a regular at Lo Han's," Felicity said. "We should talk with him."

"Already went. Lo hadn't seen Mattie in three days. And I also checked with a barman at the Mineral Palace Saloon on Prospect Road, where Mattie went most nights. But she didn't show up there the night she was murdered."

"I appreciate you sharing the information. And I'll wager the blacksmith's shop is somewhere between Mattie's shack and the saloon." He grunted again, which told Felicity she was right.

They walked toward Viceroy Street. Even without a solid line of demarcation, Felicity could tell they had crossed a border between the higher-priced prostitutes in the so-called joy houses and the cheaper women of Viceroy Street. The buildings became shabbier. She glanced up at Pike. His eyes fixed on the face of every man they saw. As he did, he placed his hand on the gun at his hip, as if an enemy might appear at any moment.

Pike caught her looking at him and stared straight ahead. "More than fifty girls live in the cribs," he said, as if directing her attention elsewhere.

"How fascinating." As interesting was who Pike was searching for among those faces.

They stopped at a block of shacks. A handwritten sign proclaiming DO NOT ENTER BY ORDER OF THE SHERIFF had been posted on the door to Mattie's room. He opened a lock on the door. "I had a deputy do this on the front and back door so no one would disturb the place before I had a chance to inspect it."

"A good way to preserve evidence," Felicity said.

"How do you know so much about a sheriff's work?" he asked.

"I read."

He gave her a harder stare.

"I mean I read all the time."

"I suppose that explains a lot."

She smiled. "I hope so."

Inside the crib, torn lace covered the front window. An unmade iron bed stood in one corner and a hickory chair in another. A washbasin and lantern topped a beat-up chest of drawers. A hat with a red ostrich plume hung on a hook. Felicity watched as Pike rummaged through the chest, which held three dresses, under-clothing, and stockings. He picked up a brush next to the chipped washbasin and pulled out a long blonde hair he let drop to the floor. A shabby black suitcase lay under the bed.

Felicity moved, and a floorboard squeaked. She lifted the board.

"Sheriff." She held up more than one hundred dollars tied with a black ribbon. "This rules out robbery as a motive."

Pike took the money. "Since Mattie didn't have any family, this'll go to the county poor fund to help other unfortunates."

On the other side of the room, a blanket had been tacked over a doorway leading to a small kitchen with a wood stove, table, and one chair. On a shelf were plates, coffee mugs, canned fruit, and rusted tins of flour, coffee, and sugar.

"A wretched life," he said.

"Considering the hidden money, Mattie Morgan was probably saving to leave town," Felicity said. "Lamentably, she waited too long."

When they stepped outside, the ground rumbled with the noontime explosions at the mines.

"Most of the girls of the line sleep at this time of day. We're going to wake a few." Pike knocked hard at the crib next to Mattie Morgan's. KITTY was painted above the door. "Wake up. This is Sheriff Tom Pike."

Kitty didn't immediately answer, so Pike slammed his fist on the door. From the other side came banging and feet stomping on the floor. A reedy woman with stringy black hair opened up and put her hand to her eyes to keep out the sunshine. Her skin was cragged as wood from a fallen aspen tree. No gauging her age on account of those many nights with men, Felicity thought. The woman's squinting eyes settled on Pike's badge.

"Christ almighty, Sheriff." Kitty wore a torn nightgown. Yawning, she let them in, scratching her upper leg. "Whatever you're here about, I didn't do it."

"Someone killed Mattie Morgan last night behind the blacksmith's."

Kitty stopped scratching and collapsed on the bed. "Poor old Mattie."

"Sit up, Kitty."

She did, and drew up her legs to her chest. She stared knives at Felicity. "And who's this? She some Salvation Army camp angel here to save my soul?"

"No one of importance, just a person who's interested in Mattie Morgan," Felicity said.

"You see Mattie last night?" Pike sat on a rickety chair across from Kitty.

"No, sir."

Felicity turned to the wall to the left. Someone snored in the room next door. The girls could probably catch every sound they cared to listen to through the thin walls. "Did you hear Mattie moving around in her room last night?" she asked Kitty, to Pike's chagrin.

"Yeah. She entertained a customer until about midnight."

"Recognize the man's voice?"

Kitty shook her head no.

"You hear Mattie call the customer by name?" Pike said.

Another no. "Too busy with my own clients to worry about hers."

"When did the man leave?" the sheriff asked.

"He finished his business in short order. Mattie took off a little after that. Almost done, Sheriff? Need to get me some sleep. Tonight is Friday, a busy time on the line."

"A little longer. Did Mattie or the other girls ever talk about a man who threatened them with a knife?" the sheriff said.

Another headshake, although one quick as a hummingbird's flight. Kitty's eyes flicked around the room and away from the sheriff's face. Her foot shook under the nightgown. From the woman's movements, Felicity expected she was lying. She looked over at Pike, who appeared to be thinking the same thing.

"Tell me the truth. Don't be afraid," he said. "I promise to keep this between you and me. Oh, she won't say anything, either." He pointed to Felicity.

Kitty whispered. "Two toughs from a gang out of Helena been bullying some of the girls. They say they'll protect us, but they just want to take our money. If we refuse, they promised to give us a good scar so we can't charge as much."

"Their names?"

"Hank Ransom, or so I heard. Can't miss him. Tall as you. A big man with lots of hair and a mustache black as a raven at midnight. He's keeping company with another fella who reminds me of a human skull."

"They threaten you? You can make a complaint, you know, and we'll take them before Judge Howard."

"They didn't touch me. I did see them pull a knife on another girl in back of the Lost Horse Saloon the other night. Don't want to make no complaint, Sheriff. They'll kill me dead."

"I'll protect you."

"You couldn't even protect ol' Mattie."

Pike sighed. "You're right. I should have."

He didn't fake his response, Felicity was sure. Here was an honorable man.

Pike got to his feet. "Thanks, Kitty. Until we arrest this killer, I want you and the other girls to be careful. Don't go out late at night by yourselves."

Kitty yawned. "Poor Mattie girl. Never did have much luck. Think I can have her new hat, Sheriff?"

"We'll see. Get some sleep."

For the rest of the afternoon, Felicity watched Pike interview most of the girls who lived in the nearby shacks. They echoed Kitty's statements. No violent customers carrying knives. Answering with a sizable amount of reluctance, a few did mention threats from the big man fitting Hank Ransom's description. One girl said Ransom and his companion called themselves the Midline Gang. None of the girls, however, was willing to testify against the men, all saying they wanted to live one more day.

Outside the last shack, Pike smiled at last. "We may have gotten a lead on our killer."

But not the one I seek, Felicity thought. Despite the prostitutes' comments about this Midline Gang, the similarities of the wounds on the victims in Placer to those in London could not be explained away.

"Sheriff."

"Call me Tom. Since you've made yourself my unofficial deputy."

"Then Tom, how about that dinner? I'm starving."

"I'm surprised you have an appetite left after all you've heard."

"Good or bad, knowledge always makes me hungry."

CHAPTER 12

Felicity held out her mug for more coffee. The American brew tasted stronger than the English version. Eye-opening strong. She wanted the lift. Although she had been on the case for one week, impatience made her nerves shift to the top of her skin. Every sound caused her to flinch.

That morning Felicity had received a telegram from the London physician she had hired to care for her friend Jackson Davies. The doctor reported that he was progressing but recovery would be slow. Felicity had already written Davies telling him about the trip to America, that she had started her investigation, and was most encouraged. She had hated to deceive him but didn't want him to relapse.

Sipping the strong coffee, she knew she had to step up her inquiry, because if this *was* the killer from England, he would soon kill victim number three.

Felicity and Pike sat in a small place called Bell's Café off the town's main street. On their way there, a school bell sounded far off, and Pike's eyes lowered. Most telling.

The food was simple and plentiful, and she was indeed hungry.

"Your mind is on something other than Placer." Pike stirred sugar into his coffee.

If he could read thoughts as he claimed, she had to be careful. "Just homesick for English tea."

He laughed.

"What?"

"I'm not saying you're lying entirely, but I wouldn't want to play poker with you. You'd bluff on each hand and win every pot."

She smiled. "I have no idea what that means."

"No matter."

"You're not married, are you, Tom?" Felicity said abruptly.

He choked on the coffee.

"Clearly, the question disturbs you." She scooted her chair in for a better look at him. "From your gentle treatment of the women we talked with today, I deduce you were taught to respect women. You've been in love, but something went wrong and there was no marriage. Your intended was probably a schoolteacher. When the school bell sounded, sorrow shaded your face."

"Son of a . . ."

"Too close to the truth?"

"Felicity Carrol of England, you're the most exasperating woman in either country, I'm willing to bet."

"I like to consider myself determined."

He wiped his mouth with a napkin and folded his hands. "I *was* engaged to a schoolteacher. Three months before we were going to enter the church, she left. She decided she didn't like the rugged life here in Placer. She moved to Chicago, last I heard."

"I'm sorry. My curse is that I sometimes say what's on my mind before people want to hear it. One other thing."

"Oh no."

"When Helen and I arrived on the stagecoach, the first thing I noticed about you was how you stared at every male passenger. In fact, every man you pass on the street. Who are you looking for, Tom?" She was quite familiar with searching for a man.

He sat back in the chair. "Somebody tell you about me?"

"Not at all."

"I'm looking for the son of a bitch who killed my father."

"He was a sheriff, also. Robert Lowery told me that."

"John Pike was not only a good lawman but a good pa. He was the one who taught me to respect women and the law."

"What happened to him?"

Pike looked out the window. "It was a nice spring day like this. I walked to the courthouse carrying his lunch in a tin pail. Fried chicken and a piece of corn bread." He turned his face toward hers. "At the corner of Main Avenue, I saw him wavering in the middle of the street. His big Colt hit the ground first. Fingers of red opened over his chest. Pa went to his knees and fell over on his side. Two men had robbed the Bank of Placer and shot him. They rode right past me."

"My God. You saw their faces."

"They are seared into my head like a brand on cattle. One had wild eyes and a smashed nose. The other man's eyes were lifeless as a rusted blade and his right cheek bled from where my pa had grazed him with a bullet, or so said witnesses later. I ran to my father and took him in my arms."

"Did he say anything?"

"He told me he loved me. Then his eyes turned hollow as a glass figurine. I was eleven."

An image came to Felicity of a similar scene. In their London house, she had held her dying father. But he had made no such declaration of love to his daughter. Instead, he had pulled his hand away from hers.

"What'd you do, Tom?"

"Joined a posse headed by my pa's deputy and friend Roo Spitzer. We dogged the killers' trail for two days only to lose it. I came back, and we buried my pa on the hill."

"And you never gave up the search."

"Never."

"You were just a boy."

"I became a man. Like my fiancé, my ma had left years before. Not having their own kids, Roo and his wife took me in and loved me as if I were their own. But every day, I practiced with Pa's gun. An hour on each hand. I paid an old Paiute Indian to teach me how to read trails and worked three jobs to save money to offer a reward for information about the men who shot my pa."

"And did you?"

"When I was seventeen, I tracked down one of the two robbers. I learned their names were Sam Ace and Mike Highland. A little of the wildness had left Highland's eyes when I caught up with him tending bar in Cheyenne, Wyoming. Refusing to surrender or tell me the whereabouts of his partner, Highland drew his weapon. I killed him."

"And you're still looking for Sam Ace. That's why you search every man's face. Seeking that one singular one."

"I believe he'll return to Placer one day. Just an unexplainable feeling, like the kind I get when I know someone's cheating at cards or lying. What keeps me going is the image of Sam Ace making the big swing with boots kicking air."

When he spoke the narrative, he had no emotion. After all this time, he had become the teller of his own story. But he still sought vengeance.

"What, no smart remark?" he said.

She shook her head but felt guilty she had lied to him about her real reason for coming to Placer. She wanted to trust him, but not yet.

He grinned nervously. "That's the most I've talked about my pa's death in a while."

"I'm glad you told me."

Then, as if to not talk any more about his father, Pike glanced toward the café's kitchen. "What'd you put in my coffee, Josiah? Mine tailings?"

A voice shot back. "Then don't drink the coffee, dammit." In the kitchen, Josiah Brown chopped onions and cried with a face as doughy as raw biscuits. The broad-chested man yanked off a dirty apron and tramped outside. Pike put two dollars on the counter.

"Come on. This man might have words we want to hear," the sheriff told Felicity, who bristled at following orders but did so because it might aid her investigation.

They went through the front door of the café and round to the back. The eatery was located on the eastern boundary of the Red District. "This is a good place for news about illegal doings about town," Pike said.

Josiah Brown stood against the wall smoking a cheap cigar. "Gosh almighty. Don't you ever take a day of rest, Pike?"

"Nah. What have you heard about the Midline Gang?"

The cook eyed Felicity. "Who's she? Your sister?"

"I'm his unofficial deputy," Felicity added.

The cook tossed away his cigar. "Ha-ha. Funny."

"Tell me, Josiah," Pike said.

"You ain't getting nothing from me. You put me in a bad humor. I don't even want my penny smoke."

"Josiah, who got you out of prison six months ago?"

"You did."

"Who got you this job?"

"You did," the cook answered with reluctance.

"Why?"

Brown kicked dirt. "So's I can tell you what I hear around Placer."

Pike withdrew a more expensive cigar from his vest pocket and handed it to Brown, who lit up with a match from behind his ear. "Tell me about the Midline Gang."

One side of his mouth broke into a grin. "They come to town to control the painted ladies."

"One of them a big man with a black mustache?"

"Yup. His friend always wears a green plaid vest." Brown took a long puff and whistled out the smoke.

Pike tapped Brown's boot, waiting for more information.

"Good smoke, Sheriff. Makes a man feel well off even if he ain't."

"They carry knives?" Felicity said.

"Can't say. But they got guns."

"Where can I find these two gentlemen?" Pike said.

"Anywhere there're soiled doves and gambling cards."

A woman with a face red as her hair stuck her head out the door. "Josiah, finish that stogie and come back here! A passel of customers walked in. Prove you ain't worthless as I think you are." She went back inside.

"I'll be right in, you harpy from hell," Brown yelled. "Can't believe I married her," he told Felicity and Pike.

"Do you believe those Midline brutes killed the girls of the line?" Felicity asked.

Brown shook his large head. "I'm betting no, ma'am. They're businessmen. They don't want to waste all the good talent."

Pike handed him another cigar and five dollars. Felicity gave him a gold piece.

"Come back anytime, ma'am," Brown said. "Pike, don't need to see you so soon."

Felicity and Pike headed to Main Avenue. "I must say, your method of investigation is quite exciting, Sheriff."

"Glad you approve."

"You do realize one man killed both women."

Pike slowed. "When Big Lil died, I thought the murder a one-time occurrence, like a flash flood in a drought. But with

Mattie's death, I might have to agree with you, much as it pains me."

A few yards away from the courthouse, Pike stopped. A man with white hair stood in front of the doors.

"What is it?" Felicity asked.

"Mayor Jonathan Reiger," the sheriff spat.

"Not one of your favorites, I gather."

"Reiger owns the largest mercantile in town, as well as a bank, restaurant, and hotel."

"Why don't you like him?"

"Prostitution, the bars, and gambling palaces are the biggest sources of crime in town. But they also attract lots of people and their money to Placer. Reiger and the other city commissioners own a lot of businesses. In the Red District, the mayor alone runs three saloons and a gambling house. So they want me and my deputies to keep the peace without costing them or the town too much cash."

"Despicable."

"No, just politics and commerce. I do suspect Reiger's padding his income with illegal activities, but I can't come up with any proof."

They stopped in front of the courthouse. "Mr. Mayor." Pike greeted him with forced politeness.

The mayor leaned on a cane topped by a carved silver head of a bear. A man of compact build, he had broken veins in his cheeks that gave his face a perpetual flush. His white hair was neatly trimmed and his pricey suit was pressed to a shine. "I'd like a word with you about these killings, Sheriff."

"I didn't think you wanted to say howdy. But first, may I present Miss Felicity Carrol. She's a writer from England. Mayor Jonathan Reiger."

"Mr. Mayor." Felicity curtsied because of his title. It occurred to her that this was the first time she had done so since arriving in America. Curtsies were just so . . . English.

"Charmed." Reiger took her hand and kissed it. "Maybe we should talk later, Tom."

"Really, I should be going. A pleasure to meet you, Mayor. Sheriff." Felicity curtsied again and headed off but turned a corner and headed back to the courthouse. She wanted to hear what the mayor had to say about the murders, if anything.

The men remained where they stood. She hid behind one corner of the building.

"Are these killers local men?" The mayor puckered his thin lips.

"Don't know," Pike said.

The mayor tapped the top of his cane against his right palm. "You don't sound too confident about finding this criminal, Tom." He spoke with an inflated resonance as if his words rolled around in his chest before tumbling out of his mouth.

"The killer will be arrested, tried, and hanged, Mr. Mayor. You have my word. How's that for confidence?"

"I know we've had our differences in the past, but I do trust your skills. Otherwise, we may have to elect a new town sheriff."

"Good. I could use a rest."

"No more of your smartness, Tom. And as for this foreign woman, I hear she's going around town asking a lot of embarrassing questions about these crimes. Think she'll portray Placer in a bad light?"

"She won't."

Felicity smiled.

The mayor puffed out his rib cage. His face implied a leer. "She *is* the most beautiful gal to set foot in Placer. A real lady."

"That and more."

The mayor pulled out a comb and slid it through his hair. "Maybe I should present her with a key to the city or extend an official welcome."

"And how is Mrs. Reiger these days? Still suffering from a cold?" Pike grinned.

"You have lots of work to do if you're going to catch a killer." Reiger scowled, spun on his heels, and strode away.

Felicity walked back to her house. Pike was right about the mayor. After meeting Reiger, she wanted to check the contents of her bag to make sure her money was still there.

After dinner, she typed up her notes about what she had learned as well as her deductions and thoughts. Based on the cruelty of the murders and the killer's directing his knife at prostitutes, Felicity ruled out this so-called Midline Gang threatening women in the Red District. The cook at the café where she and Pike had eaten was right in his assumption. Men who made a living off of prostitutes would surely not kill them. Intimidate and scar them, yes, but not murder them.

She also disregarded butchers or any other laborers working with a knife. Unless she was very wrong, and she didn't believe she was in this case, the killer knew anatomy and, therefore, was educated.

The killer must have known one other thing—Mattie Morgan's habits, her route to and from her crib to the saloon and opium den. Perhaps he had even tracked her after she got his attention as a possible target. As a result, these murders might not have been as random as they at first appeared. He knew her movements and had waited in the shadows of the blacksmith building. She suspected the killer had also stalked Lily Rawlins.

Retiring to her bedroom, Felicity wrote a letter to Jackson Davies. She informed him about the murder of another prostitute and how the wounds matched those of Lily Rawlins, meaning the same man had killed both. The mutilations on both of the women in Montana also echoed those of the Whitechapel killer, but she needed more proof before she could be positive Jack the Ripper had arrived in America. At any rate, the leads were strong enough that the trip to Montana had been more than justified.

She didn't write about too much else. She didn't want to sound too beaten down from the lack of clues steering them toward discovering the identity of the murderer. Still, she was honest about one aspect of the case:

> *Jackson, so many new inventions have been created. Machines playing music. A device carrying voices on a wire. Automatic machine guns raining bullets. Flying balloons. So many more. The world is spinning into a new age. Somehow, these murders in Whitechapel and now in this mining town of Placer strike me as bizarre forerunners.*
>
> *A new kind of killer for a modern time.*

CHAPTER 13

A breeze rustled Felicity's skirt and brought a delicate scent from the wildflowers growing thick on the hills above Placer. The lovely scent, however, did nothing to veil the one of human decay as Mattie Morgan was buried at Pauper Grounds.

A small group gathered around the hole into which the plain pine box had been lowered by two men. At the head of the grave, the Reverend T. Phoenix lifted both hands to the sky as if to yank God down to join him. His shoulder-length white hair and blue eyes were striking in the late-afternoon light, offset by a preacher's outfit: black coat, white shirt, and thin black tie.

"Lord, this woman did wrong as those five whores of Babylon. She let her body be used as a temple of sin and temptation and not as a temple of pure womanhood. But Lord, she is also an example to us all that we should not sin." His voice boomed. "Give her your blessing and let her stand at the heavenly gates of your kingdom if you so choose."

Wearing a black taffeta dress, Felicity separated herself from the four mourners, who were all women.

One of the women in a worn dress presented Felicity a shy smile before returning her focus to the service. The woman, who could have been eighteen or younger, held on to a white crocheted shawl marred by a ragged hole in the back. Felicity felt protective of this person she had not even met. The girl's older companion, however, turned her head to throw Felicity a contemptuous stare. Both had red lips as well as dark-rimmed eyes and painted-on beauty marks. Their profession was clear.

The other two women at the funeral, who appeared to be a society matron in her late thirties and her daughter, piqued more of Felicity's interest. In a fine dress of deep blue, the older woman was taller than the younger one. She clasped gloved hands in front of her waist, providing the very picture of dignity. Under a wide-brimmed hat, the older woman's upswept hair was the color of harvested wheat. As if she sensed someone looking at her, she turned to Felicity. Her face was as attractive as it was aloof.

Felicity held her breath.

She was the smiling woman in the photograph. The one Felicity had taken behind the blacksmith shop where Mattie Morgan's body had been discovered. Felicity bowed her head slightly, and the woman did the same.

The reverend's voice built momentum. "Forgive this sinner as you forgive all sinners, no matter their great vices and weaknesses. Let us bow our heads and say amen."

Only the two well-dressed women did so. The other two kept silent but didn't hide their disgust at the minister. Felicity did not blame them. No one wanted to be told their lives were sinful and hell was all they could ever expect.

Reverend Phoenix slammed his Bible shut. As he marched to his horse, he passed the four mourners. "Hope to see you at church on Sunday. Not too late for you, my dears."

He tipped his large black hat to Felicity before riding away. The older well-dressed woman set off for a shiny black carriage. Felicity had never seen a female radiate so much self-assurance, not even herself. The woman raised a finger for her younger companion to follow, and they boarded the carriage.

The other two women remained at the grave site. Felicity approached them. "The reverend could use lessons on how to comfort the living."

"Bastard," said the older woman, who had black curls high on her head. Her brown eyes were murky and her face wan, as if she had spent too many nights with uncaring men. "The Reverend Phoenix claims he wants to save us, but he don't even like us. All that talk about going to heaven. He couldn't find the place if it was nailed to his ass."

Felicity had to smile at the woman's turn of phrase.

"What are you grinning at?" The woman glared.

"The accuracy of your description."

"You don't sound American."

"I'm British."

"Who are you?" asked the younger woman with more curiosity than suspicion.

Felicity introduced herself as a writer of crime stories. "I'm working on a book about a killer who seeks out . . ." She needed a subtle way to address their work.

"Us strumpets?" the young woman said.

"Us whores." The black-haired woman leaned into Felicity. "In spite of your fancy airs, you come off as a person of pure tribulation. Why in the devil's name should we tell you one blasted thing?"

Felicity didn't back away. "Because I want to know why your friend was killed and most brutally. Can we go somewhere and talk?"

"About what?" the black-haired woman asked in a raspy voice.

"About Mattie Morgan. About the sort of man who stalks, murders, and mutilates humans."

"That ain't no man." The woman's mood relaxed.

"He is the devil himself," the young woman added.

"I agree. Please honor me by being my guests for a late luncheon. I'm new in town, so you'll have to select the restaurant."

The one with the black curls snorted. "If you're buying, we have just the place."

★ ★ ★

Felicity and the two women had just taken a seat in the Nugget Café when she noticed the sheriff standing in the street and glaring at her. Throwing down his cigar, he stomped toward them. She didn't want him interfering with her interviews of the women. "Excuse me, ladies. I must talk with the sheriff."

"Better you than me," remarked Nellie Smith, the woman with the black curls and full red lips.

Felicity met Tom Pike outside.

"What are you up to?" he said.

"We're going to have something to eat."

"I know those girls."

"You do? I'm shocked."

"Not that way. They're girls of the line."

The two women watched her and Pike through the window. Felicity waved. They waved back. "I find them very pleasant. They'll help with my writing project."

"This is no game, Miss Carrol."

"I agree completely. May I also point out that when you're upset, you address me as 'Miss Carrol.'"

"That's probably because I'm usually cross with you."

"Now excuse me, I mustn't keep them waiting any longer. It's very rude. Good afternoon, Tom." She retreated to the café.

"If you learn anything, you better tell me, or I'll arrest you for interfering with the law."

She gave a slight twist of her head. "Of course, I'll share any information."

Pike mumbled something as he walked away. She couldn't make out the words but guessed he wasn't complimenting her dress.

"You in trouble with the sheriff?" the younger woman asked when Felicity rejoined them. She called herself Beth Ray and was a pretty girl with wavy light-brown hair.

"I'm in constant trouble with the sheriff. But enough of that. What do you recommend to eat?" They sized up the bill of fare written on a chalkboard above the counter.

"The beef steak," Nellie said.

"I like the fried chicken," added Beth.

"Chicken does sound good." Felicity summoned the waitress to take their order, including coffee and a piece of pie for each of them.

"I've never talked with a writer before. Where do we start?" Beth said.

Felicity pulled off her gloves. "With Mattie Morgan."

Beth's eyes darkened with grief. Nellie's remained defiant.

"I'd like to know about her. I heard she came from San Francisco," Felicity said.

Beth nodded. "Mattie's man brought her to Placer so he could dig for gold. She said he made so many promises to her. Promises of marriage, riches, and children. Her own dress shop. He even bought her a silver wedding ring, placing it on her finger and telling her they were good as hitched."

Certainly it was the ring Felicity had found at the foot of Mattie Morgan's body.

"When his dreams of gold petered out, her man went to work for the mines, but he tripped on a cable and fell more than one hundred feet into a shaft. A hundred feet. Must have been like a dive into hell."

"Terrible."

"They buried what was left of him in the cemetery up on the hill. She loved that man and hadn't loved anyone since, least that's what Mattie said. Without enough money to go home, much less open a dress shop, she sold herself in Placer." Beth's voice lowered. "Mattie had earned lots of money in the brothels, but her fixation on opium drove her down to the cribs."

Nellie said nothing but glanced at Felicity with an obvious mistrust. Her eyes were jaundiced with weariness and cynicism. Beth, on the other hand, appeared open and friendly. When she spoke, she was no longer an experienced girl of the line but a young woman of hope and possibility.

"Poor Mattie went days eating just bread and cheese and stuffed papers in her boots to make them last, all to save the dollars and coins. Another year and she said she'd have enough for a train ticket to Denver so she could open her dress shop," Beth said.

That supported Felicity's theory about the money hidden in Mattie Morgan's room.

"Did Mattie ever talk about encountering a gentleman in a long black coat wearing gray gloves, white spats, shiny boots, and a black bowler hat? A customer or perhaps a man following her?" Felicity said. "Come to think of it, have you seen anyone like that?"

The women shook their head.

"Most of the gents go to the brothels," Beth said.

Felicity sat back. "I'm amazed that a woman such as Mattie Morgan, who was a talented dressmaker, who saved her money and planned to leave Placer, turned to opium in the first place."

"We all moved to Placer with dreams of getting rich, one way or another." At last Nellie had stopped answering Felicity's questions with scorn. "Men can mine and do other labor, but this world is not forgiving for women folk who don't have a man or family to support them. They have to depend on trading what they got."

"A lot of girls have the same story, ma'am." Beth dug into the chicken when the food arrived. "Mattie smoked opium to deal with it."

"Felicity, please. What kind of men come to see you?"

"All kinds. Lonely miners with no one to love. Husbands growing tired of their wives. Boys who've never been with a woman," Beth said. "Most of them are very nice to us. A few even give us gifts."

Nellie hooted. "We get the dregs at our cribs." She chewed as she talked. "Beth is one to coat the world in pretty colors. She didn't mention the drunks who sweat all over you or who haven't taken a bath in five years. Then there're the ones who can't do anything unless we speak filth to them."

Felicity found it difficult to swallow the food in her mouth. Never before had she heard such honest chronicles. But then, what had she expected they were going to chat about? Needlework and cooking? She swallowed. "In the last four months, have you ever encountered a man who brandished a long thin knife or who appeared violent or mad?"

"One man slapped me around because I stole his watch. 'Tweren't nothing like what happened to Mattie or Big Lil. Word is they were sliced up like ham." Nellie sampled the apple pie.

Beth shook her head no as she ate her pie with delicacy.

"Did Mattie or Big Lil have anything in common?"

"You mean besides being dead?" Nellie lit a cigarette.

Felicity didn't take offense at the woman's harsh tone. The prostitute's response reflected the life she led, one of endurance and survival, however the means. "I mean, were they friends?"

"Not that I know of. They lived on different sides of Viceroy Street."

"A week before she died, Mattie told me she was scared of the Midline Gang," Beth said. "They want to run the girls of the line and take our money. They're threatening the gals who don't go along."

"I've heard about them. Your lives can be very dangerous," Felicity said.

Nellie put out her cigarette on the side of her plate. "Comes with the territory."

"One other thing. Who was the tall woman at the funeral?" Felicity took a bite of the apple pie, which was quite good.

"That's Mrs. Albert. She runs the White Rose brothel on Mineral Avenue. A real classy place."

"A madam? That is surprising. I believed she might have belonged to a charity organization that helps the girls of the line."

"Nah, she runs whores." Nellie smirked and lit another cigarette.

"She's like you, Miss Felicity, a real lady even though she owns a joy house," Beth said.

Nellie puffed on the cigarette. "But Mrs. Albert is prickly as a pear. She likes her soiled doves young and stupid. That was one of her girls with her at Pauper Grounds. And I tell you this." She waved her cigarette. "Mrs. Albert may act like she got manners, but she beats the gals who don't do what she says, or if they don't please the customers. 'Least that's the word around town."

Felicity's cheeks heated like a sunrise. Nellie laughed.

"Nellie, Miss Felicity is a lady," Beth said. "She's not used to our kind of talk."

"She asked, didn't she?" Nellie picked her teeth with the fork. She leaned over the table and her gaze focused on Felicity, who shifted under the scrutiny. "Beth girl, if I had it, I'd bet one hundred gold pieces our Miss Felicity here has never been with a man. Hell, she never even been close to one."

Beth placed her fork down. "Miss Nellie, I do believe you are right."

The women giggled.

"I haven't met a real virgin since '79," Nellie said to Beth.

Felicity glanced around the place, which was empty at that hour. "Ladies, please. We're in a public establishment."

"She's a virgin, all right," Nellie proclaimed.

They laughed, and Felicity could not help but laugh, too. So much so, she wished she could loosen her corset.

Beth winked. "When you find the right man, all you have to do is ask us for pointers on how to keep him happy when the lights go out."

Nellie displayed a mouth of brown teeth. "We won't even charge you for the advice."

After lunch with the women, Felicity returned to her laboratory. She inserted a clean white sheet into her typewriter. She typed:

TRAITS OF THE KILLER

Preys on prostitutes
Skilled in use of knives
Knows human anatomy
Wears gloves
Red hair?
Physical strength
Left-handed
Does not molest victims
Cunning
Leaves coins and ring behind. A kind of ritual?

Such a short list.

Since none of the victims in Placer or Whitechapel had been robbed or violated, the motive was not money or sexual hunger. Something else drove the killer. An objective to kill a certain victim in a certain way. This urge was pure emotion. A warped passion ending in death.

She thumbed through German physician Wilhelm Wundt's *Textbook of Human Physiology*, in which he wrote about the new study of consciousness and how the human mind could be examined just like a body could be probed for diseases by a doctor. Wundt concluded that the unseen conscious manifested itself in outward behaviors.

The theory was nothing new. The ancient Greeks had recognized illnesses of the mind. A Persian scientist born in AD 850 had even written of emotional disorders with symptoms of anger and aggression.

Perhaps she was taking the wrong approach. Concentrating too much on the physical science. She should also take into account the science of the mind. How unrestrained wants and disorders could rule the physical being. This newer science captivated her. She loved the exactness of mathematics, chemistry, and medicine. Yet a review of the soul, spirit, or whatever the term was for what went on inside a person's head seemed infinite and testing.

She typed again:

Insane

He must be mad to commit such horrible killings. Yet the murderer wasn't like the howling lunatics of a bedlam. He was intelligent and methodical, as proven by his skilled surgeries on the victims and the fact that he had eluded capture this long. Some knife wounds did display a near frenzy, while there was a method to others. So his madness, though virulent, had design. She added to her list:

Not only kills women but punishes them

The almost punitive wounds to the victims' female organs supported her supposition that the murderer had a convoluted motive.

Hates women?

The streets of Placer and London were filled with easy prey—shop girls, waitresses, vendors. He could have had his pick. But he chose prostitutes, and maybe not just because of their availability. Back home, she had read social commentary portraying all prostitutes as promiscuous, hence their convivial contacts with men to fulfill unchecked cravings. While that might be true in a few cases, she believed women ended up selling themselves because of poverty and illiteracy. They had no other prospects in life or couldn't survive on pay from what was considered honest employment. From what she had learned about Mattie Morgan, the young woman had evidently found she earned more money as a girl of the line than as a seamstress.

What was it about these women of the night that enraged this man to the point of such violence? She slapped at the keys.

Focuses on prostitutes
  Why?
  Their availability?
  Perceived as promiscuous and immoral?

Like Whitechapel in the East End of London, the Red District of Placer was the perfect place to hunt his particular quarry. Adding to the tragedy was that even without a maniac tracking them down, most of the prostitutes were probably destined for an early death. From drink, disease, or other violence.

Felicity withdrew her hands from the typewriter keys. Beth and Nellie were right to make fun of her naiveté. She had been sheltered behind thick walls and lived in books for years. Although she had spent the last year seeking out killers, their motives had been profit, revenge, or borne out of a rage that came of a specific moment. All concrete reasons for crimes after a fashion.

But this killer.

This killer's reasons were obscure and justified only in his skewed mind.

Felicity decided she could no longer follow the old ways of reason. To catch the killer, she would have to think like him. To see out of the eyes of a man who despised the women who sold their bodies.

The idea chilled her.

CHAPTER 14

Taking up the reins of the wagon, Felicity assured Helen and Robert Lowery of her safety. "It's early afternoon. I shall be perfectly fine."

"As long as you get back by dark, Miss." Helen wrung her hands with worry nevertheless.

When Felicity swiveled back in her seat to wave, she noticed Lowery holding Helen's hand. In all the violence she had seen recently, their small gesture gave her optimism and another reason to catch those out to destroy the goodness of life.

Felicity had not mentioned to them that she had hidden a crossbow and quiver of bolts under a blanket in the wagon. A craftsman in Italy had assembled the weapon from Felicity's own design, which improved upon the medieval weapon in power and accuracy as well as being lighter and sleeker. With intense practice on the grounds of Carrol Manor, Felicity had been able to load a projectile in a few seconds and strike the center of a target one hundred feet away. When a groundskeeper had asked why she wanted such a weapon, she had replied that it was for a hunt, which wasn't strictly a lie.

She had also purchased a derringer for the trip to America but preferred the crossbow because it felt somewhat more civilized,

which she admitted was a stretch. Historians believed the crossbow had been created in the fifth century in China and that the
weapon had been used greatly during the Middle Ages. Besides the
possibility that she might actually have to use the weapon in self-
defense, the only thing that upset her was that a medieval crossbow
had been used to kill her friend in the first case she had ever investigated. The very case that had set her on this course of solving
murders. How ironic that she might now catch a murderer with
the weapon that had ignited her quest for justice in the first place.

So armed, she ventured into the Red District. The place
renowned for decadent pleasures at night presented little of those
attributes in the day. Because of the proximity to the smelters on
the nearby hills, the air stank of sulfur. The eyes of the people
walking along the streets were vacant, as if they had pursued gold
too long and finally surrendered to disappointment. The young had
become old. The old, primordial. Their heartache was as perceptible as the grime layering the scruffy wooden buildings. A man
with shadows for eyes kicked at another man who had fallen asleep
in front of a saloon. Torn curtains covered broken windows. The
body of a dead dog rotted in the middle of the street. Bars probably
lively at night now appeared forlorn. The parallels between this
area and the East End in London were extraordinary.

Felicity drove on. She could have been driving through the
Whitechapel district in the East End, with the horses clomping over
cobblestone and not dirt. Reins loose in her hands, she reflected
not on the way ahead in Placer, Montana, but on the time past. To
another ride back in London.

Standing on the stairs, Felicity had watched her father put on his
coat and hat and was determined to know where he was headed.

She was thirteen. She asked Helen to fetch her cloak and summon a hansom cab. With fright turning her blue eyes into deep crystals, the older woman did so but said nothing.

After dinner at their London house, her father would usually retire alone to the library to read and drink whiskey. Often, he just pulled on his cloak and left, and Felicity had begun to recognize the signals of when that would happen. He smoked one cigarette after another. His eyes flitted over the walls. His fingers tapped out an almost restive message on the chair. When he did go, he didn't say a word to his daughter. He rarely talked with Felicity anyway, and her attempts at conversation were met with terse answers or silence. All she knew about her father had come from Helen. But tonight Felicity wanted to know more, and she was resolved to follow him.

"He's just off to his club," Helen said with apparent uneasiness.

"We shall see." And Felicity stepped out the door.

Felicity watched as her father's carriage stopped in front of another affluent house, where a man wearing a top hat and a gentleman's clothing emerged and joined him. In the feeble light, Felicity couldn't see the other man's face. They drove to the East End and Whitechapel, its most infamous district, and continued farther until they stopped in front of a tall gray stone house. Her father exited the carriage, the other man behind. At his knock, the door swung open. A red-haired woman wearing a blue skirt and nothing more greeted her father. Within her opaque face, her red lips parted. A black ribbon circled her neck. Samuel Carrol and the other man walked in as if they had come home. They were laughing. Felicity had never heard her father laugh.

In the hansom cab, Felicity sat back with exhaustion more than anger or embarrassment and told the driver to take her back to the London house. She was most familiar with her father's neglect of her. But she grew ashamed to have witnessed another side to him that she didn't care to know after all.

Felicity's hands tightened on the reins with another memory. When she was younger, she had had nightmares about the spirit of her dead mother roaming Carrol Manor in a spectral white gown, only to be torn apart by a creature formed from shadow. When she woke up screaming, Helen would hold her and say, "My dear, when you open the door to a dark place, more darkness will rush in. You must close the door."

"How?" she would ask.

"Think about cheerful roses and beautiful rainbows," Helen had advised.

But Helen was wrong.

Under the hot sun of Montana, Felicity could not stop the dark memories. The door had opened. But never mind thinking of roses and rainbows. Moving forward was the best way to keep them out.

Felicity flicked the reins to hurry the horses along.

ENTER AND BE SAVED proclaimed the banner over the door of the Church of the Morning. Under the banner, THE REVEREND T. PHOENIX had been carved onto a piece of wood. Felicity pulled the wagon over. Located in the Red District, the church appeared to have been converted from a barn. The inside reeked of cheap candles. In the windowless building, Felicity walked over the uneven dirt floor, past rows of nicked benches, to the front. On one side stood a tall pulpit. At the center of the church, a splintered wooden cross tall as a man hung from the roof. She bent down. Speckles of what appeared to be dried blood spotted the ground underneath it. Rising, she inspected the bottom of the cross. More spots of the dried blood.

"Have you come to be saved?"

Felicity spun around. "You frightened me."

A voice echoed. "I ask that of all who enter here. Do you seek salvation, young lady?" Reverend Phoenix had entered from a side door. He wore a white apron.

"I seek truth." Felicity introduced herself and repeated her story about being a writer. He listened and nodded.

"That explains why so clearly a refined young lady attended the funeral of such a sinner."

"Mattie Morgan was a victim of murder."

"Not an unusual end for a whore." He smiled. "I do appreciate writers. They're like the scribes in the Old Testament. Come into the kitchen. I'm preparing stew for the hungry." His charm had an edge, like a pillow stuffed with feathers and thorns.

At a table, he diced beef into cubes and added them to a large boiling pot on the wood-burning stove. In the back of the kitchen, a door opened to a small, simple bedroom. "I'm not a good cook, but I can make a dinner to fill the bellies of the unfortunate. They must listen as I talk about God. The price for a meal."

"Your service for Mattie Morgan was quite powerful." Felicity tried to be tactful.

"I want to help these women reject their sinful lives and find heaven. I have made this mission my life's work."

"You made that incredibly obvious, Reverend."

His penetrating gaze was probably useful for a minister to win converts, as if his congregation peered directly into the eyes of God.

"How were you acquainted with Mattie Morgan?" she asked.

"She attended services a few times. Before her untimely death, she told me she wanted to repent her sins and be baptized. Save the Lord." He chopped potatoes.

"And Lily Rawlins? Did you know her as well?"

"She, I am afraid, refused to accept the Lord. I still said words over her grave. The least I could do in hopes that God would take pity on her wretched soul." Flecks of red meat covered his hands, which he clamped together on the table. He lifted his head with a beguiling expression of belief. "She was weak, and women are much weaker than men, not only in body but in spirit. The Bible tells us so."

"I must have missed that passage." Felicity glanced at a kitchen pot on a hook and wanted to throw it at the man's head for his inane views, unhappily held by most men. However, just the thought of tossing the pot was gratifying. She pressed on. "Do you think the women were murdered because they were prostitutes?"

"I'd rather ponder their futures in the afterlife of heaven than their pasts of sin." He smiled and sliced onions for his stew.

"You didn't answer my question, Reverend." Felicity gave her own winning smile.

"Miss Carrol, has it crossed your mind that these killings might have been the will of the Almighty? That they were examples of what happens to those who make their living in sin? I don't mean to sound harsh, but I am a man of God."

As Phoenix spoke, he tapped the knife on the table, his white hair silvery in the light. Felicity organized her observations. The reverend was powerfully built. The prostitutes knew him. He could easily get close enough to kill. As a minister, he'd rise above suspicion. Although he used his right hand to cut the vegetables and spoke with an American accent, that might be part of a role he had adopted in the new world. At Mattie's funeral he had mentioned the whores of Babylon. There were five of them, and there had been five victims in England. The red hairs she had found on Mattie Morgan's body might have belonged to a customer after all.

And what about the spots of blood under the cross in his church?

Felicity easily envisioned him hiding in the gloom, a knife in his hand. Shuddering at the prospect, she needed more facts to count him as a suspect. "You must be busy with the many sinners in town, Reverend." Her throat dried at the words.

"I'm blessed to have a large flock to guide to that magnificent place of God."

"Phoenix is an unusual name. Not your real one, is it?"

"I used to be a drinker, fornicator, and gambler. I cheated men out of their money and took foolish pride in my wiles." His voice rose in power as he continued. "But one night as I lay in my own vomit on a street, an angel appeared to me as the morning sun rose in the sky."

"An angel?"

"She took on the form of a nasty whore. Without moving her lips, the angel's words appeared in my heart. She told me to minister to others like her." His eyes and hands pointed upward. "So I placed aside my whiskey, women, and cards and took up the Bible. Like the phoenix of old, I changed into a new man out of the ashes of my own transgressions."

"Such a vision would change anyone." Felicity watched as he renewed his stew making. The man was deranged, but enough to kill? "How long have you lived in Placer?"

"Since February of this year, and I've been blessed every day."

"Why this town?"

"The whore angel whispered the name of Placer in my dreams."

"A smart angel, to be sure." Felicity's suspicions about Phoenix amplified. He had come to town before Lily Rawlins was killed. Now she had to check on his whereabouts at the time of the murders. "By the way, your stew smells delicious."

"I agree with you." A woman stood in the side doorway. The sunlight at her back obscured her features.

"Mrs. Albert," the Reverend said. "What a nice surprise."

When the woman stepped into the kitchen, Felicity took notice of a dewy face devoid of garish paint—most odd, she believed, for a madam. Mrs. Albert even had the presence of an aristocrat. She wore a silk dress of the darkest purple with a tasteful, even subdued, hat.

"You must be the writer working on a book about the unfortunate murders. How interesting." Mrs. Albert spoke with a refined southern accent.

"Felicity Carrol is my name, but how did you know?"

"Girls talk, especially the girls in the business of giving pleasure. How fascinating you entered a field so dominated by the male of the species."

"I recognize you from Mattie Morgan's funeral," Felicity said.

"A tragedy." Mrs. Albert handed Phoenix a small purse of coins. "For your efforts, Reverend."

"You're most gracious, Mrs. Albert." He addressed Felicity. "She's one of the more generous contributors to our work at the mission, as are many of the women who operate those houses of degradation and wickedness."

"We do what we can." Mrs. Albert took out a watch from her purse. "I must run."

"May I visit you sometime? I'd like to talk with you as part of the research for my book," Felicity said.

"Come anytime. You'll find us at the house with the white rose over the door."

Phoenix focused his eyes on the madam. "Have you accepted Jesus as your savior from a wicked life?"

A wispy smile lit on Mrs. Albert's lips. "Not yet." She went out the door.

Felicity also took her leave of Reverend Phoenix, but she wasn't through with him. Not at all.

★　★　★

Jeremiah Sutton loved horses more than people.

Felicity could tell because his face took on a contented serenity as he groomed the animals at his livery stable. He cooed to them as he brushed their manes. When talking with the two-legged kind of animal, however, Sutton's gnarled features stiffened to the consistency of saddle leather. His business was located directly in back of the Church of the Morning, and he hated the Reverend Phoenix with everything his mean spirit could muster and then some.

"I wanted that building to expand my business, but the religious jackass bought it out from under me and filled it with holy-holies. He invites painted ladies and other malcontents to his so-called church all hours of the day. Makes me sick."

"My gracious. What behavior for a man of God." Felicity spurred his ire. She wanted Sutton to spy on Phoenix. She thought the reverend's religious insanity might be masking one more fiendish, particularly now that she had spotted the blood drops. After leaving the church, she had scouted around for a suitable candidate, and she knew she had one as soon as she mentioned Phoenix's name to Jeremiah Sutton.

"Man of God, bah." Sutton's spittle on the ground was dark from tobacco and animosity. "Phoenix keeps his horse at my stable and pays good money; otherwise I'd piss in his eye."

"In that case, I have a proposition, and it must be our secret."

"I'm a married man. I don't dally with other skirts."

She exhaled with patience. "This is not that kind of proposition, Mr. Sutton."

"Then let's hear it."

"I must know the times and dates Reverend Phoenix leaves his church after dark. Your help will be amply rewarded. Is it possible to observe him without being seen?"

"I'm here most days and live upstairs. I can take in everything from my bedroom window, both his front and back doors."

"And you don't mind the night work?"

"Don't sleep much anymore. I've lived too long for it to do any good."

"Excellent. I'll give you a notebook to write what you see, specifically times and dates," She also presented him a fifty-dollar note. "And you must not speak of this to anyone."

He snatched the money as if it might disappear. "I won't even tell my wife. She don't need to know my business."

"Excellent."

"Why do you want to know the comings and goings of that man anyhow?" He raked coarse fingers over his whiskers.

"I represent a family he might have wronged. I require proof of his guilt."

"Good enough for me." Sutton patted the neck of a mare. "Come on, girl, we're getting paid to keep an eye on the son of a bitch next door."

CHAPTER 15

Electricity had not yet arrived in the Red District as it had other parts of the large town. As a result, the glow of kerosene lamps and candles began to appear in the windows of the shops, bars, and gambling houses lining its dirt roads as the sun dropped behind the mountain. Lively fiddle music started up in one of the saloons. Inside, men shouted conversations over the noise. Smoke emerged from gambling palaces like puffs from a young dragon. A hurdy-gurdy house sounded of a jig and feet stomping on floors. Felicity glanced inside the open doors as she passed in her wagon. Men danced with brightly daubed women, and other men danced with each other probably, because there were no more females available.

Sheriff Tom Pike had warned her the place could be dangerous after sunset. Given the dubious men eyeing her, she contemplated whether she should have better heeded his words. But she wanted to see the streets at night, how the killer saw them.

The Red District had transformed into a place of infinite gloom despite its attempts at merrymaking. Male customers were already knocking on the doors of the girls of the line. An older woman stood on a small porch and stretched. A cheap camisole and bloomers covered her voluptuous body. Outside another shack, the face of a younger girl was a decorated facade, a tired doll with scarlet lips and cheeks. Men staggered into and out of the several saloons and gambling houses along the street. Tinny music floated from brothels like a siren's song.

At the end of one building, the name MATTIE remained painted over the door. In the middle of another building were the names of Beth and Nellie. She hoped they would be safe.

Turning the horses toward home, Felicity tugged on the reins at a noise.

A woman yelped in pain. "Help!"

The sound came from an alley between two of the buildings straight ahead. Stopping the wagon, Felicity grabbed the crossbow and flung the quiver of projectiles over one shoulder. She was incensed that other people on the street ignored the woman's distressed cries. Loading the crossbow, she sprinted toward the woman's calls. Pressing herself against the front of a building, she peeked around the corner into the alley. A man held his right arm over a young woman's upper chest, pinning her to the wall. With his left hand, he outlined her face with the point of a knife. The man was dressed like a banker in a tidy brown suit, but packed it with bulk and sinew. His description matched that of the thug mentioned by the girls of the line. A member of the Midline Gang recruiting prostitutes with intimidation and threat.

The woman's body shook. Perspiration wet her forehead. "Please, don't hurt me," she pleaded.

"I won't hurt you, my little dove, not if you agree to work with us." The man's knife outlined the woman's lips.

"Don't need no whoremaster taking my hard-earned money." She immediately cowered at her bravery.

"I prefer *manager*, even *partner*. We'll treat you good." With his left hand, he slid the knife point along the woman's throat. "We're businessmen who want to work with you and the other girls. What I'm offering is one good investment. Truly is. You get our protection. We get part of your earnings. You get to live. We get to let you live. The American way."

The woman whimpered.

"Shut up!" The man's shout blew back her hair. "I'll give you a remembrance of what will happen if you don't join us." The woman screamed as the knife point drew a sliver of blood over her chest.

Felicity ran into the alley. "Let her go." She pointed the crossbow at the man's heart.

He wheeled in her direction, wearing a sneer cruel enough to wilt flowers. His shiny black hair was parted in the middle. A thick mustache obscured his entire lip. She had never seen such disdain on a face.

"Who you supposed to be? Robin Hood?" he said.

"That's exactly who I am. Now release that woman."

"Let that woman go?" he said in a horrid imitation of her English accent. "What do you know? The British have arrived." He pushed his arm tighter against the woman, causing increased sniveling and tears. He continued in a vicious voice. "We're talking business. You'll have your turn. And I'm not afraid of your little bow and arrow. Women can't shoot for shit."

Felicity aimed and fired. The bolt passed so close to the man's head, she swore it grazed his cowlick. As the bolt stuck in the wall, she reloaded, beating her record.

The man dropped his arm, and his hand went to his head as if he expected to find a projectile embedded there. The young woman scampered off into the night. His angry face was as terrifying as his knife. "Ha, you missed."

"A warning shot. The next one won't be."

The man marched toward her. Too late she noticed his eyes darting to the left. Someone seized her right arm tight to make her release the weapon. The crossbow fell. Her dress ripped at the sleeves. The unseen man seized her left arm and held them both behind her back. She gasped at his strength and was irritated she hadn't looked around for the first man's accomplice. Beth, Nellie, and Pike's informant had all mentioned *two* men threatening women. *Some savior, Felicity Carrol.*

"You got lots of spirit. I like that. Your customers must pay a lot," said the burly man with the mustache.

"I'm not a prostitute. Even if I were, you and your cowardly friend would never be allowed through my door." Although panicked, she needed her concentration and wit. These men wanted to hear her scream and cower. They wanted to feel power over her. She wouldn't oblige, which might discombobulate them enough to attempt an escape.

She spoke in a contemptuous tone. "Using a knife against women is probably the sole way to demonstrate you are men. Outwardly, you're rank and uncouth. Underneath, you're weak and stupid. The worst example of manhood I've ever encountered."

"I'll show you who's a man." Snorting venom and the smell of onions, he clutched her cheeks and aimed his tongue at her mouth.

"If you place that thing in me, I'll bite it off and spit it on the ground." She was surprised those words came out of her, but she was mad about his assault on the woman and upon her. She fought against the grip of the silent second man.

The burly man withdrew his tongue back into his mouth. "Ben, we're going to have to teach this gal some manners."

"Yeah, let's teach her." His partner's breath made Felicity's eyes water.

"You got a disrespectful mouth." The burly man flipped his knife with his left hand and caught the blade by the tip in front of her face.

An iron knife. Single-bladed, thick, and nicked. Attached to a wooden handle, the blade was almost two inches wide and at least eight inches tall. This was not the weapon that had killed Lily Rawlins and Mattie Morgan.

The burly man leaned in close to her face and smirked. "Still, you are pretty. I may want to keep you for myself."

"Cleaning a pig sty is more desirable. Now do your worst, barbarians. You won't hear me scream. In fact, I'll laugh at you."

From the brief confusion on the big man's face, he hadn't expected that response. She prepared for the knife. Her body constricted in anticipation of a blade and an end to her new beginning.

"Let her go," said Sheriff Tom Pike.

The pressure on her arms loosened. She pivoted around.

With his Colt, Pike struck the head of the second assailant. A bald hulk of a man in a black coat, green plaid vest, and striped pants hit the ground. Pike pointed his gun at the bigger man holding the knife.

"If you hadn't been talking, I couldn't have gotten the drop on them," the sheriff told Felicity. "Thank you."

Pike had insulted her, but she wasn't irate. She scooped up her loaded crossbow and aimed at the bald man who sat on the dirt rubbing his head.

"Throw down the knife or I'll blow a hole in your hand." Pike cocked his gun at the burly man.

"You don't scare me, Mr. Law."

"Then how come I can hear your knees knocking?"

The man dropped the knife.

The sheriff ordered the men to stand against the wall and tossed two sets of metal handcuffs at their feet. "Put 'em on. You're under arrest for assaulting this young woman."

"She shot an arrow at me." The big man motioned his head to the one stuck in the wall behind.

"It's called a bolt. Sheriff, I did so because he was attacking a woman. He cut her chest with that knife." Felicity straightened her clothing.

"Where is she?"

"The woman ran away after I appeared. But I'll sign a statement about what I witnessed and how they threatened me and the other woman."

"Good enough," Pike said.

"Ain't good enough for us," spat the burly man.

"Shut your mouth," Pike said.

After the men were handcuffed, the sheriff removed guns stuck in their belts under their coats, along with a truncheon in the jacket of the bald man. Pike shook his head as he packed their weapons in his saddlebag.

"This is a rough town. We're protecting ourselves," the burly man said.

"You have enough weapons here to hold off an army."

"That woman approached me to have a good time." The man flashed a gold tooth in front.

In two strides, Pike put his hand around the man's throat. "You disparage her name one more time, I'll take off my badge, beat the hell out of you, and then your partner just for good measure."

The power of Pike's threat made the men recoil and Felicity jolt. His attractiveness had increased tenfold. Blast. The sheriff's charm had sneaked up and held her like an amiable summer evening. She'd be thinking about him that night—against her will.

She tightened her hold on the crossbow.

Stop it, Felicity, you're no damsel in distress, she told herself. *It's merely western chivalry. Remember, the last man you felt drawn to turned out to be a murderer.*

"You all right?" Pike asked her.

"As rain, Sheriff," she said with composure. While she couldn't escape his allure, she could deal with it. With the sheriff's horse tied to the wagon, Felicity drove behind Pike as he walked the two men to the jail. She had one hand on the reins and another on the crossbow on her lap in case the men gave the sheriff any problems. The men glared at anyone who looked at them on the street and spit. Now that the danger had passed, Felicity's heartbeat accelerated with relief, so much so that she swore Pike might hear the thuds. After they traveled a few streets, they met one of Pike's deputies, who helped escort the men.

The red-brick jail stood behind the courthouse. As the men were led away to the cells, the big man gaped at Felicity. "We'll see you soon, Miss Robin Hood."

"You even think about her and you're dead," Pike answered, as dangerous as his Colt.

Within an hour, the sheriff sat behind the large wooden desk in his office while Felicity gave her statement to a deputy, who wrote down everything in what she considered first-rate penmanship. She signed the paper and the deputy left, closing the door behind him.

"Want to tell me what you were doing in the Red District? And with a crossbow?" Pike said.

She glanced at her watch. "My word. Eight o'clock. Helen must be frantic."

"I sent a deputy to tell her you were safe."

"I appreciate that." Her hair in disarray, Felicity took out the pins and let it fall. "By the way, how did you find me?"

"I went to see you, and Helen told me where you were headed. Luckily, I arrived in time."

"I'm perfectly able to take care of myself."

"You were doing a damn poor job. I had to save you from those men."

Felicity disliked Pike's condescending attitude. His charm diminished at that moment. Primarily, she was exasperated at *having* to be saved. "Thank you!"

"You're welcome, dammit!"

"No need to curse."

"You're upsetting everything you touch."

"The only thing I appear to be upsetting is you. Besides, I was close to freeing myself from that entanglement before you arrived."

"You've done nothing but cause trouble since you stopped in my town. Nosing around, asking too many questions, going where you shouldn't go." Pike stood up.

So did Felicity. "You should have been asking those questions about the murders."

"I have been. You just haven't noticed because you think you're right all the time."

"Well, I am right." Their tempers expanded with each statement. "Those men are members of the Midline Gang. They're trying to take control of the prostitute trade in Placer. They were recruiting that girl when I came onto the scene."

"I know that."

"Beth Ray talked about them at luncheon. She said Mattie Morgan was afraid of them also."

"Why the hell didn't you mention this before now?"

"There hasn't been much time."

"That's no excuse."

"I should have told you, Sheriff." She meant it, but she fussed with the torn sleeves on her dress.

Pike came around to the front of the desk and crossed his arms. "Those men killed Big Lil and Mattie Morgan because the women refused to cooperate."

"Your conclusion is entirely incorrect."

Pike huffed. "The man with the knife used his left hand. Our killer is left-handed. That's what you said."

"True, but the knife he put in my face had a single-edged blade. The knife used on Lily Rawlins and Mattie Morgan was thin and double-edged. I must also point out that the man's blade was wider and longer and wouldn't have matched the wounds on the victims.

Just check the postmortem report. Besides, it's illogical for men who want to make money from prostitutes to kill their inventory, so to speak."

Pike leaned against his desk. His eyes didn't leave her face, and his stare seemed strong enough to hold her to the spot. "Why'd you really come to Placer? And don't give me the I-am-a-writer horse bunk. I know people, and I know you're lying every time you open your pretty mouth."

"My reasons are personal."

"When it comes to murder, nothing is personal."

Felicity began to tremble and put her arms around herself. Lying to Pike was tiring, and the attack *had* frightened her.

"You're shaking," he said with care, as if a bit of his anger had subsided.

"They tore my favorite dress." She did lie again.

With great tenderness, he rubbed her arms. Putting her head against his chest, Felicity was tempted to close her eyes and sleep. He smelled of horses and tobacco. His rough fingers touched her skin where her dress had torn, and the trembling lessened. Astonishing.

"You've been through a lot today. Never saw a woman so brave."

What was it she heard in his voice now? Was that admiration? She began to perspire from its tenderness. She needed to get the blazes out of that office and fast.

"Better?" he said.

"So stupid of me to quake like a scared child."

"Yes, but understandable." He sat her back in the chair. "Now, why did you travel thousands of miles to this godforsaken town?"

"Sheriff Tom Pike, you are formidable."

"You can trust me, Felicity." He took her hands.

Her bones weighed as much as the mountains around Placer. For the sake of her investigation, she had to trust him. If she told him the truth, he might extend her more cooperation. Either that or send her packing. Yet she had to take the chance. Arguing with him was exhausting, and she'd rather place her energies in the investigation.

She sat up. "You're correct. I'm no writer. I didn't come here to research a book."

He grinned with apparent satisfaction.

"But I'm also very fatigued." Rising out of the chair, she straightened her dress.

"Where you going?"

"It's late. I'll tell you all tomorrow when we've both had some rest." She always resisted using her gender to get her way and hoped this western sheriff would give her the night. She did need sleep and hadn't had a restful one for several nights.

"All right, then. Tomorrow."

Felicity opened the door. "I will say one thing tonight. One reason I came here was to help a friend."

"Must be a good one to come all this way."

Her throat constricted with the startling reminder of him. His illness. His friendship. "He is. His name is Scotland Yard inspector Jackson Griggs Davies."

★   ★   ★

Although it was nearly midnight, lights welcomed Felicity back to the house on Bullion Boulevard. Pike rode his horse as she drove the wagon. He didn't say anything, and for the first time in their acquaintance, neither did she.

They drove down Main Avenue, which was lit by electric lights. Echoes of an Irish tune arose from a bar on the corner. Riders on horses, people in carriages, and those walking out of nearby restaurants and the theater flowed along the street. It was an easy and optimistic atmosphere. Felicity watched Pike, now stoic as the limestone walls of the courthouse. His eyes still sought out his father's killer among every face he passed.

"Go inside now. It's cold," he said when they reached her house.

Gathering her crossbow and quiver of bolts, she watched him ride away.

Inside, Helen slept in a chair in the sitting room. Tremendous humiliation seized Felicity as she watched the older woman. She had caused a fitful night for her friend.

The older woman stirred and woke. "Thank God you're here, Miss Felicity. Even though the sheriff's deputy told me you were safe, I couldn't sleep. I wanted to make sure you made it home, even with that awful weapon in your hand." Helen drew her robe around herself.

Felicity placed the crossbow on a hallway table. "I apologize for worrying you so, Hellie. Sometimes I'm very careless and forget that you do worry about what happens to me. You're the only one who ever has all these years."

"Nonsense. Everyone at Carrol Manor cares for you."

Felicity smiled and pressed her lips to Helen's cheek. "Hellie, this has been a rather eventful night. Actually, make that quite extraordinary. But I'm famished. What do we have to eat?"

"I have bread, cheese, and a bit of lamb from dinner."

"That sounds absolutely superb."

"I'll bring it to you in the dining room."

"Nonsense, I'll come into the kitchen."

Helen stared at her as she sat at the table. "You do seem different, Miss."

"Do I?" Felicity had forgotten to pin up her hair, which lay in waves about her shoulders. She smothered a fat piece of bread with butter. Never had anything tasted so delightful. Despite desperate weariness, her senses vibrated and her mind zipped from possibility to possibility. The realization of almost being stabbed by the two unpleasant men in the alley. The decision to share the truth about the trip to Montana. Her exhilaration at surviving the night caused everything to feel vivid and stimulating. The taste of the coffee. The smell of the lamb on the plate Helen served her. The air itself. Felicity's fingertips pulsated as she ran them over the wooden table. Then there was the upsetting response to Pike's touch. And her thoughts about Jackson Davies back home.

Steady girl. Sip your tea, she admonished herself.

Helen gave her another slice of bread. "You always did have a good appetite, especially when you're so involved in your investigations."

"A bit disquieting, I know." Felicity wasn't going to tell Helen about what had happened in the Red District alley. She had already caused too much worry that day and would save the story until the morning.

Under the modern electric lights, Felicity was comfortable in the house on Bullion Boulevard. When she was younger, Carrol Manor had seemed as inflexible as the stone from which it had been constructed. She had considered herself an interloper there because the manor belonged more to her father and grandfather. The place reflected little of herself, except for her first laboratory, the one she had accidentally set on fire. With simple cabinets and gingham curtains, this small kitchen so far from England was infinitely more congenial.

"Hellie, you must be tired as well. Please pour yourself a cup of tea and sit with me."

"Anything wrong, Miss?" She did take a seat and cup.

"This reminds me of how you used to tuck me in at night. The circumstances are different, but the feeling is not." She placed a hand over Helen's. Her friend gave the smile Felicity loved. One of gentleness and complete acceptance.

"Yes, it does feel like that."

They drank tea in silence until they both were yawning.

"It is frightfully late. We both should get to bed." Felicity stood up.

Helen wrung her hands together. "Miss, do you really think we should have come here?"

Felicity placed her hand on Helen's shoulder. "More than ever, my dear."

CHAPTER 16

Judging by his face, Sheriff Tom Pike might have been staring perdition squarely in the eye. "Lord Almighty. What is this?"

"Murder," Felicity replied.

In her crime laboratory, Felicity stood by the exhibit like a teacher of death. Using string, she had divided one wall into five separate spaces. In each space, she had pinned newspaper clippings about the five Whitechapel murders as well as copies of the police photographs of the bodies. Under the information about the earliest victim in London, Mary Ann Nichols, Felicity had posted the newspaper clippings about Lily Rawlins's murder and photographs of the alley where her body had been discovered in Placer. Next to that were clippings and photographs of the second Whitechapel victim, Annie Chapman. Underneath were the grisly photographs of the deceased Mattie Morgan, along with the drawing Felicity had sketched indicating the placement of wounds.

In the three remaining spaces were the *Times* clippings about the other Whitechapel murders, along with coroner photographs of victims Elizabeth Stride and Catherine Eddowes and the gruesome photograph of the remains of Mary Jane Kelly at Thirteen Miller's Court. Beneath sat a long shelf holding five neat stacks of papers.

On another wall was a map of Whitechapel with hat pins where the bodies had been discovered. Red ink dots on a map of Placer illustrated the sites of the murders of Lily Rawlins and Mattie Morgan.

"Over the course of four months last year, five prostitutes were savagely murdered in or near an area of the East End of London called Whitechapel," Felicity said. "The whole of Scotland Yard focused on the crimes. Hundreds of people and suspects were interviewed, but the killer was never apprehended. He vanished like a London fog."

"My God." His eyes didn't leave the photographs on the wall.

"Sheriff."

He faced her.

"You should know there's another name for the Whitechapel killer."

"What?"

"Jack the Ripper."

He said nothing, which made her nervous.

"You have heard of Jack the Ripper?"

Pike crossed, then uncrossed his arms. "Placer may be remote, but we're not the end of the damn world."

"Good, then you are familiar."

"You're talking about *the* Jack the Ripper?"

"The same."

"What does this have to do with my town?" His hand shot out toward the photographs of the London victims.

She took a breath before answering. "I believe Jack the Ripper has come to Placer."

His eyes again went to the wall.

"I've uncovered solid correlations between the slaying of Mattie Morgan, Lily Rawlins, and the five victims in Whitechapel, England." She had said out loud what she suspected and feared.

Pike shook his head so hard, strands of his longish dark hair fell into his eyes. He shoved them back behind his ears. "It can't be."

"I assure you it can."

"Why are you so dang sure it might be him?"

"Because of the manner in which the crimes were committed both in London and in Placer. For each of the Whitechapel murders, I have copies of reports from the Scotland Yard investigations, postmortems, and inquests." Felicity held up one stack of papers. "I also have photographs of the letters written by Jack the Ripper."

"How in God's name did you get all this?"

"Through a solicitor in London. The payment of pounds provides all manner of opportunities."

"You rich or something?"

"Very something." She unpinned a small photograph from the wall and held it out to Pike, turning her head away. "This is what Jack the Ripper did to Mary Jane Kelly, his last victim."

Pike's eyebrows furrowed. "I've never seen anything like it."

"His barbarism increased with each killing, but Mary Jane was his sick masterpiece."

He placed the photograph facedown on the counter. "Hold on. Hold on, Miss Carrol. I've got suspects in my jail. The Midline Gang. They used a knife to threaten you and the other woman. That makes them very good suspects," Pike said with an antagonism Felicity knew wasn't directed at her.

"They had no motive for killing the two women." Her voice was calm.

"The gang made examples of the women who didn't want to be a part of their plan."

She began to speak, but he held up his hand to stop her. "Sure, they carried the wrong type of knife, as you claim," he continued. "That's not to say they didn't have more than one blade."

"What of the mutilations?" Felicity pointed to a photograph of Mattie Morgan's body behind the blacksmith shop.

"They're animals. I'll get a confession or enough evidence to hang them."

"Prostitutes murdered in the same fashion thousands of miles apart? Mathematically, the odds are staggering."

"If you're correct—and your assumption's as large as the Rockies—then why the hell did Jack the Ripper come to Placer?" His voice became gruff as the roads leading to town.

"Because this place has one of the largest red-light districts west of the Mississippi. I even heard that while on the train from New York." She held out a stack of papers to him. "Here are the reports on Jack the Ripper's first victim and Dr. Lennox's report on Lily Rawlins. You'll find the type of wounds are almost identical. There are also striking similarities in the wounds between the Ripper's second victim, Annie Chapman, and Mattie Morgan. In each case, the murderer demonstrated he is thorough, an expert in human anatomy and removing the organs, and he is absolutely barking mad."

She held out one photograph. "Jack the Ripper laid out coins in a semicircle at the feet of Annie Chapman. He did the same with coins with Lily Rawlins. He also left a ring at the feet of Mary Ann Nichols and Mattie Morgan. All part of his ritual. Just read the reports."

"Wait a minute. What ring?"

"The one I picked up." Felicity retrieved the ring from her packet of clues. "The only fingerprints on it belonged to Mattie." She anticipated his irritation. He didn't disappoint.

He held out his hand for the ring and closed it tight in his fist. "You should have told me. You can't hide evidence."

"I'm sorry. I got carried away."

"You mentioned a Scotland Yard inspector as the reason you came here," Pike said.

"Inspector Jackson Davies put his soul into solving this case. And when he couldn't discover the identity of the Whitechapel killer, he became seriously ill. He gave me a *New York Times* article about the killing of Lily Rawlins and how it resembled the work of Jack the Ripper. Inspector Davies is convinced her death and the London murders are connected."

"That doesn't explain why you're here."

"I promised him I'd make the trip to Placer and find the murderer. But I came not only because of a promise to my friend. This killer must be stopped." The truth of it broke in her voice.

"So you're hoping if you track down Jack the Ripper that your inspector will be healed?"

"I believe he will. But as important, a murderer will be captured and tried for his crimes."

Pike stood in front of the exhibit on the wall. "You're obviously rich and a society girl; why the heck didn't your inspector send the Pinkertons or other professional detectives to chase this killer? Why you?"

"I have indeed inherited a fortune and have been privileged to gain a good education in science, medicine, and other disciplines. In the past year I've been using those resources to help solve murders that have gone unsolved. I work with Scotland Yard on such cases and can provide references from the Metropolitan Police. Would you like for me to send for them?"

He waved his hand and went back to studying all the work she had put on the wall. "For once I think you're telling me the truth."

"Sheriff. Tom. We want the same thing. Justice. We can work together to find this madman. He butchered women in England. He did the same to Mattie Morgan and Lily Rawlins in Placer. Unless he's caught, he'll continue killing. This is his nature. And when he is done here, he'll move on to other towns."

"I'm going to have to ponder what you told me."

"That's all I ask. Well, that and to please keep my real reason for coming to Placer a secret."

He gave a nod of agreement. "Can I ask you a question?"

"Of course."

"You ever play with dolls when you were a little girl?"

"Yes, but I took them apart."

He laughed. "That figures."

After Pike departed, Felicity returned to her laboratory. Sitting at the counter, she reread reports from Scotland Yard about Mary Jane Kelly's death in Thirteen Miller's Court, although the facts were embedded in her remarkable memory. While the other killings were shocking, the killer had saved his worst for last. It was as if the Ripper had wanted to leave London something to remember him by before he left. The case also stood out to her because of its inconsistencies—more than with his other killings.

No one had been seen entering or leaving Mary Jane's room at Miller's Court. No sounds woke neighbors, although police estimated the killer must have spent two hours at his grisly work. At the inquest, a female neighbor testified she had seen Mary Jane the next morning, hours after Mary Jane was killed. The woman recognized her dress and bonnet. Was it merely the ramblings of a hysterical neighbor or clues not yet explained? Why had the Ripper stopped after five killings? Why had he treated Mary Jane's body with more cruelty than the others?

Simply, why?

★ ★ ★

Felicity cursed the squeak in the hallway floorboards.

"Where you off to, Miss?" Helen came out of the kitchen, hands on hips and resolve on her usually friendly face. Robert Lowery followed, holding a mug of morning coffee.

Felicity didn't want to tell Helen her destination to spare her friend another day of concern. "I'm going to find a doctor to examine me after my encounter with the ruffians from last night." To help with her story, she pointed out the purplish bruises on her upper arms from where the smelly man had held them behind her back. She considered the marks her welcoming memento of life in the West. "Know of a good doctor, Robert?"

"Well, there's Doc Lennox."

"A disagreeable man."

"Yeah, he is. There's also Doc Phillips. His office is on Main. A good sort. Want me to drive you, Miss?"

"I can find my way. You two have a good time." She winked at Helen, who blushed.

"Be careful," Helen said.

Felicity smiled. "Always, Hellie."

While Sheriff Tom Pike deliberated on the information she had given him—she hoped, anyway—Felicity would continue her investigation. She set out for the Red District again, this time to interview Mrs. Albert, the brothel madam she had met at Reverend Phoenix's church. Mrs. Albert had obviously known Mattie Morgan well enough to attend her funeral and therefore could have important information about the victim.

Before that, Felicity wanted to check with Pike to make sure he realized the men he held in jail had nothing to do with the murders.

At his office, Pike sat at his desk, his face the color of the gray walls behind him.

"You okay?" she asked.

"My stomach is coiled as an old bedspring from what you told me and what's in those postmortem reports. I close my eyes and see those murdered women. But darn if your train might not be on the right track."

"Does that mean you believe me?" A small smile involuntarily came to her lips.

"Maybe," he said. "The wounds and mutilations on the victims in England and Placer were pert near the same. The deceased were all prostitutes. The blade used thin, long, and smooth. The evidence left behind, nonexistent."

On his desk lay a knife.

"Isn't that the one taken from the Midline Gang?" Felicity picked it up.

"A Springfield Armory hunting knife, a standard issue to soldiers. A single-edged blade two inches wide and . . ."

"One that couldn't have made the smaller cuts on the bodies of Mattie Morgan and Lily Rawlins," Felicity finished.

Pike tasted brew in a cup, scrunched up his face, and threw the liquid out his open window. "My coffee went cold." He stood up. "I'm going to talk to those men to see what they know."

"I'm going with you. They almost killed me. You owe me that."

"No good arguing with you, I can tell."

"No good at all."

"The man who attacked you calls himself Hank Ransom. The other is Ben Jenkins," Pike said as they walked. "And please, don't interrupt. I have my ways of interrogating a suspect."

"I look forward to observing your methods."

The two prisoners were eating breakfast. Pike stepped into their cell but motioned for her to wait outside.

"Nice grub you serve here," said Ransom, whose chest appeared even broader in the day. He sopped up gravy with a biscuit on the tin plate and brushed crumbs from his mustache. "And such nice company." He tossed Felicity a lusty wink.

Jenkins sat on the other bunk. Slimmer with a doltish way, the man ate with care as if trying not to spill.

"Your partner hasn't said anything since we locked you up." Pike had his back to the cell's metal door.

"Ben is a man of few words." Ransom continued chewing.

"I can see that. Well, you both better say something; otherwise I'm charging you with the murders of Lily Rawlins and Mattie Morgan, two girls of the line."

"We didn't finish off no soiled doves, nowhere, no how. Me and Jenksy were thinking about opening up our own joy house in town. That's why we were talking with them girls. We politely asked them to join our business."

"Yeah," Jenkins said.

"You threatened two women with a knife," the sheriff said.

"That young British gal shot at me with some contraption. Don't that count for anything?" Ransom pointed at Felicity with his fork. She nodded at him in return.

"You held a knife to her face. Now tell me everything you can about these dead women," Pike said.

"A dead whore is a pure waste, that's all I can say." Ransom burped.

"You murder them?" the sheriff asked.

Ransom sneered. The eggs he had eaten plastered his teeth. "I love women. I'm a businessman and not a killer."

"If you want to save your hides, tell me the truth. Where were you Thursday between eleven at night and three in the morning?"

Ransom scratched his head. "Let me recall. Oh yeah, me and Jenksy played poker at the Longbow Gambling House over on Slag Street. Right, Ben?"

"Yeah," the man muttered.

"For how long?" Pike said.

"Till 'bout two thirty in the morning; then we walked back to our boarding house on Vein Boulevard."

"We lost a lot of money," Jenkins volunteered.

"Who'd you play poker with?"

"Don't recollect, Sheriff. But the owner served us drinks all night. He'll vouch for us. We tipped him pretty good. Right, Jenksy boy?"

"Right," his accomplice grunted.

"You still had time to kill Mattie Morgan. Her body wasn't discovered until five in the morning. Anyone see you at the boarding house when you returned for the night?"

Taking a cigarette from his pocket, Ransom lit up. "Sheriff, sorry to say, no one."

Finally, Jenkins lifted his head. "The manager of the boarding house was cleaning the floors. We went to our rooms and slept. She'll tell you we didn't kill none of them hussies."

"If you didn't, then who did?" Pike said.

Ransom and Jenkins cocked their heads at each other. Jenkins shrugged and scratched his slim belly.

"My partner and I thought up some ideas, what you might call conjectures," Ransom said. "Those girls of the line were done in by a doctor or butcher who went plumb crazy."

Jenkins nodded his head in agreement.

"Why do you say that?" Felicity asked, and Pike tossed her a harsh stare.

Ransom chewed his food slowly. "I'll tell you, Miss. Whoever sliced up those women knew what lay inside a body. All me and Ben can tell you is where to insert our man parts."

Jenkins lifted his head to snicker along with Ransom and then continued eating. Felicity noticed that Pike delivered the men a powerful stare for using such language in her presence. How quaint. She had seen the bodies of murder victims, so not much else would disturb her, least of all foul language from this pair.

"Seriously, Sheriff, the jackass cutting up those chippies is reducing our profits and scaring off potential business partners. If I knew the identity of the bastard, I'd cut *his* throat," Ransom said.

"Then you admit to being members of the Midline Gang."

"The what gang?"

"Now you're being funny," Pike said.

"Hey, what about our case? When do we get out of here?" Ransom asked.

"The judge hears the evidence next week. You might get one year in prison if you're lucky and the judge is in a good mood. But then you're going to Helena. Word got out you're my guests, and Helena law wants you for malfeasance in that town. If your stories don't check out, it's the noose for killing the women in Placer."

Ransom grinned. "They will. Can I have seconds?"

Without asking this time, Felicity followed Pike in her wagon to the gambling palace, where the barman confirmed Ransom's story about what time the men had left. At their boarding house, the hefty manager said Ransom and Jenkins had returned at three thirty in the morning, drunk and making so much noise she had told them to hush.

"See any blood on their clothing?" Felicity asked before Pike got out the question.

"No blood."

"Sure they didn't leave after you saw them?" The sheriff wedged in the query before Felicity could open her mouth.

The manager yawned and shook her head. "I worked until six and didn't see them go out again."

Pike mumbled a curse and asked to see their room.

Not waiting for him to ask, Felicity helped search, looking first in the small chest of drawers.

On the bed, Pike placed a rifle and three more handguns as well as ammunition he had found under their mattress.

"No long thin knife." But then, she hadn't believed they would find one.

She and Pike also timed the ride from the gambling house to the blacksmith shop and to the boarding house two miles away.

"No way the men could have killed Mattie Morgan, mutilated her, cleaned up afterwards in the trough, and gotten back to their boarding house in time to be seen by the boarding house manager," he said to Felicity.

"I know," she said. "I just wanted to hear you say it."

They returned to the courthouse. She noticed that the sheriff's face tightened, probably from the disappointment of finding no evidence to link the two men to the killings.

As they neared the courthouse, he exclaimed, "Damnation in a handbasket."

Felicity hoped the swearing wasn't for something she had done, but she wouldn't be surprised if it was. Jackson Davies had frequently let go of curses when she had proved her point about a case, though he was rather accomplished at murmuring them under his breath. No, the sheriff had cursed because he'd seen the mayor in front of the courthouse. Mayor Reiger was smiling, but it wasn't so much welcoming as it was scary, with peaked eyebrows and too many teeth.

"Miss Carrol."

"Mr. Mayor." She curtsied.

The town official directed his attention to Pike. "Word is you have two suspects locked up. I'm proud of you for solving these killings, Tom." He had to reach up to pat one of the sheriff's shoulders.

"Thanks, Mayor. Too bad they may not have committed those crimes."

"It's too early in the day for jokes," Mayor Reiger said, the scary smile gone.

"I have no evidence to use against them in court. Witnesses place them nowhere near the murders."

"That is most unfortunate." Reiger smacked the tip of his cane down on the sidewalk.

"There is a silver side. The men assaulted two women and are part of a gang trying to take over the prostitution trade in town. So I call that fortunate they're all locked up."

"Good lord. What about the man killing the girls of the line?"

"I have every deputy sniffing out clues and witnesses. But the murderer seems to live in the darkness."

"Since your investigation is proving ineffective, I will suggest to the city commission we offer a reward for information about this monstrous criminal. It might help where you have failed."

"It might."

Felicity didn't want to be there while the mayor insulted the sheriff. Pike was due that for letting her follow him as he interviewed witnesses. "I should be heading home, gentlemen."

Reiger ignored her. "Five hundred dollars should be a sufficient incentive."

"It should," Pike said.

The mayor stepped into the street and patted his chest, as if letting in more air. "Such an ideal day, Miss."

"Yes, it is," Felicity said.

The mayor glanced at his watch. "Placer is a good place to live, except, of course, for these women getting cut into little scraps."

CHAPTER 17

Unlike the dilapidated shacks and buildings along Viceroy Street, most of the brothels on Mineral Avenue were tall, red-brick buildings. They looked perfunctory as banks, except for the sound of popular tunes played on pianos without much skill. Behind one brothel, a thin black woman hung sheets on lines. At another, a naked young woman stood at a window brushing her brown curls. Her cheeks were rouged and her stare blank.

At the end of the avenue stood the White Rose. The three-floor wooden structure resembled a home in the English countryside, which amused Felicity. The Queen Anne–style house had been painted white with green shutters and gables. Trimmed hedges enclosed a lawn. White roses bordered a stone walkway and lined the sizable porch. Above the door a white rose was captured in stained glass. A grassy hill rose in back of the brothel.

A tiny Chinese woman wearing colorful silks and a fierce expression answered Felicity's knock.

"Miss Felicity Carrol to see Mrs. Albert, please."

With a crooked mouth, the woman closed the door and left Felicity standing on the porch. A younger Chinese woman swept, keeping her head toward her work. The older Chinese woman returned. "This way."

Felicity had anticipated decor as tawdry as what she had seen at Sue's Place. Instead she found good taste. The Chinese woman walked Felicity past what appeared to be the main parlor, which took up most of the first floor. Elegant wallpaper covered the walls. Almost demure paintings of landscapes hung on the walls, along with decorative mirrors that could have been found in any proper affluent home, be it in America or England. Over a shiny oak bar hung a huge canvas of a naked woman in repose, apparently a popular image in brothels, but this one was more classical than vulgar.

A bald man in a clean white shirt and green suspenders polished the top of the bar with fluid movements. A black man in a blood-red suit picked out a tune on a piano in one corner. Spittoons were polished as new silver. Dotted around the room were various sets of S-shaped tête-à-tête seats for the temporary lovers. Vines and hearts were sewn into the red velvet fabric. Tatted lace curtains decorated the windows. If the nuns who had created the lace found out where it had ended up, they would probably faint or recite additional rosaries, Felicity supposed.

She hadn't told Pike about her plan to visit the madam, nor about the times they had met at the cemetery and at the church run by Reverend Phoenix. Neither had Felicity mentioned her suspicions about the crazy clergyman. Although she was beginning to trust the sheriff, she didn't trust him enough to share her preliminary assumptions. She required more information before she could present any findings to him—if she found any, that is. From dealing with Scotland Yard and Inspector Jackson Davies, she had learned that law enforcement officers appreciated the kind of evidence they could understand and touch. Her deductions were sometimes too elusive for them.

She was fortunate that Sheriff Pike was off to interview barbers and butchers about the killings, probably so she wouldn't do that before he had the opportunity. At any rate, she didn't have the heart to tell him the enterprise would amount to a waste of time. The killer was far too intelligent to hold such a job. He was far too skilled with a knife and in knowledge of human anatomy. But Pike had to make that discovery for himself. Further, it would keep him busy elsewhere.

Barely tall enough to reach Felicity's chin, the Chinese woman led her to a small, stylish parlor with a fine Oriental rug on the floor. A settee of royal-blue brocade dominated the room. Chairs were painted with spring daisies and inlaid with mother-of-pearl. Porcelain lamps were set on round tables covered with embroidered white cloths.

"Missy Albert will be here soon. You no touch nothing," the servant said abruptly.

"You have my word." Felicity smiled with innocence.

"Better not." The woman left.

On the mantel were finely carved figurines of angels holding up a clock between them. Felicity examined them. The carvings were perfect.

She got a whiff of something. A hint of jasmine in the room.

"I've always loved that piece."

Felicity reeled at the voice. Mrs. Albert stood behind her. The woman had the lightest of steps. "It is exquisite."

"Part of the furnishings that came with the house. It was owned by a miner who gambled away his fortune."

"Well, he had good taste."

"Please sit. I've sent for tea," she said.

"Thank you for seeing me without an appointment, but you did say to drop in," Felicity said.

"You're most welcome anytime. It's pleasant to have civilized company in such an uncivilized place."

The Chinese servant brought in a fine silver pot and delicate cups. While she poured, Felicity observed her hostess. Mrs. Albert's posture was impeccable, her dress flattering, and her manner refined. She would have fit in at any of the parties of the wealthy that Felicity had attended at her father's insistence.

From her purse, Felicity withdrew a notebook and fountain pen in her guise as a writer. "What can you tell me about Mattie Morgan?"

"A very nice young woman who indulged too much in the drug of the East. Mattie wanted a job here, but I don't allow such behavior under my roof."

"You must have thought a lot about her to attend her funeral."

"Unlike other girls on the line, Mattie had an agreeable demeanor." The madam drank her tea with almost excessive grace. "She occasionally sewed dresses for me and the girls in this house. Despite her location on the line, she was very clean and smart."

"Were you also acquainted with Lily Rawlins, the other murder victim?"

Mrs. Albert gave a long, resonant laugh. "Heavens, no. She worked the lower part of Viceroy Street and was quite grotesque. I saw her once. Fat and vulgar, but she did wear very pretty shoes."

"There does appear to be a clear line between the girls of Viceroy Street and those on Mineral Avenue."

Mrs. Albert poured more tea. "More like a vast breach between the women who offer themselves for cheap and those who put higher value on their talents."

"Very observant, Mrs. Albert."

"So I've been told. For instance, you were born in privilege but don't flaunt your wealth."

"Why do you say that?"

"Just by looking at your dress, speech, and manner, only a fool would think you were common." Her southern drawl lilted with delight at her observations. "You're also a brave young woman to visit this house, given your social standing."

"Social standing means less and less, especially in this country."

"That's easy to say for a woman who enjoys such standing in the first place."

Mrs. Albert had gotten the best of her on that point. Felicity raised her cup in salute and then took up her pen and paper again. "Have any of the women who work here ever reported a man who displayed, shall we say, strange and violent behavior? Specifically, a man carrying a long thin knife?"

"I don't stand for any violence in my house."

"Then your answer is no?"

The older woman dipped her chin with appreciation. "I applaud your straightforwardness. Women are too often dim or taught to hide their cleverness."

"I've been accused of taking frankness to an extreme."

"I'll wager a man made that accusation."

"Why, yes, as a matter of fact, and the answer to my question?"

"The girls have never mentioned such a man, yet the fellows who do visit are lustful, and that is a type of brutality. Is that sufficient?" Mrs. Albert stirred a spoonful of sugar into her tea. "Most of our male visitors come from the upper end of Placer society. Lawyers, judges, businessmen. We do see miners and cowboys, but only those who have more money to spend on their pleasures."

Felicity glanced around. "Your establishment does exude refinement."

Mrs. Albert lowered her head. "Why a long thin knife?"

"Pardon?" The question threw Felicity.

"You mentioned a man who might carry a long thin knife."

"According to postmortem reports, it was the type of weapon used on Mattie Morgan and Lily Rawlins."

Before Felicity could continue, a young woman draped in a sheer white robe tramped into the room. Under the robe, the woman wore white bloomers and nothing more.

"Mrs. Albert, you just *got* to talk with Belinda. She's stealing my corsets again. You should throw that no-good whore into the street. She steals from all the girls." Her colored-red mouth warped with irritation.

Mrs. Albert set down her teacup. She stood tall over the young woman and took hold of her forearm. "Can't you see I'm occupied with a lady? I'll talk with Belinda later. Now apologize to our guest for your inexcusable rudeness." Her voice went even deeper. "Mean it."

The young prostitute cringed. Felicity noticed one new welt in the middle of the woman's back. Another ridge appeared on the young woman's upper arm. From the injuries and the girl's cowering, Felicity thought Nellie might have been right about Mrs. Albert's whippings. What disturbing and contradictory conduct for a woman who presented herself as refined.

Mrs. Albert let go of the young woman's arm. A red handprint remained.

"Sorry, ma'am," the young woman said to Felicity. She then curtsied and ran out of the room.

"They're like children. I have to watch them every minute. They tend to be lazy and untrustworthy. Most are uneducated and uncouth, but I try to teach them manners and how to act like ladies. It's good for business. I can charge more that way."

Mrs. Albert's tone implied contempt for the women who worked for her, but she smiled graciously as she disrespected them.

"I'll take your word for that," Felicity said.

Mrs. Albert smiled politely. "So you're writing about a killer?"

"One who hunts and mutilates prostitutes. Given your business, what do you think would motivate a man to commit those crimes? I mean, for my book."

Mrs. Albert sipped her tea and placed down the cup after a moment. "I believe he might have been hurt by them."

"What do you mean?"

"Perhaps his mother was a soiled dove. When his life proved disappointing, he blamed her and all in that occupation for his failures."

"A fascinating theory. Perfect for the profile of a mad killer." Felicity spoke the truth to the woman. A good hypothesis she hadn't thought of.

"How exciting to help a writer with her book." Mrs. Albert giggled like a young girl asked to dance at her first ball.

"Speaking of profiles, Mrs. Albert, you don't fit one of a woman in charge of this establishment."

"How kind of you to say."

"You appear educated, with all the attributes of a lady. Pardon me for being so personal."

"I'm the daughter of a butcher and a serving girl in Atlanta, Georgia. I labored in the tobacco fields and married for love, but my dear, dear beloved husband died and left me little money. I traveled out west for a fresh start. Along the way, I studied diction and learned to read and write. I worked diligently to act like a lady, because more doors open for them. Surely you must understand that."

"How'd you end up in Placer?"

"Mining towns boom with commerce, so they made a perfect place to seek my fortune. Operating a service to gentlemen provided an opportunity to make money, and business has proved highly lucrative. Although I'm sure my late beloved husband would be shocked."

"You must have loved him very much."

With one hand, Mrs. Albert raised a delicate handkerchief to her eyes. "He meant the world to me and gave me so much."

Felicity tilted her head. Mrs. Albert exhibited no grief or tears for her long-lost love. No regret or bravery for having to carry on without him. Her expression settled into one of pure fulfillment. Perhaps Mrs. Albert had blamed *him* for how her life had turned out. She said he had died and left her destitute.

The woman leaned toward Felicity. "You are quite exquisite, my dear."

Felicity's cheeks flushed from the piercing scrutiny.

"I suppose you hear that often. I don't have to tell you how much of a burden beauty can be," Mrs. Albert said.

No other woman had ever mentioned this to her. Mrs. Albert seemed to have what the Hindus described as a third eye to see beyond what lay immediately in front of her. Yet Felicity wanted to keep the focus off her life. "You do make an excellent cup of tea. The best I have had in town. Although Dr. Lennox serves a close second. Ever met him?"

"An odd man with private ways."

"Such as?"

Mrs. Albert sipped tea and set down the cup. "I'm sure you have already heard the rumors about him."

Felicity shook her head.

"The doctor has a reputation for not liking the company of women, including his own patients, but he spends a lot of time with the girls on Viceroy Street. And the fouler, the better, for him. When he visits, he always carries his black bag. One can only imagine what goes on behind those doors."

"Were Lily Rawlins and Mattie Morgan among the women he visited?"

"I couldn't say, but then, it is only a rumor."

"What's your impression of Reverend Phoenix?"

"Another strange man. His sermons sound more savage than saving."

"Yes, they do."

"One evening I dropped by his church with a donation and found him wiping blood from his hands." She fluttered her eyes as if flirting.

"When did this take place?" Felicity attempted to submerge her piqued interest.

"Sometime earlier this spring. He told me he had just butchered a pig for his stew. Still, he appeared nervous, like I had caught him doing something not written in his Bible." Mrs. Albert changed the subject. "And I'm very happy you like the tea. A British brand, which makes it the best."

Felicity rose. "I've taken up enough of your time."

Mrs. Albert walked her to the door. "Come and see me again, that is, unless you're worried about scandal."

"Scandal is the least of my concerns."

"Good. There's so much else to dread in the world."

On her way home, Felicity thought over the madam's contradictions. Mrs. Albert had exhibited ladylike graciousness, yet the girl who interrupted them had exhibited fear of the woman, as well as bruises. The madam had attended the funeral of Mattie Morgan, but in the photograph Felicity had taken, Mrs. Albert wore a demure smile while passing the place where Mattie had been most brutally slain. She spoke with openness but clearly hid more than she said.

Sheriff Tom Pike boasted that he could read people. But Felicity believed even he might have trouble with an accurate appraisal of Mrs. Albert.

CHAPTER 18

At five thirty that morning, Robert Lowery alerted Felicity to the news of another killing in the Red District. As she dressed, she kept thinking, *Not again, not again.* Not another life.

But a new thought pushed into her head.

Victim number three.

By the time Felicity arrived at King General Mercantile, throngs of people had gathered around, chattering about the possible identify of the deceased.

"Jess, get those people back over there. Marty, do the same on the other end of the street," Pike called to his deputies. "Don't want nobody closer than three hundred feet of this place."

Stretching out their arms, the deputies pushed back the people who had arrived for a glimpse of the body. Felicity put her head down with a smile. Pike had adopted one of her suggested investigative techniques, namely, maintaining the integrity of the crime scene.

The sheriff spotted her and walked over. "She can come closer," he told a deputy.

Holding her satchel, she followed Pike. "Sheriff, why are you being so cooperative this morning?"

"I sent a telegram to Scotland Yard asking about you."

"And?" She smiled inwardly, knowing this would vindicate her actions in Placer.

"An inspector down there communicated back, to my surprise. He replied that you could be annoying, arrogant, and overbearing, but you had helped them capture several murderers."

She held her head higher. "Is that all?"

"No. That I should at the very least listen to what you had to say."

While justice had been her reward in the other cases, the support of Scotland Yard amounted to the most pleasing bonus. But time for the business at hand.

"What happened here, Sheriff?" Although he had invited her to call him Tom, she thought it most appropriate to address him by his title in front of others. This was something she also did with Jackson Davies. Her friend back home hadn't said anything, but she suspected he appreciated the gesture.

"The killer worked her over worse than the others," Pike answered solemnly as they walked.

"Her identity?"

"Don't know, but from her outfit, she's a girl of the line, a prostitute." He stopped so quickly she bumped into him. "You may not want to see this, Miss Carrol." He probably didn't want to call her by her first name in front of his deputies either.

She held up her satchel. "After what I've told you, you must realize I can handle the sight of blood and mayhem."

"Doc Lennox is on a medical call outside of town, so he'll examine the body later at Quigley's. I left everything as we found it until you could make your inspection. The killer did leave something else behind this time besides a body."

"What?"

"You can't miss it."

Felicity lifted the blanket covering the body. The dead woman lay on her back, hands placed at her sides, her throat cut. The knife had also been whipped along both sides of the mouth, which gave the victim the ghastly appearance of laughing at her own funeral. With that and the odd placement of the woman's head, the killer seemed to be taunting them. The mutilation to the victim's face also reiterated the culprit's warped war on the prostitutes. His determination to disfigure them in extreme ways. To punish them even more.

The bottom half of the victim's cheap green velvet dress had been lifted up and saturated with blood, as had the dirt around the body. As with the other victims, a clean incision had been made in the girl's abdomen. The deceased's eyes were open as if calling to Felicity to find out who had done this.

Listen to her.

From the satchel, Felicity removed a magnifying glass and inspected the victim's clothing. No red hairs as had been on Mattie Morgan's clothing, but she spotted long curly black hairs that probably belonged to the victim. Clutched in the right hand, however, were several strands of shorter wavy red hair. The woman must have grabbed at the assailant trying to free herself, Felicity deduced as she took samples.

The victim's left hand held a beaded purse. Using her pen, Felicity inspected the contents and counted six gold pieces. She covered the body with the blanket.

Felicity lifted her head and focused on what had been painted on the wall about forty inches above the body.

$$痛苦$$

"You read Chinese?" Pike had crouched down to look at the symbols.

"I speak four other languages, but sadly that's not one of them. I have studied Chinese history, but unfortunately, I can't translate this."

She touched one of the black grainy letters and smelled her fingers. "This isn't chalk." After scraping a sample of the material into an envelope, she drew the Chinese symbols in her notebook. Then she fetched her camera from the wagon and took photographs of the body and the symbols left by the killer.

"This is quite extraordinary. After the murder of Catherine Eddowes in Whitechapel, police found a piece of her bloodstained clothing nearby. On a wall above it was written, 'The Jews are the men that will not be blamed for nothing,'" Felicity recited from memory.

"What does that mean?"

"Who can say for sure? But we know this murderer is cunning. In Whitechapel, I believe Jack the Ripper attempted to shift blame for his crimes to Jewish people. So this"—she pointed to the Chinese symbols—"may be another distraction."

"And in Placer, he tried to place his ugly deed at the feet of the Chinese. He's playing games with us."

"Perhaps." She looked up past the blood spatters. Above the body was a second-story window.

"That's the bedroom of the people who run the store. They slept through the murder," Pike said.

"May I speak with the person who found the body?"

He motioned for her to follow him inside the store.

In the back room, a thick-waisted woman with dark-brown hair and glasses sat on a chair, colorless as a napkin. Standing next to her was a thin, pallid man, also wearing glasses. She held his hand. The woman's teeth rattled and she trembled.

Pike kneeled down. "Mrs. King, this woman is a writer all the way from England. Can you please tell her what you told me?" His voice was calming.

Mrs. King's nod was almost imperceptible. She breathed in a copious amount of air. "I rise each morning at four thirty to enjoy a cup of coffee. Such a tranquil time before my husband and son wake and business picks up from the men heading home or going to work at the smelters and mines."

Her eyes darted to the front of the store. "I started a fire in the stove and put on the coffeepot. As is my habit, I sweep off the long wooden porch while waiting for the coffee to brew. Passing wagons and horses usually kick up a thick layer of dust. You know that, Sheriff."

"I do," Pike said.

"Many times I have to shoo away drunkards who fall asleep on the benches in front of the store. This morning as I swept, I noticed a red footprint at the end of the porch nearest the alley. So I walk around the building. A woman lay on the ground near the store's brick wall. I think it's just another drunk and I tell her, 'Hey, you. Wake up and go home.'"

The largest of tears skimmed down Mrs. King's ample cheeks. Felicity touched her hand and handed her a handkerchief from her pocket.

"The woman didn't move, so I walked closer." Her mouth shuddered. "Blood spread outward from the woman's body as if she had sprouted red wings. I screamed and fainted away."

"The sheriff said you heard nothing the previous night," Felicity said.

"I wake at the sound of a mouse scurrying over the floor, but I didn't hear anything last night. That poor girl was killed right under our window." Her eyes fluttered and she swooned. Her husband caught her and fanned her face with a piece of white cloth.

"I have a few more questions," Felicity said, and was sure Pike was not approving.

The woman took in more air. "Go ahead."

"Did you or Mr. King know the victim? Had she come in the store?"

Mrs. King shook her head.

"I recognized her but didn't know her name," the husband said.

She asked about whether they had also seen a man in the black coat dressed as a gentleman. The shopkeepers hadn't.

Mrs. King cleaned her glasses on her apron. "Since our store is on the northern border of the shameful Red District, the prostitutes and other scoundrels frequenting the place do come in here to buy their necessities. They're good customers and don't ask for credit, but I don't dare admit that to the other members of the Methodist Ladies' League." She put the glasses back on.

"I suspect Mrs. King will have nightmares about this for a long time," Felicity said when she and Pike left the store. "Now I'd like a closer look at the bloody footprint on the porch."

Felicity took a measuring tape from her satchel. The print was a touch over ten inches in length. Thin sole. She looked at Pike's cowboy boots. The shoe had not been tapered. Not a boot. A dress shoe. She took a photograph.

"I'd like a copy of that," Pike requested. He then summoned one of his deputies. "We got to get rid of the Chinese symbols on the wall." He directed him to fetch water and a brush from the store.

"Why?" Felicity said.

"They'll cause grumbling among the townsfolk, and I don't need additional aggravation right now."

"Such as?"

Someone yelled behind them.

"A damn Chinaman did this," called a man with a deputy's badge. His undersized head mismatched the rest of his body, which boasted a massive chest and arms. His wide-set piggish eyes contracted. "We should have run the Chinese out of Placer years ago. These murders are some heathen rite."

"That kind," Pike told Felicity.

Others in the crowd hollered, "Damn Chinamen!"

"Heathens!"

"Run them out on a rail!"

Newspaperman Clark Andrews scribbled hard. Pike frowned.

"Damn. News of the Chinese symbols will be in the *Gazette* this afternoon," the sheriff said to Felicity. "We'll move the body to the funeral home as soon as the wagon gets here."

"Who's the instigator, Sheriff?" Felicity said.

"Marty Smith. Regrettably, he's one of my deputies." He motioned Smith over. "Marty, shut your mouth and quit stirring up the people. Hurry the wagon so we can get the body out of here." The other deputy arrived with water, and Pike had him clean away the symbols.

Smith spit. "You're destroying evidence a Chinaman killed that woman."

"I said get the wagon!"

Red-faced, the deputy hustled away.

"Killers!" some of the onlookers bellowed. "Foreigners!"

Pike strode over to the grumbling crowd. "Everybody go about your business. Give this dead woman some respect. Shoo now."

With loud complaints, the crowd began to break up. Felicity respected Pike's handling of the difficult situation. A wagon rolled up. Pike and an older deputy wrapped the body in a blanket. As they placed it in the back, a young boy with a face sparkling from perspiration sped up to them.

"Sheriff Pike, Sheriff Pike."

"Kind of busy here, Luke."

"Somebody left a package for you at the jail." The boy bent over to catch his breath.

"Be there soon as I finish here."

The boy wiped the sweat off with his shirt sleeve. "Caleb said you better come quick pronto. There's blood on the parcel."

"Frank, finish up here." Pike darted to his horse and sped off.

With all speed, Felicity gathered her equipment and drove her wagon to the courthouse. At Pike's office, she made her way around four deputies looking down at his desk. On it sat a shiny black wooden box atop a crumpled page from the *Gazette*. Smears of blood dotted the newspaper. On the box lay a human heart, which had been washed clean. Felicity took a closer view. The deputies did not move.

Pike held a note in his hand. "This was folded up inside the box."

"May I?" Felicity used tweezers to hold the paper.

I leave you the rest of her hart. It tasted of sin. I do enjoy your litle town. I want to stay as long as I can or at lest while the hunting is good. My ink is running dry. I need to plenish my supply. I am a forever poet of blood.

Dearest regard,
Your friend

In the light of the window, she peered at the note with her magnifying glass and placed the paper near her nose. "The killer wrote this in blood."

Everyone in the room stared at her.

Pike stood and glared at his deputies. "What the hell are you standing around for? Find this damn killer. Talk to every person in the Red District if you have to, look under every rock and in every doorway, but don't come back here without something. Caleb, you stay."

The deputies rumbled out except for an older deputy with a round gut over his belt.

"Caleb, who left this at the office?" Pike said.

The deputy shook his head. "Found it on the counter after I got back from the outhouse."

"Get back to work."

Felicity's attention remained on the box.

"That's not the worst." Pike moved the heart around.

She leaned in. A part of the organ had been torn away. "Teeth marks."

Pike sank back in his chair.

"Now do you believe, Tom?" Felicity said. They were alone in his office.

"Let's say you might not have to persuade me much longer."

"What a relief. Convincing you was like trying to cross the Atlantic in a paper boat."

"The what with a what?"

"Never mind. Look at this." With care, she spread out the newspaper. The torn-out front page carried the story about Mattie Morgan's killing.

"He does favor theatrics," Pike said, as if tasting something bitter.

"May I make a closer inspection of the note, the newspaper, and the other thing at my laboratory?" She pointed at the heart.

"What do you think you'll find?"

"Anything I can. But let's start with this."

Using her handkerchief, she picked up the box and pored over it with a magnifying glass. Gold-embossed dragons emblazoned the four sides. "This appears to be of Chinese manufacture. Dragons are a symbol of power and fortune in that culture." She turned it over. "The box reveals nothing about where the item was made or purchased. And the murderer left no fingerprints."

"I'd be stupefied if he had. This man *is* clever and careful. An awful combination for his line of work."

"We must obtain more information about the box and where it came from. Do you know where we can start?"

He stood up and put on his hat. "Little China."

CHAPTER 19

The smell of exotic spices, cooking chicken, lye soap, and opium wafted out of the doors. Driving her wagon, Felicity closed her eyes and breathed in the East. She opened them. Not China at all but an Americanized version. What Chinese people had brought with them and adapted to the West.

Restaurants, laundries, boardinghouses, stores, opium dens, theaters, and herbalists advertised their names in English along with the translation in Chinese. Multicolored paper lanterns hung outside many shops. The majority of the people she passed on the streets of Little China were indeed Chinese. A few wore western clothing—cowboy garb on the men and dresses on the women. But most of the men wore a black or blue tunic over white baggy pants and thick-soled black shoes, their black hair in a queue down their back. The women wore large gold earrings and dressed in silks.

Pike tipped his hat at the Chinese people, and they bowed back out of clear respect. "They came here to work on railroads, in mines, and on their own claims. As the big companies took over the mining in Placer and the small claims dried up, many sailed back home. Even before they left, they were robbed, beaten, and a few killed, according to the chatter around town. But the Chinese won't talk to me about how they're treated." Melancholy shaded his voice.

"I saw a Chinese section near Pauper Grounds, where they buried the murdered women," Felicity said.

"They're not allowed to bury their dead in Placer Cemetery. An anti-Chinese coalition once flourished in Placer, but these days only a handful get together to drink and bad-mouth the Orientals."

"How foolish to hate people because they're different." Different race, different class, different gender. Just different. Felicity disliked prejudice as much as ignorance, and they were basically the same thing. Prejudice was ignorance about those who were different and not appreciating the distinctions.

Pike stopped in front a large mercantile on Tailings Avenue. "This is Da Long's place. Da could be called the unofficial mayor of Little China." He smiled. "I'm sure he'd love the title."

A chime tinkled when they entered the store. A young Chinese man placed iron pots on shelves while another swept. They smiled and waved when Pike entered.

The mercantile offered the usual canned goods and vegetables, but the store also sold traditional Chinese clothing for women and men, ceramic teapots and cups, jade and brass figures of their gods, incense sticks, and small vials of what Felicity gathered were Chinese remedies.

Chinese customers browsed in the store along with those who weren't Chinese.

"Immigrants from the Irish to Swedes like it here as well. Da's prices are the best in town," Pike said.

"Ah, Sheriff, no see you in a long time. You want some of that balm for your sore leg?" Da Long sat behind the counter at the back of the store. He wore a neat black suit with his queue down his back. He was well-built and compact.

"The leg is fine, Da." He introduced Felicity to the Chinese man.

"My pleasure, sir." She bowed. She had read once that bowing equaled respect in that culture.

Da Long bowed back. "You have very good manners. Better than Americans. British, eh?"

"Yes. Ever been?"

He shook his head. "Interesting country with its empire. But I'm too old and worn out to visit." Long rubbed his shoulder.

Pike laughed. "Don't let Da Long fool you, Felicity. He's fathered nine sons and built up this business from nothing. He also owns a laundry and herbalist shop. As a young man he worked on the railroad and set dynamite to blow holes in the mountains. He's still tough as the track he laid for the steam engines."

Da Long's laugh was as high as Pike's was low, but it fell away quickly. "Enough of jokes, Sheriff. You two are here to ask about the writing where the lady was killed."

"How'd you know, Mr. Long?" Felicity said.

"Know everything when it comes to Chinese people. That's part of my business." He picked lint off his tidy suit.

On the counter, Felicity placed her drawing of the Chinese symbols written on the wall of the King store. "What do these mean?"

Da Long scrunched up his nose. "They mean pain."

"The killer wrote it on a wall over a woman's body," Felicity said.

Da Long lit a pipe and blew out smoke smelling of peppermint. "Someone wants you to think this bad thing was done by Chinese."

"My thoughts exactly," she said.

Pike looked from Felicity to Da Long, who both shook their heads in accord.

"Maybe this man ain't so crazy a coot as people say," Da Long said.

"He is smart, Da, but also very crazy." Pike lit a cigar. His gaze fell on the section of the store with shelves of teapots, colorful clothing, and other items from China. "What can you tell me about this?" He placed the dragon box on the counter.

Da Long rotated it in his hands. "Don't sell nothing like this, Sheriff."

"You sure?"

"Want me to take an oath or something?" Da Long's smile was impish. "I can tell you everything I sell."

"Know who might have sold this?" Felicity said.

Da Long shook his head so hard his queue whipped around his neck. "No one I know, and I know everybody in Little China."

"Can you tell us anything about this box or where in China it came from?" Felicity said.

Another headshake and another puff on the pipe.

"Must be for jewelry, I'm thinking." Long looked Felicity up and down. "You're one nosy woman."

"My most enduring trait," Felicity said.

Da Long gave another high laugh. "I like you, lady. You got jade in your spirit." He then turned to Pike and put on his trade face. "I'll take the box off your hands for a good price."

"It's crime evidence and not for sale."

"Too bad. I tell you this. Chinese man is not to blame," the shopkeeper said firmly, and handed back the box.

"How can you be so sure, Mr. Long?" Felicity said.

"If the wicked man were Chinese, his name would be running round Little China like a yapping dog. Even my little father who is ninety and half blind could tell you who he is." Long took a long drag of his pipe and wheezed out the smoke. "Sheriff Tom, lady,

Chinese people want to live in peace, and that means not murdering white women. We don't want trouble, but trouble sometimes comes looking for us."

One of the young men working in the store ran up to his father and rushed out his words in Chinese. Da Long answered and waved his hands upstairs. Felicity promised herself to learn the language as soon as she got back home.

"What's going on?" Pike said.

"Number-five son says there's angry men outside yelling bad things about Chinese," Da Long replied.

"You stay here, Da. You too, Felicity," Pike said.

"I'm afraid not," she answered.

The sheriff grunted and rushed outside, drawing his weapon as he did. A step behind, Felicity ran to her wagon to grab her crossbow. Nine men headed to Da Long's store and yelled, "Damn Chinamen! Leave our women alone! Godless murderers!"

A stout man with long black hair and harsh features marched to the front of the group. He held a wooden stick with a worn banner reading PLACER ANTI-CHINESE COALITION.

"Who's that?" Felicity asked Pike.

"Charles Montgomery. A man who's married to constant trouble."

Montgomery's severe eyes and reddened cheeks flaunted hate. His hands were rocks. "Our coalition predicted this. These foreign influences bring nothing but corruption to our community. They've taken advantage of this country but give nothing in return. They're not people but mongrels." As he spoke, he stamped the stick on the ground. "Somebody in Little China killed those women. I say we find him and hang him," he yelled to a roar of approval.

Felicity had never witnessed such hatefulness, which made the air turbulent and taste of metal shavings. The street had cleared of all the Chinese people, which was a wise move in the face of such irresponsible bile.

"Stop this now, Montgomery," Pike shouted.

Felicity noticed a young thin Chinese man walking toward Da Long's store on Tailings Avenue. She had to warn him away. Before she could, Pike's troublemaking deputy Marty Smith rode onto the street. He also spotted the young man.

"Look what I got!" the deputy bellowed.

Almost in perfect synchronization, the enraged men whirled around and started to run after the young man, who sprinted away in evident panic. Smith lassoed the young man with a rope and yanked him down the street to the store.

"Let go of that man right now," Pike shouted.

Smith towered over the young man, whose teeth chattered. The deputy picked up his prey and shook him. "Tell us who killed those women. Talk, dammit."

The young man uttered a stream of Chinese. With disgust, Smith slugged the young man in the stomach. He became a lump on the street.

Pike fired his weapon in a warning shot. From behind, three men held Pike's arms. "You're all going to jail for this," the sheriff said, struggling to get away.

"Hang that Oriental!" people yelled.

"You failed your job, Sheriff. Now it's our turn." Montgomery handed Smith a rope. The crowd's pitch changed as if a collective fervor held them.

Smith fashioned a noose and placed the rope over the young man's neck. The other end he swung over the rafters outside Da Long's store.

"We'll make an example of him. The other Chinamen will run out of Placer and never look back. Take the end of the rope," Smith ordered.

Several men fell in line and took up the rope. The Chinese man cried. Smith's arm dropped as a signal. "Pull!"

The rope tightened. The young man rose in the air and began to choke. People in the crowd hollered even louder.

A bolt sliced the rope, and the Chinese man dropped onto the store's wooden porch.

Everyone looked toward the shot's origins and quieted. Standing in the street, Felicity aimed her crossbow in their direction. "Step away from that man."

Da Long and five young Chinese men all came out of the store, holding rifles pointed at the crowd.

Pike pulled away from the men and picked up his gun, which had fallen in the dirt. "You heard the young lady."

Smith seized the Chinese man by the scruff of the neck and raised him high enough that his feet barely brushed the ground. "Tom, one of these heathens slaughtered those girls. Someone has to pay, and I say we start with him."

"Turn him loose." Pike's tone held menace.

Smith only lifted the Chinese man higher off the ground.

"Don't make me shoot you, Marty." Pike aimed the weapon at him. "I will if I have to."

Smith loosened his grip on the Chinese man, who slumped to the ground.

Making his way through the people, Montgomery took a stand in front of Pike. "Sheriff, a Chinaman left his calling card at the body. Why aren't you doing your job?"

"I am. But there's something called a court of law, and we have no evidence or witnesses to indicate a Chinese man killed those women. One thing I do know is that someone's trying their hardest to convince us of such a thing. And if you don't like how I'm doing my job, you can vote me out next election. Hell, I'd welcome it.

The job is too much damn work and I have to deal with asses like you."

"White men couldn't have murdered those women."

"Oh yes, they could. Think about this, all of you." Felicity addressed the crowd. "If a Chinese man committed this crime, why incriminate himself by writing Chinese symbols on the wall?" She had never spoken to a such a large group before, but fortitude beat down any nervousness.

"Who are you?" Montgomery said.

"A concerned citizen who doesn't want to see innocent men harmed."

"A Chinaman murdered those women for an evil Asian rite," Smith said.

"The killer left a bloody footprint near the store, and it didn't match the traditional shoes worn by a Chinese man," Felicity said. "In addition, I have studied Chinese history, and I can assure you there is no such ritual involving murder."

Everyone turned to Pike.

"She's right. The real killer wants to make everyone think a Chinese man was responsible." He held out his hands to the crowd. "We'll capture this murderer and do so in a proper and lawful way. We'll have a trial and not a late-night lynching. Now everyone go home. If I see this kind of behavior again, I'm running you all in for attempted murder."

"You and who else?" Montgomery placed his hand on his holster.

"Behind you." Pike pointed to several deputies standing in the street. They all had their weapons drawn.

"Git home, everybody," Pike commanded.

The men began to disperse. As he left, Montgomery threw Felicity a stare hateful enough to melt silver. She curtsied.

"Not you." Pike grabbed Marty Smith's shirt and tore the deputy badge off his chest. "Until tonight, you have served Placer well, so I'm not going to run you in for what you did to that boy. But I don't want to see your face in my town—ever—or I'll charge you with assault. One more thing, for the young man you terrorized." Pike punched Smith in the face. Smith crashed to the ground.

Picking himself up, Smith got on his horse and took off. Pike helped the young Chinese man to his feet. Da Long and his sons lowered their weapons.

Felicity held her breath at the actions of the sheriff. A lawman of the West for sure.

"Nice to see you, men," Pike told his deputies.

"We heard people were working up a fever down here and figured you might need a few more barrels," an older man answered.

"I did." The sheriff then ordered two of the deputies to ride around Little China in case more problems erupted.

"You did good, Sheriff Tom. You too, nosy lady," Da Long said.

The sheriff patted the man's back. "Thanks for your guns. The excitement is all over. Can you please help this young fellow? Tell him . . ." Pike bit lips searching for an explanation.

Felicity had an answer. "Tell him that fear makes people act like animals. But he can also thank the good people like you, the sheriff, and his deputies."

"And a lady with a bow and arrow," Pike said.

"Crossbow and bolt, really," she said.

Da Long spoke Chinese to the young man, who still trembled. "I also told him that some people are just sick in the head."

The young man's voice quivered as he responded.

"What'd he say?" Pike asked.

"He agree."

"I shall never forget you." Felicity held out her hand to Da Long, and the man took it. His skin was soft, but his grip strong.

"You okay too, lady."

Da Long looked at the fallen anti-Chinese banner on the ground. "See what I mean? Trouble comes looking for us."

CHAPTER 20

At the Quigley and Son Funeral Parlor, the body found behind the store had revealed little more than what Felicity already knew. Judging by the type and degree of the stab wounds on the body, the prostitute had been killed in the same manner as the two other victims in Placer. Same knife and mutilations. Unlike pretty Mattie Morgan, this victim's face portrayed heartbreak even in death.

At her house, Felicity worked with concentration and determination as if the outside world didn't exist. Acquiring knowledge had filled the emptiness in her life. Now she hoped the science and facts she had garnered would serve her when she needed them most.

Under a microscope, Felicity compared the red hairs obtained from Mattie Morgan's body with those she had collected from the hand of the newest victim. They appeared alike in color and length. What could be the meaning of red hairs on both victims?

She answered her own question. They had to be related. From that, she created an image of the killer. Dressed like a gentleman in a frock coat and black hat. Under that hat, wavy red hair.

As for the other grisly piece of evidence, she found that the victim's heart left at Pike's office had been extracted with neat cuts at the connecting veins. No surgeon could have removed it better. A perfect specimen, except for the teeth marks, which she measured, but there was nothing unusual about the bite formation. With tongs, she turned the heart over. Such a small thing to keep a person alive, she marveled. From her medical studies, Felicity had learned about the function of the vascular organ to move blood throughout the body. Yet the heart had come to symbolize more—the emotional center of a human, capable of love, empathy, and pity. Now, on the counter in her laboratory, sat one excised by a man with none of those qualities. Empathy least of all.

The note to Pike had been written on common parchment. She put it up to her nose. An undefinable smell, vaguely fruity. Almost sensual.

Smooth, oval blood marks dotted the edges of the newspaper. She experimented with how they had been made. Earlier, she had asked Robert Lowery to bring her a vial of blood from a butcher shop. She dipped two of her gloved fingers into the blood and touched a page from another newspaper. The result: the same mark. Meaning the killer had worn gloves when he wrapped the heart and box in the paper parcel that was delivered to the sheriff's office.

From an envelope, she withdrew a sample of the black grainy material that had been used to write the Chinese symbols on the wall of the store. Placing the specimen in a pan of water, she separated a tiny chunk of the grit and washed it. After viewing the piece under the microscope, she whistled at the discovery of calcium phosphate. The killer had written on the wall with ground bone mixed with ink. Human or animal bone, she could not tell.

Her excitement heightened at the next test for evidence the killer could not conceal—his handwriting.

The Whitechapel killer in London had sent three pieces of correspondence to the Central News Agency, which had written scandalous accounts of the murders in the East End. One note had been signed JACK THE RIPPER, a name that had become synonymous with terror over the course of those months and even beyond. The most nefarious letter came dated 15 October 1888 and was delivered to the president of the Whitechapel Vigilance Committee, whose volunteers had patrolled the streets during the killing spree. With the greeting FROM HELL, the note arrived with part of a human kidney thought by police to have come from Catherine Eddowes.

Felicity compared the handwriting in the note sent to Pike with that in the photograph of the Ripper's "From Hell" letter, as it had come to be called. She studied each word and how the letters were connected. Some people deemed graphology a modern science, but handwriting research dated back to 1622, when University of Bologna philosopher Camillo Baldi had published work on the subject. Baldi wrote about how a person's nature could be exposed in his handwriting. For example, if the handwriting was uneven with ascending lines, the person tended to be dominating. Even earlier, the great Aristotle had written that a person's handwriting expressed his sentiments, thoughts, and desires.

In the Jack the Ripper note and in the one sent to Pike, the letters *y*, *f*, and *g* had identical elongated tails. The words in each were written in the same forward slant, as if the writer's urges drove him headlong. The letters rose to spiky points, a sign of the writer's forcefulness. In the note to the sheriff, the killer had pressed his pen hard onto the parchment, as if he had stabbed at it with the kind of violence he used on his victims. Despite his attempts to disguise himself in the notes, his distorted personality had surfaced on paper and in blood.

Aristotle or not, however, courts of law didn't accept handwriting comparisons as evidence.

When she completed the examination, she stood and paced. The conclusion was irrefutable. The same hand had written the notes.

Jack the Ripper *had* come to America.

She sat down hard. The murderer had eluded all of Scotland Yard. How was she going to find him? She was also afraid—she'd readily admit that. To actually face a man so comfortable with slaughter was terrifying.

Exhausted, she went downstairs to read, hoping to submerge her uneasiness in a novel or biography for an hour or so. The former owner's library had a good selection of both, and she chose one, but all she could think about was Jackson Davies and his obsession with finding Jack the Ripper. Why he so diligently tracked the monster in human form. Her mouth watered with nausea. She felt what must have sickened her friend—his failure to stop the madman who seemed to live in the darkness and devour all hope.

★　★　★

A boy who could have been doused with all of Placer's dirt stood on Felicity's porch. He stomped anxious feet, leaving dust rings. She had been sitting in the library trying to read when he tapped at the window.

"It's after nine, little boy. You should be in bed," she said.

"My grandpa Jeremiah says you should come quick to the livery stable. He wants to talk with you. Something about the reverend."

"Let's go in my wagon," said Felicity, grabbing her crossbow on the way out. Thankfully, Helen had gone to bed early and didn't awaken easily.

When Felicity arrived, Jeremiah Sutton told his grandson to scat and led her to the livery stable for what he called a private chat.

"Did the Reverend Phoenix venture out the night of the latest murder?" she said.

Sutton licked his finger as he consulted the pages in the notebook she had given him. He found the right page. "Here it is. The night the girl was killed behind the King store, Phoenix came back to his church at ten. He didn't leave until six the next morning."

"Are you positive? He might have left on foot or if you dozed off."

"No, he stayed put and I didn't sleep."

"Oh." She had lost a suspect. Pike had estimated that the latest murder had taken place between one in the morning, when the Kings' son had returned home from drinking, and five in the morning, when Betsy King had found the body. Betsy's son had seen nothing behind the store when he stopped to relieve himself against the back wall.

"If that's all you have to share with me, Mr. Sutton." She prepared to pay him and leave.

The filthy boy ran into the stable. "Grandpa, Grandpa. The reverend carried another big burlap bag into his church."

"He did the same thing last night," Sutton told Felicity. "That's what I wanted to tell you."

"A bag?" Felicity felt foolish for hurrying to meet the old man.

"Something in the bag was moving and crying."

Now she wasn't so foolish. Mrs. Albert had seen the reverend's hands covered in blood. Blood stained the floor under the cross in his church. Maybe the reverend had sneaked out undetected on the night of the killing. "Mr. Sutton, we've got to see what he's up to," she said.

Sutton scooted his grandson out of the stable. "I know the place. We can sneak up to the old hayloft. We'll get a real good view." He snapped his suspenders.

"Excellent."

"How you gonna climb in that skirt?"

"I'll manage, Mr. Sutton. We must hurry."

Outside, music and voices resonated from the saloons up the street. The breeze had changed direction and brought another sound from the church. Someone bawled and yelled inside.

"Hear that?" Felicity whispered to Sutton.

"I ain't deef," he whispered back.

She followed as he crossed the road and began to climb short, thick wooden planks nailed into the back of Phoenix's building. Loud organ music started up inside—a hymn she couldn't name. Startled, she felt her foot slip halfway up, causing her chin to slam on one step, but she didn't cry out or slow her progress. As she rubbed her chin, she envisioned how her late father might react to this activity—shimmying up a building in the middle of the night to watch a supposed man of the cloth doing something involving blood. A storm rousing the English Channel would pale next to his outrage. Then again, he might just ignore her as he had most of her life.

Spry for his years, Sutton opened one side of the wide door in the loft and slithered inside. When she reached the loft, he had already lifted a trapdoor so they could see into the church below. The stink of mouse droppings was oppressive.

Lighted candles in front of the large cross gave them enough illumination to see. A burlap bag big as a person writhed below the cross as Phoenix played a hymn on the organ. When he ended the song, he opened the bag and clutched the throat of a calf that bellowed and skittered. He pulled a thick knife from his coat and uttered a bizarre, choppy language. Felicity didn't recognize the words.

"What's he saying?" Sutton whispered.

"Speaking tongues, I suspect. A common phenomenon of people in the throes of religious hysteria."

The reverend pointed the knife upward and killed the calf. His eyes rolled back in his head as he raised his bloody hands toward the cross.

Felicity and Sutton looked at each other.

The old man shook his head. "That man's nuttier than a nut cake," he whispered.

She nodded.

After a few minutes, Phoenix put the calf's body in the burlap bag, then began to scoop out the bloody floor dirt with a shovel and placed it in the bag also.

Felicity had seen enough, and they left as silently as they had entered.

"That explains the blood," she said when they returned to Sutton's livery stable.

"What, Miss?"

"Nothing. Mr. Sutton, you did a fine job of surveillance, but I'll no longer need your services." She handed him two twenty-dollar gold pieces. "A bonus."

"You mean Phoenix ain't guilty of that wrong you were talking about, young lady?"

"Yes, Mr. Sutton. And sacrificing animals, no matter how disgusting, is not against the law."

"Too bad."

The next morning Felicity returned to her laboratory, going over the facts again as if a new clue might appear. Helen rapped, brought in a tray with breakfast, and placed it on the counter where Felicity sat.

"Not sure how you can eat in here, Miss." She kept her eyes away from the crime photographs.

"It is difficult sometimes."

Helen placed her head down and made an X in the floor with her shoe.

Felicity placed down her fork. "All right, my dear, what is it?"

"After dinner Friday, may I take the rest of the night off? I'll clean up early the next morning."

"Whatever you want, Hellie." Embarrassment colored Felicity's cheeks. "And forgive me for neglecting your needs. I've been so preoccupied with this case."

"I've been taking my regular Sundays and Mondays off, Miss. Robert—I mean, Mr. Lowery—has been showing me the country."

"Hellie, you may have any night you wish, or day, for that matter."

Helen raised her head. "Sunday's fine; it's just that Mr. Lowery is taking me to something called a hoedown at a church."

"What is that?"

"A kind of dance, Miss Felicity."

"Ah, a social engagement."

Helen blushed. "Not at my age, Miss."

"At any age, Hellie. And I have noticed Mr. Lowery is very attentive to you. Smitten, really."

Helen's blush deepened.

"You know it's perfectly all right and wonderful you have a new friend." Felicity pulled money from her purse and placed it in Helen's hand. "I want you to buy a new dress for the dance."

"That's not necessary," Helen said, though she appeared moved by the gesture.

"Yes, it is. You deserve all happiness. He is a good man."

"Aye. That he is, and thank you, Miss. Excuse me now, but this room is quite petrifying. The faces of those dead women make my skin go cold." She curtsied and closed the door behind her.

Felicity studied the photographs of the women killed by Jack the Ripper in England and his new victims in Placer. The women's faces *were* frightening. Not only because of the way they had died.

They were not at peace.

CHAPTER 21

Sheriff Tom Pike's emotions were stamped on his face as if put there by a steam press. And they revealed disappointment. "I spent a good part of the day talking to anyone who carries a knife," he said, accompanied by a massive sigh.

"I take it you found no leads." Felicity said. They stood in her laboratory. She had invited him over to talk about the case.

"Butchers are slaughterers by trade. There are three of them in Placer, and I started there." He paced, waving his hands about. "The only thing I learned was that butchers are dull as their blades. Then I talked with chefs at the restaurants, but they accounted for their whereabouts. Then bootmakers, but their knives were—"

"Stubby and thick." From his bothered expression, she knew she was right. "I suppose you interviewed barbers next."

"I did. Straight razors make perfect killing tools. I skipped the ones I knew and went to those I didn't. But none of them . . ."

"Fit the profile of our killer. Your formidable intuition told you so."

"I wish you'd quit that. Yes, none of them were clever enough to carry out these killings. I doubt they knew how to write in English, much less Chinese."

"You shouldn't be so hard on yourself, Tom. The inspectors at Scotland Yard followed the same leads with the same outcome."

"I do have one bit of good news. The victim's name was Rose Johnson."

"How'd you identify her?"

"A man who stokes coal at the Ross Smelter came in and said he'd spotted Rose the night she was killed. Before going home, he stopped for a drink at the Shady Lady Saloon. He come round the corner of Rich Street and saw Rose talking with a man. But he didn't think nothing of it because of Rose's line of work."

"Did he see the man's face?" Felicity's hands tightened.

"Too dark. But he said the man wore a bowler hat low over his head. No hardworking fella. He had on one of those fancy coats." Pike reached to his knee.

"A frock coat."

"Yeah. Also gray gloves and black shiny shoes. The man motioned for Rose to follow, and they went behind the store."

"The few witnesses who may have seen Jack the Ripper described a similar outfit. At least he's consistent in his dress. How was your witness even acquainted with Rose Johnson?"

"How do you think?"

"Oh." Silly question. "Why didn't the stoker come to see you earlier?"

"He wanted the five-hundred-dollar reward the city has just put up to find the killer," Pike said.

She could have offered more but hadn't thought about a reward. The fact that the witness couldn't identify the killer amounted to another setback.

"Since the stoker didn't see the man's face, I couldn't arrest anyone, so he won't get the money. We did promise not to tell his wife about his acquaintance with the late Rose Johnson," Pike said. "Now I hope you have something more helpful."

"Quite."

"Let's hear your scientific evidence."

Taking in a breath, Felicity began with her strongest proof. She explained the substantial matches between the handwriting of the Jack the Ripper letter and the note sent to Pike. As she talked, he held the letters side by side.

"Why'd he misspell words in both notes, do you suppose?" Pike asked.

"I believe he did this on purpose to throw suspicion elsewhere, on someone less intelligent," Felicity said.

"He's constant in his methods, if nothing else. Maybe it's how we catch the bastard." He started to light a cigar but threw it out the window. "Dammit. Jack the Ripper *is* in my town."

"I'm afraid so."

"You realize if I tell anyone else about this, they'll throw me into an insane asylum and you alongside me."

"Probably."

"You got anything to lead us to this murderer?"

"Regrettably, it's not definitive." The paper on which the killer had written the note to Pike provided no clues, she told the sheriff. Given the absence of human skin under the victims' nails, they hadn't scratched their assailant.

When she reported on the ink-and-bone mixture used to write the Chinese symbols, Pike arched an eyebrow. "The man is mad as a dog with rabies."

"But smart enough not to leave fingerprints or any other evidence, Tom."

"I read a newspaper story about how fingerprints will be used to find criminals someday. That kind of science is the future of the law, I'm guessing."

Felicity nodded and reported her findings about the red hairs she had discovered on two of the bodies. She encouraged him to peer at one under the microscope.

"Know how many red-haired men are running around Placer?" Pike said.

"Let me guess. A lot?" She didn't mean to sound flippant with such a serious topic.

"Anyway, this doesn't prove a red-haired man killed those women. The hairs might have belonged to one of their clients."

"Yes, but red hairs on two of the victims, and one victim grasping strands in her fist? More than coincidence. And here's another disturbing item."

"How much worse can it get?" Pike said.

Felicity pointed to an autopsy photograph on the wall. "Elizabeth Stride died on the thirtieth of September, 1888, in Whitechapel, London. A jewelry salesman happened on her body in Dutfield's Yard at near one in the morning." In the photograph, the lower portion of Stride's body had been covered by a black cloth. "From the fewer number of wounds compared to the others, the Ripper apparently had been interrupted and ran off. He didn't get his fill of death."

"Why do you say that?" Pike studied the photograph.

"Forty-five minutes after the discovery of Stride's body, police found the body of Catherine Eddowes at Mitre Square less than a mile away." She pointed to the spot on the map of Whitechapel. "The killer had finished his customary job of mutilation on poor Catherine." Felicity handed him the autopsy photograph. Blood had been smeared over the lower part of Eddowes's face. A line of postmortem stitching rode down her body.

"Two murders in one night. Unbelievable." Pike pulled out another cigar from his pocket.

She lit the cigar for him. He placed his hand on hers as he blew out the match and let it linger. Felicity tasted him on the edges of her tongue. Salted sweat and sage.

"Cigars help me think." He took in the smoke and blew it out slowly. "Didn't your London police have any good Jack the Ripper suspects?"

"Several. A boot maker, various criminals, and even Mary Jane Kelly's former lover. But Scotland Yard couldn't connect any of the suspects to the killings."

"That's just dandy."

Felicity sat across from him. "One of the most famous suspects was Dr. James S. Drury, a prominent London surgeon."

"Why him?" He exhaled smoke.

"The good doctor had frequented the Whitechapel prostitutes for years. As a surgeon, he knew anatomy, and the knives used by the Ripper resemble those found in a doctor's bag. Not to forget that Drury practiced medicine at the London Hospital, a stone's throw from Whitechapel."

"I'd call him one perfect suspect."

"Admittedly. A *Times* writer once quoted an inspector's suspicions about Dr. Drury. But the newspaper summarily dismissed the writer because the doctor had friends in the highest of places."

"How high?"

She looked through one of her orderly piles of papers, found the clipping, and gave it to him. "His Royal Highness Prince Albert Victor, the Duke of Clarence, otherwise known as Queen Victoria's grandson."

Pike whistled. "Why didn't they arrest the son of a bitch?"

"Dr. Drury committed suicide a few weeks after the murder of Mary Jane Kelly. He drowned himself in the Thames. A passerby spotted a suicide note under a rock on the shore, but authorities never recovered his body."

"What'd the note say?"

She saw the words in her memory. "'I die, but I am not at fault. Signed J. Drury.'"

"That's one way to cheat the hangman."

Felicity sat by the open window. A breeze fluttered the curtains. She had a sense of protection in the room, as if evil lay in wait outside. "Inspector Davies had gathered a detailed report about Dr. Drury. The surgeon had a peculiar upbringing. At age five his father died. But his domineering mother loved the company of men. Within one month, she married again, and his stepfather was less than kind. All of those circumstances might result in a man with a murderous resentment against women."

"Married?"

"Yes, which conflicts with a grudge against females."

"On the other hand, some women can bend a man to crazy." Pike stubbed out the cigar.

"After Dr. Drury died, the murders stopped. Jackson believed the surgeon *was* the killer and justice had been served when the man drowned himself. Then Jackson read about the killing in Placer. And here we are, trying to find a ghost in the night while blindfolded."

They both stared at the wall of frightful photographs for a while. At last, Felicity readied paper and fountain pen. "Let's take the offensive. We make a list of possible suspects."

"Well, you can rule out barbers, butchers, cooks, and shoemakers."

"And we can omit the Reverend Phoenix." She related the story of the sacrificed calf.

"I always knew that man was off," Pike said after she had completed the narrative. "I still can't believe you shimmied up the side of a barn to spy on him." He gave her a smile. "Yes, I can."

From the wall, Felicity took down the photograph of the bloody footprint marking the sidewalk at the King mercantile near victim number three. "From this and the coal stoker's description, the suspect dresses like a gentleman. He's also smart enough to write Chinese symbols to try to throw us off his trail."

"Very good."

"I have my moments, Tom."

"Still gives us lots of possible suspects."

To her list, she added *A gentleman* and *Educated*. "The last murder in London took place in early November 1888. Lily Rawlins died in late March. So the killer had to arrive even earlier to establish himself with a new identity in Placer. Taking travel time into account, he could have arrived here between late November and January of the following year."

"Good God, Felicity. People move in and out of Placer all the time to work in the mines and smelters. Last census, we had more than ten thousand people, and they come from all over the country and the world."

"But we're dealing with a man who knows human anatomy and can wield a knife like a surgeon, which reduces the numbers considerably." She stood. "Oh my heavens. Dr. Lennox."

"What are you talking about?"

"Lennox fits the description. Mrs. Albert told me he seeks the company of prostitutes."

"Why were you visiting brothels?"

"Mrs. Albert knew Mattie Morgan, and I wanted to question her. I'm so thick. I didn't see this connection before."

"You're not stupid, but you're leaping on a wild horse and letting it take you for a ride."

"I never leap."

"The last thing we need is your flights of scientific fancy. We want evidence."

"Lennox has red hair, the same kind as on the bodies of the women."

"He examined those bodies at my request."

"Not the last victim. He was gone that day and had to inspect the body later at the funeral home. Here's one more revealing clue. When I had tea at his house, he had cups with Chinese markings but refused to say whether he had ever visited China. He didn't want to discuss his personal life at all."

Pike pursed his lips. "I don't blame him. You were snooping."

"He *is* Dr. Drury."

"That London doctor killed himself."

"With Scotland Yard closing in, Dr. Drury could have faked his suicide. He simply wrote a note and left England. The doctor had performed in several plays while he attended Oxford and had a reputation as an excellent actor." She paced this time, propelled by her hypothesis.

"If the killer worked as a doctor back in England, that's not much of a disguise."

"A physician would be above suspicion. Besides, how many people in Placer even know about Jack the Ripper? They'd simply not associate the two."

"With this imagination, you *should* take up writing." Pike sat by the window and breathed in the breeze.

"Not imagination. Pure logic. You certainly could use some." She stopped pacing and planted her feet in vexation at this man. "I have facts. Why can't you see the obvious?"

"Because it's not." From his stiff features, he was just as irritated at her.

Helen knocked and came in. "Sorry to bother you, but supper's ready."

Felicity took a breath to steady herself. "No bother, Hellie. We'll be right down."

Helen closed the door.

"Let's continue the discussion later. This talk upsets Helen so. She's happy tonight, and I don't want to spoil her mood. She's prepared a proper English dinner, roast beef and Yorkshire pudding for Robert Lowery and me. Please join us."

He took in a long breath. "Smells good, and I haven't had my supper."

"We can argue later."

"Look forward to it."

At their London house they usually dressed for dinner, but Felicity had skipped the tradition in Placer. That evening, Pike was dressed up in black pants and a jacket and white shirt instead of the denim, vest, and woolen shirt he usually wore. Felicity hadn't noticed until they sat down to eat. She had had another man on her mind, namely Jack the Ripper.

In the dining room Helen lit candles on the table. Under her large white apron, she wore a new black silk dress. Lowery wore a tweed suit, replacing his usual attire of wool shirts and denim. The part in his hair could have been made by an ax.

"Robert, you're very handsome tonight," Felicity said.

"And Miss Helen, you are a vision," Pike said.

"If you aren't a man of words."

"Only to women who warrant it." His smile dazzled.

Helen giggled. "Dinner is served."

As they ate, Pike told them about how he had grown up in Placer. His father had been a miner. Disliking the work under the earth, he had taken a job as a deputy and worked his way up to sheriff. "A job he was born for. He wanted to make sure there was law in this wild town, that no one was treated unfairly, and that justice was served. So you see, being a sheriff is in my marrow."

Lowery added that he had tried mining himself but detested working in the dark. "Rather be in the sunshine and air. Forget the gold."

The Americans enjoyed the English dishes.

"If this good grub and women like you two are any indication,
then I'm going to have to cross the water to England," Pike said,
wiping his mouth with a napkin.

"Then you must visit Carrol Manor," Helen said. "We live in a
fine old house. We'll treat you like a king."

"Or at the very least, an earl," Felicity said.

When they finished, Helen started to gather the plates. "Hellie,
please leave the cleaning until tomorrow. You two have a dance to
attend," Felicity said.

After Helen and Lowery left, Felicity blew out the candles on
the table and switched on the electric light. The dinner had left her
in a better mood after their disagreement, and Pike looked as if the
same was true for him.

"Getting back to the investigation . . . there's a favor I must
ask," she said.

"I can only imagine."

"Can we remove Rose Jackson's eyeballs?"

He stood up, knocking over the chair. "That I didn't imagine.
Are you plain loco?"

"Loco?"

"Crazy."

"I can assure you, I am not. I don't understand your objection.
Men can be so emotional."

He picked up the chair. "Why in heaven's name do you want
eyeballs?"

"The retina of the eye preserves the last image it sees. Using
photographic processing, we can capture that image. We might see
the murderer's face."

"The killer already tore up poor Rose Johnson. Leave her in peace. Besides, it may not work."

"You're the most unreasonable man on earth."

"You ever shot a photograph through an eyeball?"

"No, but the theory is sound."

"Enough." The firmness in his voice could have held up the foundation of the house.

"I don't care for your tone." She rooted her feet. The disagreement flared again.

"How's this? You're coming with me."

"Where are we going?"

"To a dance. I had planned to attend and wanted to invite you until you began fighting with me."

She smiled. "The foe down?"

He laughed. "That's *hoedown*."

"I came to America to chase a killer. I didn't bring an evening gown."

"You could wear a flour sack and still be the prettiest gal there."

"Save your compliments." Felicity disliked dances, but she needed a night away from the case to clear her thinking. "Give me ten minutes."

★ ★ ★

Every window in the brick building of the Methodist Church shone with lamps and life. Felicity and Pike entered as women's skirts eddied and banked and men danced them around to nimble music provided by a group of men on a guitar, banjo, and fiddle. Children dashed in and out of the church. A line of older women put their heads together in talk. Felicity laughed at the joy in the room. The dances she had attended back home came off stiff as a bodice forged from iron.

Pike removed her dolman wrap of red brocade. She noticed he flashed a bit of pride at having her on his arm. She had worn the nicest outfit she could find among her clothing. White lace rimmed the low, squared collar of her top as well as the hem of the three-quarter-length sleeves. The blouse helped adorn her somewhat plain dusky-blue velvet skirt. She wore simple pearl earrings. Around her neck she had tied a black ribbon with a cameo that had belonged to her mother. A comb decorated with purple ceramic lilacs held her hair in place.

"The music reminds me of the Irish tunes the servants play back home," she said.

"This should have been your real welcome to our country. Music, dancing, nice people. Not what you've seen so far in the alleys and the streets of the Red District."

Felicity waved to Helen and Robert Lowery, who danced past them. She had never seen her friend so lively. Helen budded in America, all to the music of a fiddle and banjo and a nice man at her side.

"I'm not familiar with this type of dance." Felicity watched the couples glide over the floor.

Pike took her hands. "It's a quadrille. Follow me."

Relax, she told herself. *Let yourself be led. It's just a dance.* As he swung her about the floor, an involuntary laugh erupted from her. At the end of the song, they met Helen and Lowery.

"Hellie, you're a wonderful dancer," Felicity said.

"So light on her feet," Lowery added. His eyes took on the polish of a new moon.

"You both are full of blarney," Helen answered.

The band played a waltz. Felicity liked the pressure of Pike's hand on her back and how his other hand cradled hers. "I do feel guilty having a good time," she said.

"We do what we can. You can't track a trail at night."

Over punch and a table full of cakes and pies, a gathering of mostly older women told Felicity they loved her accent. Another well-dressed woman decked out with gold jewelry introduced herself as the mayor's wife, Mrs. Reiger. When Mayor Jonathan Reiger arrived to say hello, Felicity curtsied.

"No need to do that, Miss Carrol. This is America." However, the mayor broke open a smile.

"In England, it's a proper greeting for elected officials."

"See that," he said to those around him. "You should be thankful I don't order you all to bow to me."

"Jonathan, you finish getting the electric lights installed, and we'll think about it," replied a slim man with a drooping mustache.

"You must shop regularly in Paris. Is it as divine as I've read?" asked Mrs. Reiger.

"To be honest, I find Parisians colder than the Atlantic."

The women laughed behind gloved hands.

"You're a hoot, Miss Felicity." A man patted her back.

"Is that good or bad?" She looked to Pike.

"Good."

Everyone laughed again.

A well-fed older woman sitting in a corner summoned Pike with a gloved hand. Her white hair and face could have been carved in porcelain. She wore expensive silks and a pearl choker.

"Who's that?" Felicity asked.

"Mrs. Winston. She wants to be introduced to you."

"Who is she?"

"The richest widow in Placer. Her husband owned half the copper mines around town. When they were starting out in business, she worked alongside him hauling out ore and swinging a pick just like a man."

"Remarkable."

"But she got so rich and forgot about where she came from. Now she's the queen bee and all the society ladies are fearful of her sting. One word from her and you're an outcast in town."

Felicity didn't fear being an outcast. She already was one. "Then please introduce me."

With an exaggerated gesture, he bent his elbow. She hooked her arm in his, and they approached the local royalty.

"I heard you're a writer. Isn't that a man's profession?" Mrs. Winston emphasized each word as if it had been worth a bar of gold.

"The Brontës, Jane Austen, and your own Louisa May Alcott might disagree, Mrs. Winston."

"Where's your chaperone?"

"Dancing."

Mrs. Winston coughed behind a chubby hand and cast a net of disapproval to two other matrons sitting on both sides of her. She turned back to Felicity with cheery eyes and an attack. "How reckless for a young woman to gallivant around town as I have heard you do and endanger her reputation." The woman's voice remained pleasant. "Young women must guard their standing like the precious commodity it is. They do so with proper behavior and impeccable manners. You, however, appear to be tossing your reputation away like dirty bathwater."

Pike glanced up at the ceiling, apparently waiting for a storm.

Felicity licked her lips. She had hoped the women of America could understand the liberty she was enjoying. Then again, she had fought off worse treatment back home.

"I appreciate your concern, Mrs. Winston. But women are the stuff of more than reputation. For example, you."

"Me?"

"You labored with your late husband in the mines. I can only imagine what the other ladies in town must have said about you back then. How they probably gossiped when you worked with a pick and shovel. Yet you persevered, discarded such criticism, and helped your husband build the life you now enjoy. I admire your bravery and strength."

The older woman pulled back her lips not so much in a smile but as a flag of truce. "Have a good evening, Miss Carrol."

"And you, Mrs. Winston."

Felicity held out her arm, which Pike took. Smiling, he walked her to the dance floor. As he twirled her around the room, Felicity spotted Dr. William Lennox chatting with several men in the corner of the church hall. "Tom, he's here."

"Don't." The sheriff's voice held a warning.

"I believe I shall ask him to dance." She headed off before he could stop her.

She heard the word "Damnation" behind her.

"Dr. Lennox, good evening," she said.

He bowed like a board cut in two.

"I'd love a dance." Felicity held out her hand.

The other men didn't conceal their envy and looked at the physician. "Delighted, Miss Carrol," Lennox said, though he sounded anything but as he held out his hand for her to take.

"Do you miss Scotland, Doctor?" she asked. He was actually a fine dancer.

"As much as you must miss England, Miss Carrol." Even while dancing, his hands were powerful against her hand and at her back, as if he could crush her with ease. Close to him, his hair appeared a deeper red in the light. She wished she could pluck one off his head to compare with the samples at her laboratory.

"How did you happen to find your way to Placer, Doctor?"

"Remote mining towns have few physicians. I wanted to be of service." A twitch quirked his right cheek.

"How noble." Another tactic. "I suppose you have many colleagues in England and Scotland."

The twitch passed to his left cheek. "A few."

"Were you acquainted with Dr. James Drury? He was a rather well-known London physician." She expected his forehead to perspire, his muscles to tense, an escape through the door. Nothing happened.

"His name is unfamiliar."

The music ended. He bowed again. "Good evening, Miss Carrol."

"Dr. Lennox."

He left her alone in the middle of the floor.

Pike took her elbow. "You have the guts of an Apache who just declared war on the United States." The band played another waltz.

"Dr. Lennox is concealing something," she said as they danced around the hall.

"People who come to Placer are mostly running away from the rest of the world."

"I'm going to find out what he's hiding." She spoke matter-of-factly. "And I don't comprehend your reluctance to believe he might be the murderer we seek."

"Lennox isn't a friendly man, but that doesn't make him a killer. I've worked with him since he arrived."

"When?"

"Mid-December."

"Ha. It fits the time frame." They danced faster to the slow music.

"I couldn't have missed the signs," Pike said.

"Your intuition is unscientific. The facts point elsewhere."

"Once you get an idea in your head, you don't let it go, do you?" He pulled her tighter.

"No. I suggest we continue waltzing or else we'll have another row."

"What?"

"An argument."

He pointed a thumb outside. "Let's have that right now."

"At your service, Sheriff." She emphasized his title because the entertainment part of the evening was indeed over.

He led her outside, past the horses and carriages. The music faded away.

"I don't care whether the mighty Scotland Yard does call you a good amateur detective. You're a willful know-it-all in a whalebone corset," Pike said.

"And you're an obstinate oaf with a star." She pressed her finger at his badge.

"Your mind's a steam engine." Their voices rose.

"Your head is filled with the same material covering the streets."

"Oh hell. Can I kiss you?"

"No."

He blinked in surprise. And much to hers, she grabbed his collar and kissed him hard. She hadn't envisioned her first kiss. She had never had the time. Not that this was the right time, smack in the middle of a murder investigation, but there was a necessity to feel life after so much death, so she kissed him. It was nothing like she had read in books.

It was much better. She tasted him. She breathed him. She shared herself. She tried another kiss, this one slower and gentler. It was good science to repeat the experiment. And, well, just good. The words of Christopher Marlowe came to her as Pike kissed her again, his arms encompassing her. *Make me immortal with a kiss! Her lips suck forth my soul: see, where it flies! . . . Come give me my soul again. Here will I dwell, for heaven be in these lips.*

Tom Pike might not have had heaven in his lips, but he had enough to make her fingertips heat up.

"Why, Miss Felicity Carrol," he said, and smiled.

As he was about to kiss her one more time, Felicity pushed away and steadied her breath. "Now that that's out of our systems, can we get back to working on this case?"

He laughed so hard he gasped for air, and she slapped his back to help him catch his breath.

CHAPTER 22

Sheriff Tom Pike flipped eggs with great prowess. Felicity drank his good coffee and sat at the table in his white two-story house a few streets from the courthouse. Surrounded by a white picket fence and a carpet of daisies in the front, the place appeared to belong to someone other than this tough lawman. The sitting room projected hominess with a black couch and a shelf of books, including plays by William Shakespeare. The open door to his bedroom showed a worn rug on the floor and a blue-and-white quilt over a brass bed.

After their argument and kisses, Pike had invited her to his house to talk, though not necessarily about arguing and kissing, he said. There, she still felt the vibrations in her stomach from his embrace. But she also thought of Jackson Davies and was distressed—as if she had somehow betrayed him. Her attraction to the sheriff was clear, yet when she had seen Davies so ill, she had realized she would do anything for him. That included traveling all the way to Montana.

Mostly, she felt very far from home and bewildered over her feelings about these two men. Such emotions had no chemical formula she could study or chart. They didn't add up like mathematical equations. Sipping more of the strong coffee, she decided to put away the confusion *and* the kissing for now, although the latter was very pleasant. A killer had to be caught.

She did laugh at one thought.

"What?" Pike said.

"A young woman of English society kissing a man not her fiancé in the middle of a street is considered most shameful. Not to mention going to his house unchaperoned at night."

"I'm sorry to have compromised you."

"Luckily, I'm not that type of society woman, and this isn't England. In this place and in this time, the old rules seem ludicrous."

"Then hallelujah for America." He flipped the egg again.

"Not only an upholder of the law but a good cook," she said after tasting what he had prepared.

"You should taste my beans." He winked. "And I can't believe you called me an oaf."

"I meant every word. And your term for me? Ah yes, a know-it-all in a whalebone corset." She laughed.

"You really live in a castle back home?"

"Not that big. I do believe my grandfather had wanted to be a duke or lord when he built the monstrosity. He bought thousands of acres of gardens, pastures, and woods."

"Thousands?"

"I know. Disgracefully aristocratic."

"My house must be a disappointment."

She took in his kitchen, which was painted the color of a sunflower. "Your home is quite charming."

"Whatever you do, Felicity, please do not call this house charming in front of my deputies. I won't be able to hold up my head in a saloon on Saturday nights."

"Agreed."

"Is England as green as I've read?"

"Like residing in one immense pastoral painting. Sometimes it can be a bit annoying. I do like variety."

He looked out his window. "A helluva change from all this black metal and smelter stacks."

"London has its share of smokestacks. What makes up for it is the history under your feet. You could be tracing the very steps of Henry the Eighth, Queen Elizabeth, Keats, and of course, Shakespeare." Her head motioned toward his parlor. "And you're an admirer of the Bard, as evidenced by your books."

"When I was a boy, Edwin Booth and his company performed *Hamlet* at the Majestic on Main Avenue. My ma took me. The play caught me like a bear in a trap." His eyes illuminated at the telling. "The swordplay and intrigue. When I got home and told my father, he rolled his eyes. That is, until I mentioned how four people died in the final act. He liked that action. 'Better than a dime store novel,' he said."

"Where's your mother now?"

He brushed a hand to rule his hair. "In San Francisco, I last heard. She loved to laugh and read. But this place is tough on women. She had tried with all her guts but couldn't handle the winters or the mining fever. So she boarded a stagecoach and left when I was ten. She told me I belonged in Placer with my pa. That was the only thing I agreed with. Once in a while I get letters from her."

Felicity put her head on one hand and listened to his animated storytelling. Although she disagreed with the way he approached the crimes, he was a decent, bright, and wise man. An orphan like her. "Why'd you become a lawman, Tom? Did you really want to follow in your father's footsteps, or was it something you were expected to do?" He sat up at her question. "Has no one ever asked that?"

"You're the only one."

"Well?"

"I used to watch my father as he walked down the street. He was the very figure of the law and right and helping others. After he was killed, I wanted justice for him by finding his killers, and I came to like the idea of serving up justice for anyone who needs it."

"That is well said."

"Although lately the notion has kind of slipped away." He topped off their coffee. "Speaking of parents, just how did your ma and pa ever allow you to head off to America and get involved in such foul goings-on?"

"My parents are dead."

"I'm sorry."

"My mother died when I was young. My father passed more than one year ago."

"Was he an investigator too? That why you took it up?" The question sounded playful.

"No, a businessman. Now, I must be getting back." She wanted to stop more inquiries about her family.

"What about this Scotland Yard inspector fellow? He your fiancé?" He placed her wrap around her shoulders.

"Jackson is my friend. If I was engaged, I wouldn't have kissed you."

He smiled at that. "Well, he has a good friend to come all this way and put herself in danger."

"He would have done the same for me."

The sheriff put his hands on her face and drew her to him.

She gently stepped away. "I admit you've inspired in me an urge to become more intimate. And I do have a spectacular curiosity, especially after my readings in medical school, but I don't have the time to indulge. Not with what's before us—the finding of the Whitechapel killer."

His arms fell to his sides. "You make spooning sound like a science experiment."

"Spooning?"

"Courting. Kissing."

"Ah, another American term."

"But you might be right. This isn't the time. But I wish it was." He smiled, and she returned it.

"Tom, what of my theory about Dr. Lennox?"

He kissed her cheek. "I think you're wrong as hell."

★   ★   ★

The next morning Felicity sent a telegram to Morton & Morton asking the London solicitors and their staff of excellent investigators to check on whether William Lennox had graduated from the University of Edinburgh Medical School in Scotland as well as provide any other information on his background. She also requested a photograph of Dr. James Drury.

In her excitement at the best lead so far, she almost sent a telegram to Jackson Davies, but decided against it. She didn't want to raise his hopes only to splinter them before she had proof that even the sheriff couldn't dispute. A few days before, she had received a letter from Mrs. Joanna Davies, who reported that her son was improving each day, although he was still plagued by nightmares. Since her arrival in Placer, Felicity had written regularly to Davies about what had happened so far in the investigation, but she was careful not to send his illness into relapse with news of the continued murders and lack of a viable suspect. Until now, anyway.

At the telegraph office, Felicity chewed the end of her pen. In order to convince Tom Pike that the doctor was indeed a viable suspect, she had to break open the mystery of William Lennox.

Stopping by her house to gather her investigative tools, she headed to the physician's office. After tying up her horse, she watched the front door from a corner. Within an hour, Lennox came out and locked the door.

She rushed to the back door and knocked. If his servant answered, her plan would have to be postponed. She knocked again. There was no reply, but there was a locked door. From her satchel, she took out a rolled piece of cloth holding a slim file and skeleton keys on a ring. She sighed at her good fortune. Dense trees around the yard hid her intentions. Felicity inserted one of the skeleton keys into the lock of Lennox's office, but the door didn't budge. Withdrawing the key, she used the file to shave off bits. She kept filing and trying the key until the door opened. To prevent leaving traces of her visit, she got on her hands and knees and blew away the shavings into a lush hydrangea bush to the side of the porch. She had learned the trick from reading Scotland Yard narratives about robberies.

Sneaking inside, she had to hurry. The sun filtered in through linen curtains and crept along the floor with each passing minute. She tightened her hand on the satchel.

She had noticed the doctor's preoccupation with neatness on her first visit. In glass cabinets, medicine bottles had been organized by size. Forceps, syringes, bandages, and other equipment were in orderly rows. In Lennox's surgery, she opened a cabinet drawer.

"Eureka," she dared to say aloud.

Surgical knifes of all shapes and forms lay on white cotton fabric. Her interest pinpointed the double-edged catlin, an inch wide and six inches long with a short ebony handle. The knife definitely could have made the wounds in the prostitutes. She reached out to touch it but quickly withdrew her hand, as she didn't want to leave her fingerprints on the polished handle.

At Lennox's desk, she opened more drawers, using care so as not to disturb a stack of papers neatly arranged there. She reviewed the documents, which were reports on various patients. She hooted an exasperated breath. They were typewritten. She had no samples of his writing to compare with the Jack the Ripper letter and note to Pike.

As upsetting, the names of Rose Johnson, Mattie Morgan, and Lily Rawlins weren't among his patients.

Felicity, she asked herself, *when has this ever been easy?*

Another drawer held blank sheets of paper, along with ink and a pen. She took out one of the sheets to match it with the note sent to Pike. She also scraped off the dried substance on the pen's tip and placed it into an envelope to determine later if the pen had been used to write the note in blood.

Another drawer held medical journals. In the last drawer were clipped newspaper articles about the deaths of the three women. This was good proof, but not enough.

Like his parlor and office, Lennox's private residence was sterile. There were no portraits of family. Nothing personal demonstrated he even lived there. From a hairbrush, she lifted several strands of his hair for comparison to those she had picked off the clothing of the victims.

In his bedroom hung two more watercolor paintings—one of a castle in a meadow and another of a lonely stretch of beach. She leaned in. Lennox hadn't signed the paintings, which she thought strange.

In a tall wardrobe hung six black suits and several white shirts. The pockets were empty. According to the labels, the suits were made by Harbingers in London. Putting the suit fabric to her nose, she smelled alcohol. Not surprising, given Lennox's occupation. Below the suits were four pairs of black leather shoes in a perfect line. Dress shoes. Shoes that could have made a bloody print at the King mercantile. A dark coloration stained the sole of one. From her satchel, she withdrew a dropper and applied to the spot a mixture of hydrogen peroxide and tincture of guaiac from the guaiacum tree. The resulting robin's-egg blue indicated blood.

Although excited, she could hear Pike's contention. The doctor had probably tramped in the spilled blood while inspecting the bodies. Unfortunately, that was a good explanation. She measured the length of the shoe. An inch longer than the bloody print at the crime scene. Sitting back, she chewed her lower lip at the discrepancy.

Still, his knives and the blood on his shoes gave her cause to continue the search. Add to that his disposition of detachment fitting the makeup of a pitiless killer. Besides, he might have used different shoes when he killed those women.

Impulsively, she swept her hand over Lennox's hanging suits and shirts. Her father's wardrobe had had the same tidiness. A memory brushed over her like a dry wind. Her father had always insisted his shoes be lined up like soldiers on a field. She was seven. During a rambunctious game of hide-and-seek with Helen, Felicity hid in her father's wardrobe and displaced the shoes. Her father, not Helen, opened the door. His neck muscles pulsated as he yelled, "You careless child. See what you've done."

She never again played hide-and-seek.

"Get your head into what you are doing," Felicity whispered.

A black physician's bag sat on top of the wardrobe. Inside were bandages, balms, tweezers, small scissors, and a folded single-edged surgical knife. No sign of blood. Most unusual for a doctor's bag and exasperatingly contradictory for the bag of a killer.

And the shoe size. The shoe size.

The front door creaked. She froze. A most unwise thing to do, she admitted.

Move.

She couldn't make it to the back door in time, so she slipped beneath the four-poster bed and barely took in air to slow her heart's frantic beating. Halfway under the bed, she couldn't push forward. Her skirt became entangled in the metal springs. She jerked at the fabric. A rip, but she freed herself. Felicity slid toward the headboard up against the wall and held her satchel close to her body.

Lennox marched into the room. She recalled his brisk walk, as if he always had places to go. He paced in front of the bed with raps of his shoes. After a few minutes, he went into the other room. Perspiration covered her forehead. *He can't kill you in his own house*, she reassured herself. *How can you be so sure?* an inner voice answered.

The light through the curtains turned a dusky orange with the coming sunset. He clicked on an electric light in the bedroom. Felicity pushed herself closer to the wall and wished she could disappear into the dark wood. Someone knocked at the back door. Different footsteps sounded, lighter and rushed. Must be his servant.

"About time. I have an appointment and want my dinner now," Lennox said.

"Yes, sir. Sorry, my wife . . ."

"I don't care. Get my dinner."

"Yes, Doctor."

"And your fingerprints dirtied the glass doors on the cabinet in my surgery. You know how I loathe that."

"Sorry, sir."

Her head went into her hands. Those were her fingerprints.

The clattering of dishes and pans came from another room, along with the smell of cooking beef. The doctor paced in the bedroom. What had made him so agitated? Guilt over the murders? Worry he might be caught? Most likely, his ache to kill thrashing about in him attempting to break loose. Six weeks had passed between the murder of Lily Rawlins and Mattie Morgan, then two weeks between Mattie Morgan and Rose Johnson. Why so many days between the first and second? The answer was logical, even for a killer. He wanted to gauge whether he had gotten away with the crime. So he waited until he believed it safe enough to stalk another girl.

Felicity scooted back against the wall.

Silverware clinked against dishes in the other room. Then came the sound of the dishes being cleared away and washed. Lennox said nothing in all that time. Within an hour, the servant left Lennox with a "Good night, sir," which the doctor didn't acknowledge. Lennox returned to the bedroom and changed his shoes. He sat on a chair across the room for a time. Felicity didn't breathe when he stooped to tie his laces. He turned off the lights and walked out. The front door closed.

Scrambling from under the bed, she clipped her thigh on the wooden post and mentally cursed at the pain. She noted that Lennox had taken his doctor's bag from the top of the chest. Making her way to the medical cabinet, she opened the drawer. One of the catlin knives was missing.

Rushing out the back door, Felicity ran to her horse and rode until she spotted Lennox's slower-moving carriage going around the street corner. She gave enough distance between them that he didn't notice her pursuit, aided by the dusky evening that had come to Placer. After a few turns, she knew his destination.

The Red District.

With leisure, the doctor drove onto Viceroy Street and stopped his carriage a short distance from a set of cribs. Felicity let the reins relax in her hands. Good, Lennox had passed the doors of Beth Ray and Nellie Smith up the street. After checking in both directions, the doctor knocked and entered one of the shacks. The name Jo had been painted over the door in a fancy script. He carried his doctor's bag and wore gray gloves.

Getting off her horse, Felicity hid across the street in an alley between a gambling house and a cheap hotel. She rebuked her rashness. She had no weapon if attacked or to subdue the doctor if he was set to kill again. No crossbow or even that little pistol.

Her mind sped to the story of how the Persian army had attacked the mighty Greeks in 401 BC. They had used slings.

She ripped a long strip of fabric from the bottom of her petticoat. Biting each end, she quickly braided the fabric, forming a cradle in the middle. From the ground, she chose two egg-sized stones worthy of David knocking down Goliath.

She glanced at her watch. The doctor had been inside the shack for five minutes. Making sure she had no witnesses, Felicity ran to the other side of the dark street and put her ear against the door. A murmur of voices, but no sounds of a struggle. She couldn't give in to indecision. She had to save the woman inside. Felicity hurled one of the rocks at the door and dashed back to the safety of the unlit alley across the street.

A curvy blonde woman in a tired corset and gray skirt opened the door. Seeing no one there, she closed it, but not before tossing a curse to the unknown person.

"Thank goodness," Felicity whispered from her place of concealment.

After another few minutes, the doctor walked to his carriage as if on a summer eve's constitutional. Blood didn't saturate his gloves. Felicity knotted her hands in puzzlement. Lennox boarded his carriage and rode off. Someone had probably spotted him entering the prostitute's room, so he couldn't harm the woman. That had to be the answer.

Footsteps crunched the gravel behind Felicity. She twisted about.

"Howdy," a voice boomed from the shadows behind her in the alley. The silhouette of a man with a rounded belly entered the dim light a few feet from where she stood. His calling card was a pungent mix of whiskey and sweat. "How much do you cost?"

"You're very mistaken and very odious," Felicity said. Behind her back, she placed the remaining stone in the fabric sling and backed up into the street.

"Come here and give me a taste." The man breathed through his nose. A dreadful noise.

Felicity continued toward her horse tied to a post near the alley. The man lumbered closer. His feral eyes skimmed her body.

"I'll pay you good."

"Please leave me alone, or I'll be forced to injure you." Felicity twirled the sling in her right hand.

With a base laugh, he ambled toward her.

"I warn you. I'll use this weapon."

"I'll take you right here on the street and save my money." He hurried as best he could in his drunken state.

Her right arm made a swift rotation in an overhand throw; she stepped forward and released the projectile. The stone smacked the man in the middle of his chest. With a grunt, he fell back like a chopped tree. Felicity rushed to him and kicked his foot. He wriggled in pain and moaned.

"Good, you're alive." She rushed to her horse.

CHAPTER 23

Sheriff Tom Pike smiled when he saw Felicity ride up to the courthouse, but then shook his head. Her expression must have told him this was more than a pleasant visit.

"I followed William Lennox to Viceroy Street tonight. There he entered the shack of a prostitute named Jo. Please check on her, Tom. I believe she's safe, but she may have information about the doctor. I couldn't get over there myself because a big man accosted me in an alley." The words emerged in a torrent.

"What big man? What the hell are you talking about, and why were you spying on the doctor?"

"We can discuss that later. We must hurry." She jumped on her horse, and he followed. She suspected the only reason he did was to placate her.

In the Red District, they stopped in front of Jo's shack. Felicity breathed relief. The big smelly man had picked himself up from the place where she had knocked him over. She'd save the story about how she had smashed him in the chest with a rock for another time. Pike's face edged on anger, most probably at her.

The sheriff pounded on Jo's door. As he prepared to give it a kick, the woman opened up. She still wore a gray skirt but had removed the corset. Her tremendous breasts made Felicity's cheeks flush.

"Who's next?" The woman could have been helping a customer at a store. She wore lewdness like a hat. "Why, Sheriff Pike. I've seen you around town. I hoped you'd come visit me. I'll even give you a good price, the one I save for our city officials." Up close the woman appeared to be in her thirties.

Jo peeked around him to see Felicity standing there. "Hold on. Is she with the women's league to run us out of town?"

"This is law business. Let us in," Pike said.

"*Entre vous.*" Jo had a husky voice. "That's how they say it in Paris, or so I read on a bottle of toilet water."

The woman was safe, so Felicity forgave her misuse of French.

"Put some clothes on," Pike said as they entered. The room gave off a briny smell.

"Suit yourself." Jo donned a lacy red robe, which didn't do much to conceal her body. She sat on the rumpled bed. "Who's the gal?"

"I thought you were in danger," Felicity said.

"Aren't you an angel of mercy." Mockery dominated Jo's voice.

"You know Dr. Lennox?" the sheriff asked.

"Who?" Jo's blue eyes went up to the ceiling.

"A well-dressed man with red hair and beard," Felicity answered.

"Don't know nobody like that."

"Jo, you're lying to me." Pike lit a cigar for himself and the cigarette Jo had placed in her mouth.

"Oh, him." The woman worried the ground as she spoke.

"What'd he want?" Pike said.

"What every man wants who knocks on my door." Jo's legs slid open. Her black-lined eyes glistened and concentrated on Felicity's face as if to test her.

"Jo, I don't hear nothing like the truth coming out of your painted lips," Pike said.

"That's the naked truth. I'd swear on my father's grave, if I knew where it was." Her eyes shot back to the floor.

"Did Dr. Lennox hurt or threaten you?" Felicity said, and she could feel Pike's exasperation at her interference.

Jo dared to grin. "Miss, he didn't get nothing he didn't pay for."

"We'll protect you if he did threaten you in any way," Pike said.

"Oh, I'm sure. Now 'scuse me, Sheriff. Men will be knocking on my door with more than questions."

Pike said nothing as he and Felicity returned to the now dark courthouse. The place had electric lights, and he lit up his office. He sat behind his desk and motioned for Felicity to sit across from him.

His silence infuriated her, but she placed her hands on her lap. A flare of temper wouldn't help make her case against the doctor. "That woman was clearly lying."

"You're right."

She hadn't anticipated his consensus. She straightened. "Then arrest him."

"Tell me why, dammit."

Felicity reported what she had seen at Lennox's office. She didn't mention the difference in size between the doctor's shoes and the print at the crime scene at the King store. The other evidence overpowered the point.

"That's all you got?" His tone stiffened with doubt.

What was it about police officers and only wanting a certain kind of evidence? "You're being intolerably stubborn, Tom. Have you forgotten about the knives in his surgery? They're exactly the kind used in the murders."

"He's a doctor. He has knives."

"Then ask him his whereabouts on the nights of the murders. See if he can come up with witnesses."

"I hear no good reason to even ask those questions." His antagonism surfaced. "And I should run you in for breaking into the man's house."

"Under Montana law, a person who suspects another person of malfeasance can take whatever means possible to bring the person to justice."

"Where'd you read that?"

"In the law books at my house."

He walked around the desk. "You don't carry a badge, Miss Felicity Carrol. You're a rich girl from England with a grudge. You're putting too much weight on science and not enough on people. What's under a man's skin ain't found with your microscope and in your books. Dr. Lennox is no killer, and that's how I read it until you convince me otherwise."

The way he talked, they were strangers again. Not two people who had shared ardent kisses the previous night. If she had allowed emotion to lead, she might have been hurt. But she hadn't. Still, her whole body clenched because he had snubbed her facts. She'd had this same disagreement on her earliest investigation with Inspector Jackson Davies.

"We have evidence, Sheriff." Her voice held resolve.

"If we take your so-called evidence to a judge, he'll throw it out and you and me with it." He slapped his hands on the desk.

She sputtered with vexation at his attitude and the prospect that she would forever be having this constant fight with lawmen. A few tears escaped. Not bothering with her handkerchief, she roughly wiped at the tears with the back of her hands. "I've not wept like this since my pony Maurice died. I hate when females do nothing better than shed tears."

"Face up to it. The trail's dried out. That's why you're really crying. You can see how dangerous this is becoming." Pike took a white handkerchief from his vest pocket and dabbed at her cheeks. "I didn't mean to be so rough."

She sat up and blew her nose. "I'm sorry for not uncovering enough evidence to suit you."

His head went into his hands. "Felicity, you are giving me a gut ache."

★   ★   ★

At Pauper Grounds, Rose Johnson went into the ground with two witnesses standing by. Reverend Phoenix seemed to be performing for Felicity and the gravedigger alone, the latter of whom chewed tobacco and leaned on his shovel.

With one hand, Phoenix raised a Bible upward. With the other, he beat on his chest. "Rose Johnson could be counted as another whore of Babylon, but we're all sinners unless we do your good work. We must strive to live without iniquity, or else our immortal spirits will fall down into the bottomless pit. Amen."

The gravedigger, a runt with skin the same color as the ground in which he worked, started filling in the hole. Felicity threw in a handful of dirt. Dust to dust. The gravedigger might as well have been burying all her expectations to convict William Lennox. The scrapings from the tip of his pen had been just dried ink. Not enough proof to bring Lennox to justice.

"Nice to see you again, Miss Carrol, even if it's at the bone garden," Phoenix said.

She detested his almost vindictive send-off of these murdered women, but he did at least care enough to appear at their graves. Mr. Quigley the undertaker had told her no other clergyman would say the holy words over the bodies of prostitutes, murdered or otherwise.

"Since you minister to the women in the Red District, Reverend Phoenix, I trust you'll warn them about this maniacal killer roaming the streets. They must use all caution."

"The church is open day and night, so they can run there if they are in danger."

"I do feel I'm battling something I cannot win." She hadn't meant to sound so dispirited or confide in the calf-killing crazy man. "I'm talking about my writing, of course," she added.

"Trouble and obstacles await anyone who challenges the Beast. He is quicker, smarter, and more enticing than any angel of God."

"I didn't mention the devil, Reverend." But she was in fact tracking evil.

"As my mother used to say before she drank herself to an early grave, you don't have to seek out the devil. He waits for you." He tipped his wide-brimmed hat and got on his horse.

The gravedigger whistled as he shoveled earth onto the wooden box. The clumps broke on the cheap coffin. *Thump, thump, thump.* The branches of nearby aspens quaked in the breeze like the wings of insects.

Felicity pictured Beth Ray and Nellie Smith in the ground. Each in cheap coffins, their ashen bodies disfigured by a knife, their clothes knitted with blood.

She hurried to her wagon and drove toward the Red District.

★ ★ ★

When Beth Ray answered the door, she didn't wear the red lips or rouge of a prostitute. She could have been a young girl coming in from a country day, rosy-cheeked from sunshine on a tranquil pasture. Her tawny hair was in a braid, tied with a white ribbon. She wore a pink gingham dress and clean apron.

"Hello, Beth. I'm sorry to visit unannounced, but I wanted to talk with you and Nellie," Felicity said.

Beth glanced up the street. "What if someone sees you here, Miss Felicity? You shouldn't be here. You're a lady."

"I'm also your friend, I hope. May I come in?"

Given the unpainted wooden walls and marred floor, the word *drab* was insufficient for the room. A splintered chest and rocker sat in one corner. In another corner stood a potbelly stove with a pile of wood on one side. In back of the main room lay a kitchen, which held a small table with two chairs. Still, the floor had been swept, and the open window brought in fresh air. A quilt with flower designs covered the bed.

"I brought you these." Felicity handed Beth a bunch of roses she had stopped to pick from the front of her house on Bullion Boulevard. Felicity had placed the flowers in a ceramic vase she'd found on a shelf in the library.

"How pretty, and they smell good." Beth could have been a child receiving a toy. She placed the vase on the chest of drawers. "Brightens up this old room."

"Flowers have that power."

"Try the rocker, Miss. It's not too uncomfortable."

Felicity didn't sit. "Another woman has been murdered."

"I know. The news traveled through the Red District like a wildfire in summer. I guess she didn't live too far away from me. Another girl of the line. The killer's got something against us."

"I'm worried about you and Nellie."

"Don't have to worry about her. Nellie pulled up stakes as soon as she heard about the latest killing. She didn't like this town anymore 'cause of all the girls being attacked. She said she never had much luck in her life so she'd probably end up like them."

"I'm glad she left for her own safety." From her purse, Felicity pulled out four fifty-dollar bank notes and held them out to Beth. "Please take these. You can go to another town. You can make a new start someplace else, someplace safer."

Dimples set in Beth's cheeks, but she didn't take the money. "You're the first person who's treated me nice in many, many years." She sat on the bed that squeaked. "Always wanted to go to California. Even the name sounds of paradise. A place with no winters. Fruit on trees growing all year round. A chance to dip myself in the warm waters of the ocean. 'Least that's what a miner told me one night. He wanted me to go with him."

"Why didn't you?"

"Because it was the throwaway talk of men after they lay with you."

Felicity sat on the rocker. "Beth, how did you end up here?" Her knowledge came from books, and this young woman's resulted from the life she had lived. Felicity needed to know more than what had been written on a page.

"My daddy was a bad, bad man. He beat all of us children and my mother almost every day for years. We suffered something terrible at his hands. He was mad at life and took it out on us."

"I'm sorry." Here was another girl who had experienced injury at the hands of a parent. Felicity, however, showed no bruises from her father's neglect, not outwardly.

Beth smiled. "I endured by closing my eyes and making up stories about traveling to foreign places. I'd dream of marrying a rich king who'd order my pa torn to pieces by voracious dogs. Or that Indians would capture, torture, and scalp him."

Felicity was surprised at the violence, but perhaps that was what Beth's father had encouraged with his own. "What happened?"

"The day before I turned sixteen, I cooked up chicken soup. Me and my pa were alone. To the pot, I added two handfuls of flypaper to percolate the poison in them. I served him up a big bowl. After the second helping, he died. I stole one of the family horses and lit out."

Beth continued as if telling a story about someone else. "With no prospects, I became a soiled dove. For someone with no education, I make money. As important, I control the men who want to pay for me. If I don't like their faces, I close the door on them."

She gazed at Felicity, waiting for a response. "Never told that to anyone."

Felicity's sense of justice teetered on the edge of a sword. Should Beth be arrested, or had she carried out a sentence on a man who deserved it? At that point Felicity couldn't say.

"You're not condemning me, are you, Miss?"

"For someone so injured, I don't know how I can. All I can say is that justice has a means of finding us, one way or another."

"Then I hope I can escape it for what I did to my pa. If I can find my way to California, I'll wade out in the ocean and be baptized as a new person."

"I know about reinventing yourself, Beth. You're a smart woman. You can be anything you want to be." Still, Felicity couldn't help but be frightened for her.

Beth got up from the bed with another squeak. "I appreciate the thought, Miss Felicity. But don't matter where I go. Everything will be the same. The men. The beds. In Placer, I got lots of friends at least. A man at the Red Rose Gambling House even talks about marrying me."

"You'll be leaving behind a place stalked by a horrible murderer. Please, consider my suggestion." Felicity placed the money on top of the small chest. "The bank notes will be here if you change your mind. Few people receive a second chance, Beth. This is yours. Take it."

Beth smiled. "I'll think about it."

"Until you leave town, promise me you won't go out after sunset."

"I promise, Miss Felicity."

"That's a start."

She glanced at the small kitchen area. "I wish I had tea to offer. English people love tea."

At last, Felicity smiled. "I do like coffee."

"Got some on the stove." Beth headed toward the kitchen but stopped and turned around. "Hold on. Something's different about you since the last time we talked."

Felicity's cheeks heated.

The young woman slapped her knee with laughter. "I want to hear the whole story over a cup of brew."

"Honestly, this is a very private matter." Felicity did want to discuss her fledgling experience with a woman of, well, numerous ones, but would not out of respect to Tom Pike.

"Come on, spill the details, Miss Felicity."

"I have no comment." She smiled larger than she should have.

Beth's eyebrows rose with mischief.

"What?"

"You've been with the sheriff. I seen how he looked at you in front of the café. Like you were heaven on two legs even though he was mad."

"We shared a kiss."

Beth motioned for more details.

"All right, kisses. That is all, I can assure you."

"That's a start." Beth threw her head back in a laugh. "You don't need any pointers, do you, Miss Felicity?"

"No, thanks. I've always been a good student."

"Good. Then I'll go get your coffee."

That night, Felicity sat on the porch of her house in Placer. Below she had a good view of the lights of the town. The brighter spots in the center of town where electricity had arrived. The dots of light at the mines and smelters. The darker area of the Red District.

The night became pitch and lifeless after a covering of clouds shrouded the full yellow moon. The clouds thickened, and lightning flared up behind them. Rain would come soon, she thought, and wrapped her shawl tighter. She had always loved the smell of rain back home in England. The freshness and renewal it brought. She hoped the same would happen so far away from Carrol Manor, but still her skin chilled, because the clouds and sky were full of turmoil. The rain started pinging on the roof.

She couldn't seem to move other than rock back and forth on the wooden chair. She was weighed down by the events of the day, by Beth's story and a floundering inquiry. She had a good suspect in Lennox but couldn't uncover enough evidence to use against him. All those circumstances seemed to bind her. She could have been sinking helplessly under a deluge of rain. Down to where there was no freshness or renewal. No light at all. The chillness of her skin turned to stiff cold, just like it did for the murdered or those soon to be.

CHAPTER 24

Felicity took her final photograph of the body. Sunlight had scattered the storm clouds of the previous night.

The victim appeared to be in her twenties and heavyset. Spread over the ground, her black straight hair resembled the beaks of hungry ravens. She had died wearing a cheap red velvet dress, red stockings, and black boots. The yellow feathers in her trifling black hat had dried to a pitiful sight.

Rain had washed the blood from the neck wound, which was identical to those of the other victims. The woman's sad dress had been hiked up. An incision along the right side of her abdomen stopped short halfway up.

Taking care not to slip on the mud, Felicity packed up her camera. "What's her name?"

"Teresa Sweet," Pike said.

"A girl of the line?"

"She worked in a brothel. And forget about finding any good footprints in all this mud."

Felicity bent over. Sloppy ruts that might have been footprints marked the brown muck around the body. A few of the holes were filled with water colored red by blood. Mud clung to Felicity's skirt as she stood.

The body had been found in a large stand of white-barked aspens. Less than six yards away was a dirt path that wound through the trees. She and Pike walked to the path. Standing there with a deputy was a slender man with white hairs sprouting irregularly from his chin. The hair on top of his head was also white and scattered. His hair and clothes were covered with sawdust and mud and his fingers looked coarse as sand. The nails on his right hand were black-and-blue, as if he had hit them with a hammer. His appearance told Felicity that he worked with wood. He leaned on a thick branch from an aspen tree and rubbed his left knee.

Sheriff Pike introduced Billy Stuart to Felicity, keeping her story that she was a writer interested in crime. "He works as a carpenter at the smelter."

She had been right about his profession.

"Tell us what you saw, Billy," Pike said.

"It was about three in the morning and I was making my way back to my boarding house on Sluice Street. After a full shift, the pain from my bum knee hurt awful, so I thought I'd take Digger's Lane to make the trip shorter."

Using the aspen as a crutch, he walked a little up the path to illustrate his story. "I was about here, I guess, when I heard what sounded like the moans of a sick dog. I look over and see a man bent over a woman lying on the ground. The moon was full, so that helped. The man held something in his hand. Even with little light to see by, I'd been in enough bar fights to sense the presence of a knife."

Stuart hobbled off the path. "I yelled, 'Hey you! What you doing to that woman?' and I went toward them. That bastard straightened and made his way through the trees. I followed. I had read about the murders of the girls of the line in the *Gazette*, so I gave chase. And I remember reading about the reward money, so that put a fire under my old feet."

With difficulty, Stuart turned and headed up the path, with Felicity and Pike following. She heard Stuart's knee cracking.

"Did you see his face?" Felicity asked.

"Now, ma'am. It was just too dark. I forgot about the ache in my knee and ran quick as I could. I didn't have no gun. Don't carry them. But I yelled, 'Hold it, you son of a bitch!' and hoped the man might turn around, but he didn't."

The dirt path ended at a set of wooden steps leading up a twelve-foot incline to Ore Avenue.

Stuart pointed at the stairs. "Right here, the man slipped. I reached out and touched his pant leg but couldn't get a firm hold. The man kicked at me, leapt up, and reached the street above. By the time I climbed up there, the man was gone. Agony plunged into my knee and my face smacked onto the dirt of Ore Avenue. I dragged myself up to the street and started yelling for help, but the street was deserted."

His shoulders sagged. "I made my way back down and found a tree branch to use as a crutch. Then I found the woman and lit matches. Her eyes were open, but she was dead. I picked up her hand. Still warm."

"Was the man dressed as a gent?" Pike said, beating Felicity to the question.

"Yes, sir. Long black coat, hat, nice pants and shoes."

"I applaud your keen observations, Mr. Stuart," she said.

"Call me Billy. I'm just sorry I didn't see that bastard's face." His rough cheeks went vermillion.

"You said you heard noises first," Felicity said.

"Didn't sound like no man. Sounded like something with claws and teeth and hooves. An animal with rabies, but also howling in pain. Gives me the shivers to think about it." Stuart rubbed his sore knee harder. "If I'd only spotted him ten minutes earlier, the poor girl might be walking around today."

"You did all you could to apprehend the madman," Felicity said. "You don't have to be sorry for anything."

Pike placed his hand on the older man's shoulder. "Go on home now, Billy. Take care of your knee."

Still using the branch as a cane, Billy Stuart staggered away.

"Any other witnesses see the killer?" Felicity asked Pike.

He took off his hat and slapped it against his hand. "At that time of night and between shifts at the mines and smelters, the streets are empty. You've seen the Red District at that hour. Too many places to hide."

"What about the reward the city is offering?"

"Didn't amount to spit." He kicked at the dirt.

"What's really bothering you, Tom?"

"In London, Jack the Ripper didn't finish cutting up Elizabeth Stride, because he'd been interrupted. So he murdered Catherine Eddowes the same night."

"What are you getting at?"

"He's going to kill again, and very soon."

CHAPTER 25

TO: FELICITY CARROL

PLACER MONTANA, UNITED STATES OF AMERICA

   FROM: MORTON & MORTON, LONDON, ENGLAND

     NO RECORD OF WILLIAM LENNOX ATTENDING UNIVERSITY OF
EDINBURGH MEDICAL SCHOOL.

     NO INFORMATION OF LENNOX PRACTICING MEDICINE IN ENG-
LAND OR SCOTLAND. PHOTO OF DR. DRURY DIFFICULT TO OBTAIN.
NO FAMILY LOCATED. WILL CONTINUE EFFORTS.

JOSHUA MORTON

With the telegram from her solicitors, Felicity hurried to Pike's office. When his deputies told her he had not yet come to work, she rode to his house and knocked hard. He answered with half of his face shaven.

"So what?" He handed back the telegram after reading it.

"Ask your Dr. Lennox why he lied about going to medical school in Edinburgh."

"Did he tell you he went there, or did you just assume it because he's Scottish?" Pike grimaced from a nick.

Felicity didn't want to answer. "He was terribly ambiguous."

"How about the notepaper you stole from his house?"

"Similar to the one sent to you."

"The same paper?"

"My results are inconclusive."

"Any blood on his pen?"

"No. You sound like a lawyer."

"*Someone* needs to remember the law around here." Pike walked to his bedroom with Felicity at his heels. He finished shaving. "Why are you so dang convinced Dr. Lennox is guilty?"

"Along with what I've found, he's cold and calculating. The very essence of a killer with no conscience." Glancing at herself in his mirror, she perspired as if a dying star flared inside her.

Pike wiped the shaving soap off with a towel. "You're not talking about Dr. Lennox, are you?"

Her knees shook under her dress. "Who else could I be talking about?"

"Go ahead and tell me. The words are on your tongue. I can almost see them sitting there."

She sat in a chair across from him. "You have the most irritating habit of dissecting everything I say. I should know what I'm talking about."

"If you say so." He headed to the kitchen, where he poured a mug of coffee.

His statement jolted her momentarily, but she pursued him. "Jack the Ripper will go on killing in Placer, and other towns, unless he is stopped."

"For once we agree. But you haven't given me anything solid enough to make me believe the doctor butchered those women."

"He has the skill and personality. He had the opportunity." He snorted at that. "And Tom, I feel the truth in my bones."

Pike donned a triumphant face.

"Why are you looking at me like that?"

"You're finally learning not all facts come from under a microscope."

"Nonsense."

He put on his hat, Felicity still trailing him. "Where are you going?"

"To find our man. You coming or not, Miss Carrol?"

She sped to catch up with him.

At the three-story brothel on Slag Street where Teresa Sweet had lived and worked, Felicity and Pike talked with the madam and other prostitutes, who said Teresa had left around eleven.

"She told us she was going to see Bill Mandrake at the Riding Horse Saloon on Viceroy Street. Most nights she did that," said one woman. "Teresa and him were sweethearts."

The dead's girl room revealed nothing.

"Much nicer than the cribs of Viceroy," Felicity said as she and Pike inspected the room. A new brass bed. Tiffany lamps, thick rugs on the floor. Lace curtains. Even a writing desk.

"The madams protect the brothel girls." Pike looked through a small trunk in the corner.

"At least inside these walls."

They stopped at the Riding Horse Saloon, where Pike wanted to interview Teresa Sweet's lover.

"This might not be the work of your killer at all, but a deadly lover's spat," Pike said before entering.

"This wasn't a crime of passion. It was a crime of madness," Felicity said.

A young man with the robust cheeks of a farm boy, Bill Mandrake slowly cleaned the bar with a rag. From the redness of his face, he had been crying.

"Teresa left here a little after one. I read in the newspaper about the other murdered girls, and I pleaded with her to stay until my shift ended at three and then I'd walk her home."

"Why didn't she stay?" Pike asked.

"Teresa said the madam wanted her back by one thirty or else she'd fine her twenty dollars." Mandrake bowed his head as if he had served his last drink. "I wanted to marry her. Teresa called me foolish because she considered herself tainted, but never was there a gentler girl."

"Did a man dressed in a long dark coat, bowler hat, and gloves come into your saloon? Someone perhaps paying special attention to Teresa?" Felicity asked. The man replied with a shake of his head.

"And where were you last night?" Pike asked the barman.

Mandrake's face lost its color. "I'd never hurt Teresa, but I understand you asking." He waved over an older bull of a man. "Seth, please tell the sheriff. Did I leave the bar last night?"

"No, sir. Bill stayed here until three this morning."

"Never saw him leave?" Pike asked.

"No, sir." The man left to help customers at the other end of the bar.

"Then I am sorry for you loss," Felicity said.

Bill Mandrake's eyes became wet with tears. "If women aren't safe in this world, then who is?"

With Felicity at his side, the sheriff proceeded to knock on every door within a mile of Digger's Lane asking anyone if they had seen the suspect who had run from Billy Stuart. Not one had. Last, they made a stop at the Quigley and Son Funeral Parlor.

"All right, let's see what you can do," Pike said.

Felicity smiled.

While Pike and Marcus Quigley stood off to the side, Felicity took a magnifying glass from her satchel and carefully inspected the victim's clothing and body. To her chagrin, she found no red hairs anywhere.

"She wasn't violated," Felicity said after scrutinizing the lower part of the body.

"How do you know?" Pike said.

"No traces of seminal fluid nor bruising around her legs or groin. Then again, there were no indications of rape on any of the other victims."

"That's what I like about Miss Carrol," Quigley said. "She don't hold nothing back."

"Marcus, you and I are going to have a long talk one day," the sheriff said.

"'Bout what?"

"Not telling me about her earlier visits."

"She bribed me, Tom. I'm guilty."

Felicity's nerves tingled from having Pike watch her work. As if he might be grading her investigative skills.

When inspecting the wounds, she called Pike closer. "They match those on the other women. The same knife was used on all of them." She explained the difference in the cuts made by single- and double-edged blades.

Pike rubbed his large hands over his face as if just waking up. "Marcus, please remove one of the eyeballs of this lady."

Quigley didn't flit an eyelash. "I've had worst requests. Which one you want?"

★   ★   ★

In the darkroom located in the cellar, Felicity prepared for the photograph and its development. Upstairs, Pike nosed through the kitchen for something to hold the eyeball so they could shoot the light through the lens and onto the photographic paper. She had also asked him to bring down a metal funnel. If Helen should return, Felicity had advised him to merely say she needed the kitchen tools for one of her experiments.

Returning to the cellar, Pike held a wire ladle, knife, and funnel. He used the knife to make a small hole in the bottom of the ladle to hold the eye. Around the cellar, he located four bricks and set the ladle handle between two of them to place the eye about three feet from the surface of the counter as per her instructions.

"Excellent, Tom."

"If anyone had told me I was going to help take a photograph through a dead woman's eye, I'd have locked them up for being monkey drunk."

"I'm not sure what that means. Let's crack on, shall we?"

Working by kerosene lamps, she and Pike carefully detached the two electrical wires tacked to the ceiling, along with the light-bulbs and the power switch. Pike ran the bulb over the food shelves and power switch into the darkroom.

He withdrew the victim's right eyeball from the white cloth in which Quigley had wrapped it. At Felicity's direction, he placed the eyeball in the spoon of the ladle with the lens facing the counter. Pike scrunched his face as he touched the slimy orb.

Felicity dipped her head in approval of the arrangement. "We're going to stimulate the nerves in the retina of the eye and simultaneously shine a light at the back where the retina is located. The victim's last image will be projected onto the photographic paper. Such is the scientific theory."

"How do we get a dead woman's eye working again?"

"I'm going to break one of the lightbulbs, dislodge the filament, and place the carbon rods against the eye. The electric current will travel through and fire up the nerves."

"Makes sense, I think. Wait. I once read a book about this kind of thing."

"*Frankenstein* by Mary Shelley. Reanimation of the flesh."

"I thought you called this science, not storytelling."

"Why can't it be both?" She rolled up her sleeves. "The metal funnel will concentrate the light. If you don't mind, I'll stimulate the eyeball."

"Be my guest."

"Don't touch the ladle; otherwise you'll receive a little shock."

"All right, Miss Frankenstein, let's get this over with."

Closing the black curtain around the darkroom, Felicity lit the candle under the protective yellow lantern to provide enough light to see what they were doing while preventing exposure of the photographic paper. On the lip of the counter, she broke the glass bulb of one of the lights and lifted out the delicate filament with a thinly rolled piece of paper. Underneath the ladle holding the eye, Felicity placed a piece of photographic paper.

Pike held the remaining lightbulb in the funnel and pointed the tip at the eyeball to concentrate the light.

"Let's turn on the power." With her free hand, Felicity flicked the switch. She touched the broken bulb to the left side of the eye. After ten minutes, she hit the power switch.

Both let out a breath as if they had held all the air in their lungs.

"I hope it's enough time to expose the paper," she said.

"Me too. It's beginning to smell like fried eyeball in this cellar."

While Pike reattached the electrical lines to the ceiling, Felicity set about developing the photograph. Pike rewrapped the eye to return to the undertaker to bury with the victim. Finished with his work, he watched over her shoulder as an image started to appear on the paper floating in the developer bath.

"I'll be damned," Pike said as the photograph took form.

The grainy figure of a slender man standing at what appeared to be the top of Digger's Lane formed on the paper. A streetlight from Ore Avenue illuminated his back and muddied his face. From his outline, he wore a long coat and bowler hat.

"We can't see his face." Felicity dried her hands on an apron she wore.

More than anything, she had wanted to see the face of Dr. Lennox, or should she say, Dr. James Drury of London, England.

Without a clear identification, she had to go to her alternate plan. Shadow the physician at night to obtain proof enough to have the man arrested. She was as sure of his guilt as she was of anything.

"I'm afraid our experiment failed, Tom. We can't see his face."

Pike held the photograph, his stare intent. "But you've exposed a real man and not a phantom. The trouble is, he's turning my whole town into a damn slaughterhouse."

CHAPTER 26

The next morning as Felicity put her hair up with pins, she heard Helen's hurried steps to her room. She bade her enter before Helen could even knock. The older woman's face flushed with apprehension.

"What's wrong, Hellie?"

"A young man from London." She handed Felicity his card. "It can't be good news. He's green as a fish."

Felicity read the card.

RICHARD FRANKLIN
JAMESON & SONS, SOLICITORS

"Hope nothing's wrong at the manor," Helen said. "Hope no one is hurt."

"Nonsense. He probably has some papers for me to sign. Mr. Jameson loves for me to sign papers."

Still, Felicity hid her nervousness from her friend. Martin Jameson wasn't the kind of man to send a colleague all the way to America for paperwork or on a whim. Something *was* wrong.

Downstairs, Felicity watched Richard Franklin through the glass library doors. He stood stiffer than a guard at the palace. His dark walrus mustache made the young man look more like an aged senior partner. His face held uneasiness. Now Felicity became worried, too. She must hide her own nerves.

She entered the library and extended her hand. His handshake was taffy. "We've met before, Mr. Franklin."

"At your father's funeral."

"Oh yes." Felicity motioned for him to sit and shut the door. "Nothing wrong at Carrol Manor, I hope."

"No, Miss Carrol."

"The mills and shipping company still running at optimum efficiency and profitability?"

"Yes, Miss."

"Then why, Mr. Franklin, have you traveled so far to see me?"

He glanced around the room.

"We're quite alone, Mr. Franklin."

"Two weeks ago, our office received a communication that has caused Mr. Martin Jameson, Senior, much discomfort. He immediately asked me to make the trip, given he hates sea voyages." His voice was crisp as a new pound note. "The subject proved so sensitive, Mr. Jameson didn't want to send a telegram or letter and believed a personal visit was in order." He held out an envelope.

FOR THE EYES OF MARTIN JAMESON had been typed on the front. The letter inside was also typed.

Mr. Jameson,

It has come to my attention Miss Felicity Carrol is delving into murders in America not unlike those committed by the infamous Whitechapel killer. If she continues, her business enterprises shall be in great danger. I have in my possession information linking her late father Samuel Carrol to those horrible crimes in the East End. Disclosure will insure she loses all her assets and income. Unless she terminates this careless endeavor, I will not hesitate distributing the material to The Times of London and other newspapers. I trust you will see to this matter.

Yours truly,
I. W. Beck

There was no signature.

"Who is I. W. Beck?" she said.

"We don't know. We made inquiries but could locate no such man. Obviously an alias."

"Exactly what's the danger to which the unknown Mr. Beck is referring?"

The young man cleared his throat. "I am speaking as Mr. Jameson."

"I understand, and what does he have to say?"

Patches of red expanded on his thin cheeks. "You see, your late father was a good friend of one of the Whitechapel suspects."

Felicity closed her eyes. "Dr. James Drury." Each letter scraped her tongue.

"Quite so. Mr. Carrol and this person were regular visitors to the women in those, ah, establishments for which Whitechapel is famous."

"The man in the top hat and coat." The man she had seen getting in the carriage with her father the night she had followed him on one of the visits to the brothels.

"Pardon me?" Under his mustache, Franklin nipped at his lower lip. He had the subtlety of a marching band.

"What else do you have to tell me?"

"The fact that Mr. Samuel Carrol befriended such an infamous man is worrisome enough. But Scotland Yard also interviewed your father about the Whitechapel murders."

"As a suspect?"

The luster of perspiration appeared on the young solicitor's forehead. "Mr. Jameson didn't say, but I'm sure this threat only reflects your father's association with Dr. Drury. However, release of the information could damage the name of Carrol Mills and Shipping. The companies could lose their clients, and you would lose the greatest source of your wealth."

"I thoroughly researched the Whitechapel case . . ."

"Your father and Mr. Jameson made sure his name did not appear anywhere in connection with the case." Franklin swallowed hard.

Which explained Martin Jameson's weird behavior when she had mentioned Whitechapel before she left England.

"In other words, my father and Jameson bribed police officials to keep his name out of their reports and therefore out of the newspapers." Felicity stood and gazed out the window.

For so long she had witnessed the worst in her father. Since he died, she had been accepting the pain he had imposed on her. Yet somehow the fact that others knew his weaknesses caused a new and different kind of misery.

"Mr. Carrol ceased to become a suspect when he proved he had been out of town at the time of the last murder."

"How fortunate."

"Mr. Jameson urges you to return to England straightaway and set aside these matters."

"My work is not complete here."

"If that's your decision, I'm afraid all will be gone upon your return. Your family's businesses will be ruined by this man Beck if he follows through on his threat."

Her wealth had been a burden all her life, but it had also allowed her to learn what she pleased and work on murder investigations. Was she prepared to have nothing? A faint smile crept over her face. She could always teach school or become a private detective for the Pinkertons.

Franklin must have guessed her thoughts. "Miss Carrol, consider the hundreds of people who work for your mills and shipping line. And the money you set aside for your older servants could also be in jeopardy."

"Helen. Mr. Ryan." Her real family could be in jeopardy.

"For a start."

"You've given me a lot to contemplate, Mr. Franklin."

"Tomorrow, I'll begin the journey back to England, Miss Carrol. What shall I tell Mr. Jameson?"

"That I thank him. May I keep the letter from Mr. Beck?"

Franklin handed it to her.

"By the way, how did this arrive? There's no postage mark."

"It simply appeared on the desk of one of our clerks."

"Doesn't it strike you as peculiar this Mr. Beck asked for no money? This has all the markings of blackmail. Yet he demanded nothing."

"Mr. Jameson thought it singular as well. He suspects Mr. Beck meant the note as a warning and may only have the family's best interests at heart."

"Then Mr. Beck has the most extraordinary way of showing concern."

Richard Franklin took his leave politely and silently, as most English gentlemen did.

Though not meaning to, Felicity had crushed the letter in her hand. Returning to her laboratory, she straightened the paper on the counter. A good-quality stock, but nothing unique.

Still, the letter carried another message. In England, she had told no one about her reason for visiting Montana except Jackson Davies, and he wouldn't have told anyone, she was sure. This proved one thing. The killer believed she was close to identifying him.

Dr. James Drury knew about her father's nightly activities. He lived, and his name was now William Lennox. Lennox knew about her interest in the Placer murders. Somehow he had had the letter delivered to Jameson's office in London. Lennox must be tied to the murders, and soon. He had already killed four women. If he held to his pattern, he would take his fifth victim and leave for another town to begin his wicked ritual all over again.

A soft rap at the door disturbed her thoughts.

"Miss Felicity, do you want supper? You've been in here for hours." Helen peeked in the door.

"Come in, Hellie. I'd like to ask you something."

The older woman did but kept her eyes on the rug.

"You knew about my father's visits to Whitechapel, didn't you?" Felicity hoped her voice did not betray disappointment.

Helen kept silent.

"Please tell me."

Helen clenched her hands together. "We just heard stories, Miss. When you followed him that night in London, I realized you had discovered his secret too."

"Did he go to those houses while my mother still lived?"

"No, Miss." Her answer was impassioned. "He loved her so. Only after she passed on, years after."

"I'm sorry, Helen. I had to know."

Helen touched the doorknob to leave but stopped. She turned back to Felicity. "It pains me he's still hurting you, Miss." She went through the door.

Helen understood her heartache, and that comforted Felicity.

In case the threat of I. W. Beck was real, Felicity had to wrap up this investigation quickly. Starting tomorrow, she would watch the doctor's house each night and follow him when he ventured out. She'd have to observe him stalking another prostitute and stop him before he could murder the girl or her.

The word *perilous* didn't quite cover this endeavor, because how did one detain a madman? Her mind hustled through the pages of the medical and chemistry books she had read in school. An ethyl alcohol derivative, chloral hydrate, would render him unconscious at once. But she had to get close enough to inject him. There might be another way to deliver the sedative. Perhaps a blowgun like those used by the Maya? The ever handy Robert Lowery could make her one at her direction.

The day's illumination had died, and she hadn't noticed she now sat in a dark room. She switched on the electric light. By nightfall, Felicity had formulated the drug to tranquilize the killer. But her fingers had been turned to metal by what she faced.

He wants you to fear him. He wants you to run home. He wants . . .

CHAPTER 27

Tugging the shawl tighter around her shoulders, Felicity stood in front of the house. Her body was slow with fatigue following the visit from the London solicitor and preparation of the chemical to capture a killer. She should have been sleeping, but as the killings continued, she had found sleep difficult. Perhaps because of the ashen faces in the photographs hanging in the room next to hers and the madness she couldn't grasp. The murderer she could not stop. She now understood why most women preferred refuge behind lace curtains, children, and afternoon tea. Malevolence, chaos, and death hid beyond in the night.

Crickets clicked in the bushes. Smoke from the smelters' stacks puffed white in the dark sky. How could she ever sleep well again after everything she had seen? Since her father died, she had not experienced the same compression of loneliness on her soul, but she felt it tonight.

"Miss Felicity!" Robert Lowery rode up to her.

"What happened, Robert?"

"I was playing poker with the jailers in the courthouse when Tom Pike ran in and told the deputies he needed them to get to the Red District. Another girl was killed. This one in her own crib. I hurried on back here." Breathing hard, he got down from the horse.

"Did the sheriff mention the victim's name?"

"Someone called Beth."

Grabbing the reins from the older man, Felicity leapt on the horse. She dug her heels into the animal's sides. She couldn't hear the horse trot through the streets nor the shouts of men as the galloping threw dirt into their faces. She didn't see the dog snapping at the hooves. She only heard a reverberating clamor rolling in her ears.

In front of the cribs, she slid off the horse and didn't bother to tie it up. Pike stood on the porch lined with lanterns. When he saw her, his jaw muscles tightened. Felicity charged to the door. Pike caught her by the waist and held firm. "No."

She struggled.

"You don't want to see this."

The struggling didn't stop. "Let me go."

He released her.

More lanterns had been placed on the floor of the crib. The killer's insanity was manifest in the wild spatters spotting the walls and ceiling. What remained of Beth Ray lay on top of the bed. The naked body appeared to have been carved away to misery, muscle, and mortality. The whites of her eyes appeared stark and condemning. They were the eyes of all the victims of murder.

Felicity noticed the open carpetbag on the chest. Beth had intended to leave town with the money she had given her. Beth could have been saved. Felicity peeked inside the carpetbag. At the bottom sat a liver.

Tearing outside, Felicity saw Dr. William Lennox walking up to the shack. She charged the doctor and slapped his face so hard her hand stung. "You did this, you murderer! You butchered Beth and all the others." Her fists beat on his chest. "You preyed on the weak. Monster! You sent that letter. But I won't run away."

Lennox put his arms up against her fists but remained silent. As she pulled her arm back to strike again, Pike grabbed her and dragged her away.

She shook off his hands. "Tom, he slaughtered them all. What more do you want?"

"The doctor was delivering a baby outside of town and only just arrived back," Pike said. "He didn't kill Beth Ray. He didn't kill any of the women."

For the first time in her life, Felicity Margaret Carrol of Surrey, England, fainted.

★   ★   ★

Felicity awoke and blinked. Her eyesight blurred. Two invisible iron vices wedged her head between them. When she could see clearly, Dr. Lennox was holding her wrist and counting heartbeats on his watch. He set her hand on the bed, addressing Pike and Helen, who stood nearby. "She'll be fine. Just needs bed rest." To Felicity, the physician said, "By tomorrow, you'll be your old inquisitive self again."

When Felicity tried to sit up, a wave of dizziness compelled her back down on the bed.

"Please, Miss Carrol. No sudden movements."

"All this talk of death and murder, I'm surprised we're not all sick in our beds," Helen said protectively while she patted Felicity's forehead with a moist cloth. She threw a stern stare at the sheriff and the doctor.

"Hellie, help me to sit up, please." Helen's touch was so familiar. The older woman's hand on her back. Fluffing the pillow. Her soothing nature, giving love beyond her wages. The immense care of a mother. As Helen pulled back, Felicity kissed her cheek as she had so often as a little girl. "Thank you, my dear, dear Hellie."

"My pleasure, Miss Felicity. Always has been. Now I'm going to fix you a bowl of broth." Before she left the room, Helen addressed the men with, "If you gents cause my lady any additional upset, you'll have to deal with me."

"We'll take good care of her, Helen," Pike said.

Helen went downstairs.

With effort, Felicity looked into the doctor's face. "I apologize for my appalling suspicions, Dr. Lennox. I'm ashamed of my behavior towards you. Forgive me."

The man remained dispassionate. "I probably did make a terribly good suspect." A modicum of pride went with the statement.

"You certainly did. For instance, the visits to the girls of the line."

"Even ill, you demonstrate a tremendous amount of fortitude." Lennox straightened and gave Pike a nod.

"Dr. Lennox is treating the prostitutes for syphilis," the sheriff said.

"Why didn't you say so in the first place, Dr. Lennox?" Felicity said.

"Because such diseases aren't mentioned in polite society, Miss Carrol, particularly to a young woman of good breeding like yourself. Besides, I promised to keep my patients' identities a secret."

"Tom, how did you know?"

"After your telegram, I had a long sit-down with the doctor. He confided in me about tending to the prostitutes. The women who he's treating backed up his story."

The honest talk gave Felicity strength. She sat up a little more, but her head still felt as if it might explode at any second. "Why couldn't my solicitors find your name among those who practiced medicine in England or Scotland?"

Pike leaned in. "A real good question, Doc."

Lennox placed the medical equipment in his black bag. "Because I caused a death." His voice quivered the slightest bit. He sounded like a person then and not an emotionless metallic creature. "My real name is Donnan Brody. In Scotland, I was troubled by the treatment of syphilitics. The dejected creatures who worked the streets. Many weren't even allowed into hospitals for care. As terrible, the use of mercury to treat the disease often killed the patients."

"It's no simple cure," Felicity said.

"Quite. Patients suffer from mercury poisoning. And this was my treatment for a fourteen-year-old prostitute from Edinburgh. I pasted a mercury ointment over her and placed her in a sweat bath. She died as a result, but not without great anguish." He closed the medical bag.

"You were only adhering to the recommended treatment, Doctor," Felicity said.

"She still died at my hands, Miss Carrol, and nothing would change that. I traveled to America. Changed my name so I could continue helping these unfortunates in my own way with new treatments not involving the use of mercury."

"Newer techniques frowned upon back home," Felicity said.

"Most certainly."

The doctor had proven he was human. "You make me doubly ashamed, sir."

"No need." Lennox's kindness vaporized. He picked up his medical bag. "Now I must see to another patient. I hope, Miss Carrol, my story won't become part of your crime book."

"You have my promise, Doctor."

Lennox walked out the door.

"I'm such a fool, Tom."

"The prettiest I've met in a long time. But yes, a fool."

"Because of my preoccupation with the doctor's guilt, I couldn't find the real suspect in time. If I hadn't been so stubborn, Beth Ray might be alive today." A strident pain hit her left temple, which she rubbed. She longed to sleep but had more to confess. "I wanted the doctor to be guilty. He is so like my late father."

Pike held on to her hand as she spoke.

"Weakened by my birth, my mother died of consumption. I was six months old. I was five when my brother died of pneumonia. He was seven." The words came easier than she expected, as if they had always been near the surface.

"And your father blamed you for the death of your mother."

"Not to mention that I lived and they didn't." Felicity took his hand. "Once again, you see to the heart of things. An uneasy land lay between me and my father. I had found, however, that science and reason will never betray or hurt you. Until now." She gave a weak smile.

Pike's breathing remained steady, as if he balanced the air in the room. "You're not to blame for Beth Ray."

"I didn't stop Jack the Ripper from knocking on her door."

"If that's the case, then I'm as guilty as you. But we aren't." His smile was sad. "Stopping this killer is like stopping hell itself."

After Pike left, Felicity pulled up the quilt, lay back, and closed her eyes. She slept several hours and then woke. Sunset colored the room ocher. Her ears rang from the stillness. She splashed water on her face in the basin. Through the windows, a glowing red layer sat above the horizon. Particles in the air from the smelters daubed the sky with the magnificent hues. How ironic that ugly smoke could result in something so radiant.

Felicity contemplated the chamber of horrors she had created on the wall in her laboratory. She began removing the photographs and news articles about the crimes in London and in Placer. Doing so, she also recounted her transgressions.

She had wrongly accused Dr. William Lennox.

She had not saved Beth or the other women.

Jack the Ripper had won. The butcher of Whitechapel and now the Red District of Placer, Montana, had triumphed. His name should be Jack the Conqueror. His insanity had vanquished enlightenment. His violence dominated science.

Never having met failure in her studies, she encountered it now. The selfish need to prove herself a great detective could mean destroying the livelihoods of people back home if she didn't quit this investigation.

And what of Jackson Davies? His reaction to abandoning their shared mission? He had almost died from a fixation on the killer.

Felicity placed the papers and photographs in a trunk. She would just have to help her friend get through this failure, and she hoped he might do the same for her. Her love of education had always sustained her. Well, she *had* continued her education in Placer. She had learned evil could win.

It was time to go home.

CHAPTER 28

Helen Wilkins dotted away tears with a handkerchief. Her nose gushed. "I don't mean to carry on so, Miss Felicity. I've come to like this place."

"So have I, Hellie." Felicity had expected some reaction when she told Helen about her decision, but the older woman had stunned her with its force.

"I've met such nice people here," Helen blubbered.

Felicity sat next to her. "If it's any consolation to you, I'm going to ask Robert Lowery to come with us to England. We could use another good man at Carrol Manor."

"Oh, Miss Felicity." Helen grinned.

Felicity used her handkerchief to dab at Helen's tears. "If you like, you can extend him the invitation."

Her voice lifted with delight. "I wanted to ask but not get above my station."

"There are no stations between us. Only friendship."

Helen dried her face with her apron, curtsied, and hurried out.

Felicity heard the kitchen door open and close. A while later, Helen and Lowery entered the library where Felicity sat, still exhausted from the night before.

"Miss Felicity, I'll work hard for you," Lowery said.

"I have no doubt. And one more thing." He and Helen both stopped smiling, because Felicity had taken on an exaggerated seriousness. "As Helen's employer and, more importantly, one of her oldest friends, please tell me of your intentions, Robert."

The color left his cheeks. Helen laughed like a fresh country girl and elbowed his ribs. "Go on then."

Lowery straightened so much Felicity worried he might break in two. "I'd like permission to marry Helen."

"While her brother is not here, I hope I may be a good substitute." She didn't hesitate. "You have my blessing. But would you like to remain here or return to England?"

Helen and Lowery took each other's hands. She whispered to Lowery. He whispered to Helen.

"If it's all the same, Miss, I'd like to be married as soon as we can so my dried-up old brother won't have a thing to say," Helen said. "And we both decided to go back to Carrol Manor. Robert's never traveled and he'd love it there."

"Then please, do me the greatest of honors. Allow me to make those arrangements," Felicity said.

"I have no words," Helen said.

She hugged Helen and shook hands with Lowery. "Your faces are reward enough."

"We best get back to work. Come on, Robert. Much to do." Helen ushered him from the room. "Miss Felicity, you rest and I'll bring in your tea."

Felicity walked up to her room and sat on the bed. Since she had made her decision to go home, her chest had never seemed to fill with enough air. Her muscles weakened at the thought that she had been bested by the killer. As she lay on the bed, resolve abandoned her. But she didn't remain there long. She had a wedding to plan.

★　★　★

Sheriff Tom Pike had called the Placer Grand Hotel the nicest in town, and he wasn't wrong. While not up to the standards of the fine hotels in London, the Grand exhibited luxury nonetheless—notable for an isolated town such as Placer. In the dining room, goblets sparkled and the napkins resembled tamed birds. A marvelous place for a wedding. However, Helen and Robert Lowery wanted to be married in the garden of the house on Bullion Boulevard. Lowery had already asked Judge Simon Winslow, a friend of his late employer, to perform the ceremony.

Felicity talked with the manager of the Grand Hotel to hire a cook and waiters for the wedding, as well as obtain the use of tables, flowers, and the other settings for thirty people. The manager revealed himself to be an exacting man with a trim mustache. His black suit shone like obsidian from ironing. But his glacial attitude thawed when she mentioned she'd spare no expense on the event.

"I can assure you, Miss Carrol, the nuptial party will be impeccable." He had a voice prissy as satin.

"Quite. I also want to reserve the wedding suite for the couple." She paid in full for everything.

His eyes gleamed at the money.

Felicity had asked Helen and Lowery not to tell anyone about their return to England. She hadn't told Pike of her decision and admonished herself for her cowardice. She could face the Midline Gang, but not the sheriff. Not yet. Walking on Main Avenue, she passed the Alhambra Theatre. The marquee read THE MERCHANT OF VENICE, which would be performed that weekend. Dinner and the theater. Her gift to him, since she had nothing else to give.

She had not found Jack the Ripper.

★　★　★

Tom Pike grinned as she presented the tickets. "This makes me even happier than the time I caught five cattle rustlers up near the MacKay River."

Felicity laughed.

"I'm joshing you. I only arrested three of them."

"Still very impressive, Tom." She sounded too cheerful.

He lost his smile. Suspicion lit on his face. Who could blame him after all her mistakes and deceptions?

"Hold on, Felicity. What's the real reason for all this?"

She planned to save the news of her pending departure until after the dinner and play when they were alone. She'd lie until then. "To express my gratitude for how much you have helped me since I arrived in Placer."

"To be honest, there were lots of times I wanted to put you back on the stagecoach."

"How very kind you didn't."

"And Bob Lowery told me you're throwing a wedding party for him and Helen. I'm going to be his best man."

"Brilliant." She needed to hurry out of his office so he couldn't start reading her mind. "Must run. I'm meeting Helen at a dressmaker."

"I'll let you go, but only for a while."

At a fashionable shop on Main Avenue, Felicity chose a dress for Helen's wedding and one for herself for the evening with Pike because she hadn't brought anything suitable for such an engagement. She chose a violet silk with puffed shoulder straps and black lace at the waist and hem. Blue brocade made up the train. She also purchased long black gloves and satin slippers. As she stood in front of a mirror in her new outfit, her eyes were rusted as old tin.

"A picture of loveliness," proclaimed the Irishwoman who owned the shop. "The gown needs a little altering, Miss Carrol. You can pick it up tomorrow morning."

Helen emerged from another dressing room wearing the wedding gown Felicity had selected, made of cream brocade and draped white lace, decorated with orange blossoms. In Helen's hair were two mother-of-pearl combs painted with white roses that Felicity had picked out for her.

Arms out, Helen revolved in front of the mirror. "I can barely believe it's me."

"You look like a queen, Hellie."

"I do feel rather like Victoria." Helen pushed out her chest.

"Prettier."

"Mrs. O'Malley," Felicity addressed the dressmaker, "Helen will also require a trousseau. Let's see, a traveling outfit, two day dresses, a cloak, an evening gown, robe, shoes, and undergarments."

"Please, Miss, this is too much." Tears gave Helen's eyes a touching luster.

"Unless you're Henry the Eighth, you get married once. So the traditions will be conducted with all respect and ceremony."

"But you hate tradition." Helen teased her mistress.

"Not today. I'm merely returning the love and kindness you have given me all my life."

Helen suddenly hugged Felicity, who breathed in her smell of good cooking. "Excuse my forwardness, Miss." Helen quickly put down her arms.

"That's the best gift you could ever have given me."

★　★　★

Felicity drove the wagon to Quigley and Son to pay for a proper funeral for Beth Ray. The rest of the murdered prostitutes had been buried in a plain pine coffin by the county. Admittedly out of guilt, she wanted more for Beth.

Marcus Quigley offered to upgrade the coffin to one painted white and lined with blue silk. Felicity approved. He also would transport the coffin to the cemetery in his new black hearse, pulled by two white horses bedecked with black feathers. The likeness of two angels holding a vine of roses would decorate Beth Ray's headstone.

"Marvelous job, Mr. Quigley, but do you have to bury her in Pauper Grounds? Can't she be interred in the regular cemetery?"

Quigley scratched at his head. "People don't like those wantons buried next to decent folk."

She handed him a fifty-dollar bank note. "A man such as yourself could sidestep such an absurd notion."

"I believe I can." He accepted the money. "I'll be ready tomorrow."

"Can you also manage to locate another minister besides the Reverend Phoenix to preside at the service?" She handed him more money.

"Leave everything to me." Quigley winked.

Felicity thanked him and rubbed her temples, which had not stopped pulsating since the night of Beth Ray's murder.

"I suppose you want to see Beth's body for your usual inspection. The doctor and sheriff already made theirs, but they called it too mangled up to tell them much."

Felicity had not come to the funeral parlor to examine the remains of the young woman. "Not this time." She started for the door, but pivoted. "Well, maybe a quick review."

Quigley gave an extravagant bow. "After you, Miss."

With a swish, Marcus Quigley drew back the bloodstained sheet. Felicity staggered. Away from the little room in which Beth Ray had lived, worked, and died, the body appeared even smaller and more broken. Felicity walked around the corpse, while Quigley took his usual place on the stool in the corner.

"Never seen a human body treated so, Miss. Not even the time we buried a miner who got caught in an explosion."

Felicity leaned in and sniffed. "Jasmine. Mr. Quigley, did you use a scent on the body?"

"No, Miss. She came in smelling like that. Even stronger when they brought her to me."

"I didn't notice it the night she died." Then again, her fury at the sight of Beth's body had blocked out her other senses. She'd been deaf and blind to all except the murder and her hatred of Dr. William Lennox.

Quigley dug grit from under his nails. "I'm surprised the girls of the line could afford such nice-smelling perfume. Maybe the man who did this wanted to cover the stink of what he had done."

"I've seen all I can bear." She turned away from the body. He replaced the sheet. "Mr. Quigley, you've been most accommodating and kind to me."

"Just part of the service."

Felicity started for home, but the jasmine lingered in her nose, and so did a question about the murder. She drove to Beth's crib. As soon as she entered, she took a deep breath. The jasmine scent. Feeble but unmistakable. She rummaged inside the chest of drawers and on the shelves but couldn't find any bottle of jasmine-scented perfume or toilet water.

The mattress had been taken away, leaving behind the rusted metal springs. Several sets of reddish footprints covered the floor, no doubt from the sheriff, his deputies, and others who had trodden through the blood as they inspected the murder scene. She managed to discern one pair of bloody footprints belonging to men's dress shoes in the small kitchen in the back. The prints were alike in size and shape to the one on the sidewalk at King General Mercantile where the third body had been found. The bloody prints stopped in the middle of the kitchen.

Scratch marks on the floor indicated that the table had been shoved to one side. Dried red splashes covered the tabletop. A ceramic water basin had been smashed on the floor and swept into a corner. Several pieces of the broken basin had smears of blood on them, but no obvious fingerprints. Covered in blood, the killer must have cleaned up before leaving Beth's room.

Felicity checked the floor leading to the flimsy back door. No bloody tracks out there. *He had taken off his shoes.*

Outside the back door, a wooden step led to dirt marred with footprints in every direction. Three wooden privies stood about thirty feet behind the shacks. The door to one whined open, causing Felicity to jump. A tiny woman with curly brown hair emerged, smoothing the front of her dress.

"Free now, honey," the woman said.

"Pardon me?"

Her thumb shot back at the privy. "I'm done with my business if you need to use the outhouse."

"Oh, no thank you."

"Suit yourself." The woman began to walk away.

"Excuse me, but were you acquainted with Beth Ray?"

The woman halted and turned around. "I knew the poor girl. What relation are you?" She gave Felicity a going-over with her eyes. "You ain't no soiled dove, are you?"

"I was her friend."

"That makes you my friend, too." The woman extended a tiny hand with silver rings on several of her fingers. "The name's Kate. I live next door. Pleased to meet you."

"Felicity, and the pleasure is all mine."

Taking paper, a tobacco pouch, and matches from the front of her tattered dress, Kate rolled a cigarette and lit up. "I saw what happened to Beth. It was terrible."

Felicity blinked hard. "Yes."

"The sheriff already asked me lots of questions." The cigarette dangled off one side of her mouth.

"What did he want to know?"

"If I heard any noise coming from Beth's place the night it happened."

"Did you?"

Kate scratched under her arms. "Not a damn thing except that squeaking bed of hers. Not one scream from poor Beth."

"What else?"

"About the time of this and that."

"Time?"

"The sheriff said Beth left a saloon about ten. I didn't hear her come back to the crib because I was entertaining a gentleman, who left about eleven or so. Trouble is, the handsome sheriff must have had his times all mixed up." Kate sat on the step of Beth's back door.

"Why?"

Kate took a long drag before answering. "See, I got this stomach ailment, and when my innards say I must go, then I must go. Anyway, my stomach starts tossing, which is a sign to git to the outhouse in a hurry."

"What time?"

"Way past midnight. On my way back from the outhouse, I heard someone behind me."

"The killer?"

"Beth."

"Are you certain?"

"Didn't see her face. It was dark. But I could tell it was Beth because she was wearing her favorite green dress and green velvet bonnet. She was also in a hell of a hurry. She had something under arm, a parcel like. I called, 'Where you going, gal?' But Beth didn't answer and ran into the back alley behind the privies."

"Positive about the time?"

Kate's chin lowered with a nod. "Yes, ma'am. When I went back into my room, I asked another of my gentlemen about the time, and he said twelve thirty. I thought that was a little late for Beth to be going out. But she must have come back and that's when someone done her in."

Felicity's face scrunched with bafflement. "That's odd."

"About twenty minutes after I saw Beth out back, a man must have come looking for her company. Then I heard him yelling, 'Murder, murder, murder.' We go outside and he's running down the street calling for help."

"What did the sheriff say when you told him you had seen Beth in back of the cribs?"

Kate stood and stretched. "He said one woman looks like another when it's dark outside." She tossed off her cigarette. "I did drink a tad too much whiskey that night. But I could have sworn I saw little Beth."

"Kate, did Beth ever own a jasmine scent?"

"Don't know, but we can't afford such niceties."

Felicity gave the woman a ten-dollar gold piece. "For your troubles."

Kate bit the coin and appreciated its authenticity. "Poor Beth. Maybe I saw her spirit running to heaven is all."

Returning to the shack, Felicity combed through Beth's clothing for the green bonnet and dress. There weren't there. Like the other evidence Felicity had gathered, Kate's story added up to another mystery.

On her way out, Felicity saw the vase she had given Beth had been knocked to the floor. Rose petals were scattered about. Someone had torn them from the stems.

★   ★   ★

Marcus Quigley made good on his promises.

A black carriage with two striding horses transported Beth Ray's white coffin to Placer Cemetery. Wearing a fine black coat and hat, Quigley drove the carriage himself. An old preacher with a bulbous nose and squinting eyes behind wire-framed glasses sent Beth off with soothing words for the dead and prayers of resurrection. Standing across the grave from the preacher, Felicity held a bouquet of roses from her garden. Tears irritated her eyes, but she dared not close them because images of Beth's torn body flashed in waiting. Those images had already occupied her dreams.

No one else attended the service.

"Ashes to ashes and dust to dust, so shall we all return, but our spirit is eternal." The preacher could have been a grandfather burying one of his own. "And so we bid goodbye to the body of Beth Ray and pray her spirit is already in heaven. Amen." He closed his Bible. As he passed, the preacher shook Felicity's hand. "Sorry for the loss of your cousin."

Felicity looked at Quigley, who shrugged his shoulders. That answered her question as to how the undertaker had managed to bury Beth Ray in Placer Cemetery. The minister boarded his small buggy and drove off.

"Did we do right by her?" Quigley had his black hat in his hand.

"The service was lovely, Mr. Quigley."

He gave an appreciative nod, placed his hat back on, and left.

Yes, Mr. Quigley had done right by Beth Ray, but she had not. The woman's killer remained free and unpunished. Felicity tossed the roses onto the coffin.

CHAPTER 29

When Felicity opened the door to Sheriff Tom Pike, his face went tender with admiration.

"You're the most beautiful woman in Placer, maybe in all of Blackwood County or Montana."

"Such an exaggeration, but thank you. If I may offer a compliment, you're incredibly handsome tonight."

He wore a black evening coat, dress shirt and vest, bow tie, and polished shoes. "The man who sold me the suit said I needed a top hat. I told him I did not want to be no undertaker at Quigley and Son."

She smiled. "Don't you feel exposed without your gun?"

"My Colt is under the seat of the carriage. Never know when you might have to arrest somebody, especially when I'm with you."

Felicity rushed about gathering her purse and wrap. She didn't want to tarry, even though she had made sure the trunks they had packed were out of view.

On the street stood a black carriage headed by two black bays. A brawny man with a gray mustache and bald head held the reins.

"Felicity Carrol, this is my friend, Magnus Cunningham," Pike said.

"A pleasure," said Cunningham. "Tom here says he wanted to demonstrate he could be a gentleman like the ones running around back in England. I told him best not be wishing for too much."

"Good ol' Magnus. He loves fooling about." Pike tossed him a threatening look and helped Felicity into the carriage.

"I do ask one thing tonight, Felicity."

"What?"

"No murder talk during dinner."

"We can save it for dessert."

They dined at the restaurant in the Regent Hotel, a newer building of red brick and white stone on Main. Like the Grand Hotel, the Regent boasted luxury. Waiters in pristine aprons. Candles in cut-glass vases. Fresh flowers.

"The cook came all the way from Denver." Pike had one eye on the menu. "That's what he told me when I put him in jail for cheating at poker last month."

"Let's hope he cooks better than he plays cards."

Pike ordered wine to go with their roast-beef dinners. Despite the good food, Felicity had little appetite, thinking ahead to how she would end the evening by telling him she was going to leave. What she had observed at Beth's shack also continued to bother her.

During dinner, they talked about the politics of their respective countries. He asked about living under the rule of a queen. She asked about President Benjamin Harrison. The conversation was trite compared to their most recent talks about homicide.

They walked to the theater after dinner. Pike asked his friend to pick them up after the play ended at about ten.

The soft lighting from the four-story brick theater welcomed them. Felicity had purchased two seats in one of the boxes. Their entrance warranted the attention of many in the audience, with nods and twinkles from opera glasses. As Pike lifted off Felicity's satin dolman wrap, his lips brushed her shoulders.

"I still wouldn't mind another kiss," he said.

"I'm not sure one would be enough for either of us," she added.

The town's wealthiest were in attendance. The theater neared capacity with men in expensive dress clothing and women on their arms wearing the latest fashions from New York and San Francisco.

"This appears to be a sold-out performance." Felicity pointed out the box next to theirs, which remained empty. "Except for that one."

"Belongs to Mrs. Albert. The theater manager says she reserves the box no matter the play. Sometimes she comes, other times not. I met her a few times when she showed up for performances."

"What do you think of her?" Like it or not, his instincts were good.

"She's different."

"How?"

"Most madams are either very businesslike or overly sociable. But Mrs. Albert is more like the headmistress of a girl's school. Rigid as a tree." His eyes already were on the stage.

"Think she has secrets, Tom?"

"A barnful. And she's the type who won't tell you a damn thing unless it benefits her."

Before Pike could say anything more, Mrs. Albert swept in wearing an elegant black evening dress with a high collar. "Sheriff."

"Ma'am."

"And good to see you again, Felicity. A friendly face in an unfriendly crowd." Mrs. Albert glanced at the audience below. A few females in the lower rows didn't hide their distaste. "Some of the women in this town don't usually welcome my presence."

"Anyone who appreciates the theater deserves esteem, Mrs. Albert," Felicity said.

"I don't have the opportunity to attend every play, but my dear beloved husband adored theater productions." She sat. "This is one of my favorites."

"'This bond doth give thee here no jot of blood; The words expressly are "a pound of flesh,"'" Felicity recited in her best theatrical voice.

"The best of currencies."

Before Felicity could ask what she meant, the curtain went up.

The company, which had traveled from New York, presented a lavish and enjoyable production. Felicity had read all of Shakespeare's plays and sonnets during a prideful attempt to soak in English literature. She had attended many of Shakespeare's plays staged in London. His words belonged on the boards. During the production, Felicity often glanced at Pike, who appeared to have been conveyed to the Venice streets of Shylock.

At the beginning of Act III, Felicity smelled jasmine.

Felicity shifted in her seat. The scent originated from the box next to them. With a delicate gesture, Mrs. Albert held a black lace handkerchief to her nose. In the dim lights of the theater, her eyes were black things. Pike's assessment had been correct. Mrs. Albert had a distance to her. The sides of the woman's mouth turned up in superiority, as if everyone else had no meaning on this earth.

On the stage, the character of Portia took on the disguise of a young man to defend Antonio, the merchant of Venice. Shylock had threatened to collect the "pound of flesh" after Antonio defaulted on his loan. The tall, red-headed actress who played Portia delivered her dialogue with a commanding deep-toned voice, never more so than in Scene IV.

"And twenty of these puny lies I'll tell, that men shall swear I have discontinued school above a twelfthmonth. I have within my mind a thousand raw tricks of these bragging Jacks, which I will practice."

Felicity's flesh quivered at the lines. Her clothes rubbed her raw. She glanced to the side. Mrs. Albert had left her box. The play continued.

"My God, your hand is freezing, Felicity," Pike said.

She didn't realize he had even touched her.

The curtain at last dropped to an appreciative audience.

"Thanks again." Pike kissed her cheek.

"Delighted you enjoyed the play, Tom."

"You must have seen lots of plays in London. My God, the very center of Shakespeare's world." He placed her wrap around her shoulders.

"My beloved father could never get enough of the theater." Her voice lifted with sarcasm.

Her beloved father not so beloved.

Mrs. Albert's beloved husband.

The scent of jasmine.

Bruises on the prostitute at the White Rose brothel.

Drury's missing wife.

A female in man's clothing.

Someone wearing Beth's dress.

A thousand raw tricks of these bragging Jacks.

All the air seemed to evaporate from Felicity's body. She had been duped.

Pike touched her hand. "About dessert and maybe that kiss."

"I must return to the house."

"I love your spirit. These evening clothes must have stirred up your passions like a wind on the plains."

"Tom, please. Let's go." Her voice conveyed only urgency and grit.

"What the hell's wrong with you?"

"I have to leave now." Picking up her dress, she hustled past him, out of the box, and to the stairs of the theater.

In the carriage, Pike concentrated on his folded hands. His face muscles were taut. She had noticeably angered him with the way she had acted at the theater and her silence since then. But she couldn't mention her new theory. He wanted to kiss her but not believe her. Not after what had happened with Dr. William Lennox. Pike no longer trusted her deductions or methods.

When they arrived at her house, she charged out of the carriage before Pike could get out to help her down.

"Wait." He jumped out, caught up to her, and took her arm. "What's going on with you? Something's under your saddle."

"I'm ill."

"You're lying again."

Felicity gnashed her teeth at what she needed to do next. "How dare you. I have had enough of your vulgar suspicions and uncouth behavior. You're no gentleman. You're a primitive with a badge." She slapped his face. "Leave me alone."

Lifting the fabric of her gown, she dashed inside and up the stairs. She didn't want to see how she'd hurt Pike, who remained on the street. Slamming the door, she glanced back through the window as he drove away in the carriage.

She had already packed her equipment in one of the trunks and had to dig out the vials, microscope, and books. At the bottom were the newspaper clippings she had taken off the wall. She dug into the piles of papers and pitched aside the ones she did not need. At last, the article she wanted, though the words were already stored in her formidable memory. The *Times* of London report about the suicide of Dr. James Drury, dated November 20, 1888:

RENOWNED SURGEON
VICTIM OF SUICIDE DROWNING

Dr. James Drury forged a name as a talented surgeon who befriended a prince. Later in life, however, he suffered under infamy as an unofficial suspect in the shocking Whitechapel murders that plagued the city's East End.

On the morning of November 20, Mr. Martin Rossell, a bricklayer, was walking along St. Katherine's Way when he noticed a piece of paper under a rock less than five feet from the edge of the Thames. Curious, Mr. Rossell picked up the note, on which was written, "I die, but I am not at fault. J. Drury." Mr. Rossell, however, did not see a body floating in the river and summoned police to the location. After a thorough search by the Metropolitan Police, the body of Dr. Drury was not recovered from the river, and authorities abandoned the effort by early evening.

Thirty-five-year-old Drury worked as a surgeon at the Royal London Hospital on Whitechapel Road. He had lived what appeared to be an extraordinary life. A successful doctor, he cultivated a friendship with His Royal Highness Prince Albert Victor, the Duke of Clarence, whom the physician had met at a charity benefit. Later in life, the two men could often be seen at various London social events.

However, all that ended after the death of Mary Jane Kelly, a known prostitute, on November 9, 1888, in her room at 13 Miller's Court. In a November 15 article in the Times, Dr. Drury's name was mentioned as one of the suspects in the violent murders of Kelly and four other prostitutes in Whitechapel by the killer who was dubbed Jack the Ripper. The Times quoted a former inspector with Scotland Yard who did not wish his name mentioned. The inspector called the surgeon "a person of interest" in the investigation, but he did not elaborate.

The self-proclaimed Jack the Ripper mutilated the women in such a manner that police believed the fiend knew well the anatomy of a human body. The killer, who extracted organs with the skill of a surgeon, remains at large.

Dr. Drury left behind a wife, Emily. They had no children.

Felicity didn't need to look for the paper; she recalled every word of a Scotland Yard document about the murder of Mary Jane Kelly.

Mrs. Michael Magpie, who resided upstairs from Mary Jane Kelly at Miller's Court, reported to Scotland Yard inspectors that she looked out her window at five in the morning and saw a woman outside the building. Although she did not see the woman's face, Mrs. Magpie recognized a dress and shawl often worn by Kelly. Inspectors say Mrs. Magpie must have been hysterical because of the murder. Doctors place Kelly's time of death at two earlier the same morning.

The letter dropped off at Jameson's office had been signed by *I. W. Beck*, a name Felicity thought familiar, but she couldn't pinpoint how. She sought another report and found it buried among others. The primary officer on the scene of Kelly's murder had been Inspector Walter Beck.

I. W. Beck.

"Bloody hell." The curse words she often overheard from the kitchen help slipped out and were appropriate.

The killer wanted to play games. She would play.

Throwing down the papers, Felicity bolted up. Making use of scissors to snip away her bodice and bustle, she tore away the gown for a quick escape from the clothing. Fortunately, Helen had gone out with Lowery; otherwise Felicity might have been slowed by questions. Although her hands trembled and were clumsy, she accelerated her movements. She donned a brown sealskin skirt with leaf patterns at the waist. Undoing the two buttons on a white blouse, she replaced her flat-heeled silk slippers with sturdy riding boots. A simple paisley shawl added to the costume.

Using her small finger, she outlined her eyes using ash from the fireplace. With a hat pin, she pricked her fingers. The blood reddened her cheeks and lips. She shook her hair loose, tied a white ribbon around her neck, and donned a pair of black gloves. In her mirror, she approved of the effect. Into a purse went the tools required to free locked doors. From the trunk she dug out a vial and wrapped it in a handkerchief, which she slipped into the top of her corset. Also in the purse she placed the derringer she had purchased but never used, along with an extra bullet.

Felicity held out her hands. They were steady and warm.

Time to play the killer's game of disguise.

No more deductions and science. She had traveled far for this night and had never been so close to meeting Jack the Ripper.

CHAPTER 30

From a vantage point in a dark alley, Felicity watched the front and back doors of the White Rose brothel and waited for an opportunity to enter unnoticed. She had left her horse tied up in front of another brothel down the street.

A group of one dozen men approached the building. They were loud, drunk, and provided her the chance she needed. When one of the men slammed his fists on the front door of the brothel, Felicity darted to the back door, which was unlocked. She glanced into the empty kitchen. Off to one side, a door opened to a small bedroom apparently belonging to the Chinese maid, given the many Chinese artifacts inside. And probably where Mrs. Albert had obtained the box with the dragons embossed on it. With caution, Felicity crept across the kitchen. She heard the Chinese maid mutter in her native language as she let the men in the front door.

The men were a noisy lot. Shuffling feet, belching, swearing, and laughing. The best of diversions. From the sitting room at the front of the house boomed the sound of a Stephen Foster song hammered out on the piano. The men yelled for service.

"You wait here. Girls come to you. Then choose. We got best in town." The maid spoke loud above their uproar.

"Send those gals now," bellowed one man, receiving laughing approval from his companions. "We've been saving up money to come here instead of going to the girls of the line."

"I want the pick of the good ones. Don't send those ugly trollops like last time," another man said.

"No ugly girls here. Mrs. Albert make sure." Annoyance clipped the maid's voice.

"Where is Mrs. Albert? We want to deal with her," a third man said.

"She no here. If Missy Albert here, she no let you talk dirty in her house." The maid went up the front stairs.

More male laughter and bad singing of "Camptown Races" emanated from the sitting room. Felicity sped up a back staircase leading from the kitchen. When she reached the second floor, she peeped around the corner. The Chinese maid rang a bell at the end of the hall. Eight women dressed in corsets, bloomers, and silk nightgowns in various colors walked out from a line of doors on each side of the hallway. They strolled to the set of stairs facing the front of the brothel. The men hooted at the women's appearance. Sounds of talking and a popular tune on the piano gained volume. The women's laughter sounded false as pyrite.

The third floor proved accessible only from another set of stairs at the back of the house. The location made sense. Mrs. Albert wanted a room as far as possible from the women she detested, a place of privacy. Her own way to leave the house undetected. Felicity started up the stairs and then continued along the vacant hallway. In the middle, two doors faced each other. She tried one, which opened. In the light from the full moon through a window, she saw bed frames stacked against one wall. Across the hall, the other door did not open. Using the tools, she worked on the lock, stopping often to listen for footsteps coming up the stairs.

The lock gave way with a click.

It was a storage room with shelves of sheets and towels, furniture, and nothing more. Closing the door, Felicity edged along the wall. At the end of the hallway stood a short set of stairs. At the top of the stairs was another locked door. Felicity worked on the lock and opened the heavy door. Her stomach wrenched. She gagged at a powerful scent of jasmine. The room seemed to tighten around her as if she lay in a coffin. Undoubtedly, the feeling arose not only from the smell but because she was very much in the lair of a killer. She suppressed her fear and began her examination. Because the window faced the front of the building, she dared not light the oil lamp. The moonlight through the sheer curtains provided enough illumination.

This was no ornate boudoir of a madam.

It was an English-style bedroom, with sturdy wooden furniture dominating the room. A reserved coverlet of burgundy was folded on the bed. A Bible lay on a table. Felicity picked it up and thumbed through. Ink had been splashed on some pages. Others had been ripped out.

Inside a dark wood armoire hung expensive dresses. Felicity felt around the bottom. Nothing. Her foot caught on the post of bed. She fell forward, placing her hands out to stifle any sound of her stumble.

Felicity remained on the floor. She listened for footsteps in the hallway. For discovery. For worse. She heard only the noise of the men who trod up the front stairs to the girls' rooms on the second floor. Doors slammed shut. Men whooped.

In the sitting room, the remaining men maintained their singing and loud talk, probably in anticipation of having their turn with one of the women. She breathed out relief. No one had heard her. Turning her head, she glanced under the bed. A trunk lay underneath. She slid it out. Locked.

Felicity worked on it with her tools. She pushed up the lid. Lying on its side was a black doctor's bag with the initials JD in gold lettering on one side.

James Drury.

From the bag she lifted out a long mahogany box holding several surgical knives, including three catlins. From the imprints in the velvet, two catlin knives were missing. The trunk also held two folded black frock coats, trousers, and white shirts, along with two pairs of black leather boots, spats, and gray gloves, one pair of which was smeared with blood. A neat pile of proof.

But the knives and clothing were not enough for Felicity that night. Closing the bag, she locked the trunk and slid it back under the bed.

Perspiration wet her blouse. She wiped at her forehead with her sleeves. After locking the bedroom door, she whirled around, down the short set of stairs, and right into the solid arms of the man standing in the third-floor hall. His breath stank of cheap cigars and beer. He wore a dingy plaid shirt and pants stiff with sweat and dirt.

"You must be new," he slurred.

"I've been around for a long time." The American accent moved easily off her tongue. "I have to go. Another man expects me." She tried to slip around him. He seemed to take up the entire hall. They were alone.

His arm went to her waist. "Forget him, sister. I got to say, you're the prettiest whore I've laid eyes on. Mrs. Albert charges ten dollars for her girls, but I'd pay a bag of gold nuggets for you."

"You couldn't afford me. Now let go before I call Mrs. Albert or the maid."

"Mrs. Albert ain't here, and my friends're waitin' for their turn with a gal. I don't want to wait." His tongue circled his lips. He glanced to one of the doors and grabbed Felicity's wrist. "Let's head to your room. I'll pay ya twenty dollars. You can keep all the money for yourself and not share it with the madam."

Though he was unsteady with intoxication, she couldn't use force against this man. She grinned with an idea. "You do interest me, and I'll take your offer. Let's keep our voices low so no one will hear us." She put her finger up to his lips.

He whispered. "What do they call you?" He still held on to her arm.

"Elizabeth." Felicity batted her eyes. The only name she could think of at the moment. "Free my wrist, and I'll give you a sample of what you can get for your money." He relaxed his hand. Her hand slid between her breasts, as if to move apart the clothing. She removed the handkerchief-wrapped vial and hid it in her fist.

"You're going to be special." He tugged at his pants.

"How right you are." She led him to the empty room and closed the door behind them.

"Don't you want to go to your bedroom?"

"This is more exciting. Something you won't soon forget."

"All right then." He panted.

She pushed at his shoulders. "Now sit on the floor, and we'll have a good time." Pure instinct motivated her.

"Git on with it." He gurgled a laugh and sat. His big legs went straight out. His upper body swayed a bit. "Hope I can get up from the floor. Been drinking since five today."

Sucking in her breath, her hand slid over this thigh. "Relax now." She dipped behind him, leaned in, and whispered into his ear. "You can taste how sweet I am. Now close your eyes." She should have been an actress.

Yelping with pleasure, he closed them. She uncapped the vial with her teeth and doused the handkerchief with chloroform. One of her arms shot around his neck. With her other hand, she shoved the handkerchief against his mouth and nose and held it there with all the force she could muster. To help, she braced her knees against his back and kept her head away from the sweet but effective smell. The man struggled and then fell back unconscious in a few breaths.

Winded, she shot up. No more time to waste. If the Chinese maid found the hulk of a man, she might believe he had passed out in a stupor in the empty room. The smell of the chloroform would dissipate by then.

Felicity rushed out the door.

★   ★   ★

Felicity's boots pounded the dirt as she ran. Each step smacked with her imagined insight into the killer's mind.

After five murders, the town of Placer was done, the killer probably thought. Staying longer might result in an arrest and the noose. But victory had to be relished. Over London's Scotland Yard and, now, the western lawmen. None comprehended a task both artistic and justified. Ahead were more towns, more fallen women. More punishment. Time to enjoy the freedom to stroll the streets and mock them all.

And there in an alley off Viceroy Street, Felicity Carroll caught up with Jack the Ripper. The murderer leaned against a wall staring at a young prostitute across the way.

"Good evening, Mrs. Drury. Mrs. Emily Drury." Felicity stood about twenty feet behind the woman.

Emily Drury turned without rushing. She wore a black double-breasted man's frock coat with a velvet collar and silk lapels, black trousers, a white shirt and black tie. Her large hands were encased in gray gloves. A thin dark mustache lined her upper lip. She took off the bowler hat and bowed to Felicity. On the woman's head sat a short wig of red hair.

Replacing the hat, she offered up a gracious, "Miss Felicity Carrol." Her voice imitated a man's. "You're a clever girl."

Perspiration streamed between Felicity's shoulder blades now, although her limbs iced over like ocean waters. She aimed the derringer at the woman's heart. "An inspired disguise. You deceived us all, Mrs. Drury."

"How thoughtful of you to notice. Yet wearing a disguise is not against the law, my dear girl. For example, your own costume is very effective. Unless you have taken up whoring. Perhaps you have. The girls do gossip about you and the sheriff."

Felicity shuddered at the insanity in the voice. Simultaneously bestial and articulate as Satan's orator. She edged forward, hoping to force the woman into the muted light of the street. Mrs. Drury didn't accommodate her. "How you must have congratulated yourself for outsmarting the law both here and in England. Who would believe a woman could commit such atrocities?"

"You're babbling, dear. I can't understand you."

"All those medical books in your husband's library. You learned anatomy from them, as well as how to use a surgical blade."

"Tish, tish, tish." The mad smile deepened on Emily Drury.

"After you killed Mary Jane Kelly, your clothes were soaked with blood. So you put on her dress and bonnet so as not to draw attention as you escaped, which is why a neighbor claimed she saw Mary Jane the next morning. You did the same when you killed Beth Ray."

"Such a vibrant imagination."

"How ironic your husband was suspected of the Whitechapel murders. But he couldn't accept the shame of his exposed activity in the brothels and killed himself."

"Tish, tish, tish."

"You shouldn't have used the jasmine scent when you killed Beth Ray." Felicity raised the gun. How easy it would be to put a bullet into that diseased brain.

Emily Drury moved toward Felicity. "The whore stunk with fornication. In such a small space, I had to mask the odor or else I'd swoon." She had dropped the man's voice. Her speech turned polished as the knife she took from the jacket pocket. She now talked like a refined British woman who could have been discussing the weather and not the murder of women.

"The coins you left under the bodies?" Felicity said.

"My, you are a curious little creature. The last payment for the harlots, until they roasted in hell."

"And the ring at the feet of Mattie Morgan?"

The killer moved closer. "Just an amusement, and I do love my little jokes. And 'Jack the Ripper' was most inspired, if I do say so. How surprising people made such a fuss over the death of those wretched whores. I created a such furor by dispatching loathsome women. Incredible."

"The letters to the sheriff and news agency. Ah, and eating the organs. Another jest?"

"Amusing to no end."

"How inspiring to deflect the blame onto Dr. Lennox."

"You were more than willing to believe in his guilt. Although I hoped the letter I had delivered to your solicitor might frighten you away."

"But here I am. You're coming with me to the sheriff's office." Felicity pushed the gun farther in front of her. "Drop the knife."

Emily Drury's head flew back with a guttural laugh. At once, she stopped. "You really think I'll confess to a judge? You're quite out of your element. Just a foolish English schoolgirl with too much money and time."

"I want justice for the women you killed."

"They weren't human. They were nothing but offal. I heard you were friendly with Beth Ray, and I admit I couldn't miss the opportunity to make her and you suffer." She smiled.

Beth *had* been targeted because of her. Felicity's jaw locked with anger. "You're the animal. Not them," she managed to say.

Felicity and her adversary stared at each other. At once, Emily Drury screamed and ran at Felicity with the long catlin knife in her left hand. Felicity fired and hit the woman's shoulder. She still charged. The insane had the power of ten, Felicity had read and gulped now at the veracity of the statement.

Emily Drury swiped the knife at Felicity, who bent backward to avoid injury. A stinging raced over the top of her right cheek, a little more than a thumb's length from her eye. The small gun went flying. Felicity's arms shot out at the woman and shoved hard. The swing with the knife had thrown Emily Drury off balance and she crashed on her back, but still held on to the knife. Felicity stepped on the woman's wrist to force her to release it. When she did, Felicity kicked the knife away into the dark alley. Spinning around to retrieve the derringer, Felicity reloaded with the extra bullet in her pocket.

She aimed the gun at Emily Drury's heart. "Get up slowly."

The woman's legs swept at Felicity's. The air left Felicity's lungs as she banged onto the dirt on her back.

Emily Drury picked herself up and ran.

Gun in hand, Felicity rallied. The woman darted west up Viceroy Street, where the number of houses and buildings turned sparse. Felicity cursed at having to wear the skirt, which created the flapping sounds of a distressed bird as she ran. Blood from her cheek wet the front of her blouse. With her sleeve, she swiped at her face. Ahead of her, Emily Drury maneuvered through the inky alleys and streets, still going west.

On the hill ahead, a scattering of lights lit the smelters and mines. Soon the houses disappeared altogether and the killer headed right to where Felicity did not want to be. The barren land around the mines and smelters appeared unforgiving in the day. At night, it resembled an even harsher landscape resplendent with hiding places.

Emily Drury darted through a yard of timbers and climbed over a huge stack of wood. Ignoring the splinters wedging into her hands, Felicity pursued and dared not blink. She didn't want to lose sight of the killer sprinting ahead. Too many shadows loomed in which the murderer could disappear. The woman spun left toward the smelters. Felicity picked up her skirts and reached to within five feet of the woman, who laughed. Emily Drury had lost her bowler and wig. Her brown hair whipped over her back.

The killer reached piles of dirt and rock taken out of the earth. Scrambling up a mass more than thirty feet high, she sent rocks onto Felicity climbing below her. One rock banged Felicity's right hand. She lost the derringer and didn't have the time or enough light to hunt for the weapon among the rocks.

Felicity had to keep moving.

As they clambered over another pile of dirt and rocks, Felicity realized they could be running forever. She had to slow the woman, who scampered toward a line of metal structures above the mine shafts. She would try with words.

"Your beloved husband. What a joke. He must have known what you were. That's why he courted the solace of prostitutes. That's why he threw himself into the Thames," Felicity shouted at her.

The woman skidded to a standstill. Felicity also slowed, but crept toward Emily Drury with caution. They stood under a giant metal scaffolding erected over a shaft. An electric light on a pole shone on their faces. Felicity's lungs were scorched from running, but she did a quick reconnaissance for a weapon to use against Emily Drury. Thick snakes of electric cables plunged into the blackness of the hole. Out of it arose the clang of metal against rock.

"Stupid girl. You don't know me," Emily Drury said through her own racked breathing. "Think my husband really killed himself? That pitiful soul who had to pay strumpets to convince himself of his manhood."

"And you hated those women for that, didn't you?"

"But your father loved them, and quite frequently. In fact, Samuel Carrol introduced my husband to those disgusting houses. The lecherous vermin."

"Don't talk about my father."

"Can't bear the truth? The truth is, Samuel Carrol loved the whores more than you. I heard him and my husband talking in the library one night. Your father couldn't even bear to look at you. He found comfort in their arms."

The woman was as clever and dangerous as she was insane.

"Your mother couldn't compare."

"Shut up!"

Neck muscles tightened, the woman ran toward Felicity.

Felicity had to move. She knew Emily Drury had a second knife and only waited for the chance to plunge it into her.

Behind them, two workers appeared out of the blackness and into the light. "Get outta here. This is dangerous. No place for women," one of them yelled.

Emily Drury rotated on one heel and headed right for a building resembling a gigantic iron box.

Walton Smelter proclaimed the sign over the door the killer entered. A few feet behind, Felicity bumped into a man exiting the door. His body exuded heat.

"Hope you're looking for me." Soot smudged the man's face.

"I am not. Move aside." Felicity pushed through the door of the smelter.

She had entered the underworld. Hades. Fire and brimstone.

Crushers reducing the ore to gravel created a din, shaking Felicity's legs as she ran through the immense building. Great round ovens were stacked one on top of the other along one section of a wall. Men shoved coal into the ovens, which melted the ground ore and freed the precious metals within. Fiery sparks flitted about like unholy fairies. The temperature created an invisible but thick layer Felicity had to penetrate. Her every intake of air seemed to contain flames and smoke. In front of her, Emily Drury tore off her frock coat, apparently to deal with the temperature.

As Felicity passed, men hollered at them to get out, while others dismissed the intruding women and just fed the fires.

A spark fell on Felicity's skirt, and a ball of flame sprouted. Without slowing, she picked up the fabric and banged out the fire. From the ground, she grabbed an iron pipe long as her arm. Taking a sudden left, Emily Drury shot through a side door of the smelter. Felicity did the same. Once outside, they scurried along on a narrow path between the smelter and a hill plunging downward into blackness. Molten slag flowed out of the building in a ditch wide as a creek. The fluid mineral waste coursed down the slope in a deadly golden ribbon. Emily Drury hurdled the ditch. As Felicity hopped over, the slag's fever stung her legs.

In a clearing past the smelter, Emily Drury awaited her. "You're never going to stop, are you?"

"No."

"I expected this day to come. When my secret would be discovered and all good things ended. I didn't expect someone like you. I had the whole of Scotland Yard on its knees with impotence."

"I assure you, everyone will stand up when you're sentenced to die."

Emily Drury inched nearer. "I'm already under a death sentence, Miss Carrol. My husband brought syphilis to me from those houses. Syphilis. The unclean. Now you'll join the girls of the line you're so fond of."

From her pants pocket, Emily Drury whipped out another knife and charged Felicity. Swinging hard, Felicity aimed the pipe at the woman's arm. Emily Drury twisted hard from the blow, but the knife slid over Felicity's upper left arm. With the pipe, Felicity struck the woman's back, making her spin again, but she righted herself and ran down the hill. She tried to maintain her footing on the slope but slipped on the gravel and rode downward on her back.

Felicity touched the wound on her arm. Just skin, no muscle affected. She gave chase, but she couldn't stay on her feet either and careened toward the bottom of the hill, still carrying her pipe weapon. Along the right side poured the molten stream of slag, which ended in a sizable pool at the bottom of the hill. Her eyes watered from the heat.

The killer slammed into the ground, missing the pool by mere feet. She sprang up and held the knife out to thrust into Felicity, who skidded out of control on the slope. In the light from the slag, Felicity could see what the woman planned. When Felicity hit the bottom, she held out the pipe to deflect the blade. Felicity scrambled to her feet. While Emily Drury raised her arm to strike again, Felicity swung the metal at the woman's chest. The killer flew into the molten pool.

Emily Drury didn't scream as she melted into the red-hot mass.

★   ★   ★

Two smelter workers scratched their heads at the sight of the young woman sitting on the ground tossing rocks into the molten pool.

Dried blood crusted on her right cheek. More blood drizzled down her arm.

"You need a doctor, ma'am," one of the workers said.

"Probably." More rocks into the pool. They plopped in the slag.

"What happened to the man you were chasing?" one of the workers asked.

"I sent her back to hell." Felicity tossed in another rock.

CHAPTER 31

"I now pronounce you man and wife," Judge Simon Winslow said with solemnity as Helen and Robert Lowery stood under the gazebo.

Lowery took the face of the new Mrs. Lowery in his hands and kissed her so gently that Helen cried. The small gathering clapped; a few of Lowery's friends gave a yip of cowboy proportions as another shot a gun into the air. Tom Pike whistled and stomped his boots.

Felicity clapped loudly and shouted, "Well done."

Following the ceremony, guests extended personal congratulations to the couple. Felicity watched and enjoyed the happiness of people she loved.

"Now, Robert, you take care of this woman. Never has there been anyone as kind and accepting," Felicity said to the new husband.

"You have my promise, Miss Felicity."

"I'm sure you won't disappoint me."

"Forgive me for being so bold, but I have come to look upon you as a daughter in the time you've been here. I hope you'll some-day consider me a second father."

As much as Felicity wanted to, she didn't cry. "That I will," she answered in a voice husky with sentiment from such a splendid offer. She hugged him.

Felicity turned to her friend, "And Hellie, my Hellie."

"Bless you for all you have done, Miss. I've never known such happiness." Helen's face opened like a new morning.

"Then I'm happy, too."

"Next time, it'll be your turn at the altar." Helen held up her ring.

"I doubt that," replied Felicity, and they both laughed.

For the wedding dinner, the guests sat at tables set up in the garden behind the house on Bullion Boulevard. On the white tablecloths were bowls of flowers from the garden. The hotel waiters Felicity had hired served healthy portions of lamb, chicken, potatoes, green beans, and rolls on china plates. Lowery's friends enjoyed the beer Felicity had included in the menu, along with wine and a superb lemon cake and fruit.

As the sunlight weakened, waiters lit candles on the tables and paper lanterns Felicity had purchased from Da Long's store for the occasion. She had also hired a small band that played while couples danced on sheets of board laid down on the ground. Helen and Robert held each other as if they had done so for years.

Weary, Felicity sat in the gazebo located off to the side of the garden and watched the party continue on into the evening. She ran her finger over the purplish scar on her cheek. Dr. William Lennox had done a tidy job of stitching the cuts on her face and arm. In his usual unfriendly bedside manner, he had informed Felicity her cheek would forever be marked.

"Doctor, the wound I'll carry from now on will be on the outside, not the inside," she had replied. As expected, he did not bother to ask for further explanation or seem to care.

After Lennox stitched her up, she'd gone directly to the telegraph office. This news couldn't wait.

TO: INSPECTOR JACKSON DAVIES

JACKSON, THE CASE IS CLOSED. JUSTICE IS SERVED. BACK HOME SOON.

FELICITY

During a court inquest into the death of Mrs. Albert, the presiding judge often squinted his eyes at Felicity as she testified that Mrs. Albert had admitted to killing the five prostitutes in Placer. His bushy eyebrows rose at Felicity's explanation of how the woman had gone insane. Felicity had told them where to find proof of the woman's guilt, which included the knives and men's clothing in the trunk under the bed at the White Rose brothel. Blood stained the soles of the dress shoes and the gloves found in the room. Felicity said she had discovered all this while doing research for her book on the crimes. Though she disliked lying to a judge, she needed to keep up the fiction that she was a writer in case the story ever got back to England. Tom Pike knew the truth and wouldn't tell.

Faced with threats of jail as an accessory to murder, the Chinese maid confessed she had seen Mrs. Albert dressed as a man in a frock coat and bowler hat leaving her bedroom on the nights Mattie Morgan and Beth Ray died. Mrs. Albert had warned the servant to mind her business lest she be kicked out into the streets.

The maid also identified the Chinese box sent to Sheriff Tom Pike as one she had thought she'd lost. Mrs. Albert's handwriting also matched the note sent to the sheriff, though the presiding judge discounted the evidence.

Felicity and Pike had agreed not to mention the names of Emily and James Drury, nor the Whitechapel killings or Jack the Ripper. The people of Placer and the judge might consider the tale too hard to digest. The mayhem had ended, which was all that mattered. More to prove herself to Pike than anyone else, Felicity had asked her London solicitors Morton & Morton to send a photograph of Emily Drury. Pike couldn't deny Emily Drury and Mrs. Albert were the same woman.

Given the evidence from the brothel, the admission of the Chinese maid, and Felicity's testimony, the judge ruled that Mrs. Albert had murdered the women in Placer. Felicity suspected the judge believed her story only because of the injuries to her face and arm, and because she was a nice young Englishwoman with no reason to lie. After the inquest, Felicity gathered all the case documents and photographs of the murder victims in England and Placer and had them shipped ahead to Carrol Manor. The proceeds from the sale of the house on Bullion Boulevard were reserved for a fund so Dr. Lennox could continue his medical care for the prostitutes and help any woman who wanted to leave the profession. Everything orderly. At least most everything.

She wrapped up the whole affair with a telegram to solicitor Martin Jameson. She informed him that he no longer had to worry about the threats to the Carrol name and businesses. She had personally dealt with Mr. I. W. Beck.

With all items of death behind her, she proceeded to plan the wedding, and she thought she had done a good job of it when the day arrived. Through the evening, the wedding guests enjoyed the good food and drink in the garden, lit by lanterns hanging from the trees.

Sheriff Tom Pike joined her in the gazebo. They sat listening to the music. She had already apologized to him for the way she had acted at the theater, and he had accepted it after hearing the reason why. Despite all the crime still going on in the wild mining town, Placer seemed calmer that night. Her emotions were just as clear. She could not imagine him anywhere but Montana, and she belonged in England. "I will miss you, Tom."

"And I you, Felicity Carrol. Even though you almost got your-self killed and refused to tell me what you had learned about the murderer."

"Would you have believed me?"

The sheriff smiled. "Probably not."

"I got my man, so to speak, even if she turned out to be a woman." She placed a hand on his. "I'm sorry you haven't yet found the man who killed your father," she said.

"Me too."

"Until that day, I'm sure you'll be searching every face in town until you find his."

He looked out over the lights of the town he protected. "Sure as the sun blinking over the mountains in the morning." He nod-ded slowly. "I will keep looking until I don't have to anymore."

She looked up at the stars. They seemed to be winking with truths that night. "I guess we'll all keep searching until we don't have to anymore."

CHAPTER 32

Felicity sat in their regular spot at the Café Royal on Regent Street. She checked her watch. Five past one.

Tapping her foot, she began to doubt her decision not to visit Jackson Davies the moment she, Helen, and Robert Lowery had docked in London a few days before. She should have asked Helen and Robert to take care of the luggage, hailed a hansom, and gone to see her friend then and there. She should have rushed up to his room and told him the whole story.

Tapping her spoon against her teacup in the café, she scolded herself. She shouldn't have been so enigmatic and smug in her communication to her friend. But she had too much to tell and couldn't do it in a letter or telegram.

Then Jackson Davies appeared. His face had thinned and he appeared older. Traces of white infiltrated his fine dark hair, and his brown eyes hinting of a forest were shaded like a late afternoon. Clearly he had lived through a serious illness. But his face lightened when he saw her, and he ran over. Felicity had no idea how long they hugged. He had never before shown such personal affection, and Felicity had to admit she held on just as much to him.

"Come, our tea's getting cold," she said.

"You're rich; buy us another pot," Davies said.

"I've missed your cheek, Inspector." Felicity waved over the waiter and asked for another pot and to start their lunch she had ordered.

"Oh my God," he said.

"What?"

"Your face."

She touched the scar left by Emily Drury, now healed but measuring a good two inches. "Ah, my souvenir from the killer. You're not repulsed by it?"

"You're twice as beautiful."

"Inspector Jackson Griggs Davies, never have I heard you utter so much poppycock. And that's saying a lot." Her finger outlined the scar on her face. "You do realize no eligible bachelor in England will marry someone carrying such a mark."

"Nonsense. Who wouldn't want the woman who stopped Jack the Ripper?"

"I did, didn't I?" She didn't say it with pride. Only as a fact.

"Yes, you bleedin' did. And I want to hear every detail."

For the next hour, she told him about what had transpired in Placer, Montana, which sounded even farther away now. She left nothing out, except kissing Sheriff Tom Pike. He had given her another before she and Helen left. A nice memory, which it would remain. Her story took them through lunch and several pots of tea.

Davies sat back in his chair. "A woman. All this time, a woman."

"A very disturbed one."

'No wonder the Yard couldn't find the killer. We were looking in the wrong place." He pounded one hand into the other.

"She had us all deceived, Jackson. No one would have believed a female capable of such violence, but she's human and humans are very capable. You've seen samples of that in your work." Felicity closed her eyes with the awful truth of it—she would always have cases to probe and killers to apprehend. To prove herself over and over.

"But why, Felicity? Why did she do it?"

"Emily Drury was insane, and that insanity took revenge against prostitutes. Her husband had been a customer of the prostitutes in Whitechapel and passed on to his wife the dreaded disease of syphilis."

"My God."

"One thing, Jackson."

"Hmm?" he said, almost adrift in his own thoughts.

"I don't believe we should mention the real identity of Jack the Ripper. Primarily, no one would believe me. I've always tried to stay behind the scenes and to keep scandal away from my family business to keep people working. Can you live with that?"

He answered sooner than she expected. "Jack the Ripper got justice in a fiery pit. That's good with me." Davies took her hand. "But how are you? You look tired."

"Better now that you're recovered. When I couldn't find the killer in Placer and the murders continued, I experienced some of the obsession and defeat you must have gone through, Jackson."

His eyes blinked tears. "Then you understand?"

Using her handkerchief to dot at them, she said, "Completely." He nodded in accord. She sensed a stronger connection had formed between Davies and her. More than friendship, but one of experiencing the same terrors and, hopefully, conquering them for now.

He yanked at the lapels of his jacket. "I'm back at work, you know."

"That's brilliant!"

"I can't repay you for what you've done, my friend."

"You already have."

"Then may I ask you another favor?" Davies said in a most serious tone.

"Of course."

Pulling out his familiar work notebook from his jacket, he consulted a page. "Last night, a schoolteacher named Michael Peters was murdered. Someone stashed his body under a pile of clothes at a laundry off of Fleet Street. He had five pounds in his pants. Everyone who knew him liked the man. Now, here's the darnedest thing."

"What?"

"Whoever killed him sealed his mouth with wax."

"Oh, my."

"Can you examine the body and tell me what you think?"

"My pleasure, Inspector." Now she was truly home.

★   ★   ★

The case Jackson Davies mentioned did intrigue her, especially after Felicity inspected the body at the London coroner's mortuary. The wax used to close the mouth smelled of turpentine, chalk, and shellac, ingredients that went into sealing wax. Yet the wax felt grainer and also carried a smell that told Felicity the material was used to seal wine bottles. Davies smiled and said the victim's brother owned a wine shop and that gave him a lead. He headed off to arrest the brother, she surmised.

Finally, she headed home to Carrol Manor with Helen and Robert. When she arrived, she found the estate in fine shape, and the servants welcomed her. Helen had a grand time introducing her new husband to everyone.

"I like England, Miss. Very green," Lowery told Felicity.

"Very good, Robert." She had asked him where he might want to work on the estate, and he had told her on the grounds.

"I'd like to be outside and then come home to my loving wife."

She introduced him to John Ryan, who was in charge of the grounds. After a few days, the men appeared to be on their way to becoming friends.

Summer had come to the land, and Felicity enjoyed the season and peace. Although she realized she would soon get bored with all that summer and peace.

A week after returning, Felicity headed to a nearby clearing of rock and dirt behind the house. She had asked John Ryan and Robert Lowery to help her move all the files, notes, reports, newspaper articles, and photographs pertaining to the murders in Whitechapel and Placer, Montana. They were placed into a pile, which she doused with a good helping of coal oil.

"Want Robert and me to take care of this, Miss Felicity?" Ryan asked.

"We'd do a good job," Lowery added.

"I know. But I must do this myself. You two fine men go have a cup of coffee. Cook has made an outstanding apple tart with your names on it."

Both men nodded and headed off to the manor, talking as they went.

Taking a box of matches from her pocket, she lit one and threw it on the pile, which exploded into flames. Stepping back, she watched the papers curl and whiten into ash. Onto the pile of fiery papers, she added the hurtful memories of her father. His neglect and disapproval. His inability to show any love for her. She had carried the feeling so long, she feared its burden until she died. In Montana, she had even suspected an innocent man of murder because he reminded her of her father, revealing her own resentment against him for not loving her. A resentment mighty as her heartbreak.

She also tossed onto the fire the guilt she had taken on over his death. The moment had come for release. There was too much to do in this world. Bits of red-lined ash floated up into the sky like unfulfilled wishes, but one of her wishes had been realized. That she find her way in the world.

The apple tart cook had prepared sounded like her idea of heaven—if she believed in one. Felicity turned back to the house and breathed in sugar and contentment.

ACKNOWLEDGMENTS

I'm most grateful for wonderful online resources, including Visible Proofs: Forensic Views of the Body (U.S. National Library of Medicine), Casebook: Jack the Ripper, The Victorian Web, and Victorian Crime & Punishment, as well as the websites of the Metropolitan Police, Daily Mail, BBC, British Library, and Victoria and Albert Museum, not to forget Wikipedia. Thanks to Chris and Heidi Sanders for providing insight into Montana mining. Thanks to my pal Bonnie Dodge for her encouragement. Much gratitude goes to my great agent Elizabeth Kracht, who believed in this story, and to Faith Black Ross for helping it sing on the page. Always thanks to my loving, supportive family, who've always believed I had stories in me.